"This house was my sanctuary when I most needed one."

Julianna spoke quietly, as if bestowing a confidence. Every word went straight to Edmund's heart. "You were my protector when I had no other. I owe you past what I can ever repay. If you want me to stay, you have only to say the word."

If she had drawn a fixed bayonet and plunged it into his chest, she could not have inflicted so deep and gaping a wound. For a moment, Edmund could find neither the breath nor the courage to reply. Then the harsh lessons of his childhood came to his rescue. Bury the hurt— bury it deep.

Without turning to look at Julianna, he spoke as if her offer did not matter to him in the least. "Any debt you owe me may be discharged by making my nephew a loving and faithful wife. I will file an annulment petition before the week is out."

Dear Reader,

Entertainment. Escape. Fantasy. These three words describe the heart of Harlequin Historicals. If you want compelling, emotional stories by some of the best writers in the field, look no further.

We think Deborah Hale is one of the best *new* writers in the field. Her debut book, *My Lord Protector,* is a sigh-inducing "older man, younger woman" romance set in Georgian England. Here, Julianna Ramsey is forced by her elder stepbrother to marry while her betrothed, Crispin, is away at sea. Unknown to Julianna, the stern, wealthy man who offers for her is her fiancé's uncle—he'll "protect her" until his nephew returns. Loyal to the memory of Crispin, Julianna and Edmund must fight the forbidden love that burns between them. Don't miss it!

The Bride of Windermere by Margo Maguire is another terrific first book. In this heartfelt medieval tale, a rugged knight falls in love with a woman he has been sent to protect on her journey to see the king. And Jackie Manning returns this month with a sparkling Western, *Silver Hearts,* featuring a doctor turned cowboy and the feisty Eastern miss he rescues.

Rounding out the month is *Joe's Wife* by Cheryl St.John. Tye Hatcher, the town bad boy, returns from the war to prove his worth. He marries the widow of the once most popular man in town, Joe, and must live up to the memory of him. Keep a hankie close by!

Whatever your tastes in reading, you'll be sure to find a romantic journey back to the past between the covers of a Harlequin Historical®.

Sincerely,
Tracy Farrell, Senior Editor

ase address questions and book requests to:
equin Reader Service
3010 Walden Ave., P.O. Box 1325, Buffalo, NY 14269
an: P.O. Box 609, Fort Erie, Ont. L2A 5X3

My Lord Protector

Deborah Hale

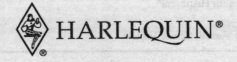

HARLEQUIN®

TORONTO • NEW YORK • LONDON
AMSTERDAM • PARIS • SYDNEY • HAMBURG
STOCKHOLM • ATHENS • TOKYO • MILAN • MADRID
PRAGUE • WARSAW • BUDAPEST • AUCKLAND

ISBN 0-373-29052-7

MY LORD PROTECTOR

DEBORAH HALE

After a decade of tracing her ancestors to their roots in Georgian-era Britain, Golden Heart winner Deborah Hale turned to historical romance writing as a way to blend her love of the past with her desire to spin a good love story. Deborah lives in Nova Scotia, Canada, between the historic British garrison town of Halifax and the romantic Annapolis Valley of Longfellow's *Evangeline.* With four children under ten (including twins), Deborah calls writing her "sanity retention mechanism." On good days, she likes to think it's working.

Deborah invites you to her one-of-a-kind web site to catch the flavor of eighteenth-century London, from a cup of the most decadent chocolate to scandalous tidbits of backstage gossip from the Green Room at Drury Lane. To get there, follow her author's link on the Harlequin web site http://www.romance.net.

To Judy Gorham,
who read this book before anyone else knew
I was writing it.

Chapter One

October 1742

"**D**early beloved." The curate's whistling treble voice echoed through the vast vaulted emptiness of St. Martin's in the Fields, one of London's most fashionable places of worship. "We are gathered in the sight of God to join this man and this woman in the bonds of holy matrimony, which is an honorable estate.…"

Honorable estate? Julianna Ramsay could barely contain a shriek of bitter laughter. *Bondage—certainly.* She wanted to tear the prayer book from the curate's plump fingers and hurl it through the massive window above the altar. She longed to scale the stone pillars and batter the hypocritical smirks off the faces of those smug plaster cherubs.

"If any here can show just cause why this wedding should not take place, let him speak now or forever hold his peace."

Jerome's blunt fingers tightened around her wrist. Julianna cast her stepbrother a sidelong glance. Unshaven and disheveled from the previous night's debauchery, he glared back at her with eyes as black and pitiless as his conscience.

Thick lips curled in a gloating sneer. *By all means, sister,* he wordlessly urged her, *indulge in a fit of hysterical fury. I'll see you shackled in the bowels of Bedlam before the day is out.*

Summoning every ounce of composure, Julianna fought to

master her impotent rage. Her features cold and rigid as a marble effigy, she focused her answer into a scornful look. *I would not give you the satisfaction, Jerome.* Refusing to meet the curate's questioning glance, she clenched her lips to imprison the words of protest she dared not utter.

A raw autumn wind keened around the church's lofty spire, nearly drowning out the words of the wedding service. The little curate cleared his throat and pitched his delivery louder. "Dost thou, Julianna, take this man to thy lawful wedded husband..."

Reluctantly, Julianna's gaze shifted to her bridegroom, Sir Edmund Fitzhugh. He could not have looked less like Crispin Bayard, the man she had hoped to wed. Thinking of her handsome young sweetheart, Julianna's heart quailed. The words she must soon speak would destroy any chance of a future with Crispin.

Oh my love, her soul cried out across the miles that separated them, *how could you have abandoned me to this?* Even as that anguished question rang in her thoughts, a countering voice of reason objected. How could Crispin have known, when he sailed for the South Seas, that her father would shortly die bankrupt, leaving her at the mercy of her feared and despised stepbrother?

An expectant silence wrenched Julianna back to the present. Jerome prompted her with another bruising squeeze of her wrist.

"I do." She fairly spit the words.

The curate smiled indulgently. No doubt he mistook the force of her answer for eagerness to wed a man of wealth and position.

"And dost thou, Edmund, take this woman to thy lawful wedded wife, to live together under God's holy ordinance..."

While his attention was fixed on the clergyman, Julianna stole a look at her bridegroom. She would have guessed him a former sea captain, even without Jerome's telling. The intrepid set of Sir Edmund's broad shoulders and his wide stance bespoke years spent on a pitching quarterdeck. His large hands looked capable of nimbly lashing a sail or holding a tiller steady in rough seas. His firm jaw, slightly cleft chin and the stern line of his mouth all suggested a temperament resolute—even obdurate. His deep-set eyes, which seemed to search out some distant horizon, were cold and gray as the North Atlantic.

Where was the pitiful old wreck she'd expected to find at the chancel steps this morning? That had been Julianna's desperate plan to foil her stepbrother and to keep herself unsullied for Crispin. When Jerome had demanded she take a husband immediately, she had sent her trusted cousin, Francis, to seek a bridegroom too old and decrepit to consummate their union. Since then, she'd not had a private moment to ask Francis how he'd fared. Noting his complacent manner, she'd assumed all was well.

Jerome's derisive account of Sir Edmund's proposal had made him sound ideal for her purpose. "We met at the Chapterhouse while I was posting my notice of the books for auction. He collects book and antiquities. Indeed, he is something of an antiquity himself. Affects to wear his own hair, mind you, though it's sparse enough in places to excuse a good periwig."

Antiquity? Under other circumstances the idea might have struck Julianna as amusing. Jerome had overestimated Sir Edmund's age by more than one good year. Though perhaps not in the peak of condition, her bridegroom appeared well capable of undertaking his marital duties. So much for her pathetic plan.

"...and forsaking all others, keep thee only unto her, until death dost thou part?"

"I do." The timbre of Sir Edmund's voice was deep and resonant, with more than a hint of sharpness. Such a voice brooked no dissent from a crew, a household or a wife. And, God help her, she had promised to obey.

A blessed numbness stole over Julianna. Her budding dreams of an unconsummated marriage had died stillborn. Jerome had sold off all her worldly goods—her beloved books and even her treasured harp, insisting he needed the money to discharge her late father's debts. Soon she would belong to this stern, forbidding man. Yet she was able to view it all calmly, as though this marriage were being perpetrated upon a stranger.

"Who gives this woman to be married to this man?"

"I do," said Jerome.

To Julianna's ears, those two short words rang with ten years' worth of mocking triumph. Her stomach seethed as she caught a whiff of her stepbrother's breath, putrid with stale brandy. Raising her fan, she fluttered it to disperse the fumes.

Who gives this woman? For most brides those words were a formality. In her case they could not have been more accurate. Her stepbrother was giving her away to a total stranger, with forced consent, for promises of money. Sold, like all her late father's possessions, to the highest bidder.

"In the name of God, I, Edmund, take thee, Julianna, to my lawful wedded wife. To have and to hold from this day forward. For better, for worse. For richer, for poorer. In sickness and in health. Till death do us part."

When her turn came to speak, Julianna's lips moved but the words emerged scarcely audible even to herself. Looking past the looming silhouette of Sir Edmund Fitzhugh, she addressed her words to Crispin, vowing to keep her heart only unto him.

"I, Julianna, take thee, Edmund, to my wedded husband...."

Her words were barely a whisper, and Edmund had the uncomfortable conviction his bride was staring right through him.

How dare she look so woebegone at the prospect of marrying him? his Fitzhugh pride demanded. After all, this daft scheme had been hers in the first place. When she'd sent her timorous cousin around to advance the idea, he'd found himself with no honorable recourse but to fall in with their foolish plan.

"...in sickness and in health. Till death do us part."

At that moment, the enormity of what he was doing boxed Edmund squarely in the stomach. Julianna Ramsay looked so very young in her ill-fitting black gown, her ruddy curls all but hidden by a fulsome cap. Though he was barely forty, Edmund had seen and done more than most men twice his age. Years of adventuring in the Tropics had taken their toll on his constitution. At the moment he wanted nothing more than to escape to the refuge of his library with a comfortable wing chair, a pipeful of rich tobacco and a familiar volume of Shakespeare or Marcus Aurelius.

"With this ring, I thee wed...." The words stuck in Edmund's throat as he thrust the heavy gold circlet onto Julianna's waxen finger. With effort, he managed to bark them out.

Long ago he had sworn never to marry again. Matrimony did not suit his solitary temperament. He and Amelia had made each other bitterly unhappy during the interminable months of their brief marriage. Edmund had never pretended it was all the fault of his frigid, ambitious late wife. What mad impulse had propelled him back to the altar after all these years?

Edmund stole another glance at Julianna as they knelt to receive the Eucharist. The pallid light of an overcast morning filtered through the altar window, starkly illuminating the cruel marks that marred her delicate features—a livid welt on her cheek, dark bruises on her chin, a swollen lower lip. The sight of her—young, vulnerable and so obviously brutalized, called forth every protective instinct in his being. His hands itched to close around Jerome Skeldon's thick neck. To wrest Julianna Ramsay from the power of that blackguard, he was even willing to thrust his head back into the matrimonial noose.

"Oh God, who hath consecrated the state of matrimony to such an excellent mystery…look mercifully upon these thy servants."

Edmund took a deep breath and squared his shoulders. For better or worse, the deed was done. In a stroke he had secured Julianna's safety. He would provide for her every comfort. Surely she could ask no more of him. He would resume his tranquil, well-ordered existence, and try to pretend the disquieting events of past days had never taken place.

As he rose to accept the congratulations of their small bridal party, one thought continued to trouble Edmund. If only he could be certain Crispin would approve…

Skeldon's carriage rattled over the cobbles of Piccadilly Street, bearing Jerome, Francis and Julianna to Fitzhugh House for the bridal luncheon. Slouched in the seat opposite his stepsister, Jerome drew a flask from his coat pocket and took a long pull. He gasped appreciatively at the liquor's potency.

With exaggerated care, he wiped the mouth of the bottle on his stock and held it out to her. "Will you join me, milady?"

Julianna arched an eyebrow in disdain, not daring to speak.

"Of course, you want nothing to cloud your experience of this special day." Jerome sneered. "Is that not so, sister?"

As the barb of her stepbrother's sarcasm stung, Julianna knew she had only herself to blame. The skies had suddenly opened as the wedding party emerged from the church, spewing a cascade of rain upon them. In the rush toward the carriages, she had deliberately made for Jerome's. Much as she hated and mistrusted her stepbrother, at least she knew what to expect from him. That was more than she could say of her formidable-looking bridegroom.

Jerome thrust his flask toward Francis. "You more sociably disposed than your cousin, Underhill?"

"Not I," Francis chirped. "I intend to slake my thirst at luncheon. Julianna's new husband looks to be a gentleman of quality, and I mean to do justice to his hospitality."

"Suit yourself." Jerome shrugged and took another drink.

It had been the same ever since the carriage pulled away from St. Martin's—Jerome baiting her with surly mock courtesy, while Francis made the most annoyingly good-humored small talk. Both grated equally on Julianna's raw nerves.

Heavy and tight, the gold wedding band encircled her finger like a fetter. The unnatural calm that had sustained her through the wedding ceremony was rapidly slipping away. Behind that mask of composure cowered a frightened child. Could she truly be the wife of that cold, silent man? How would she survive this day and this night, let alone the days and months and years to come? Only the look of sly satisfaction in Jerome's eyes forced Julianna to hold her head high and still her quivering lip.

The curate lurched into Edmund's brougham, water sluicing from the rear corners of his hat. "I must apologize for my tardiness." He gasped for breath. "While I was changing out of my surplice, the rector detained me for a quick word."

"I beg your pardon?" Edmund wrenched his gaze back from the window. He was still puzzling over Julianna's defection to her stepbrother's carriage. Surprised by the sudden downpour, had she simply acted on impulse? Or had she intentionally chosen the company of that sordid brute, Skeldon, over his own?

"The rector," the curate repeated loudly. "He asked me to tell you how sorry he was not to preside over your nuptials. If only you'd been in less haste, or if his engagement had been less pressing, I know he'd have been pleased to perform the service."

Removing his hat, he gave it a little shake. Then he drew out a handkerchief and began to mop the moisture from his face. "A rainy wedding day. That's considered a good omen, I believe."

Catching a glimpse of Skeldon's landau behind them, Edmund muttered, "In Surrey, we say, 'happy the bride the sun shines on.'"

The curate gave a strangulated chuckle. "And speaking of the bride, where is your lovely lady?"

Was she lovely? Edmund found himself wondering as he explained about the sudden cloudburst and the wedding party's scramble for shelter in the carriages. No, he decided at last. Not in the conventional sense. Her eyes were an odd color for one thing—the pale amber brown of clear, hot tea. Her mouth was too wide for beauty, not to mention slightly crooked. Or perhaps it was only the bruises that made it look so.

All the same, she had a fey, winsome air that touched him. Somewhere in his dispassionate, impregnable heart, Edmund shrank from the look of aversion he'd seen in his bride's eyes.

Passing through a half wall of masonry and wrought iron, the two carriages drew to a halt before Fitzhugh House, a spacious red brick mansion with many windows. The rain had eased to a fitful spatter. As Julianna alighted from Jerome's landau, Sir Edmund stepped forward to take her arm.

A servant in impeccable livery stood before the massive front doors. Sir Edmund nodded toward him. "Let me begin by introducing the steward of my household, Mr. Mordecai Brock."

The man bowed stiffly. He sported an impressive set of side whiskers, together with the most severe eyebrows Julianna had ever seen. Piercing blue eyes beneath those brows shot her a look of glowering disapproval.

"A pleasure to meet you, Mr. Brock," she lied.

The steward threw open the doors, ushering the wedding party into a large, marble-floored entry hall. A pair of elegant staircases flanked the spacious chamber, sweeping upward to the second story. The dark wood of their balustrades gleamed.

A veritable army of servants were marshaled in the entry hall—footmen, coachmen, maids of every capacity. Sir Edmund paraded his bride before them like a visiting general inspecting his troops, while Mr. Brock introduced each member of his staff. Julianna scarcely heard him.

Though their names meant nothing to her, the servants' facial expressions cut her at every turn—contemptuous, boldly curious. Having been on the most familiar terms with her father's staff, she was distressed by the obvious antipathy of these people. If only she could make them understand how little she wanted to be here. As little as they wanted her, apparently.

The inspection concluded, Mr. Brock whispered a word to his master. Sir Edmund turned to Julianna. "If you'll excuse me, there is a matter I must attend to." He motioned to Francis. "Underhill, will you kindly deputize for me and escort my wife into luncheon?"

Francis beamed. "An honor and a pleasure, Sir Edmund." As he took Julianna's arm, he gave it a reassuring squeeze.

Her Welsh temper flared. How dare the fool look so outrageously pleased with himself? He was supposed to be Crispin's best friend. Did he call this friendship—handing his comrade's intended bride over to a stranger? Using the width of her skirts as cover, she dealt him a sharp kick in the shin. Francis flinched, blinking his mild eyes with a wounded air. She flashed him an answering glare that made no secret of her ire.

As the dining room door swung open, the curate uttered a gasp of delight. Bathed in the soft glow of candlelight, Sir Edmund's service of silver, crystal and gilded china made the table glitter like an open treasure chest.

"Sir Edmund is a very generous host," said the curate.

"If not a particularly genial one," Jerome muttered. Strolling over to the sideboard, he made a great show of inspecting the wines.

Francis held a chair for Julianna. "This is certainly the feast I envisaged. Your father was always reckoned to set a good table, my dear. But this surpasses even the best of his board."

Looking up from his scrutiny of the wine, Jerome sniffed. "Father squandered his substance entertaining every ne'er-do-well in London. If he'd paid more attention to his business than to his salons, his estate wouldn't be in such bad pass now."

"De mortuis nil nisi bonum," the curate piously reminded Jerome. "Speak well of the dead."

"Speak well? I *did* well to find my sister a husband at such short notice, and her without a penny's dowry." Taking a bottle off the sideboard, he poured himself a glass of wine.

Julianna barely stifled her urge to pick up the nearest piece of glassware and fling it at her stepbrother's head.

"Ah, Skeldon, I see you have anticipated me." Sir Edmund strode to the head of the table and lifted his own glass. "Let us begin our celebration with a toast to the bride." Beneath the forced heartiness, Julianna detected an edge of hostility in his voice. Looking from Jerome to Sir Edmund, she recalled a saying of her old nurse. In times of trouble, Winnie had often complained of being caught between the devil and the deep blue sea.

"Permit me, Sir Edmund." Jerome was beginning to slur his words. "As her brother of ten years, and lately her guardian, I believe I'm best equipped to offer a salute to your bride."

Julianna felt the blood drain from her face. Salute—Jerome had used that very word last night as he'd ambushed her on the way to her room. *Did you think I would send you to bed on your wedding eve without a brotherly salute?* Fortunately he'd been drunk enough to slow his reflexes. Wriggling out of his pawing grasp, she'd escaped to the safety of her bedchamber with nothing worse than a bruised face. All through the night she had prayed she would soon become the property of a man too old and ailing to look upon her with Jerome's brutal lust.

The gentlemen enthusiastically drank Julianna's health, then settled down to the feast.

"I fear I may never dine so well again," said Francis, as the servants brought in a course of soup and jellied eels, followed by hot kidney pie.

"Stuffed woodcock." The curate poised his knife and fork eagerly over one of the birds. "Why, there are three brace of the creatures." Popping a plump morsel of breast meat into his mouth, he groaned with pleasure.

Under other circumstances, Julianna would have relished such a fine meal, but today she dared not trust a bite upon her heaving stomach. Toying nervously with her food, she noticed Sir Edmund also took small helpings. As she watched from the corner of her eye, he pushed each morsel several times around his plate before lifting a half-empty fork to his lips.

Francis more than compensated for Sir Edmund's lack of appetite, helping himself to everything as if he hadn't eaten in months and expected to fast for several more. He and the curate kept up a cheerful banter while Jerome took his refreshment in the form of Sir Edmund's stock of excellent French wines.

As the footman removed her barely touched plate, Julianna's gaze strayed to a portrait above the mantel. It showed a handsome woman dressed in the style of the past generation. In her long face and cleft chin, she resembled Sir Edmund, but the lady's lips were fuller and her eyes looked...familiar.

Curiosity overcame Julianna's reticence. She leaned toward her new husband. "Sir Edmund, is that a portrait of your mother?"

He started at the question, as though her presence had slipped his mind. Francis and the curate were still engaged in sprightly conversation, while an inebriated Jerome contributed the odd vulgar jest. Almost lost in the hubbub, Sir Edmund's words were addressed less to Julianna than to the lady in the portrait. To catch his reply, she had to lean closer still.

"Unfortunately I have no likeness of my mother. She died when I was born. That is my sister, Alice. She was some dozen years my senior and a mother to me in every way throughout my childhood. Alice has been dead fully ten years now."

He seemed on the point of saying more when Francis interrupted with a question. "Sir Edmund, we were just admiring

the Fitzhugh coat of arms upon the near wall. Is it true you are
heir to a title that dates back to the Conquest?''

With labored joviality, Sir Edmund replied in a louder voice,
''The first Fitzhugh did arrive in England with Duke William.
However, I come from a long line of younger sons. One Edmund Fitzhugh was a Knight Hospitaller in the First Crusade
and a later one fell at Agincourt, 'upon St. Crispin's day.'''

That name on Sir Edmund's lips was almost more than Julianna could bear. She recognized the quotation, from Shakespeare's *Henry V,* but never had she made the connection with
her Crispin. Julianna caught her husband's eyes upon her, his
expression inscrutable. Perhaps Jerome had told him of her true
love, and on their wedding day he meant to taunt her with it.

Under the table, her knees began to tremble. She clenched
them together, but the palsy moved up her legs. She had to
clasp her hands in her lap to still them. Light-headed, Julianna
wondered how to go about excusing herself.

Sir Edmund rose abruptly. ''Gentlemen, if you will excuse
us, I believe my wife and I will retire. My health is not the
best, and Lady Fitzhugh is likely exhausted with grief from her
recent bereavement. Please stay and celebrate on our behalf.''

Taking Julianna's arm, he propelled her out the door before
she had time to object or the others had time to reply. Behind
them, Julianna heard Jerome give an admiring whistle. ''The
old devil works fast!''

She tried to swallow the lump in her throat. It felt as big as
a whole stuffed woodcock. Perhaps it would be best to get this
over with. Nothing could be worse than waiting.

As the door closed behind them, Sir Edmund's shoulders
bowed slightly. ''I trust you do not mind leaving so soon. I
could not stand to be in the same room with that man for another minute.''

Having no idea what he meant, Julianna nodded dumbly. Sir
Edmund signaled a young housemaid. ''Gwenyth, show Lady
Fitzhugh to her rooms and help her unpack, or whatever she
needs.''

He turned back to Julianna, his face looking suddenly drawn
and weary. ''I am afraid I must make my excuses to you as

well, ma'am. I have overexpended my strength these past few days, and must rest. I will come by your rooms later. We can talk then.''

Nodding in reply to his stiff bow, Julianna trailed the maid up the staircase. Apparently she would have to wait, after all.

Chapter Two

"**Y**our rooms are this way, milady." The girl's voice carried a familiar Welsh lilt. Julianna's heart lifted at the sound. Whatever else lay ahead of her in Sir Edmund's house, she meant to have at least one ally.

"Gwenyth?" Julianna had a poor command of her grandmother's tongue, picked up mostly from ballads. Still, with a little effort she was able to put a few words of Welsh together, to ask how long the girl had been away from "home."

The response proved well worth her effort. Gwenyth rounded upon her with startled delight, quickly jabbering off an animated tale of which Julianna could only pick out a word here and there.

Julianna held up her hand. "I'm sorry. My Welsh is not as good as that. My grandmother was a Cymru from the north coast. It cheers me to hear your voice, for it reminds me of home."

"Ah-h well, to say again in English, milady—I came from the hill country north of Abergavenny two years back, when my daddy passed on. My auntie's the cook here. What she won't say when she hears you can speak the Old Tongue."

Looking into Gwenyth's beaming face, Julianna knew she had gained her ally.

Halfway down a wide gallery, the maid stopped before a closed door. "I hope your rooms will suit, ma'am. We had quite a time readyin' everything at such little notice. Auntie said if anyone had told her this past Sabbath that the captain would have a new bride before week's end, she'd have…''

Julianna stepped over the threshold of her new quarters. They had entered a sitting room, past which she could see a bedroom, and a farther chamber beyond it—a dressing room, perhaps. Looking around, Julianna wondered if she had taken leave of her senses. Though she was seeing this small salon for the very first time, it felt as familiar as her own skin.

There in the far corner stood her father's marquetry writing desk. In the center of the room was the brocade upholstered chaise upon which she had sat so recently with Cousin Francis. At the hearthside stood her little breakfast table. A tall case beside the door held books, the titles of which she could recite by heart. Not daring to move or speak, for fear of dissipating this lovely illusion, Julianna pressed her back against the door.

Though she did not trust the evidence of her eyes, her nose soon persuaded her it was no mere fancy. She smelled a compound of her father's pipe tobacco and wig powder, together with her own rose water and the ghosts of favorite meals. All underlaid with the subtle musty odor of old books. No rare spice or expensive perfume could ever smell as sweet to her. Slowly, Julianna's chest began to heave and warm tears welled up in her eyes. Since her father's death and through the past several wretched days, she had not shed a single tear. Now she found herself overcome by this unexpected good fortune.

Rushing to the bedchamber, she discovered her own bed with its familiar linens and hangings. Her lap harp rested on the pillows. Her mother's portrait looked down a blessing from the opposite wall. Julianna clambered onto the bed, crushing the harp to her bosom. She began to rock back and forth as her tears flowed unchecked, accompanied by great shuddering sobs.

''Are you sure 'tis all right, milady?'' Gwenyth ventured. ''Like I said, we'd little time from when the fellows delivered everything last evening. Are *you* quite well, ma'am? Could I get you a cup of tea…or aught stronger?''

Bounding from the bed, laughter now mixed with her tears, Julianna grasped Gwenyth by the hands and danced her about the room. Among all these familiar things, the girl had suddenly become the image of her dearest Winnie, grown young again.

"Oh, Gwenyth, I am fine. The rooms are wonderful! Give the staff my warmest thanks." Brushing away tears with the back of her hand, Julianna tried to collect herself. "I will take tea, please, and a basin of water to wash."

"I could draw you a bath, milady. Your dressing room is all set up with one. Has its own fire and a kettle to heat water." Gwenyth continued in a tone of apology, "The master does have his own notions about bein' clean, ma'am. More than once I've heard him say, 'The most savage headhunter in all Borneo smells better than the average London hostess!'"

Julianna had no difficulty imagining Sir Edmund Fitzhugh uttering so pithy a sentiment. While some might disdain his fastidious attitude, she sympathized completely.

Gwenyth's voice dropped to a conspiratorial whisper. "That's why he won't ever put on a wig, isn't it? 'A home for vermin,' he calls 'em." Together, the girls chuckled over this blunt but accurate assessment.

"I'll go light the fire, milady. Then I'll fetch your tea. By the time you finish it, the water'll be hot."

Once Gwenyth had gone, Julianna began to explore her living quarters. The little dressing room intrigued her, with its water kettle and shallow copper bathing tub. The cozy little room contained a pair of cherry-wood wardrobes from her old home, and something new to her. In the far corner sat a delightful low table with a large mirror, presumably for use in dressing her hair.

How had all this come about—her things bought at the auction and brought here to be so carefully assembled, awaiting her arrival? What touched Julianna more than the deed itself was the perceptive kindness that had anticipated her feelings and taken such pains to make her welcome. These were hardly the actions she would have expected from the stern-faced man with whom she had exchanged less than a dozen sentences. Had she misjudged him?

Reveling in the unaccustomed luxury of a private bath, Julianna continued to puzzle over her situation. As the scalding, soapy water ran over her shoulders and Gwenyth scrubbed her skin with a soft cloth, she tried to cleanse herself of Jerome's amorous assault. Would it be any better tonight, when her bridegroom came to claim her? The thought of lying unclothed and intimate with a man she knew so little made Julianna cringe and blush so furiously the roots of her hair stung. Vows, clerical pronouncements and signed marriage bond notwithstanding, she doubted such an act could be anything but a violation.

She tried to imagine herself alone with her new husband. She did not expect the lascivious brutality of Jerome, nor the gentle ardor of her Crispin. Sir Edmund Fitzhugh looked so aloof and self-possessed. She could scarcely envisage kisses from that firm mouth, caresses from those cool, capable hands or tender murmurings from that commanding voice. Yet, did she not owe a duty to the man who had rescued her from a far worse fate?

Enfolded in a cozy wrap, Julianna sat before the mirrored table as Gwenyth combed out her tangled curls and chattered on about her own childhood in Wales. The steamy warmth of the room, together with the abashment of recent conjectures, had revived the rosiness of her complexion. The firelight played glints of gold and copper through her russet hair. She'd decided to leave it hanging long for her wedding night. Draped over her neck and around her face, it might obscure the marks Jerome had left.

Her hair combed out and drying, Julianna dismissed her already faithful Gwenyth, extracting a promise that the girl would be her waiting woman. She would try to rest, Julianna told her maid, requesting a light tea later in the day.

After Gwenyth had gone, Julianna lay on her bed, staring up at the canopy. Despite so many recent restless nights, sleep eluded her. Searching the bookcase, she pulled out a well-thumbed copy of *Don Quixote* and sat down to read. She had devoted much of her sixteenth year to translating her beloved Cervantes from the original Spanish. Today, however, not even Señor de la Mancha had the power to distract her. After a half hour's dogged attempt at concentration, she abandoned the project. Where was a knight-errant when a lady needs one? Julianna wondered, returning the book to its place on the shelf.

For a while she prowled her rooms like a caged animal. Now and then, she would pause to gaze out her window, which overlooked the rear courtyard and garden. The storm had gathered force again, the wind lashing waves of rain against the thick windowpanes. In the dark glass, her reflection floated—a ghost girl weeping raindrop tears.

Something in the wild sorrow of the tempest struck a chord in Julianna's Celtic soul. If she could not keep her unease at bay, then she would drown herself in it. Drawing the hangings on her bed to create a cocoon of darkness, she groped for her harp. At last her hands closed over the familiar curves of carved ash wood. She hugged the venerable instrument to her aching heart.

Sitting alone in the darkness gave Julianna an illusion of safety. Even as a child, she had loved the dark. Darkness guarded hidden fears. Darkness kept watch over secret tears. Darkness respected private sorrow. In the cool embrace of the dark, she concentrated on the sound and feel of her harp. It was an easy armful. Carved with intricate twining knots, the sounding post rested in its accustomed place, bridging her lap and the hollow of her shoulder. She had dreaded losing it as much as she would have dreaded losing the fingers that plucked its strings. By ancient Welsh law, a person's harp was the one possession that could never be seized to satisfy a debt. No Englishman would ever understand that.

Tonight no music would satisfy Julianna's soul but the Welsh ballads her harp had been crafted to play. Its strings vibrated from the fleet undulations of her fingers as she played every haunting lament of her embattled people. How many of her ancestresses, younger than she, had gone off to marriages made by others? How many had been taken as spoils of war and used accordingly? How many, eschewing the love of mortal men, had found some barren peace in the arms of the church? So many centuries had passed, and still a woman was no more than chattel.

On and on Julianna played, long after her fingers had begun to ache, singing in a voice hoarse with unshed tears, lost in the sweet, mournful music. To one especially poignant lament she returned again and again. Composed by her ancestor, Gryffud ab yr Yneed Coch, the song was an elegy for Llywelyn Olaf, the last true prince of Wales:

"Do you not see the path of the wind and the rain?"

"Do you not see that the world has ended?" it concluded in despair.

"Oh milady, that sounded lovely!"

Julianna startled at the sound of Gwenyth's voice. In the protective cavern of her bed, she had managed to lose herself. Now she must come out and face a fate she could not escape.

"I haven't heard anyone play the harp since I came away from home." Gwenyth drew back the bed hangings. "'Llywelyn's Lament,' wasn't it? It has a pretty sound, though it is so sad."

As she laid her harp aside, Julianna wondered if Gwenyth would ask why a bride should sing a dirge on her wedding night.

Though she might have been curious, the little maid was obviously too well trained to question the actions of her new mistress. "I've brought you a bite of supper like you asked, milady. If you feel up to it."

Julianna nodded. For a moment she lingered in the doorway to the sitting room, looking back at her bed. After tonight, would she ever be able to think of it as a sanctuary again? An icy chill licked its way up her back. Pulling her wrap protectively around herself, she quickly turned to the sitting room, where a cheery fire blazed in the hearth and Gwenyth was setting the table. Never had Julianna felt such an overwhelming need for distraction and the companionship of another woman.

"Gwenyth, will you kindly do me one last service? Please sit and take tea with me?"

The girl darted a furtive glance behind her, as if expecting a wrathful Mr. Brock to materialize at her heels. "Oh, ma'am, I couldn't! Wouldn't be fitting, would it?"

"Perhaps not, but I desperately need some company. It would be a great boon to me if you would stay."

Gwenyth wavered between an obvious desire to oblige, and an exaggerated sense of propriety. "I will stay, ma'am, if that's what you'd like. But I'll take no tea. I'll just unpack a few things from your trunk while you eat.''

''Thank you, Gwenyth. That is the perfect solution, isn't it? Perhaps you can tell me something of the captain—other than his distaste for dirt. I'll admit I am not very well acquainted with my husband.'' That last word stuck in Julianna's throat.

''Dunno as I can help you on that score, milady. The master's said no more than a dozen words to me before today. You could have bowled me over with a feather when he asked me to direct you up here. Auntie Enid and Mr. Brock have worked for him the longest. They both think the sun rises and sets by the master.''

Her face must have betrayed her feelings about Sir Edmund's intimidating steward, for Gwenyth chuckled in sympathy. ''Oh, he's not so bad, our Mr. Brock. For all he guards the master like an old bulldog, his bark's a good deal worse than his bite.''

Julianna rolled her eyes. ''I hope I will not have to be bitten to find out the truth of that.''

The two girls shared a guarded laugh. How Mr. Brock's ears must be burning! Gwenyth continued her story.

''When I saw all your books go into this room, ma'am, I thought to myself, 'Whoever she is, this lady'll be a good match for the master!' He has more than one great room full of books. Spends most of his time in the library, reading and smoking his long pipe. What a black look a body gets if he's disturbed! He's not a very sociable man, you know. Why, that luncheon today is as much entertainment as we've had in this house since I've been here.''

Two sharp raps at the door made Julianna start guiltily. Dropping her pretense of unpacking, Gwenyth scurried to answer the summons. Sir Edmund stepped into the sitting room. At the sight of him, Julianna's heart leapt into her throat, suffusing her face with blood and beating a galloping pulse in her ears. Her husband looked as if he had slept—in preparation for tonight? With his jabot and waistcoat discarded and the top several buttons of his shirt undone, he cut a somewhat less daunting figure than he had at their wedding ceremony. At the moment, that was little consolation to Julianna.

"I'll come back in the morning and finish this up, shall I, milady? Unless there's something special you want out just now?"

"No, thank you, Gwenyth, tomorrow will be fine. Good night."

Bobbing a quick curtsy, the girl made her escape. Given her wish, Julianna would have been hot on Gwenyth's heels.

An awkward silence fell over the sitting room, punctuated only by the crackling of the fire and the ticking of the mantel clock. Had it been damaged in the move? Julianna wondered. It seemed to take longer than usual to count each passing second.

"Will you have a seat, Sir Edmund?" she asked in a rush. "I was just finishing my tea. The food at luncheon looked lovely, but I was too nervous to touch a bite. Will you join me?"

"Thank you, no." Sir Edmund took a seat at the far end of the chaise. "I rarely find myself hungry these days. However, you needn't stop on my account."

"I have eaten as much as I can manage." Julianna felt the appetizing little meal turn to a lump of lead in her stomach. Taking a cautious step back from the hearthside table, she perched on the other end of the chaise.

Sir Edmund cleared his throat. "I trust the accommodations meet with your approval."

Out of the corner of her eye, Julianna glanced at her bridegroom. He looked every bit as anxious and uncertain as she felt. Somehow it eased her own apprehension. Whatever else he might be, Sir Edmund Fitzhugh obviously was not practiced in the art of seduction.

A bubble of nervous laughter broke from her lips. "Meet with my approval? Are you much given to understatement, Sir Edmund? Why, I wept with joy when I saw my possessions returned to me."

His expression darkened. "They should never have been taken from you in the first place. Of all the infamous conduct... I suppose Skeldon responsible for this, and these?"

He gestured toward the bruises on her face. Mortified that

they had drawn his notice, Julianna flinched. Perhaps he misread her reaction, for he reached out and tilted her smarting chin with the subtlest of pressure, urging her to look him in the eye. When he spoke, his voice was hardly above a whisper.

"Understand, my dear, that you will never be so used in this house. I will likely be a less than perfect husband, having so little previous experience with matrimony. However, I do hold myself a cut above any cowardly swine who would raise his hand to a woman. This is your home now. You will always be safe here."

Some beacon of compassion in the depths of those inscrutable eyes, together with the reassuring gentleness of his hand and voice, touched her. Julianna's tightly bound emotions broke free, overwhelming her. Before she had time to think what she was doing, she found herself cradled against Sir Edmund's shoulder, weeping her heart out in the sanctuary of his arms.

The fine linen of his shirt drank in her tears. She could feel the warmth of his chest against her cheek. He smelled of pipe tobacco and shaving soap, and a faint spicy aroma she could not identify. She loved Crispin with all her heart, but Crispin was lost to her. She was alone in a hostile world, with only one possible haven of safety and solace. Squeezing her eyes tightly shut, Julianna raised her face to Sir Edmund's. Her lips brushed his sharp jawline, coming to rest with tremulous delicacy against his. For a moment he seemed to yield, the firm set of his mouth softening in response to the timid invitation of her kiss.

Then, without a twitch of warning, he pushed her back and leapt up from the chaise as if the upholstery had caught fire. "Have you lost your mind, woman? What is the meaning of this?"

What had she done wrong? Had she behaved in too forward a manner? "I thought…that is, Jerome told me…you wanted to breed an heir to your fortune."

"I had to tell him something." Sir Edmund made an obvious effort to regain his composure. "I couldn't very well approach a fellow in the midst of a respectable coffeehouse and casually inquire if he had a sister for sale. Besides, I have a perfectly suitable heir, as you well know, and I have no interest in sup-planting him.''

Now who had lost his senses?

''But, if you don't…I mean… Well, look here, exactly why did you offer to marry me?''

He gazed down at her with a vexing mixture of amazement and amusement. ''You don't know who I am,'' he said, in the hushed, reverent tone of one suddenly enlightened.

''I know very well who you are,'' Julianna snapped. ''However, I do *not* know what you are talking about.''

''You don't know who I am,'' Sir Edmund repeated, appearing pleasantly relieved by the knowledge. ''That explains it all—the way you looked during the wedding. Why, I've seen cheerier faces bound for the gallows.''

A guilty blush smarted in Julianna's cheeks. She hung her head. ''I meant nothing personal regarding you, Sir Edmund.''

''I should hope not. After all, I am undoubtedly the answer to any maiden's prayer.'' The dryly ironic tone of his voice made Julianna glance up. She saw his brows arched and his shoulders raised in a droll, self-deprecating gesture. This arid humor caught her so much by surprise, she could not stifle a volley of nervous laughter. Sir Edmund's features relaxed from their comic aspect into something approaching a smile.

''I thought your woeful expression might be playacting for your stepbrother. I am sorry you had to suffer such distress, but it may have been worth it to convince Skeldon of your reluctance to marry me. Perhaps that was Underhill's intent.''

''Cousin Francis? So he did come to you. I should have known better than to trust him with such a commission. He is the most kindhearted creature in the world, but…''

''But he is a very modest man, with ample reason to be so.'' A fleeting smile warmed Sir Edmund's features. ''You could have found no fault with his mission on your behalf. Young Underhill argued your case with the utmost conviction. I'll own, I took some convincing. I prize my solitude, you see.'' Casting her a wary look, he reclaimed his seat on the chaise.

''I take your point, Sir Edmund. Neither of us came eagerly

to this marriage. But what is this other business you alluded to, about your identity?''

''At luncheon, I made an awkward attempt to reassure you when I spoke of my family history. For centuries the name Crispin, like Edmund, has often been bestowed on hapless Fitzhugh infants. My father was the Reverend Crispin Fitzhugh. I also have a nephew, my sister Alice's son—Crispin Bayard.''

Her Crispin, the nephew of Sir Edmund Fitzhugh? Julianna mulled this single fact over and over in her mind, that it might take hold. ''Then you must be Crispin's 'quoting uncle'!''

''So he would often call me. And I would reply, 'A word fitly spoken is like—' ''

'' '—is like apples of gold.' '' Julianna laughed with delighted surprise. ''It is you! I can't believe it. How, for all the times we spoke of you, could Crispin not have told me your name?''

''My nephew is gentleman enough to know that talk of an aging uncle is no way to woo one's ladylove.''

''Crispin did once tell me that everything he learned about being a gentleman came from your example.''

Sir Edmund shook his head. ''He missed the mark there. I believe we both benefited from our upbringing by my dear Alice.''

Suddenly, as if conjured by their eager exchange, Julianna had the warmest, most palpable sense of Crispin's presence. Grasping Sir Edmund's hand, she wrung it heartily. ''It is such a pleasure to meet you at last.''

Then Julianna recalled that not only had she met Crispin's uncle, she had wed him. Abruptly, she dropped his hand.

Perhaps to reassure her, Sir Edmund continued. ''Crispin talked much of you before his departure. I know he would want me do everything in my power to aid you. He need never have made this expedition to the South Seas, you know. As my heir, if he'd chosen to remain in England and marry you, I would have made him a handsome settlement. He is a true Fitzhugh, however. Pride is our besetting sin, so I can hardly grudge him his measure of it. Neither can I quarrel with his taste for adventure, as I was also smitten with it in my youth. He is a good lad, and I know he'll fare well. He has been my ward since his mother died, and like a son to me in every way. Though perhaps we share a closer bond than most fathers and sons, who often grow at odds as time passes. My nephew is all the world to me.''

''And to me.'' She had not intended to say this. Whatever the circumstances, it could hardly be polite, professing to a new husband one's undying love for another man. ''What I mean to say is…and you to him. He spoke of you with great affection.''

Sir Edmund graciously ignored Julianna's gaffe, and her equally unsubtle attempt at recovery. ''Affection is far too pale a term for the fervor with which Crispin recounted your charms, my dear. Most of our conversations in the past months lapsed into a catalog of your beauty, your wit, your understanding.'' He ticked each off on a finger. ''I once chided him with Shakespeare's words. 'My mistress' eyes—' ''

'' '—are nothing like the sun…' '' countered Julianna. ''Crispin told me of it.''

''He insisted that one day I would retract those words, and so I do. Whenever you speak his name, your eyes are lambent with June sunshine.''

In response to Sir Edmund's courtly homage, the warmth of that sunshine spread from Julianna's eyes to her smile. Though she suspected it must look rather ghoulish on her battered face.

''I see where Crispin acquired his gift for poetic flattery.''

Rather than pleasing him, her compliment turned a man of mature years into a stammering schoolboy intent upon making his escape. ''Well…hardly…in any case…now that you know…that is to say, understand…the facts…'' Jumping from the chaise once again, he made a curt bow. ''I trust you will sleep well.''

As he backed toward the door, Julianna rose. ''So you will not be staying the night, after all.'' Obvious relief infused the words she had not meant to speak aloud. But her instant embarrassment seemed to restore Sir Edmund's composure.

''Much as I regret refusing such an invitation, I think it best, for many reasons, that our union remain…chaste. I regard you as Crispin's bride, residing in my house. When he returns, our unconsummated marriage should make it relatively easy to secure an annulment. Besides, the state of my health is such that the exertions of playing the ardent bridegroom might leave you a widow sooner than would be convenient.''

Astonished, Julianna did not think to smile at his mordant jest. As he turned the door handle, another thought occurred to Sir Edmund. ''The terms of this arrangement must remain in confidence. To the rest of the world it should appear we are husband and wife. I mistrust your stepbrother. There might be something to fear from him if he discovers our deception.''

''You have my word, Sir Edmund.'' If she ever told such an improbable tale, Julianna knew she would be dispatched to Bedlam faster than Jerome could ever have managed.

''Good. Good. Then once again I bid you good-night.''

With his abrupt departure, Julianna retired to bed, early and alone. Her heart seethed with a queer mix of emotions. She recognized astonishment, intense relief and profound gratitude, but puzzled over a shade of some nameless foreign feeling that defied definition. Surely it could not be…disappointment?

Chapter Three

15 December 1742
Dearest Winnie,

Christmas greetings from London to Wales. I trust this letter has reached you without delay, along with a more tangible remembrance. Besides bringing my kindest regards, it comes to reassure you of my fortunate situation. Shortly after you left London, I wed Sir Edmund Fitzhugh, a friend of Cousin Francis.

As her pen scratched softly against the sheet of thick creamy vellum, a frown of dissatisfaction creased Julianna's brow. Her words sounded so stiff and formal. Unfortunately, she hadn't the nerve to write this pack of lies in plainer language.

Gwenyth turned from her dusting. "It must be lovely, ma'am, to read all those grand books and write such a fine hand."

"I suppose it is." Julianna sighed. What had life come to, she asked herself, when her beloved studies no longer enthralled her? "If you would care to learn, I could teach you."

"I wouldn't dare presume, ma'am." Gwenyth returned to her dusting with a vengeance, vigorously rubbing the woodwork with a lightly oiled cloth. "Whatever would Mr. Brock say?"

Julianna made a face at the mention of their steward. The

last thing she needed was to provide him with another complaint against her. With a dispirited shrug, she resumed her writing.

> I live in a fine big house with many servants and every possible comfort. Our cook and her niece, my maidservant, are both Welsh. In their care you may rest assured that I am fed and attended almost as well as in days of yore.

Glancing up at Gwenyth going cheerfully about her work, Julianna breathed a silent prayer of thanks. Without the Welsh girl's loyalty and fellowship, she would have gone mad in the gilded cage of Fitzhugh House. The other maids' smirking politeness irritated her more than outright insolence. Mrs. Davies gave no quarter, even for the sake of their common ancestry. As for Mr. Brock, in the weeks since her wedding their mutual antipathy had degenerated into covert warfare—all the more hostile for the frosty civility that masked it.

Dipping her pen in the inkwell, she continued her letter.

> My husband makes me a generous allowance, so you must not think I will miss the small sum enclosed. Sir Edmund considers it in the interests of marital harmony for a wife to have her own funds.

Julianna shook her head as she penned this half truth. Sir Edmund gave her money to soothe his conscience for spending so little time with her. She seldom saw him, but for the few evenings a week he condescended to dine with her. The strained silence of those meals was punctuated by brief exchanges so banal they scarcely merited the title of conversation. She wondered if the kindness and humor she had glimpsed in him on their wedding night had been a figment of her overwrought imagination.

"There." Gwenyth looked around the room where brass, wood and glass gleamed. "Now I'd best see to my other chores. Before I go, is there anything I can get for you, milady? A bite to eat? Auntie says you scarcely touched your breakfast. She's worried you aren't partial to her cooking."

"Never fear." Julianna laid her pen aside. "Mr. Brock has already delivered me a lecture on that subject. Tell your aunt I like her meals very well. My appetite is poor, that is all."

"Are you quite well, milady? You sleep the day away—straight to bed from dinner and lying in longer every morning."

"I know." Julianna was not certain herself what to make of her strange craving for sleep. "At first I thought I was only catching up on the sleepless nights between my father's death and my wedding. Yet the more I sleep, the more tired I am through the day."

"If you don't mind my asking, ma'am...are you happy here?"

This straightforward question confounded Julianna for a moment. Finally she recovered her composure sufficiently to answer. "I would be a very wicked and ungrateful young woman not to be happy here, Gwenyth." Each word sounded as if it had been well laundered and starched. "I have a beautiful home, plentiful food, servants to do my bidding, a generous allowance from Sir Edmund." She had to bite her tongue to keep from adding, *And I have not a single friend in the world.*

"But you must miss your daddy. When I first came here after my daddy passed on, I missed him something dreadful."

"Miss my father? Yes, I suppose I do. We were such good friends. He was always teaching me something new, letting me help him with his work. He was a very special man, Gwenyth."

"You need to get out more, milady," Gwenyth advised. "Why don't you ask Sir Edmund to take you to that Chapterhouse place."

"Perhaps I should, Gwenyth." *In a pig's eye, I should,* Julianna thought to herself. Sir Edmund Fitzhugh was the most unsociable creature she had ever met. At home, he kept to his rooms or to the library with his books and his pipe. Once she had ventured to breach the solitude of that domain. He had treated her to so icy a glare, she'd speedily excused herself on the pretext of borrowing a book.

Gwenyth suddenly glanced at Julianna's mantel clock in alarm. "Oh, look at the time! Here I've been pestering the life out of you, ma'am, when I've work to do.'' Gwenyth bobbed a hurried curtsy and bustled off.

Julianna took up her pen again, determined to finish.

It will please you to hear that Cousin Francis's wife has given birth to a healthy daughter, whom they have christened Pamela. I visit once a week, but no oftener, as Cecily is recovering slowly from her confinement.

She was hard-put to muster the energy for those weekly visits with the Underhills. Only the torture of her loneliness compelled her to it. Without quite realizing what she was writing, Julianna concluded.

Last Christmas, how little did I guess that a year would see my father dead, and me a bride. I miss Papa more and more as Christmas draws near. I must close now and bring this letter to Francis, who has promised to contract an honest agent to deliver it to you. Think of me when you sing the plygain on Christmas morning, as I will think of you.

Heaving a sigh, Julianna dusted the paper with blotting powder and blew it off again. Then she folded it into a compact parcel containing three gold sovereigns, and sealed it with wax.

A knock sounded on the sitting room door.

''Come in,'' Julianna called, wishing she dared say exactly the opposite.

Mr. Brock entered, his bristling brows drawn together in a look of grim censure. What offense was she guilty of this time? Nothing she did met with Brock's approval. Several times he'd pointedly inquired of her plans to visit the seamstress, with the unspoken suggestion that her wardrobe was unsuitable and reflected badly upon Sir Edmund. Yet whenever she requested a chaise and pair for an outing, he sternly implied that her timing was most inconvenient.

''May I speak with you, madam?''

Nodding stiffly, Julianna wondered if there was any way she could stop him.

"It concerns Gwenyth, madam," said Brock, in his best mock-obsequious tone. "I was hoping you might be prevailed upon to restrict your calls on her. The poor child is hard-pressed to discharge her other important duties about the house."

"Indeed? Can your staff not spare a single maid exclusively to attend the lady of the house? You were right in coming to me in this matter. The situation must be rectified at once. I will be happy to pay Gwenyth's wages out of my own allowance."

For an instant Julianna savored the sweet triumph of seeing her adversary entirely at a loss for words.

"Thank you for bringing the problem to my attention, Brock. I will discuss it with Sir Edmund at my earliest convenience." It was all she could do to keep a straight face, watching the rapid desertion of Mr. Brock's composure.

She hoped the steward would not call her bluff, Julianna thought after he had gone. She did not wish to complain to Sir Edmund about her treatment, partly because he was so unapproachable. Besides, when she considered the alternatives to her present life, her concerns seemed so petty and foolish. From years of habit, she had grown accustomed to keeping her troubles to herself and putting on a show of complacency. Her letter to Winnie was merely the latest prop in that show.

Julianna recalled the letter. She must deliver it to Francis. But that would mean another unpleasant exchange with Brock about a carriage. She would also have to change clothes. Tomorrow would be soon enough. What matter when her letter reached Caer Gryffud? Christmas no longer held the special significance it once had.

Her father had always made a great celebration of it. There had been guests to welcome and entertainments to plan. Julianna felt a tear run down her cheek. Gifts to buy and special outings to arrange. Another tear fell, then another. Wassail and carolers. She could not summon the strength to stem the tide. Dropping her head upon her arms, she gave way to aching, lonely weeping.

In the gallery beyond Julianna's door, Edmund paced back and forth, berating himself for a cowardly fool. After all, over a pipe and coffee at the Chapterhouse, he regularly conversed with the most learned men in England. What made him hesitate to speak to his own wife? Whenever he came within ten feet of her, a wave of childish bashfulness assailed him and he could barely stammer the most tedious remark. He tried to cover his embarrassment with a mask of frigid reserve.

Only one other person had ever rendered him so frustratingly inarticulate. Often as a boy, he had squirmed between a desperate desire to please and a suffocating certainty of failure. What this slip of a girl had in common with his critical, forbidding father, Edmund could not fathom. He only knew that when he ventured a look into her strange golden-brown eyes, he saw longing and disappointment. As with his father, he had failed her without understanding how or why.

What more could she want from him? Edmund's fists clenched and his step quickened. He had showered her with everything his first wife had nagged for so vehemently: a fine house, carriages, servants, money. He burdened her with as little of his company as appearances would permit. Did the silly child appreciate all he had done to ensure her ease and security? No. She moped about the house like a pathetic little ghost, hardly uttering a word, not eating enough to sustain a sparrow.

Since their marriage, he couldn't call his home his own. The girl trailed behind him like a stray kitten, with her look of wordless reproach. She had even invaded the sanctuary of his library. Would she hound him out of his bedchamber next? In two months, she'd worn his patience threadbare. Imagine two years of this! Crispin had bloody well better appreciate his sacrifices.

Halting before her door, Edmund squared his shoulders. If he could brave this one interview, he might secure a few days' breathing space. He'd pack the girl off to her relatives over Christmas, and reclaim a measure of his cherished privacy. With luck, she might develop a taste for visiting, and get out from under foot entirely.

As he raised his fist to knock, Edmund caught the sound of a muffled sob from behind the door. Damn women and their tears! In his day, he had fought Dutch mercenaries, pirates and headhunters. None of those put the fear of God in him like a weeping woman. Grinding his teeth, he let his hand drop and turned away. Just then, Brock appeared at the end of the corridor. Determined not to be caught in a humiliating retreat, Edmund administered a peremptory knock on the door.

The abrupt summons jolted Julianna from her crying spell. Hurriedly mopping the tears with a corner of her fichu, she hoped her red eyes and sniffling would not betray her. She opened her door to Sir Edmund for the first time since their wedding night.

"May I come in?" he asked. "There is a matter I would like to discuss with you."

Had Mr. Brock fallen to telling tales? Julianna wondered.

"By all means, Sir Edmund. Do take a seat by the fire. With the air so damp and chill, it is pleasant to warm one's hands."

Seating himself, he made a show of chafing his fingers. "I believe this raw wind bodes our first snow."

"Very likely." Julianna took her seat on the chaise.

"Indeed." Sir Edmund stared fixedly at the fire screen.

Silence reigned in the sitting room once again.

Julianna swallowed a sigh of impatience. "You wished to discuss some matter with me, Sir Edmund?"

He took the cue eagerly. "Just so. It regards the servants."

This surprised Julianna not in the least.

"It had slipped my mind until Brock drew it to my attention."

Julianna frowned. *Very impolitic, Mr. Brock.* The steward had evidently realized she was even more reluctant than he to drag Sir Edmund into their quarrels.

"You see, with Yuletide upon us, some changes must be made in the habits of my household."

"Changes?" repeated a surprised Julianna. This had no bearing on her feud with Mr. Brock.

"Yes. You see, in past years, it was always our custom—Crispin's and mine, to give the house servants a few days off and fend for ourselves." Sir Edmund's eyes took on a look of private remembrance, and he lapsed into a near smile. "Mrs. Davies would leave cold food enough for the whole British navy. We would take in a concert or a play, then dine at an eating house. On Christmas Day we'd fill the puncheon and play host to the carolers.''

Sir Edmund shook his head, as if to clear it of the memory. ''This year circumstances have changed. I wondered if you might enjoy your own holiday. Take a few days and spend them with family, so the servants can still have their time off visiting.''

''I would not dream of denying the servants their accustomed holiday.'' Julianna could imagine the animosity below stairs if they had such cause to resent her. ''I will ride the stage to Bath, and take the waters.''

Sir Edmund's left eyebrow flew so far upward, Julianna feared it would remain stuck on the top of his head. ''Out of the question. Pack my bride off to Bath, unchaperoned? Beau Nash would never let me live it down. I thought…your cousin…?''

''No. The Underhills have little room to entertain a guest. I doubt Cecily would be equal to it, in any case. I trust you are not suggesting I holiday with my stepbrother, for I'd sooner throw myself in the Thames!''

Her earlier tears hovered, ready to fall again. Even as she bit her lip and willed them back, one escaped, then another.

''There now, child. I had no idea you had so little family.'' He had hardly taken the time to find out, had he?

Sir Edmund knelt beside her, swiping his handkerchief across her face, as one would do with a howling infant. Julianna felt mortified.

''We will keep the staff on, and plan some entertainment for our first Christmas together,'' he declared in a voice tinged with desperation.

Julianna pushed away his hand and his clumsy attempt to comfort her. She was not a child. She had survived worse than a lonely Christmas.

''No, Sir Edmund. I will not spoil the servants' holiday. I'm quite capable of dressing myself and finding a bite to eat.'' Something possessed her to add, ''Could we not continue your accustomed arrangement? I know I am not an agreeable substitute for Crispin...." *But neither are you.* She was barely able to stifle this biting assertion.

"Not so. I should be delighted to have your company," said Sir Edmund, evincing all the delight of a man facing tooth extraction. "You can help me celebrate, as Crispin used to. I believe he would like that."

Sir Edmund departed, obviously relieved to make his escape and likely wondering what he had let himself in for. Julianna thanked heaven that she would be free from the disapproving eyes of the Fitzhugh servants for a few days. At the moment, she could imagine no better Christmas gift.

Looking forward to her holiday lifted Julianna's spirits. The following morning found her up at an early hour, preparing for an excursion into the City. At lunch, she ordered Brock to arrange her transport, mentioning her errand with the seamstress to forestall his usual diatribe.

Being so new from girlhood, Julianna had seldom dealt with tradespeople. However, she soon found herself taken under the wing of the motherly seamstress Cecily Underhill had recommended. Though Julianna recognized the woman's obliging manner as mere merchant's courtesy, she hungered for a kind word, whatever the source. She spent a pleasant two hours in the cozy shop, ordering a modest but suitable winter wardrobe.

"These gowns should do quite nicely, Mrs. Naseby, but I would like something new, and rather special—for Christmas."

The seamstress wagged her finger. "Say no more, Lady Fitzhugh. I have the very thing. A customer ordered it, and by the time I'd got the cloth she wanted in just the color, all made up as she'd asked, wasn't the lady big with child, and me stuck with the gown. The color should suit you nicely, my dear, with that pretty hair. I believe you'll find it a perfect fit."

Mrs. Naseby bustled off to the back room, calling behind her, "I offered it to several of my other customers, but they found the cost too dear. I'll make you a good price of it, Lady Fitzhugh, just to take it off my hands."

Julianna gasped at the sum mentioned but gasped again, in admiration, when she saw the ravishing swath of lustrous deep-green silk in the seamstress's arms. She needed no urging to try it on and perform a turn before the mirror. The gown's rich hue, with ruches of cream-colored lace at the elbows and bosom, brightened her hair and complexion. Having never owned so becoming a garment, Julianna was determined to buy this one. Let Mr. Brock choke over the bill when it crossed his desk. She would remind him, sweetly, that her costume must reflect well upon his master.

From the dressmaker's, Julianna made the rounds of the milliner's, the bookseller's and the fruitmonger's, before stopping at her cousin's place of business. There she delivered Christmas presents for all the Underhills, and entrusted Francis with her letter to Winnie. Just as she was setting out for home, Jerome hailed her. This was their first encounter since her wedding. Better ten irascible stewards, thought Julianna, than a single Jerome.

"Upon my word, Lady Fitzhugh! So I have run you to ground at last, sister dear. You and your bridegroom have been keeping so low a profile, I wondered if you would ever emerge from your honeymoon. I know newlyweds are traditionally preoccupied, but Sir Edmund scarcely seems the uxorious type."

Julianna could hardly wait to show Jerome what a fool they had made of him. For the moment she affected an offhand retort. "Jealous, Jerome?"

"Of you?" His smirk deepened into a sneer. "I like a more womanly figure. You're fading away to transparency. I don't believe it suits you—playing broodmare to your old stallion."

Sir Edmund might not have won her affection, but he had gained Julianna's unqualified gratitude and respect. She would not stand to hear him spoken of thus, particularly by Jerome. Stepping past him into her carriage, she leaned toward her stepbrother and purred in his ear, "Any sane woman would give herself to my husband a thousand times, before suffering vermin like you to kiss her hand." At her signal, the carriage pulled away smartly. Not before she had time to savor Jerome's murderous look.

Julianna returned home late in the day, well laden with packages and flushed with the triumph of finally putting her stepbrother in his place. Not even Brock's bristling scrutiny could cow her.

"Have someone bring these packages to my sitting room, and ask Mrs. Davies if she can spare me a cup of chocolate." Julianna pulled off her gloves. "Pray don't glower so during this merry season, Mr. Brock. I am certain it will have a detrimental effect on your digestion."

Flouncing away from the sputtering steward, she met Sir Edmund descending the staircase. Immediately regretting her impudence, she ducked her head in shame, steeling herself for his rebuke. Much to her surprise, he passed without a word. When Julianna glanced up, his face looked grave and impassive as ever, but she detected an unmistakable twinkle in his gray eyes.

Chapter Four

"Milady!" squealed Gwenyth, "a new cap for me? What a treat!"

Holding up the daintily laced creation for inspection, Julianna passed it to her maid with a flourish and a warm smile.

"Yes, Gwenyth, you must be sure to wear it on your visit. I understand it is the latest style. It would not surprise me in the least if you received several marriage proposals, thanks to this cunning bit of millinery. So, you must promise not to desert me—unless your beau is quite irresistible! Take along these nuts and sweetmeats for your Christmas feast. Eat plenty, sleep late and enjoy yourself completely. I will expect an entertaining report of the festivities upon your return."

Gwenyth's attention strayed momentarily from contemplation of the exquisite little cap. Her brow puckered. "Are you sure you'll be all right without me, ma'am? 'Tis all very well, two men on their own for several days, but a lady needs her maid. Who will help you dress and bathe and do your hair?"

"Never fear. I am quite capable of drawing my own bath and pinning up my own hair. As for dressing—if I encounter a hook or lace that I cannot reach, what else is a husband for?"

The thought of Sir Edmund stooping to the incongruous role of tiring woman sent both maid and mistress into an irrepressible fit of laughter. Impulsively, Julianna took Gwenyth's hand. "I shall miss your company and high spirits more than all the services you do me. I wish you the merriest of Christmasses."

Two ponderous knocks at the sitting room door announced the presence of Mr. Brock. "Gwenyth, your aunt is looking for you. I believe your ride has arrived."

Holding her new cap and other Christmas bounty behind her skirt, Gwenyth withdrew. Once the steward had turned his back on her, she flashed Julianna a broad grin and a wink.

"I will also be taking my leave within the hour," Brock informed Julianna. "Do you require anything in the meantime?"

He presented such a grim aspect, she could not resist a gentle jape. "I only require, Mr. Brock, that you endeavor to enjoy your holiday. I promise to refrain from mischief in your absence—so far as in me lies."

The teasing did not sit well with Brock, who stalked off, wearing a look that told Julianna he would love to upend her over his knee and whip her like a naughty child. In reply, she abandoned decorum, thrusting out her tongue at his retreating back.

Spying through the frosted pane of her window some time later, Julianna confirmed Brock's departure, along with the last of the other servants. Momentarily overcome by the giddy freedom of a prisoner set at liberty, she let out a loud whoop and danced a clumsy pirouette across the sitting room before collapsing upon the chaise in a heap of helpless mirth.

When her laughter subsided, Julianna began to consider what to do with herself for the next two-and-a-half days. She thought of looking for Sir Edmund, but decided his reluctant company held little appeal. Then another idea seized her. What better opportunity to explore Fitzhugh House? Tossing a wrap around her shoulders, she set off.

She passed a pleasant hour lingering in the dim galleries, viewing Sir Edmund's collection of paintings—an eclectic mixture of landscapes, portraits and still-life studies.

Gradually, Julianna noticed how quiet and empty the house had become without the muted comings and goings of the servants. Her footsteps on the parquet floor reverberated down the wide, shadowy corridor, and she felt a sudden shiver of nameless unease. Pulling open the first door that came to hand, she happened upon Sir Edmund's suite. As he was not there to find her prying, she decided to indulge her curiosity with a furtive look around.

Though Sir Edmund's apartment lacked a separate sitting room, his bedchamber looked much larger than her own. An enormous, old-fashioned bed occupied a considerable space. Tall and boxlike, with plain posts of dark wood and hangings of a somber olive hue, it was practically a room unto itself. Besides a chaise and armchair, the only other furnishings were a battered sea chest and an open-shelved cabinet that housed a collection of exotic-looking statuary and lacquerwork, together with a set of brass navigational tools. Framed maps and charts adorned the walls. It gave Julianna the distinct impression of standing in a captain's cabin on some great ship. She could have sworn she smelled a faint tangy odor of the sea. A spartanly masculine domain, Sir Edmund's apartment did not invite her to linger.

On her way back to her own rooms, Julianna suddenly inhaled a familiar scent. Even before she realized it was Crispin's favorite pomade, her heart gave a happy lurch of recognition. Following the smell, she discovered his chamber. She had known, in an abstract fashion, that she was living in Crispin's home. Yet it had never felt that way, until now. The bedchamber appeared tidy and impersonal, but the cluttered little dressing room looked as if its tenant had just stepped out and might return at any moment.

A brush held strands of Crispin's chestnut curls among its bristles. The wardrobe bulged with coats that Julianna knew like old friends. Taking out a well-cut dark blue velvet, she drew it around herself. Eyes closed, she nuzzled her cheek against the soft nap of the lapel, inhaling the essence of Crispin that clung to the fabric. At that moment, Julianna returned to the gardens at Vauxhall, and the fragrant summer afternoon when Crispin Bayard had proposed to her.

In early June, the gardens were awash in a palette of pastel flowers, on a backdrop of dewy green foliage. Attended by the gallant captain, Julianna savored her first taste of the amusements offered there. They hummed along with popular airs, performed by a string consort. They viewed statuary and displays of Mr. Hogarth's engravings. They nibbled from a bowl of strawberries in the refreshment pavilion. By far Julianna's favorite diversion was wandering the verdant footpaths on the captain's arm, absorbed in polite flirtation. Finding a secluded bench, they paused to rest. Her escort grew unwontedly quiet.

"Have I tired out your voice as well as your legs, Captain?" she asked in jest, only to be taken aback by the grave, pensive set of his handsome features. "Or is something wrong?"

"Miss Ramsay...Julianna..." Upon his lips, her name sounded the most lyrical word in the language. "It is wrong of me to speak, but neither can I keep silent. With the hazardous undertaking before me, it could not be a worse time for romantic distractions...most unfair to any lady...advancing a compact of so long duration, with no assurance of my safe return..."

"Captain Bayard...Crispin..." His name sparkled on her tongue like champagne. "I believe I have kept you too long in the sun. You are not making a particle of sense."

"No wonder. Since the day we met, I have taken leave of my senses. Sense tells me it is madness to meet with you so often, when I may not tender an honorable proposal. However, the light of your beauty and the music of your voice are too sweet a madness to resist."

Languidly drawing off her glove, Julianna reached out to push that unruly curl back from his brow, as she had longed to do since their first meeting. Her hand strayed down his cheek. Crispin needed no further invitation to kiss her. Their lips made a delicious confection of berries and cream.

"Crispin, are you asking for my hand?" Julianna asked breathlessly, when he drew back.

"Could you consider it? Two years without you stretches ahead like a lifetime. Could you wait two years for me, and look to wed upon my return?"

Smiling pertly, she replied, "You have tasted my answer."

His anxious expression eased into a smile of barely containable happiness. "Ah, but I grow forgetful as well as mad," he teased. "Give me your answer again, that I may remember."

Laughing with delight, she obliged. Then, as Crispin held her, she rested her cheek against the soft velvet of his coat.

When Julianna opened her eyes, she saw that Crispin's dressing room had grown dark in the early winter twilight. She had no wish to roam the eerily echoing galleries of Fitzhugh House in this deep gloom. With a reluctant sigh, she slipped the coat from her shoulders and returned it to the wardrobe. Pausing at the door, she blew a kiss back into the empty room.

In the darkened corridor, Julianna soon became disoriented. After one or two unsuccessful attempts, she confidently pulled open her own door.

Edmund set aside his razor and bolted a swallow of brandy. *Dutch courage,* he thought, grimacing at his half-shaved face in the looking glass. *Nonsense,* another part of him countered, *just a drop of oil to lubricate my tongue.* Raising a skeptical eyebrow, he slid the blade of his razor from ear to chin in a single deft sweep. Not that he'd need to do much talking if that goose of a girl didn't soon put in an appearance. Where could she have gone? He'd noticed nothing missing during a quick inspection of her rooms. So she couldn't have run away—more the pity.

Four quick strokes shaved the stiff whiskers from Edmund's upper lip. Dashedly inconsiderate of the girl, bolting to who-knew-where, after all the trouble he'd taken to secure them a stage-side box at Drury Lane tonight. Odd she'd go missing now. Ever since she'd blackmailed him into letting her stay for Christmas, she had looked in far brighter spirits. It had been everything he could do to keep a sober face when he'd overheard the little chit saucing Mordecai Brock. Thinking back on it, Edmund grinned to himself and tipped another draft of his brandy. About time Brock had somebody to put him in his place.

Tilting his head back, Edmund held the razor poised above his neck. He started at the sound of someone barging into his bedchamber. "Who's there!" he barked—a wonder he hadn't slit his throat from ear to ear!

"It is I, Sir Edmund," came an apologetic squeak. "I lost

my way in the galleries and opened your door by mistake. Please excuse the intrusion.''

Before he could reply, Edmund heard the door close again. With a growl of vexation, he dropped the razor and splashed a palmful of water on his face. Tugging on a coat and grabbing a candle, he set off after Julianna.

''No need to run away,'' he said, puffing as he caught up with her. ''I didn't mean to snap your head off, but the noise startled me. Even as I called out, I realized it must be you. Ghosts seldom haunt new houses.''

She glanced over at him with a nervous smile, probably wondering if he meant to flay her alive over an honest mistake. Had he given her reason to think him such an ogre? With a spasm of chagrin, Edmund acknowledged the possibility.

''Besides...'' He made an effort to allay her fears. ''I have been looking for you. I reserved us a box at Drury Lane for this evening. The company is staging a revival of Mr. Congreve's *The Way of the World*. It is an excellent piece, very amusing.''

''I have read the text of the play,'' Julianna replied eagerly. ''I would love to see it performed. This will be my first time at the theater. Papa always protested I was too young. He had finally promised to take me...'' Her voice trailed off.

Fearing she might start blubbering, Edmund hurried on, determinedly cheerful. ''Then I must keep his promise.''

They reached Julianna's rooms, where Edmund immediately set to work banking the coals of her sitting room fire.

''You must dress quickly...and warmly,'' he called over his shoulder. ''They put small braziers in the boxes on cold nights, but it can take a while to heat up.''

Having completed his fire-tending chores, Edmund replaced the screen. He sat on the chaise for a few minutes, twiddling his thumbs. ''Have you eaten yet?'' he shouted in to Julianna, but received no reply. ''I thought we might take a late supper at one of the eating houses around Covent Garden. If you get hungry in the meantime, we can always buy some oranges at the theater.''

Edmund sat for a few minutes more. Then he got up and

wound Julianna's mantel clock, admiring the Flemish craftsmanship. He sat down again, drumming an impatient tattoo with his fingers on the arm of the chaise. Though he had managed to forget many aspects of his first marriage, he still vividly recalled how long it had taken Amelia to dress for any outing. Despite lengthy preparations, the result had never satisfied her.

"Sir Edmund…"

He spun about to see Julianna standing in her bedroom door, the half-secured back of her snuff-brown frock presented to him.

"May I impose upon you to finish hooking my gown?" She gave a deprecatory laugh at her own plight. "I'm unequal to the contortions required to reach the two between my shoulder blades."

"This will be a new job for me," Edmund quipped, "but I believe I can manage." He set to the task, resolutely trying to ignore the tantalizing distraction of wispy red-gold curls clustered at the nape of Julianna's neck.

When, for an instant, his fingertips brushed the warm silk of her skin, he was overwhelmed by disquieting memories of the kiss she had offered him on their wedding night—memories he had ruthlessly suppressed for weeks.

"There, how is that?" He quickly stepped back. "I think I have all the hooks matched with their eyes. Throw on a cloak, girl, and let us go before we miss the first act."

Julianna fairly danced at his side as they walked down to the foyer of Fitzhugh House and climbed into the waiting carriage. She kept up a voluble chatter about the plays she had read and would like to see performed. Edmund relaxed, sensing that he need not contribute much to the conversation. He couldn't help approving of the girl's taste in reading matter and her cogently expressed opinions.

As they took their seats in a prominent front box, Edmund felt many eyes upon them. On the nearest faces he read mingled respect and envy. How curious that no displays of his wealth had ever occasioned such covetous looks as his squiring of a beautiful young woman. Edmund scowled, trying to mask the ridiculous rush of elation that surged within him as the play commenced.

It concerned family intrigue—a battle for control over the estate of Lady Wishfort. Through the evening, Edmund found his glance often straying sidelong, to catch Julianna's reaction to a particular jest or bit of stage business. She sat indecorously hunched forward, elbows resting on the lip of the box. Her chin cupped in one hand, his young wife appeared blind and deaf to anything but Congreve's brilliant comedy.

Every nuance of the action played across Julianna's luminous, mobile features. No one in the theater that evening laughed so readily and merrily at the subtlest quip. No one clapped with such appreciative glee when a favorite character gained the upper hand. No one joined so enthusiastically in the ovation when the actors took their bows. Edmund found his own laughter and applause flowing with less than usual restraint. Never could he remember enjoying an evening of theater so keenly. Julianna's spontaneous delight was as contagious as it was refreshing.

The air had turned milder and damp when Edmund steered Julianna through the stream of exiting theatergoers. They made their way to supper on foot, through the light Christmas fog. A group of waits, the Yuletide street musicians employed by London's aldermen, was performing carols near the busy intersection of Catherine and Russell Streets. As Edmund and Julianna approached, the waits concluded a lively rendition of "I Saw Three Ships."

"My father's favorite carol," Julianna mused aloud.

In the diffuse glow of the streetlamp, Edmund looked down into her rosy girlish face. He saw a wistful luster in her wide doe eyes. Why, she was little more than a child, he realized, an orphaned child living on the charity of a virtual stranger. Who could blame her if she pined, or wept, or craved the poor comfort of his company? Edmund felt his craggy features warmed by a kindly, almost paternal smile.

"'Three Ships' is my favorite carol, as well," he said, "like many an old sailor." With that, he fished in his waistcoat pocket for a few coins to offer the waits.

Carriages clattered to and fro on the cobbles of busy Bow Street as they crossed. On a side street near Covent Garden, they entered a building whose signboard ostentatiously proclaimed it Eldridge's Select Supper Club. Engrossed in the play, Julianna had not given food a second thought. Now, as a host of succulent aromas assailed her nose, she found herself heartily famished. The warmth of the dining alcove made a pleasant change from the drafty theater box. A glass of port warmed her further, whetting her already sharp appetite to a keen pitch.

Fortunately, the food soon arrived. It was abundant and delicious: clear soup, rabbit smothered in onions, accompanied by herb dumplings, braised celery and carrots. Julianna groaned when offered her favorite Banbury cakes. If only she could have loosened the stays of her corset to relieve the pressure on her stomach! Throughout the meal, Sir Edmund ate little, as was his wont, but imbibed of his wine more liberally than usual. Perhaps for that reason he proved a surprisingly agreeable conversationalist. Julianna found their usual tongue-tied formality eased.

"Do I take it, from your rapt attention this evening, that you enjoyed the play?" he asked.

"It was everything I could have hoped," Julianna sighed.

"Fitzhugh, old fellow!" A voice rang out. "Thought it must be you. Spotted you from clear the other side of the playhouse. Thought you might come back here for a bite. Haven't seen you about the town in months. Had to indulge me curiosity and seek out the identity of your lovely young companion. Miss."

The man executed an exaggerated bow in Julianna's direction—a perilous feat for one so diminutive in height and almost perfectly spherical in shape. An ill-fitting peruke perched precariously upon the top of his head, and a roguish patch covered one eye.

Sir Edmund responded guardedly. "No, I have not been about in the evenings of late. This is my wife." He hesitated over that last word, then smiled apologetically at Julianna. "My dear, may I present Langston Carew, Esquire. Carew, Lady Julianna Fitzhugh. Her father was the late Mr. Alistair Ramsay."

"A pleasure, ma'am." The little fellow beamed. "Knew

your father slightly. Well, Fitzhugh, forgoing the bachelor's life at this late date, what? Wise man! If I could find a pretty little baggage like this to warm me old bones on a winter's night, I'd never step from me own hearth! Haw, haw!''

Sir Edmund cringed visibly. Julianna wondered if he expected her to take offense. In fact, every aspect of this comical old gallant proclaimed such honest admiration and irrepressible good humor, she felt drawn to Langston Carew. In reply to his ribald comments, she lavished upon him her most radiant smile.

Less amused, Sir Edmund fixed his mouth in an upturned grimace. His tone conveyed a forced pretense of cordiality. ''Perhaps you should think of marrying, Carew. Never too late, they say.''

''Ahem. Yes, I suppose. Well, I'll not keep you from your dinners. A merry Christmas, Sir Edmund and Lady Fitzhugh. Perhaps we'll see more of you about the town this winter!''

Sir Edmund nodded dismissively. ''Aye, Carew, perhaps.''

When Carew had retired out of earshot, Sir Edmund addressed Julianna on the quiet. ''A vulgar old devil, but not bad at heart. He was the assistant factor at Madras when I was there.''

The information intrigued her. ''You must tell me more of your adventures in the Indies, Sir Edmund.''

''Yes,'' he replied, without offering to go on.

Just as they ascended the stairs, the tall pedestal clock in the entry hall of Fitzhugh House struck one. Sir Edmund escorted Julianna to her rooms. Once again he attended to her fire, and checked the level of coal in the scuttle. Then he turned from the hearth, rubbing a smudge of soot from his fingertips.

''Mr. Handel is giving a private presentation of his latest oratorio tomorrow evening at Haymarket. I have heard good reports of the work since it was performed in Dublin. The concert will raise funds for the Foundling Hospital. As a patron, I should attend. Would you care to accompany me?''

''Yes, please, Sir Edmund.'' Julianna clapped her hands eagerly. ''I so admire Mr. Handel's music!''

"Now, now," he cautioned, "do not expect too much. This is not a public premiere, more of a formal rehearsal."

"I am sure I shall not be disappointed. Good night, Sir Edmund. Thank you for the play and the supper. I cannot recall when I have enjoyed myself more."

At her door, Sir Edmund turned and posed an unexpected question. "You miss your father very much, Julianna?"

Perhaps because his query caught her off her guard, she answered with simple sincerity. "I do—especially at this time of year. We were very close."

"I envy you." She could scarcely hear his reply. Perhaps he had not intended it for her ears at all.

Before she could reply or question, he was gone.

Hurriedly Julianna undressed and burrowed, shivering, under the bedclothes. Bright scenes from the play danced through her mind. She smiled to herself in the darkness, anticipating tomorrow's concert. Drifting toward sleep, she found her thoughts turning again and again to the enigma of Sir Edmund. Yawning, she shook her head in private perplexity. He could be such pleasant company one minute, then turn stonily reticent the next. For Crispin's sake, she wanted to make a friend of his uncle. And for Sir Edmund's sake as well. Beneath his show of cool self-sufficiency, she sensed a core of deep loneliness.

Chapter Five

The next morning, Julianna lingered in bed as long as she dared, dreading exposure to the chilly air. There were distinct disadvantages, she decided, to giving all one's servants a holiday. She had become spoiled—used to rising in a warm room with hot water to wash and a steaming cup of tea to drink. Driven by hunger, Julianna finally took a deep breath and bolted from her bed. Hurriedly, she dressed in her warmest gown. Entering her sitting room, she found the fire already burning. On her breakfast table sat a plate of buttered bread and a pot of tea, still hot. She could only smile to herself and shake her head, no closer to solving the riddle of Sir Edmund Fitzhugh.

Again that evening, Julianna considered wearing her new green silk gown. In the end, she decided it might be too bright and fashionable for an evening of sacred music. Instead, she settled on a frock of genteel gray. Its color gave her complexion a sallow cast, while the cut made her look no more than twelve years old. Julianna comforted herself with the thought that she was going to watch and listen, and not to display herself. She was beginning to regret her impulsive purchase of the stunning emerald gown she could never find an occasion to wear.

Any worries over her costume vanished with the opening bars of the oratorio. Though it was ostensibly a rehearsal, the musicians were doubtless aware of their highly critical audience and determined to perform well. London music lovers had turned out at the Opera House in force, curious for a taste of the work Dublin had received so well.

Julianna had never heard so many instruments and voices massed. In her estimation, the resulting music beggared description. The soloists' fine voices soared above the lush orchestration in melodies so evocative and hauntingly familiar she longed to sing with them. During the great ''Hallelujah,'' the very air throbbed with exultant music. Lost in the moment, she reached for Sir Edmund's hand, clasping it tightly. As the piece ended, she stirred from her trance and pulled her fingers away, her cheeks burning.

Under cover of the polite applause, Sir Edmund leaned toward her and whispered, ''You mirror my feelings precisely. I understand Handel composed this work in three weeks. Having heard it, I can only credit Divine inspiration.''

A reception for the hospital patrons followed the concert. Julianna noted with chagrin that the other ladies had all dressed in high style. Beside them she looked thoroughly dowdy and callow. Embarrassment changed to resentment when she intercepted several surreptitious glances and covert nods in her direction. Her youth, not her dress, was drawing this silent censure.

Parity in age between a husband and wife was hardly a general circumstance, she mused indignantly. It could take years for a man to earn or inherit the means to support a family. By that time he must marry a younger woman, capable of breeding. Ten or fifteen years between husband and wife would not raise an eyebrow. However, when the gap widened to a score, folks looked askance at a so-called ''Smithfield match,'' with all the mercenary implications of the Smithfield cattle market.

She could tell Sir Edmund was aware of the critical scrutiny bent upon them. He strode about, stiff as buckram and painfully civil in his introductions. With an immense feeling of relief, Julianna spied a group of familiar figures, friends of her late father. Hauling Sir Edmund in her wake, she approached the gentlemen with an effusive greeting.

Mr. Kelway squinted in Julianna's direction. Recognizing her, he called out, ''Upon my word, fellows, if it isn't our little tyrant, Miss Ramsay! My dear, I just returned from Florence and was shocked to hear the sad news of your father. He will be sadly missed.''

His companions nodded with vaguely sympathetic murmurings. Caught off guard by these expressions of condolence, Julianna could think of little by way of response.

''How kind of you to say so,'' was her subdued reply. Then she brightened. ''Gentlemen, may I introduce my husband, Sir Edmund Fitzhugh. Sir Edmund, Messrs. Smith, Nares and Kelway, fine musicians all. They very nearly wore out the strings of my father's harpsichord, but in a glorious cause.''

The gentlemen bowed and shook hands all around. Sir Edmund opened with the expected conversational gambit. ''You brought trained ears to this evening's entertainment, gentlemen. What were your impressions?''

Nares's lip curled. ''Oh, it might have been worse. I expected wonders after the laudatory notices from Dublin.''

The other two musicians reacted with sagacious nods. ''I must admit—'' Smith pointed heavenward ''—he had a good librettist.''

This caused some laughter but Nares resumed his carping tone. ''I still say this piece won't add anything to Handel's popularity. The king may like his music but everyone else disdains it, to spite German Georgie.''

Sir Edmund did not let that go unanswered. ''Society has come to a sorry pass indeed, when the appreciation of music becomes a province of politics.''

''Our friend Mr. Arne quite liked it,'' ventured Kelway. ''Though that may simply be clannishness on his part, for his sister's performance was very well received. I believe it has salvaged her reputation. Did you hear what the Dean of Dublin Cathedral pronounced upon hearing Mrs. Cibber sing her aria?''

To their questioning looks, he intoned ecclesiastically, '' 'Woman, for this, are thy sins forgiven thee!' ''

The three musicians laughed heartily.

Their merriment soon evaporated in the face of Sir Edmund's curt rebuke. ''Need I remind you gentleman there is a lady present?''

The three men reddened like schoolboys caught at mischief. Kelway muttered his apologies as they moved off. Behind the cover of her fan, Julianna cast them an apologetic smile. Privately, she found it sweetly amusing that Sir Edmund should spring to the defense of her feminine sensibilities.

The Cibber scandal was cold, albeit salacious gossip. Joseph Kelway had undoubtedly assumed she knew every unsavory detail since gossip claimed Jerome had played a particularly odious role in the whole shameful business. Still, if Sir Edmund chose to think of her as some paragon of innocence, Julianna was in no hurry to disabuse him. Having long admired Cervantes' tragicomic senor de La Manche, she was flattered to play Dulcinea to his Quixote.

Sir Edmund spoke little on the drive home. Julianna wondered if he was still privately bristling over the implied censure of their marriage. Trying to draw him out, she asked how he had come to be involved with the Foundling Hospital, under construction in Bloomsbury. He quickly warmed to the topic.

"Thomas Coram instigated it all, and he press-ganged me early in the venture. As an old fellow seaman, he played upon the soft heart our kind are wont to harbor for needy children. I have little sympathy for the gin-swilling layabouts and cutpurses that make up half the parish paupers' rolls. Still, no person of conscience can fail to pity the innocent infants who perish on the streets of this prosperous city every day, for want of care. Perhaps if there was some refuge for their mothers in the first place…" His voice trailed off and Julianna wondered if, once again, he was seeking to shield her from life's darker side.

"Suffice it to say, there are two kinds of men in this world," Sir Edmund continued in a tone of asperity. "Those who believe it is the prerogative of the strong to prey upon the weak, and those who know it is the duty of the strong to protect the weak. Unfortunately, the former far outnumber the latter."

Nodding her agreement, Julianna smothered a yawn. Not because Sir Edmund's conversation bored her—quite the contrary. But this would be her second evening in a row keeping late hours. Despite heavy eyelids, she vastly preferred the past two merry evenings to her former, cheerless early nights.

Leaning back on the comfortably upholstered seat of the carriage, she dismissed the reception from her mind. Instead, she concentrated on the beautiful music that had so touched her. Closing her eyes, she quietly hummed one especially sweet melody:

He shall gather the lambs with his arm,
And carry them in his bosom.

Poised on the brink of sleep, she pictured the gentle, protective shepherd with her husband's face.

Julianna was making music again the next morning. As soon as she had risen and dressed, she continued a Christmas tradition once shared with her grandmother. Plucking her harp by the light of the fire, she sang a *plygain*—a Welsh "dawn carol." "The love of our dear Shepherd will always be a wonderment," it began. Love in any incarnation, thought Julianna, would always be a wonderment.

Plygain sung, she felt truly in the Christmas spirit. She tiptoed down the hallway, treading with special care past Sir Edmund's door. The kitchen was in rather a litter from the past two days of foraging for their meals. She would attend to that soon enough. First she started the great cook fire and set some water to heat for washing, and for tea. While the kettle boiled, Julianna cleared away the food scraps and stacked the dishes. Investigating the larder, she discovered a flitch of lean bacon and enough other foodstuffs to make a decent hot breakfast. Thankfully, Winnie had taught her the art of cookery.

Julianna remembered the old woman's admonition. "You cannot always count on having help around, my girl. A body's come to a sad pass when they can't get themselves a bite."

She hoped Winnie would soon receive her letter and rest easy about her fate. Perhaps when Crispin returned home, they could bring Winnie back to London. She would be getting past much useful work by then, but having her with them would complete Julianna's happiness. How it would please Winnie to rock another generation of Gryffud infants in their cradles. Thinking ahead to that pretty domestic scene, Julianna let her hands work away, washing up and preparing the meal.

"Am I the slugabed this morning?"

At that casual query from the doorway, Julianna gasped and nearly dropped the platter she was washing.

"S-sir Edmund," she sputtered, "you must have a tread like a cat! I never hear you coming."

"A useful skill, perfected long ago. I do it without thinking now, and I'm afraid it often gets me into trouble." He inhaled appreciatively. "What smells so delicious?"

Julianna gave a proprietary glance around the tidy kitchen, to the savory steam rising from the cook pots. "I thought a hot meal might make a pleasant change for Christmas morning. I fried up a mess of bacon and griddle cakes. I will just set the eggs to boil and make the tea. Could you assemble the dishes and cutlery on a tray? We can take breakfast in my sitting room. It should be warm in there by now."

Sir Edmund pulled a mock salute. "Very well, zir, I have my orders." His voice was a perfect take on the Somerset accent of their head coachman, all growling "r's" and buzzing "z's".

Julianna could not help laughing. "Was your gift for mimicry also a skill perfected long ago?"

"You might say so." Sir Edmund flashed a rueful grin. "It is certainly another that gets me into trouble. If someone speaks to me in an unusual accent, I have a terrible habit of unconsciously incorporating bits of it into my own voice, until I sound just like them. People tend to think they are the butt of my fun, and take it rather ill."

With some difficulty, they managed to carry all the food and utensils to the upper floor. The fire burned brightly in Julianna's grate and the little sitting room felt deliciously warm. She and Sir Edmund both tucked into the food with a right good will. When he had cleaned his plate, Sir Edmund leaned back and patted his stomach.

"I don't know when I have enjoyed a meal so much," he declared heartily. "My thanks to you."

Julianna smiled over her teacup. "It was the least I could do, after all your kindness to me of late. Just don't let Mrs. Davies hear you praise my cooking!''

"Auntie Enid. Yes, I daresay she'd not be pleased about that, now, would she?'' This time he spoke in the cook's Welsh singsong falsetto. They both laughed.

"My grandmother always made much over Christmas," Sir Edmund mused softly. "She grew up before the Civil War. Later, Cromwell's government banned all Yuletide festivities. Grandmother always complained that Christmas was never as merry again, even after the Restoration. Since my father was so busy with church duties at that time of year, he would pack Alice and me off to Abbot's Leigh until Twelfth Night or later. I looked forward to it all the year.''

Sir Edmund suddenly recalled himself, his smile twisting into a wry grin. He drew a narrow box from his waistcoat pocket.

"Here is a small gift, to celebrate the day. You may consider it from Crispin, and me.'' The final words sounded to Julianna like a self-conscious afterthought.

"Why, thank you, Sir Edmund. That is very...oh...''

Lifting the lid, Julianna discovered a pendant on a heavy gold chain. It was a large cabochon emerald, cut very shallow.

"It opens," Sir Edmund prompted her.

Indeed, the setting was delicately hinged at one side. When Julianna folded the pendant open, the most exquisite miniature of Crispin smiled back at her. The artist had captured his likeness so perfectly that it brought both a smile to her lips and a tear to her eye. How marvelous to see that beloved face again, after all these months!

"I had it commissioned before he left," said Sir Edmund. "I thought it a very fine likeness. I knew you would treasure it.''

"Oh, I do! Indeed, I do! Thank you.'' The only proper expression of her gratitude was an impulsive embrace, which flustered Sir Edmund a trifle. He pulled back from her, clutching his teacup and raising it in the air, as if to ward her off.

"Shall we drink a toast to Crispin? To his successful voyage and safe return.''

"Oh, Sir Edmund, I almost forgot. I have a gift for you.''

Rummaging through her father's desk, Julianna extracted the book she had bought. "Just a token."

"Well, well, a book by Mr. Fielding. *Joseph Andrews.* Newly printed, is it? It must be, for I do not have a copy—until now. I admire Fielding's plays, so I trust this will be enjoyable reading. My thanks."

Breakfast over, they cleared the dishes away and dressed for church. Not for the first time did Julianna thank a merciful God for her deliverance from Jerome and for the safe haven she had found with Sir Edmund. She prayed for Crispin's safety at sea, for the success of his venture and for his swift return.

After church, they bolted a cold luncheon and prepared to receive the carolers who traditionally made their rounds on Christmas Day. The dull green fire of her emerald pendant made Julianna decide to wear her new gown, though she grumbled to herself that it was far too grand for such an occasion. Once dressed, she could not find a way to arrange her hair that suited her. In truth, it looked best falling free. Since they were not going out, she determined to leave it in this unfashionable but becoming style.

Descending the staircase, Julianna paused halfway down. When Sir Edmund looked up, she could have sworn he uttered an unintentional gasp of admiration.

"Whenas in silks, Julianna goes,
Then, then (methinks) how sweetly flows
That liquefaction of her clothes."

He quoted Herrick with a slight alteration in her favor. Julianna replied with a toss of her curls and a flirtatious smile. She was secretly more flattered by his first unguarded response than by the mannered courtesy of his words.

"Your compliments are so gallant, Sir Edmund." She fluttered her fan. "If only you would tender them more often."

His mock scowl did not conceal a discernible reddening of Sir Edmund's complexion. "Pray, do not try to vamp me, young lady," he growled. "Every wise businessman knows that any currency thrown about too freely loses its value."

Julianna poured two dippers of punch. "Are you all wise businessman, Sir Edmund, practicing thrift and parsimony even while paying court? Crispin is more the poet—lavish and profligate with his compliments." She offered him a cup. "I don't believe we ever completed the toast you proposed at breakfast. Here's to Crispin and the success of his voyage. Two years hence, may we three raise a glass together."

They soon found themselves immersed in company. Word of Sir Edmund's hospitality had evidently spread, for the parade of carolers came on and on. There were groups as small as three or four and others numbering more than a dozen. Some were workmates. Others, originally from elsewhere in the country, had come together to sing the traditional carols of their region. The tailors sang their accustomed "Coventry Carol," rendering the sweet, poignant harmonies particularly well.

Most groups entered and sang their piece, then stayed on for some food and drink. While taking their refreshment, they listened to the next group or two, then continued on their way with a few coins from Sir Edmund.

As a group from the West Country broke into a chorus of their traditional "We Wish You a Merry Christmas," the rest of the company joined in, including the host and hostess. At the end of this rousing song, a cheer went up and a voice from the crowd called out, "What about a tune for us, Sir Edmund? Ma'am?"

Julianna was about to demur, when Sir Edmund drew out her harp from beneath a table. "I forgot to mention," he whispered, "this is also part of our Christmas tradition. Do you know 'I Sing of a Maiden'?"

"You might have warned me, so we could have practiced."

"You will find our audience decidedly uncritical."

Julianna tentatively plucked out the notes on her harp, and together they sang the archaic words of the carol. Sir Edmund's deep rich singing voice blended well with her own husky tones. Their audience proved most appreciative. People began calling out tunes for her to play and all joined in the singing.

It was late when the last of their guests departed. Tired from the early morning and the activity of their Christmas celebrations, Julianna felt rather flushed from the wine punch and the press of warm bodies in the room all day.

"Shall we clean this up now, Sir Edmund, or in the morning?" She sighed, looking around dispiritedly at the dirty cups and the muddy footprints on the marble floor.

"Leave it." Sir Edmund's voice sounded hoarse and weary. "Crispin and I never touched a thing other years. Some of the servants will be back early tomorrow—those visiting in London. They can take care of it. I suggest you stay abed until someone comes to light your fires and bring your breakfast. I know I intend to." He shivered. "I believe I have caught a chill from the draft of the door opening and closing all afternoon."

"Oh, I am sorry, Sir Edmund." Julianna saw that his face also appeared flushed. "Can I get you anything?"

"No, thank you, my dear. A drop of Hungary water before bed and a good night's sleep should put me right. Good night."

As they parted ways for the night, Sir Edmund called softly after her, down the shadowy corridor, "I am glad you decided to stay for the holiday. I enjoyed your company."

"And I, yours, Sir Edmund. Rest well." Julianna hoped the pleasant companionship she had shared with Crispin's uncle over these past days might continue into the winter. Somehow, she doubted it would survive the servants' return.

Chapter Six

The return of the servants had certain benefits, Julianna discovered. It was pleasant to sleep late the next morning, without the prospect of dressing in the chilly air. She had not been awake long when a girl came to tend the fires. Gwenyth and her aunt would be spending a few more days in Chatham, visiting relatives of the late Mr. Davies. Julianna longed to see Gwenyth again and exchange the news of their respective holidays. From Hetty, who brought her breakfast, she learned that Mr. Brock had returned bright and early. She wondered how much of her recent felicity had been due to the absence of the lowering steward.

After the excitement and activity of Christmas, St. Stephen's Day proved decidedly dreary. Julianna found herself unaccountably hungry for Sir Edmund's company, though she doubted they could recapture the easy camaraderie of the past several days. There was no sign of him at luncheon. A search of the library yielded nothing more promising than a well-worn copy of *Pilgrim's Progress*. Julianna borrowed it for want of better diversion. She assumed Sir Edmund must be keeping to his rooms, perhaps nursing the chill he had taken yesterday. Mr. Brock was very much in evidence, supervising the cleanup and organizing an abbreviated staff. Late in the afternoon, desperate for any kind of human society, Julianna tried to engage him in conversation.

"You had a pleasant Christmas, I trust, Mr. Brock."

Brock continued to put the house in order while delivering an offhand reply. "Aye, ma'am. Pleasant enough."

"You stayed in London?"

"Rotherhithe, ma'am," came Brock's short reply, speaking of an area on the south bank of the Thames.

"With friends or family?" Julianna persisted.

The steward's eyes narrowed beneath his ferocious brows, but his answer remained civil. "With my brother and his family, ma'am. Will that be everything, ma'am?"

Julianna found herself enjoying the show of consternation Mr. Brock took few pains to hide. Some streak of perversity kept her from acknowledging his question.

"I expect you would like to hear how Sir Edmund and I fared in your absence." She rushed on before he could refuse. "We fared admirably, I think, though I would not care to do without our staff on a continuing basis. Did Sir Edmund tell you we attended the theater and a charity concert? The music was superb. Yesterday we hosted the carolers, and even did a little musical turn of our own. I had no idea my husband possessed such a fine singing voice. Does it not sound a thoroughly enjoyable program?" she concluded breathlessly.

His nostrils flared, and for an instant Julianna feared he meant to pick her up and administer a sound shaking. The intent blazed in his face. Brock's voice was barely under control as he growled, "It sounds a thoroughly exhausting program for one of Sir Edmund's weak constitution. Little wonder he has taken to his bed, poor man. If I had been here—"

She would not stand a lecture from this man, as if any ailment of Sir Edmund's might be her fault. "Surely your master is well past years of discretion, Mr. Brock, and capable of choosing his own activities."

The steward turned on his heel and stalked off. He had done so, Julianna suspected, to forestall doing her an injury. Well, much as he might have wanted to shake her, she wanted equally to shake him. In spite of her pert reply, his barb had struck home. She had known of Sir Edmund's poor health, noted his slight appetite and how easily he tired. Perhaps she should have gone away for a few days and given him a chance to rest, instead of enduring a succession of late nights and improvised meals. What a fine way to repay all his kindness! For what felt like the hundredth time that day, Julianna opened her locket for a glimpse of Crispin's reassuring smile.

"Alice!"

Julianna jolted awake, her stomach in knots, her breath shallow and rapid. A dream. She sank back into her pillows, laughing at her own foolishness. She had been dreaming the strangest dream about Crispin in a Greek toga and herself in a classical chiton, saying their goodbyes in the gardens at Vauxhall. He had professed his love for her, then called her by the name Alice. When she had protested that her name was not Alice, but Julianna, he had begun to shake her and demand to know what she had done with Alice.

"Alice…"

The faint, distant cry made Julianna gasp and clutch the bedclothes before her, as she had clutched the chiton in her dream. Was she dreaming still? Then, as her waking mind began to function, she realized the voice intruding upon her dreams could have only one source—Sir Edmund. Grasping the bell at her bedside, she rang it vigorously. Gwenyth soon came running to answer her summons. The girl shivered in her wrap and nightcap but looked far too alert to have been recently woken.

"Gwenyth, what is going on?" Julianna demanded. "Is that Sir Edmund I hear?"

"Oh yes, ma'am. The master's ever so ill." Gwenyth rattled off her tale in a nervous staccato burst. "Clean mad with the fever, Auntie says. Did Mr. Brock not tell you? It's that sickness he caught years ago in the tropics. He takes a spell of it every few years. He was ill the first winter I came here, see, and he almost died that time. Auntie says she's never seen him worse than this. He's been calling for his sister off and on for an hour now. Mr. Brock is at his wits' end to quiet him."

Julianna felt a sickening pang of self-reproach. "Can nothing be done?"

Gwenyth's shoulders rose in a shrug, her lips pursed. "I

dunno, ma'am. Not a doctor, am I? Mr. Brock's sent John for the barber-surgeon. Perhaps he can—''

''No!''

Gwenyth's words galvanized Julianna and brought forth a flood of vivid, painful memories. It had been dark and cold and late—just like this—on the night years ago when Winnie had shaken her from a sound sleep. Myfanwy Penallen was dying and wanted her little granddaughter with her at the end. Julianna would never forget her grandmother's blanched skin, sunken eyes and wasted body. The red-gold hair about which she had once been so vain dulled to a ruddy ash, her strength and spirit bled and purged away—almost. A dash of pepper spiced her last words, flung at Alistair Ramsay over his daughter's head.

''I'd not have died, if you hadn't tried to cure me!''

That final, venomous accusation hung in the air after the old lady's heart and breath had stilled and Winnie had taken Julianna back to her own bed. It had shaken Alistair Ramsay. No barber-surgeon ever crossed his threshold after that night. Over the years he had cultivated patronage for a rising young cadre of scientific physicians. Julianna was equally determined to allow no barber-surgeon in her house.

''Gwenyth, is there an old gown of Mrs. Bayard's about?'' she asked, a plan beginning to take shape in her mind.

''Oh yes, milady,'' the girl replied, a query in her voice. ''These used to be Mrs. Bayard's rooms, see? Before you came, they were just as she left them. When we rearranged it all for you, her belongings just got moved across the hall, and—''

''Good.'' Julianna had heard all she needed to hear. ''Go fetch me one of her gowns, and be quick about it.''

As Gwenyth departed on her errand, Julianna took a moment to collect her wits. Feeling responsible for Sir Edmund's condition, she resolved to remedy the situation in any way possible. From what Gwenyth had told her, the most urgent tasks would be to calm Sir Edmund and to keep the barber-surgeon at bay. Any action on her part would likely call down the wrath of the formidable Mr. Brock. By the time Gwenyth returned, Julianna was trying to steel herself for the confrontation.

"I hope this will do, ma'am. There are others, but I took the first that came to hand."

Julianna fanned her nose against the camphoric fumes of Mrs. Davies's mothproofing preparation. "This will have to serve. Tomorrow, make sure to have the rest aired, in case I need them. Help brush my hair up under this cap. Now, back to bed, Gwenyth. I may need your help tomorrow, so you must get your rest."

As she made her way down the dark gallery, Julianna's heart raced. Her palms felt cold and damp. She would sooner face down a great wild beast than her husband's ferocious steward. Sir Edmund's cries grew weaker, but no less agitated, as she approached his apartment. Hearing footsteps behind her, she spun around to find a young footman escorting a capped and cloaked stranger. Julianna recognized the satchel he carried.

Taking a deep breath, she thrust out her hand. "Doctor?"

The gentleman set down his case, doffed his hat and bowed over her hand. "Jonas Hanley, ma'am. I was summoned to attend Sir Edmund Fitzhugh. I understand his condition is very grave."

A poor choice of words, Julianna reflected. "I am Lady Fitzhugh, Mr. Hanley. I regret we have summoned you out at so late an hour on a cold night. I must apologize for the misunderstanding. My husband will not require your services, after all."

The surgeon opened his mouth to voice his obvious annoyance, but Julianna managed to forestall his tirade.

"Of course, we will recompense you handsomely for your trouble. John, show Mr. Hanley to the drawing room and poor him a cup of port to warm his journey home."

"But, milady, Mr. Brock'll…"

"Leave Mr. Brock to me, John." Julianna strove to interject the proper note of matronly authority. "You have my orders."

The men turned back, the surgeon huffing and clucking. Julianna overheard the young footman muttering excuses for the whims of his employers. She watched with relief as they retreated down the hallway. She knew better than to hope her next encounter would resolve itself so smoothly. Bracing her shoulders and muttering a prayer under her breath, she pushed open Sir Edmund's door.

The light in the room was dim, fortunately. Sir Edmund half sat, half reclined upon his high bed, asking again and again for Alice. Mordecai Brock leaned over his master, vainly trying to calm the sick man and induce him to lie still. At the sound of the door, Brock looked over his shoulder.

"Doctor, at last..." He spied Julianna. His face, at first a mask of bewilderment, clouded with rage as he recognized her. "Get out of here, now!" His blazing eyes declared that he would rend her limb from limb. However, the steward's body could not completely shield his master from the apparition at the door.

"Alice, you have come at last!" Sir Edmund collapsed back onto his pillows.

"Yes, Edmund, I am here." Julianna moved toward the bed. Though she addressed her words to the patient, she kept her eyes locked on Mordecai Brock, daring him to stop her.

Sweat beaded Sir Edmund's brow and his eyes were eerily vacant. Julianna put her hand to his fiery forehead.

"Lie still, my dear. Alice is here. You must sleep, while I sit with you and bathe your head." Such words would a loving mother croon to a sick child. They had their desired effect.

"Yes, Alice, I will try to rest." Sir Edmund nodded with childlike contrition. "I feel so strange. I am glad you have come. I called and called for you."

"Shh, you must not talk now, Edmund. Lie back and close your eyes. Mr. Brock, bring me a cloth and a basin of tepid water. And see that no one disturbs us, on any account."

"May I speak to you in private, ma'am?" The steward pitched his voice low, so as not to rouse Sir Edmund, but Julianna could see a vein throbbing at one temple of his rage-mottled face.

"One moment, Mr. Brock." She turned back to the bed. "Now, Edmund, I must step outside for an instant. I know you feel hot and unwell, but try to rest quietly."

Sir Edmund raised her hand to a cheek rough with several days' growth of whiskers. By contrast, his words were those of a plaintive little boy. "I will do as you say, Alice. Only, come back very soon."

Once they were alone in the gallery, with a closed door separating them from Sir Edmund, Mordecai Brock erupted in a muted explosion of fury.

"What do you think you are playing at, jade? Have you not done damage enough, cavorting around London last week, getting him run down and prey to this? I have my hands full with him and I will not put up with your playacting and upsetting him further. Now get back to bed, before I pick you up and dump you there!"

Mordecai Brock was shorter in stature than Sir Edmund. By balancing high on her toes, Julianna could look him directly in the eye, her face within inches of his.

"Do that and it will be your last act as steward of this house." Julianna strove to keep her voice firm, but dispassionate. She suspected he might strike her if she inflamed his temper further. If it happened, she would have no choice but to dismiss him. That was not her aim.

Her words must have left the steward momentarily speechless, for she was able to continue in a more conciliatory vein. "I will excuse your outburst, Mr. Brock, considering how distraught you are over my husband's illness. But, mark me, I will not show such clemency again. In the first place, not that it is any of your business, our two Christmas outings were entirely Sir Edmund's idea. Had you told me of the possible danger to my husband's health, I would certainly have refused his invitations and contrived to keep him at home. Secondly, my 'playacting' seems to have done far more good than harm. Even I can see my husband needs to relax and rest. Believe it or not, I desire Sir Edmund's recovery as much as you do. I can best accomplish that with your aid, but if need be, I will manage on my own. You have a choice, Mr. Brock, so consider well. Give me the assistance I need and the respect I deserve as mistress of this house or leave now and hinder me no more."

To Julianna, the silence that followed her audacious little speech stretched on interminably. Her legs were beginning to shake and her breath was coming too quickly. Still, she dared not flinch from Mordecai Brock's testing gaze.

At last he declared, "I will stay. Not on account of your daft threats but because you bear watching, my girl."

"A wise choice, Mr. Brock." Her voice almost broke. Drawing a deep breath, she added, with more confidence than she felt, "Your motives are nothing to me, for I can stand the scrutiny."

Rather than meeting her eye, Brock stared at a point on her forehead. "Your orders, madam?"

She felt on firmer ground now. "Have one of the girls bring the water for drinking and cooling cloths. I have already sent the barber-surgeon away."

"You have done what?" the steward thundered.

"Lower your voice, Mr. Brock, and remember your decision. I will not have those carrion craw in my house. Nor will I let Sir Edmund die of their so-called cures. They would let blood for a case of hiccups! At first light, you must go to Westminster Hospital on Chapel Street and ask for Jonathan Cail. On the way back, give him as much information as you can about this fever of Sir Edmund's. That will do for now."

Brock stalked off down the hall. When he had disappeared from sight, Julianna allowed herself to lean against the wall and let her trembling legs buckle beneath her. Her anger and indignation were spent. Though she felt a slight flush of triumph, tears sprang to her eyes. She scolded herself for such weakness. Well begun is half done, Winnie had always said. In spite of her promising beginning, Julianna knew she still had far to go. In the next room lay a feverish man who believed himself a young boy and she his long-dead sister, come back to nurse him.

When she returned to his bedside, she found Sir Edmund distressed anew.

"Please don't go away again, Alice," he begged. "My head hurts so. The light makes it hurt."

Julianna snuffed the candle and returned to sit by the bed. Where was the girl with the water she had ordered?

"There now, is that better?" She reached for his hand in the darkness.

Sir Edmund clung to her fingers. "My head still hurts, and I feel so hot." His voice sounded petulant.

"Lovely cool water will be coming soon. Is there anything else you would like in the meantime?"

"Sing me a song. I like to hear you sing, Alice. Please?"

"What shall I sing?"

"You know. 'The Scarborough Fair.' That is my favorite." He sounded indignant that she had not remembered.

"Of course. How could I forget? 'Go you now to Scarborough Fair? Parsley, sage, rosemary, and thyme...'"

Gently, hardly above a whisper, Julianna sang the old tune and every other quiet, soothing melody she could think of—airs and ballads, hymns and nursery rhymes. Between songs, she murmured the kind of endearments she could recall from her own childhood sickbed. When the water came, she bathed his fevered forehead, crooning all the while.

The late winter sun had risen when Julianna noticed Sir Edmund's breathing becoming slower and more even. His head felt cooler. The fever broken, he slept.

Julianna's own eyes were beginning to droop when Gwenyth appeared. "Mr. Brock has brought the doctor, ma'am. He would speak with you outside. I can sit with the master, if you like."

"Very well, Gwenyth. Call me right away if he wakes."

In the corridor, Julianna found Brock with Jonathan Cail.

"Dear Dr. Cail! Thank you so much for coming."

The doctor took her hand. "Why, Miss Ramsay, what a lady you have become since last we met. Though you do look like you just stepped out of an old painting."

"Excuse me? Oh, the dress!" Julianna gave a weary chuckle. "My husband was delirious last night from the fever, and calling for his dead sister. I thought the masquerade might calm his mind, and so it did."

"A wise idea. It is always best to indulge a delirious patient, if possible. Any agitation only works against the healing process."

Julianna cast Mordecai Brock a look to say she had told him so. He refused to take notice.

"I am pleased to say we will not require your services after all. My husband's fever has subsided at last. He is sleeping."

"Then I will not disturb him for the present. If what your steward tells me is true, your husband is not yet out of danger. Is there someplace private, where we may speak at greater length?"

"Why certainly. You have not yet broken your fast, I think." Julianna turned to the steward. "Mr. Brock, order breakfast for two. Then get yourself to bed. I know you have lost more than one night's sleep since Christmas."

"I believe I will sit with Sir Edmund until you return, ma'am," he replied.

"No, Mr. Brock." Julianna almost stamped her foot for emphasis. "If Sir Edmund's illness continues, I will need you rested and well to assist me. Gwenyth is with him now and he is sleeping. You must do the same. Consider that an order."

"Aye, ma'am." He heaved his words in a great sigh. Julianna doubted Mr. Brock would have any trouble obeying her command.

As Julianna and the doctor awaited their breakfast in the dining room, she asked, "What did you mean about my husband not being out of danger? What is this awful fever?"

"Of course I have not yet examined the patient, but your manservant's account of Sir Edmund's medical history was very specific and informative. He would make a fine physician."

Giddy from lack of sleep, Julianna could not suppress a laugh. "I think his manner at the patients' bedside would leave something to be desired."

Their food arrived shortly, and they continued to converse between bites. "The course of this disease is cyclical, with several periods of fever building over a span of one or two days. According to your steward, this last episode was only the second. The attack is far from over."

"What can you do for him?"

"Little, I'm afraid," Dr. Cail confessed. "Illness of any kind derives from an imbalance of the body's four humors. With fever, it is an agitation of the spleen, causing a surfeit of blood. If it is any consolation, you have done well so far. Keep your husband as quiet as possible and watch for signs of the fever recurring. It will begin with chills and headache, and then the pyrexia will mount quickly. Give him cold liquids to dilute the blood. Bathe his head with cool water until the fever subsides. I have heard there is a tonic sometimes used to good effect in the Indies. It is extracted from the bark of some tree and is quite a bitter brew. The final fever in the cycle will be the most dangerous, for it can produce seizures, or coma—even death. I suggest a quick bleeding when the fever is at its height. Now, don't pull faces. I know the treatment is overused by many of my medical brethren, but judiciously applied, it is most effective in breaking a fever.''

As they returned to the sickroom, Julianna did her best to digest all this information. ''What should I do now?'' she asked. ''And after each fever breaks?''

The doctor shrugged. ''Let him sleep as much as he will. If he wakes, get him to drink. Give him water-gruel or broth, if he will eat. Most important, get some rest yourself. You are facing a week or more before this illness runs its course. With each fresh fever, you will be harder pressed. Now, I must return to my patients at hospital. Thank you for breakfast. I will be awaiting your call.''

Julianna took a deep breath. ''I promise to carry out all your instructions to the letter.''

With a practiced hand, the physician took Sir Edmund's pulse and listened to his breathing. When he had completed his examination, Julianna posed a parting question.

''Tell me truthfully, Dr. Cail—can he survive?''

The doctor's look seemed to evaluate her ability to withstand his pronouncement.

''Truthfully, Lady Fitzhugh?'' He shook his head. ''I have grave doubts.''

Chapter Seven

A band of pressure squeezed Julianna's temples and a prickly ache throbbed behind her eyes. At times her vision grew distorted, as if she were viewing the world through a pane of old glass. Her head fell forward, then snapped up again as Sir Edmund moved restlessly in his sleep. She was beginning to envy him that sleep. Places and times outside this room had become nebulous memories. Reality was the man on the bed, his face as frighteningly gray as his wide, empty eyes. Reality was the accusatory stare beneath Mr. Brock's heavy brows.

Three…or was it four times?…Sir Edmund had been racked with chills, his flesh burning away from within. On the second day, which now seemed so long ago, Julianna had dispatched Mr. Brock to the Thames quayside. She had hoped some returning sailor or ship's surgeon might carry the tonic of which Dr. Cail had spoken. Grimly triumphant, Brock had returned at last, bearing a small dose. The physician had not exaggerated in calling the stuff bitter. Even cut liberally with treacle, it took every art of Julianna's persuasion to coax a spoonful of the foul mixture past her patient's lips.

"Mr. Barley!" Sir Edmund's feeble shout jolted Julianna fully awake. He was trying to rise, propped up on one elbow, his other hand gesticulating with unexpected vigor. "Hard astar, Mr. Barley. Get that wind behind us!"

Julianna's gaze flew to Mr. Brock, and the old seaman mouthed her a silent prompt.

"Aye, Captain. Hard astar."

Sir Edmund's head jerked back. He grasped Brock's arm. "Get aloft every square inch of canvas you can muster. That sun'll soon be setting, but we must outrun them until then."

A flash of comprehension crossed Brock's face. "Aye, aye, Cap'n. See to that rigging, boys! Hoist the mizzenmast!"

Sir Edmund's eyes glittered dangerously. "Let's prepare a little ruse for our friends, bos'n. Lash a raft together, load her with anything that'll burn and douse the works with lamp oil. Prepare to light her, and cast off at my signal."

"Aye, sir."

Sir Edmund raised a hand, as if to shade his eyes from the setting sun. He squinted past Julianna, into a distant horizon beyond the confines of the room. "Steady as she goes, Mr. Barley. Be ready to bring her hard about. I think we've put a bit more water between us. Can you still see them, Mr. Davies?"

Brock sent a sharp glance toward Julianna and shook his head vehemently. In as deep a voice as she could manage, Julianna replied, "No, Captain." She read Brock's lips. "It's too dark to see 'em, sir."

Sir Edmund's parched lips broke into a tight smile. "Then pray their eyes are no better than yours, Huw. Is our diversion ready, Mr. Brock?"

"Aye, Captain. We've just set her alight."

Julianna shook her head. Was Brock delirious, too?

"There she goes," cried Sir Edmund. "Hard about, Mr. Barley. Cut sail, bos'n, and hope they take the bait. Man overboard? Damn! Secure the rigging!"

Sir Edmund writhed among the bedclothes. Julianna looked to Brock in alarm.

"Here, sir!" The steward thrust out his forearm and clasped his master's. Sir Edmund quieted immediately.

"Hold fast now," he encouraged Brock. "They'll soon haul us aboard. Sharks? I doubt any shark would bother with the scrawny leather of our hides. She's coming to. Head up, lad. Just a minute more. Give us a little warning next time you fancy a twilight swim. Hold on, man. That's an order."

Sir Edmund's voice had risen, as if to be heard above the roar of rolling ocean swells. His hand clutched Brock's so tightly that every cord and vein stood out.

Again, Brock mouthed Julianna's line. "Easy, sir. We've got you both."

"Helm, move off smartly." Sir Edmund lay back, gasping. "Get this man a tot of rum and dry him out."

Who could have imagined Brock's voice so hushed and warm? "Aye, sir. Best dry out yourself, and get some rest."

Sir Edmund heaved a sigh. "Have Hamish McDonald take this watch...." In a lighter vein, he added, "And do inform me if we collide with those pirates in the night."

Julianna rubbed her eyes. It had been like watching a riveting drama. With an unexpectedly gentle touch, Brock disengaged his arm from his master's grip. He spoke quietly to the unconscious Sir Edmund and to himself, oblivious to her presence.

"It was the first time you saved my life, sir, but not the last. Rest easy, sir. I'd take your place now, if I could."

In that moment, Julianna saw her nemesis in a whole new light—the vigilant guardian of a master to whom he owed his life. Having also been rescued by Sir Edmund, she could sympathize with—what had Gwenyth called him?—an old bulldog. So Mr. Brock's animosity was not toward her personally, but rather to the threat she represented. That threat, Julianna thought ruefully, had not been without substance.

"He will live, Mr. Brock." She tried to reassure him, but to herself she added desperately, "He must."

Mordecai Brock did not respond with so much as a glance. Perhaps his antipathy was personal, after all. Julianna shrugged and yawned, past caring what Brock or anyone else thought of her. Her eyes closed, then flew open again at a sound from the door. John peered diffidently into the darkened room.

"I gave orders—" Brock hissed.

"Yes, Mr. Brock," the boy blurted, "but there's a man at the door. Demands to see the mistress. Says he's her brother."

Jerome! Julianna rose, the blood draining from her face. Chaotic snatches of thought swirled in her weary mind. She could feel Jerome's hands tight on her wrists. She could taste his fetid breath. Her skittery glance swept the room for a hiding place and met Brock's puzzled gaze.

"Send him away!" she pleaded breathlessly. "Mr. Brock, I cannot see him. You must send him away. I beg you."

"Stay here." Brock strode from the room.

That was one direction Julianna could not follow. She had to know what new menace Jerome was hatching. Creeping down the gallery to the head of the stairs, she held her breath, listening. There was no doubt of the caller's identity. She knew that bullying voice all too well.

"...sister, my good man."

Brock's reply was sharp. "I am not your man, for good or ill...laddie."

"Is that so?" No one could infuse his words with more mocking insolence than Jerome. "Sir Edmund is dying, they tell me. When he breathes his last, my sister will be mistress of this house. As her guardian, I will be your new master. Does that put a different complexion on the matter? Now run along and get Julianna, and we will say no more about it."

"If Sir Edmund dies," growled Brock, "you can put a torch to this place for all I care. But while he lives, if my mistress says she will not see you, rest assured you will not see her."

Mr. Brock, a bulwark in her defense? Julianna could scarcely credit the thought. Jerome stormed and threatened, but Brock stood firm. All that lay between her and the clutches of her stepbrother, Julianna suddenly realized, was a dying man. With swift, paralyzing certainty, she knew Sir Edmund would die. She must get as far away as possible, while there was still time.

Think, Julianna ordered herself. *Breathe slowly.* The idea of flight had crossed her mind back when Jerome had first threatened to commit her to debtors' prison or to Bedlam if she did not marry. Then, she had dismissed it out of hand. Without money, she could have run no farther than a prostitute's crib in Alsatia. Circumstances were more favorable now. She had two quarters' allowance, minus her small Christmas purchases and what she had sent to Winnie in Wales.

Wales!

The instant that thought crossed her mind, Julianna's plan

began to take shape. If her small hoard proved insufficient, her wedding ring would fetch a good price, as would her emerald pendant. She could never part with the miniature of Crispin, but selling the locket would bring enough capital to last her a while.

She had no time to lose. She must change into clothes suitable for traveling, pack what she could easily carry and be gone before anyone missed her. Julianna vaguely wondered what Crispin would say, two years hence, when he found out she had deserted his dying uncle. Surely he would understand that she had fled to preserve her virtue, for his sake. In the end, however, it was not loyalty to Crispin that stayed her.

As she hurried by Sir Edmund's room, mentally packing her bag, Julianna heard him call out. Her legs refused to carry her past his door. Before she could stop herself, her hand turned the knob. Sir Edmund lay quiet, his eyes closed. Had she truly heard his voice, or had it been her own conscience calling? With the flesh of his face seared away, and the wisp of a beard on his chin, Sir Edmund looked the very picture of her beloved Don Quixote. Reluctantly, Julianna realized that she had come to care, in some nameless way, for this contradictory, unfathomable man. She could not leave him to die alone.

Fool! she raged at herself. *You might as well march naked to Jerome's front door!*

Despite that, she closed Sir Edmund's door softly behind her and assumed her accustomed place by his bedside. When Brock returned, she looked into his solemn, rugged countenance with a tired smile of gratitude, which he did not acknowledge.

Brock had barely reseated himself, when Sir Edmund began to tremble and call for more bedclothes. Catching the steward's eye, Julianna nodded. He left hurriedly, in search of the doctor. Sir Edmund fought to sit up but slumped to one side. His chest heaved beneath his thick nightshirt in a way that chilled Julianna's heart.

"Help me, Alice. I can get no air!" he wheezed.

Julianna threw open the door to relieve the closeness of the room. Then she slid onto the bed behind Sir Edmund. She cradled his lank frame in her arms, almost upright, his head falling against her shoulder. Still he gulped at the cool draft from the gallery, but otherwise evinced less distress. Time crystallized like a bead of amber. Julianna's gown became soaked with sweat. She felt light-headed and she had lost all sensation in her legs.

"Can we go into the garden, Alice?"

Julianna came awake at Sir Edmund's raspy whisper. She murmured Alice's assent, relieved not to be taking part in another high-sea adventure without Brock to cue her.

"See all the roses? Aren't they beautiful? Which do you like best?"

His voice sounded fey and uninflected. Julianna fancied she could hear his words in a small boy's clear treble. She responded gently. "The pinks. I have always loved the pinks. And you?"

"I like the white ones…the rosebuds best of all." His words were suddenly infused with anguish. "Why do they all die when I touch them?"

Julianna tried to clear her foggy mind. The absurd question obviously mattered to him. "Hush now. Roses never live long, you know, especially once you pluck them."

Sir Edmund's voice continued plaintive. "I have not plucked a single one, only touched. When I touch them, they wither and die."

What could she say to such lunatic ravings?

"I have killed them all!"

Julianna could have sworn she heard tears in his voice. "Hush. It is only a bad dream. You have killed nothing."

He responded with a spent sigh, the words barely distinguishable as such. "I…killed…Mother."

Before the meaning of his words could dent her consciousness, Julianna felt Sir Edmund's body go rigid in her arms.

"John! Gwenyth! Someone come quickly!"

Brock rushed to her aid, the physician close behind him.

"Not a moment too soon." The doctor drew his lancet and made a cut in Sir Edmund's forearm. Dark blood spurted from the wound, staining the bedclothes before Brock could catch it in a shallow basin. Julianna looked away, her empty stomach queasy. The patient appeared insensible to any pain, but the spasticity in his limbs relaxed. Judging the treatment a success, the doctor applied a bandage to the incision.

"We should know shortly."

Julianna could hardly tell whether she was asleep or awake. She was too tired, suddenly, to care whether Sir Edmund lived or died, or what Jerome would do with her afterward. Almost imperceptibly, Sir Edmund's breathing slowed and his fever subsided. Once she judged him deeply asleep, Julianna allowed Brock to support his master, while the doctor eased her from her place on the bed. Jonathan Cail responded to her hopeful, questioning look with guarded encouragement.

"The next twenty-four hours will tell the tale. If this was the final fever, there is good reason for optimism. Otherwise, I doubt your husband can survive another spell. In his weakened state, I dare not bleed him again."

When the doctor had gone, Julianna and Brock waged a phlegmatic contest of wills as to who would sleep and who would keep watch over the patient. Each insisted that the other needed rest more. In the end they were both too exhausted to fight, and too stubborn to leave. All that day they sat side by side on the chaise, scarcely exchanging a word. At one point through the night, Julianna woke to find her head slumped against Brock's substantial shoulder, his arm supporting her back. Then, just after sunrise on the following day, Sir Edmund's eyelids fluttered open. His wife and steward held their collective breath.

He was barely able to croak, "Julianna, what are you doing here? Why are you wearing that old dress? Brock, get me some water. I'm parched."

The strain broken, Brock hurried to do his master's bidding. Julianna closed her eyes, dizzy with relief. The waking was brief. Once Sir Edmund again rested comfortably, Mordecai Brock was adamant.

"You must sleep, too, milady. I know how he will be once he comes to again—more troublesome and cantankerous than you can imagine. Then we will need every trick you have to manage him. You will not be up to it, if you are worn down and ill yourself. Now, for once, take an order instead of giving it. I will see you put to bed, supposing you do hand me my notice.''

Could that be a note of warmth in Brock's voice?

"No, Mr. Brock. I will stay a while longer, in case Sir Edmund needs me."

As she rose to exert her authority, Julianna had the distressing sensation of peripheral darkness closing off her vision. She was barely conscious of Mordecai Brock hoisting her up in his powerful arms. The last sound she heard was the steward's grunt of satisfaction as he strode down the hallway, to deposit her on her own bed.

Julianna was surprised to see daylight when she awoke. She felt weak as a kitten, but ravenous. Posted in the sitting room, Gwenyth appeared instantly at the feeble ring of her bell.

"I wondered if you would ever awaken, milady. Is there aught I can get for you? Bring a bite of breakfast, perhaps?"

Rubbing her eyes, Julianna yawned. "Breakfast? Gwenyth, what time is it?"

"Gone nine, ma'am, and Saturday morning."

Julianna could scarcely believe that she had slept 'round the clock. "Sir Edmund? How is he, Gwenyth? I never meant to sleep so long. I must go to him."

"Mr. Brock is with Sir Edmund, ma'am," said Gwenyth. "He gave orders you were not to be disturbed on any account. From what I hear tell, the master's come around something wonderful. Auntie Enid says he's had three bowls of her wine broth."

At the mention of food, Julianna's aching stomach growled.

"Could you get me some breakfast, Gwenyth? Tell your aunt to lay on plenty, for I am starving. While I eat, you can draw my bath and set out clean clothes. How good it will feel to wear my own gowns again!"

Oh, that breakfast! Were there ever sausages so plump and crisp? Poached eggs with yolks like molten sunshine? Savoring each mouthful, Julianna recalled Winnie's saying that hunger was better than a French chef.

As Mrs. Davies's strong scalding coffee revived her, she looked out the window for the first time in almost a fortnight. The white sunlight reflected off a landscape encased in a brittle crust of snow. Life had continued, the sun had risen and set, and she had been completely unaware of it. As she licked the last smear of butter from her fingers, the doctor arrived to report on Sir Edmund's condition.

"You can take pride in your nursing skills, Lady Fitzhugh. Your husband has come through the worst. He is more wakeful now, and alert to his surroundings. He has even begun to take food, which is always a good sign."

"My main contribution was to dig in my heels against the barber-surgeon, and call upon your services," Julianna demurred. "I cannot begin to thank you. Of course, we will see that you are generously recompensed for your time. Once he recovers more fully, I expect Sir Edmund will want to make a contribution to the hospital as well."

"We are always glad of donations," the doctor replied, "but your husband is already a substantial benefactor of the Westminster. As for your contribution to his recovery, none of my advice would have signified without you there to calm and nurse him through the periods of delirium. I must caution you, however. Your husband is not yet out of danger. Though we have temporarily corrected the imbalance of blood, his spleen remains swollen. If he should take a blow to that area or fall upon it, the swelling could burst, and he would bleed to death in a very short time. As he will be weak, and his limbs unsteady, a fall would be almost certain. Therefore, he must remain in bed for a while. Mr. Brock tells me such advice will not sit well with Sir Edmund. You must use your influence to keep him at rest."

Julianna nodded. "I understand, Doctor. I can vouch that Sir Edmund will remain in bed for as long as you wish."

"If anyone can do it... Well, I must get back to the hospital. I will look in every week or so, to check on Sir Edmund's progress. In the meantime, if you need me, you know where I can be reached."

While she soaked out two weeks of cramps and kinks in the

steaming water of her bath, Julianna digested the physician's news. Her hair washed and dressed, and wearing a clean gown of her own, she felt like a new woman. However, surveying her hollow cheeks and the dark smudges beneath her eyes made Julianna pull a wry face at her reflection. She was beginning to yawn again and contemplate an afternoon nap, when a breathless John burst through her door.

"Mr. Brock says to come at once, milady. It's the master!"

Oh, whatever could be wrong now? Julianna hurried down the corridor on the footman's heels. Not a relapse, she hoped. Sir Edmund might survive, but Julianna doubted whether she could.

Chapter Eight

Entering Sir Edmund's chamber, Julianna found him perched on the edge of his bed, trying to rise, while Brock pleaded in vain with him to lie back down. It felt uncannily as though the past two weeks had been a bad dream, and she were coming in back at the beginning. Having brought the irascible Mr. Brock to heel, could she not manage one fractious invalid? Perhaps not, if that invalid was master of the house.

"Edmund Fitzhugh, get back in bed this instant!"

Two heads snapped up, their expressions almost comic with shock. Sir Edmund recovered first.

"This is no concern of yours, and no concern of Brock's, come to that. Go away, both of you."

He would dare dismiss her after she had saved his life? Julianna's mouth compressed into a resolute line. "That I will not, until you are back in bed, resting quietly."

He met her stubborn stare with one of his own. "I feel fine. I merely wish to rise, bathe, dress and take my leisure. What is wrong with that? Brock, rather than nattering at me like an old biddy hen, you'd do better seeing this bossy chit out."

Now it would come, Julianna thought to herself. Time for Mr. Brock to get a bit of his own back.

"Not I, Sir Edmund. I have come up against your pepperbox of a wife once too often of late. By me, Lady Fitzhugh's word is law in this house until the doctor declares you fit."

Julianna's mouth dropped open, as did Sir Edmund's. She

had never seen or imagined him this angry. Little wonder the staff were so anxious to avoid rousing his temper. Twice he opened and shut his mouth, finally mastering his fury enough to hurl a single word. "Mutiny!"

The steward winced and Julianna found herself actually sorry for him. Perhaps the time had come to change tactics. Laying a hand on Mr. Brock's arm, she nodded toward the door. The look of relief on his face almost made her smile. Taking Brock's place by the bed, Julianna knelt at Sir Edmund's feet. Could she embarrass him into cooperating?

"Sir Edmund, lie down. I beg you. The doctor says it could be very dangerous for you to be on your feet."

"Harrumph! Humorous imbalance, engorgement of the spleen. The only humor I see is that anyone would credit such Hippocratic nonsense. I'm certain the danger is greatly exaggerated."

"Certain enough to wager your life?" Julianna asked.

She could see Sir Edmund's resolve wavering. With the sweet cajolery that had always swayed her father, she added, "As for what concern your welfare is to me, I vowed to care for you in times of sickness. Have you forgotten? I stayed by your side nearly every moment of the past fortnight. I will not see you casually jeopardize the life I have worked so hard to save. Would Crispin ever forgive me if you died while in my care?"

Her last salvo found its mark. At the mention of Crispin, she detected a thawing in Sir Edmund's icy glare. He drew his legs under the coverlet and lay deliberately back on his pillow. Julianna sensed he did not intend to surrender unconditionally.

"Very well," he fumed. "Let me die of boredom, and the stench of this bed, and these clothes, and myself!"

Julianna rolled her eyes. Sir Edmund Fitzhugh and his eccentric penchant for soap and water! Forcing a smile, she concentrated on keeping her voice even and soothing.

"You need not leave your bed for any of those things. You can be washed." She plumped his pillow.

"You can be shaved." She drew the bedclothes over his chest and smoothed them in place.

"As for boredom…what would you do if you were at liberty?"

"Peruse the paper, of course," he snapped. "To find out what has transpired in the world since Christmas."

"I'd be happy to fetch the latest paper and read it to you. Would you prefer the *Craftsman* or the *Gazetteer*?"

Her offer did nothing to placate Sir Edmund. "Perhaps I would prefer a chess match at Jerusalem or the Chapterhouse."

"I play well," said Julianna, her tone bright and brittle. "At the risk of sounding immodest, I doubt you could find a more worthy opponent among all the gentlemen of your acquaintance. I also am adept at backgammon, cribbage, commerce, whist…."

"How terribly fortunate." Though confined to his bed, Sir Edmund still could wield the bludgeon of sarcasm. "I simply might wish to enjoy the pleasures of the town."

Julianna crimsoned, more from rising fury than from the blatant affront to her modesty. She pretended to miss his implication. "Concerts, you mean—or theater? I can play the harp and sing for you. Read from any play you choose."

Pursing his lips, Sir Edmund dryly observed, "I begin to see where this is going."

Julianna put her hand on his arm and smiled beatifically, though she would have preferred to box his ears. "Then I take it you will be a gentleman and acquiesce with good grace."

He jerked his arm away. "Don't press me too far, wench!"

"Lovely!" effused Julianna as if she had just received a pretty compliment. "Then I shall retire so Mr. Brock and the footmen can assist in your toilette. I'm sure it will make you feel much better. I shall return with your midday meal, then stay on to amuse you through the afternoon."

Closing the door more forcefully than she'd intended, Julianna took a deep breath and blew it out sharply in exasperation. Stubborn, hateful creature! To think of all she had risked to stay by his side. She started at the tickle of Brock's sidewhiskers on her ear.

"He'll be a handful, ma'am, and no mistake. Being confined to quarters is a bitter pill for a man like the captain, who has always gone and done as he pleased. Better your pretty face to make him swallow it than my ugly old phizzog.''

Flashing the steward a comradely smile, Julianna extended her slim fingers, which he enveloped in his own large callused hand.

Julianna never quite understood what she had done to win over the implacable Mr. Brock. But as the dark, close days of winter dragged by, she began to doubt she would ever number Sir Edmund among her admirers. Even with her father, she had never endured the constant, unrelenting society of another person. Having gone from seldom seeing Sir Edmund to this forced intimacy, the former appealed to her more and more.

She did not find the substance of her duties unpleasant. In fact, their pastimes together were all ones Julianna enjoyed. Still, it vexed her that each activity came at his behest. Just once she would have relished choosing when they read, what they read, how long they read or what they undertook next.

If only this time spent together had brought her a closer acquaintance with Crispin's uncle, it might have been easier to bear. Instead Julianna felt she knew less of him now than ever. She guessed that his present enforced idleness was difficult for Sir Edmund, and he obviously resented his reliance upon her. Since she was nearest at hand, he frequently took out his frustrations upon her. She was growing heartily impatient with his constant irritability. Where was the man she had glimpsed at Christmas, and on their wedding night—the man of wry wit, quiet courtesy and perceptive kindness? There were days when Julianna wondered if he had ever existed, or if she had conjured him out of her own loneliness and need for a father figure.

Lately, because she had refused to allow the return of his pipe, Sir Edmund waxed more antagonistic than ever. In his weakened state, she knew the ingestion of tobacco smoke could not be good for him. Besides, he might drop off to sleep with the pipe lit, and burn the house down. Resenting Brock's refusal to cross her orders in the matter, Sir Edmund heaped sarcastic abuse on his poor steward at every opportunity.

Each week Julianna prayed Dr. Cail would declare Sir Edmund past danger, and able to be up and about on his own. The young physician had begun to shrink from her beseeching eyes at the end of his examinations.

"Still some swelling, I'm afraid, though your color is improving, Sir Edmund. I fear it will be a few weeks more."

Thinking ahead to several more weeks of her present existence, Julianna felt particularly cross and out of sorts. Her eyes and head hurt from reading in the gloom. Her fingers ached from being cramped round the pages of a book and from plucking the harp. Her back was sore from so much sitting in one place, and her throat smarted from the strain of constant reading and singing. If that disagreeable man had the gall to take up with her today, it would be his own lookout!

A young footman peered warily into Edmund's chamber.

"Oh, you're awake, sir," he said, demonstrating a powerful grasp of the obvious. "I'll go fetch the mistress."

Before Edmund could voice his objection, the boy disappeared. Shooting a wrathful glare at the door, he wished he could bar it with a look. Soon his tyrant of a wife would barge in with her vexing air of cheerful self-sacrifice, determined to kill him with kindness. Had he ever thought Julianna a sweet, defenseless waif? The little baggage was about as sweet and defenseless as a mongoose!

She had chained him to this bed with fetters of guilt, then proceeded to smother him with her feigned solicitude. She plumped his pillows when they needed no plumping. She smoothed his pristine sheets a dozen times a day. Next, she'd be spooning pap into him and wiping his mouth after every bite! Edmund nearly gagged on the black bile of his rage.

Worst of all, the little minx had usurped his role as head of the household without offering a sop to his pride. She'd suborned his whole crew—even Mordecai Brock. That feat Edmund could ascribe only to witchcraft. He had no say in anything these days. She'd even had the face to forbid him taking up his pipe, protesting her concern for his welfare. By heaven, once her trained puppy of a physician pronounced him fit, he'd turf the little wretch out, bag and baggage!

Without so much as a courtesy knock, Julianna marched in with a blatantly insincere smile stuck on her face.

"Sir Edmund, John told me you were awake."

She plumped his pillow. "What shall we do now?"

Edmund was tempted to tell her exactly what she could do.

"Perhaps you are tired still? I could go away and let you rest." He could hear the eagerness in her voice.

"Thank you, no, I am perfectly awake and alert," he replied in a martyred tone. "But if you would rather be elsewhere, do not feel compelled to remain here simply because I am a prisoner in this bed, and likely to remain so for who-knows-how-long."

She forcefully tucked the bedclothes around him. "If you are not tired, then I am quite content to remain. Would you care for a game of chess?"

Edmund threw up his hands. "And have you beat me again in that humiliating fashion? I think not. My intellectual powers are becoming atrophied as badly as my limbs, with so little society and stimulation."

"Some music, then?" She did not bother to disguise a rising note of sharpness in her voice.

Edmund essayed a pained smile. "Not that. Splendid as your performances are, I've grown rather weary of those interminable Welsh ballads. No doubt they are terribly stirring, if one understands the language, but…"

A bright flush crept into Julianna's cheeks. It accentuated her pallor, and the dusky hollows of her cheeks. She eyed his pillow as though she longed to stifle him with it. Edmund's conscience suffered a twinge of remorse.

"I would enjoy reading some Shakespeare," he ventured, striving to sound more amiable. "You can take your father's copy, and I will take my own. We can each read the parts for characters of our own sex."

"Very well. That sounds quite enjoyable. Which play shall we read? *Romeo and Juliet*?"

Edmund raised his eyes heavenward, beseeching the Almighty for strength. "Only if you aim to make me retch. All that tedious romantic rambling—and the melodrama. Fortunately the Bard has better work to be remembered for.''

Golden sparks snapped in Julianna's brown eyes. "On the contrary. I think it some of his most exquisite verse, and the plight of the young lovers pathetic and moving.''

He cast her a look of utter disdain. "On so cold and gray a day, who needs their spirits depressed with further tragedy?''

Julianna answered through clenched teeth. "Then what would *you* have?''

"Something to lighten the gloom—*A Midsummer Night's Dream,* to my mind Shakespeare's finest comedy. For exquisite verse, you will find none to equal the poetic discourse of the fairy king and his court. Their talk of overhung riverbanks and moonlit summer nights may transport us from this endless winter.''

"Very well,'' she assented coolly. "Here is your text. I believe as Duke Theseus, you have the first speech.''

" 'Now, fair Hippolyta, our nuptial hour draws on apace....' ''

The words of Theseus and his Amazon bride lacked the warmth of tone they implied. However, when two antagonists like Oberon and his fairy queen addressed each other, their exchanges had a bite the best of London's actors might well have envied.

As Sir Edmund took on the parts of Nick Bottom, Peter Quince and company, Julianna began to thaw in spite of herself. Her husband employed his talent for mimicry to give the characters voices from all corners of the kingdom—Newcastle to Penzance. The scenes were very droll, and Julianna found herself laughing. Then, when the scene shifted to the Athenian forest, and Oberon gave instructions to the gamboling Puck, Sir Edmund's hushed eloquence quite bewitched her:

"I know a bank whereon the wild thyme blows,
Where oxlips and the nodding violet grows....''

Julianna, a city girl born and bred, could see that pastoral bower as if before her very eyes. She sensed Sir Edmund did know of such a secret place, canopied with fragrant honeysuckle. For her part, it became easier to speak the amorous words of the enchanted Titania to Bottom:

"So is mine eye enthralled to thy shape...
On the first view, to say, to swear, I love thee."

As Sir Edmund added a braying note to the rustic accent of Nick Bottom, transformed with the head of an ass, Julianna's lips twitched. It took a mighty effort of will to swallow her mirth and reply touchingly as the besotted fairy queen. The finale, where the workingmen staged the "tedious brief scene of young Pyramus and Thisbe," was a comic masterpiece. Julianna's sides ached with helpless laughter.

"Bravo, Sir Edmund!" She applauded sincerely. "You should have gone on the stage! I owe you a vote of thanks for your fine selection. It truly has brightened a 'Midwinter Day's Doldrums.' I have laughed myself hoarse. May I have a sip of that lemon drink Mrs. Davies compounded for you?"

The juice seared her throat like liquid fire. Sir Edmund frowned and fussed over her obvious distress.

"When Dr. Cail comes to examine me," he insisted, "I will have him look you over, as well."

"Nasty dose of quinsy." The doctor winced as he peered into Julianna's open mouth.

He rattled off his prescribed course of treatment. "Send to the 'pothecary for a poultice and keep it wrapped around her throat with good Welsh flannel. Make her drink plenty of water. No talking for several days at least. And do make her get some rest."

"Yes, of course, Doctor. I feel quite responsible for my wife's condition," Edmund admitted. "I fear I have been an impatient patient, so to speak. I have drawn too heavily on her time and strength to help me endure the monotony of my convalescence. Should I inquire about my own recovery, or will I be doomed to disappointment?"

The doctor made a show of packing his bag. "Better to ask

next week, Sir Edmund, when I may have more encouraging news.''

Summoning Mordecai Brock, Edmund ordered him to put Julianna to bed and send someone to the apothecary's shop.

''Well, how is she faring?'' he asked several hours later when the steward brought his supper.

''How do you think?'' snapped Brock. ''She's in a bad way, poor lass, and all thanks to you. Why, she's worked herself to a shadow, dancing to your tune morning, noon and night....''

''Enough!'' thundered Edmund. ''Away with you!''

Over the next few days, the rest of his staff made it quietly known where their sympathies lay. No one came near Edmund, except to deliver meals, or when specifically summoned. He had plenty of time to fret over Julianna's condition and to ponder the disgraceful way he'd treated her. He did owe her his life, after all. And he'd taken perverse glee in their tacit battle of wills. What he'd resented, Edmund admitted to himself, was having that lovely, vivacious creature see him so weak and vulnerable. He'd been wrong to punish her for his punctured vanity.

Given a surfeit of the solitude he'd always craved, Edmund quickly grew tired of his own company. As a bland pudding needed a measure of honey or a dash of ginger, he needed the sweetness and spice of Julianna. Heaving a pensive sigh, he took up his book—the one she'd given him for Christmas.

He had read only a page or two when his bedroom door swung open. There she stood, shivering in her nightshift and wrap, two dainty bare feet peeping out below the hem. How long had it been since he'd seen a woman barefoot? A fierce flush of heat swept through Edmund's body. Was his fever coming back again?

''What are you doing out of bed, you little goose?'' he asked gruffly. ''Is one long-term invalid in the house not enough?''

Unused for several days, her voice erupted as a harsh croak. ''Tiresome...nothing to do...can I stay?''

Anticipating his assent, she moved toward the chaise.

''Now you have some appreciation for how I feel. Remember, I have been captive in this wretched bed far longer than your brief detention. If you intend to stay, for mercy's sake don't sit out there in the draft and take a chill on top of the quinsy.''

He threw back the bedclothes and eased himself over. ''Climb aboard! This monstrosity has room enough for a whole troop.''

How long had it been since he'd invited a woman into his bed? Resolutely, Edmund tried to suppress the thought.

''Ah!'' He flinched. ''I will thank you to keep your icy feet off my shin! There. Comfortable?'' He plumped a pillow for Julianna, in mock revenge. ''Now, as you are temporarily mute, I must provide the amusement. I'm enjoying Fielding's book. Shall I start over and read it aloud to you?''

Julianna shook her head. ''Tell me a story,'' she rasped. ''About you...where is the bank...wild thyme blows?''

For a moment Edmund puzzled her request. Then he realized what she was asking. ''You have caught me out. I do know a bank whereon the wild thyme blows. It was near my boyhood home. I believed that if I approached very quietly, I might one day find the fairy queen slumbering there. It is well I never caught her, for she might have lured me away to be her mortal servant. Though, at the time, it would have held great appeal for me.''

He sighed and looked away. ''I shouldn't jump into the midst of a long story. The fact is, I spent a rather lonely childhood.''

It went against the habit of a lifetime, talking about himself, particularly his past. Yet he could not help it, as she sat beside him looking so expectant. A force more powerful than his deeply ingrained reticence took possession of Edmund, compelling him to draw close to her in the only way he dared.

Chapter Nine

"I grew up tramping the meadows and woods around Abbot's Leigh," Edmund began. "The country there is beautiful. Green. Alive. Wild in places. You can smell the seasons changing. I must have explored every square acre between Guildford and Farnham in my day. Even back then, the Bayard wanderlust stirred in my veins."

"Bayard?" Julianna croaked.

Edmund read her puzzled expression. "Oh yes. I'm a Bayard, too. My mother was Rosemary Bayard, daughter of Lord Marlwood. Crispin's father was a cousin of ours. So you see, with Bayard blood on both sides, Crispin couldn't escape his destiny as an adventurer.

"See that chart?" Edmund pointed to the wall beside the hearth. There hung a yellowed parchment mounted under glass, its markings dulled to an antique brown. "That belonged to my uncle Walter Bayard—an intrepid explorer. He returned home to Abbot's Leigh when I was eight. All that winter, I scarcely stirred from the footstool by his chair. He had a trove of stories so fascinating that I would listen for hours on end."

Edmund shook his head sadly. "Unfortunately, Uncle Walter died before the next winter. He had filled my head with sea lore and fired my heart with a desire to explore the wide world and see all its wonders. After I finished school, I took up a naval commission to follow in his footsteps."

Edmund fell silent for a moment, remembering his departure

for Eton. He did not intend to voice the thought, but somehow
it came out. "I never saw my father so happy as the day I left
for school. He couldn't wait to be rid of me. My earliest memory is overhearing him describe me as 'the boy who killed his
mother.'" Edmund caught himself. Raising an eyebrow, he
glanced sidelong at Julianna, trying to make light of his painful
admission. "Talk of your original sin!"

Julianna's wide mouth compressed into a taut line. Her pale
brown eyes blazed with amber fury. "How dare he?" she exploded, indignantly. "Of an innocent child…and he a man of
God!"

"Hush, now. You must rest your voice, and this is my story
to tell. Besides, my father wasn't a particularly religious man
in any emotional or intuitive sense—more a theological scholar
who looked upon sacred doctrine as an intellectual exercise,
with grace the reward for complete understanding. A fine example of the Fitzhugh sin of pride, and rank heresy to my way
of thinking. Pray you never hear preaching as dreary as his!"

Edmund shut his mouth abruptly. Never had he voiced this
pent-up criticism of his father. How could Julianna understand
such feelings—she who had idolized a doting sire? As he fought
to master the tide of resentment and rejection that welled up in
his heart, Edmund felt her hand on his. It was a fine-boned
hand, but strong and capable. Hazily, he recalled that hand bathing his fevered brow and tipping a glass to his parched lips. He
looked up into eyes shining with the warm light of home at the
end of a cold and lonely journey.

"I wonder if my father ever felt any guilt?" Edmund had
never asked himself that question before. "After all, he got my
mother with child, knowing how dangerous it could be at her
age. Alice once told me he loved her very much. I never believed it. The man I knew was no more capable of love than—"

The door opened and Brock strode into the room, bearing Sir
Edmund's tea tray. At the sight of his master and mistress sharing the bed, he started and fumbled the tray. He appeared so
flabbergasted, Edmund and Julianna broke into nervous laughter.

"Here, what are you doing out of your bed, young lady?" the steward asked Julianna with a pretense of severity.

Before she could reply, Edmund quipped, "My poor bride was starved for my charming company. Can you blame her?"

Brock looked from his master to Julianna. She looked from Brock to Edmund. Then, all three sputtered with laughter.

"She was so anxious to see me, the little goose ventured out barefoot," Edmund told his steward. "Will you do the honors and carry my wife back to her own room?"

"That I will, sir." Brock fairly beamed with felicity.

"Come back tomorrow," Edmund invited Julianna. "I'll tell you all about India and the antics of Langston Carew."

She smiled and bade him adieu with her eyes. As the door closed behind them, Edmund poured himself a cup of tea. Taking a sip of the scalding liquid, he shook his head. Imagine dredging up that business about his father! He'd assumed such memories had long since lost their sting. Today he'd learned differently.

It brought back the time, as a boy, when his grandmother had lanced a boil on his leg. He had suffered the worsening pain in stoic silence for several days until she had discovered the trouble. Thirty years later, Edmund could feel the quick stab of agony, as the blade had punctured his swollen flesh. Then came a wave of relief, as poison gushed from the open wound. Edmund felt awash in that same relief now. A good thing Brock had interrupted him. Otherwise, he might have confessed to Julianna that he was as incapable of love as his father had been.

"Back for more punishment?" Sir Edmund asked when Brock deposited Julianna on his bed the following afternoon. He avoided her gaze, leading Julianna to wonder if he regretted yesterday's impulse to confide in her.

She had thought a great deal about Sir Edmund's childhood since then. She felt a certain kinship with him, since her own mother had died as a result of her birth. Thankfully, her father never held her to blame. On the contrary, he had cherished her like a treasure gained at dear cost. Devotedly as his grandmother and sister had reared young Edmund, Julianna could tell their love never quite compensated for the loss of his mother, or for his father's indifference.

"India!" she demanded in a voice still painfully hoarse. To-day, she wished to evoke no bitter memories.

"India," Sir Edmund agreed with visible relief.

Brock lingered in the room, toying with the fire irons.

"I went there after I resigned my naval commission," said Sir Edmund. "Governor Pitt took me on as his military attaché. In Madras, I fell into the dubious company of Langston Carew—the little rake."

As Julianna smothered a raspy giggle, Sir Edmund rolled his eyes. "Oh, Carew cut a dash in those days—not so portly as he is now. He had both his eyes then, and he always was the kind of glib flatterer women flock to. We made a rather ill-matched pair. I was the tall, solemn, tactless foil to Carew's impish charm. As I recall, I spent more time getting him out of trouble than I ever did on military matters. I wish I had a guinea for every duel I stood as his second."

How ridiculous, Julianna thought, that women should have flocked to Langston Carew over a man like Sir Edmund! Some-how, though, she did not care for the thought of other women flocking to him.

Sir Edmund's tales of India soon distracted her from such unsettling notions. His vivid narration transported her half a world away and two decades into the past. She could picture the splendid palaces and soaring temples, the grotesque statuary and the brilliantly garbed nobles. She swayed atop mammoth, lumbering elephants in their canopied howdahs. She thrilled to the labyrinthine intrigue of the Indian courts.

Through the highly colored tapestry of Sir Edmund's story wound the bright thread of the misadventures of Langston Carew, the comic Lothario from whom no lady was safe. One of Carew's indiscretions resulted in an ugly duel, during which he lost an eye and the opponent lost his life. On another occasion, his seduction of an Indian princess ignited the wrath of her uncle, the ruler of Hyderabad. His army stormed up the coast with French troops from Pondicherry, sacking an English fac-tory.

"It would've been a bad business, that," piped up Mordecai Brock, as he continued his show of tending the fire. "Sir Edmund sailed in and managed to evacuate the station just before the attack. He saved a good many lives, including innocent women and children. It earned him a commendation from the governor."

"Get away with you, you old busybody," Sir Edmund grumbled good-naturedly. "I only did my job and pulled Carew's bacon out of the fire yet again."

As Brock departed, he and Julianna exchanged a knowing look.

"My third year in Madras," Sir Edmund continued, "I took part in an expedition against the pirate admiral of the Andaman Islands. A bad storm hit us a few days out, demolishing the fleet. My ship was blown far off course, and finally wrecked. I washed ashore on a small island south of the Nicobars."

He went on to tell Julianna how the island people had made him welcome, much to his surprise. So popular did the young Englishman become that the headman finally presented him with a trio of wives. This unexpected revelation caused Julianna to erupt in a gale of hoarse laughter.

"Now, now!" Sir Edmund feigned affront. "It was an honorable custom there. They were lovely little things, but I never could tell who was who. I called them 'the little birds,' because they responded to my every word or action with a chorus of twittering laughter."

He looked askance at Julianna. "I can tell what you are thinking, but you may save your blushes. My interactions with the young ladies were quite honorable. I was far too young and puritan to cope with polygamy. Truth to tell, I was afraid any romantic overtures on my part would be greeted by more giggling. There's no sound on earth so calculated to extinguish a young man's ardor!"

Back in her own bed that night, Julianna thought over Sir Edmund's stories...particularly the one about his three wives. Most men she knew would have taken full advantage of the situation, but he seemed to possess a singular degree of honor where women were concerned. Was he impervious to their charms?

As Julianna continued to recuperate over the next week, she spent most of her days with Sir Edmund, listening to more tales of his adventures in the South Seas. He told her of the sunken treasure galleon he'd discovered, and how he'd used his wind-fall to buy a ship. For ten years, Captain Fitzhugh and his crew had plied the waters north and east of Java, smuggling nutmeg from the Spice Islands, trading in all manner of outlandish goods. They had lived by their wits, mindful to keep one step ahead of the Dutch and the fiendish pirates of the Celebes.

Each day, when he brought Julianna to Sir Edmund's chamber, Brock would invent reasons to hang about, eager to join in the storytelling. If she cast dubious looks over a far-fetched tale, he'd rifle Sir Edmund's sea chest, unearthing bizarre artifacts to support their account: shark's teeth, Balinese shadow puppets, feathers from the birds of paradise. With each fresh tale, Julianna's fascination grew.

She listened avidly to their reports of cannibal tribes, volcanoes and dragons. Why, Sir Edmund had lived more adventures than Julianna had read in all her books. Though he was characteristically self-effacing, she remembered his delirious reliving of one near escape and his daring sea rescue of young Brock. As the days passed, she came to see him in a new light. She pictured the young Captain Fitzhugh much like his nephew: resolute, resourceful and rather dashing.

One missing element was Crispin's easy affability. A gregarious Sir Edmund, even Julianna's imagination could not credit. Strangely though, understanding the source of his intense reserve, she no longer resented it. Rather, she began to treasure Sir Edmund's ultimate compliment—lowering the drawbridge of his lonely citadel and inviting her inside.

Chapter Ten

"Mr. Brock, is there no such thing as equanimity in this house?" Julianna sighed, as they took tea in her sitting room.

"Beg pardon, ma'am?"

Julianna caught sight of her reflection in the silver teapot. The pasty cast of her complexion was relieved only by the dark hollows in her cheeks and the circles beneath her eyes.

"As soon as I resolve one problem around here, another rapidly crops up to take its place."

"Problem, milady?" Brock was beginning to appear more at ease. When Julianna had sent for him, he'd looked precisely like a naughty scholar summoned for his first caning. "The captain's finally settled and manageable. I've never seen him better humored or more content. I'd say that's all your doing, ma'am."

Touched by this expression of Brock's hard-won approval, Julianna smiled. "There was a time I'd never have thought to hear such a compliment from you. Do you remember?"

"Aye, I recall," he stammered, "though I'd like to forget. I've meant to beg your pardon before now. I hope you can understand—when your wedding came off so sudden, I could only think you'd married the captain for his brass. Seeing your face that morning, even an old bachelor like me could tell you didn't care for your new husband. When he fell ill, I was certain you'd want naught more than to see him gone."

Brock bolted a drink of tea. "When I saw how you tended

him during the fever, I knew you did want the captain to live after all. The upshot is I was dead wrong. I hope you can see your way to forgive me?'' His last words came out at a full gallop.

''There is nothing to forgive, Brock. We each misjudged the other, jumped to conclusions, imputed false motives. Now, that's all behind us and we can begin afresh, for we have a common purpose to protect Sir Edmund. You're right in saying he's more content of late. But I fear he may be contenting himself as an invalid for the rest of his life. It's almost three weeks since Dr. Cail said he might get up, but he's done nothing of the sort. Whenever I mention it, he always puts me off.''

Her voice sharpened with asperity. ''His appetite is poor again, of course, from doing nothing but lie in bed all day. The doctor says if he doesn't soon recover his strength, it will invite another attack of the fever. In his present state, that would be the end of him. He was so anxious to be about at first. I cannot understand why he has changed so completely.''

''I don't think he'd want you to know, ma'am.'' Brock's voice dropped, as if he feared being overheard. ''But the master did try to take a few steps after the doctor gave him the word. He was that out of balance and weak in the legs, he could barely stand. I think it'll take him a while to get walking well again. For a man like the captain, he'd rather not make the effort. A bit too proud you might say, ma'am, especially with you around.''

Pride? Sir Edmund had spoken of pride as, what?—his family's besetting sin? Julianna nodded slowly.

''What you say makes excellent sense, Brock. Now, having some insight into the cause, have you any useful ideas for a cure?''

His reply came so readily, she was certain he'd been mulling it over on his own for some time. ''What about taking the captain home to Marlwood? The fresh spring air would do him good. You, too, ma'am, if you don't mind my saying so. He always liked to roam the countryside. Here in the city, there may be nothing worth the work of walking. It'd be different at Abbot's Leigh.''

Julianna could barely contain her enthusiasm. "Brock, you are a genius! I've been eager to visit Marlwood ever since Sir Edmund first told me of it. We shall go, and the sooner the better. What will we need to do to prepare?"

"Well, ma'am, I can go on ahead with a few of the staff and some luggage. The housekeeper and her man tend the place all year round. They won't be expecting us this soon. Still, I reckon a week's all we'd need to have everything shipshape for you and Sir Edmund. Would that be time enough?"

Julianna did a few mental calculations. "A perfect interval. I'll have to inform Sir Edmund of our plans and convince him it would be preferable to leave this house on his own two feet. I shudder already to think of the confrontation. Fortunately, I'm becoming used to imposing my will upon obstinate men." She winked at Brock. "I believe I'm even beginning to enjoy it."

His chuckle gave way to a shudder. "If it's all the same with you, milady, I'll leave before you tell the master. That way I'll be gone when he brings the roof down. I've fought off sharks and Sumatran tigers with little more than my bare hands but I wouldn't have the courage to take on your task."

As it turned out, Brock had not overestimated his master's reaction to Julianna's announcement.

"You have done *what!*" he thundered.

She responded with a show of innocent concern. "Sir Edmund, I had no idea the fever had also compromised your hearing. I'll speak louder and more slowly. I…sent… Brock…to…Surrey…to prepare…Abbot's Leigh…for our…arrival…next week."

Fortunately, she'd taken the precaution of standing back from the bed. In lieu of getting his hands around her neck, Sir Edmund pounded the mattress. "Damn it, woman! I'm not deaf, merely incredulous. How dare you do this without consulting me? You know I'm in no condition for a long journey into the country."

Cloyingly sweet, she replied, "Calm yourself, sir. Dr. Cail agrees with me that the coach ride to Marlwood will do you no harm. Why, it is less than a day's travel. Besides, we both feel that the country air will do you a world of good.''

Such calm and reasoned argument left Sir Edmund on shaky ground, but he persisted. ''That's all very well. But why send Brock tearing off without so much as a by-your-leave to me? A man, even an invalid, likes to cherish some notion that he is master in his own home.''

Julianna looked beseechingly heavenward. ''Exactly what would you have done if I'd asked you?''

He pounced headlong after the bait. ''Put a stop to the whole foolish business...''

She had him. ''Exactly! And forbidden Mr. Brock to go, placing him in the awkward position of choosing whose orders to obey, yours or mine. I simply spared him that dilemma since I meant to have my own way in any case.''

Sir Edmund looked sufficiently composed, or possibly dumbfounded, that Julianna dared sit on the bed beside him.

''Have I not been a good nurse and a reasonably agreeable companion to you these past months?''

''Well, of course, but...''

Her voice played an adagio of gentle forbearance. ''Truly, I have not begrudged a moment of the time. Yet, much as I've grown to cherish your company, if I'm confined to this room much longer I shall go mad. Surely you wouldn't deny me a chance to breathe some clean air and to ramble the beautiful countryside. It is your stories that have made me long to see Marlwood and Abbot's Leigh. Please say we can go! If you really do object so strongly, I can summon Brock back....''

''Hardly, if you've already gone to so much trouble.'' Sir Edmund heaved a sigh of resignation. ''I suppose I can withstand the trip. Now, leave off with your Cornish hugs, Mistress Puss, or I shall have to add cracked ribs to my list of ailments! All sweetness, aren't you, now that you've got your own way?''

''There is one slight problem still,'' Julianna ventured.

His eyes narrowed warily. ''Indeed? What now?''

''Somehow, I doubt a proud man like you would relish the prospect of being carried to the carriage for our departure.'' She rushed on, to forestall his objections. ''We have a whole week before then. If we work very hard together, I'm sure you will be able to walk out of this house, using a stick, or leaning on my arm. A far more decorous arrangement, wouldn't you say?''

''Of course, but—''

''I knew you'd agree.'' She treated him to a disarming grin. ''You are such a sensible man. For today we can work on getting you accustomed to maintaining an upright posture. Ease yourself up and swing your legs over the side of the bed. Very good! You have more strength in them than you might think. Now, I will bring the chess table and set it between us. That way, we can enjoy a little recreation while you work at maintaining your balance. If you feel tired or faint, just give the word. Tomorrow, we can work at getting you to bear some weight on your legs. I believe I shall open with a queen's pawn....''

Sir Edmund bowed his head over the chessboard. Slowly, silently, his shoulders began to shake, then heave. Dear God, had she pushed him too far? Was he ill—or weeping? Alarmed, Julianna reached out to him. With angry relief, she realized he was laughing in great gulping, wheezing spasms. Lifting a front-ranking black chessman to her like a glass for a toast, he declared, ''I believe *I* am the queen's pawn.''

She let him win the match, Edmund suspected, to assuage his poor, mauled pride. Then Julianna tucked him back into bed with an admonition to get some rest. Bestowing a hasty kiss on his brow, she bustled off to begin preparing for their journey. Edmund settled back onto his pillows and indulged in a good chuckle at his own expense.

All this time he'd been congratulating himself on rescuing Crispin's helpless light o'love. Little had he guessed that her willowy form masked an intellect as sharp, a character as strong, as the finest Toledo steel. A queen, to be sure. A consort worthy of...Crispin. Yes, worthy of his handsome, charming nephew. How ironic, how a woman so deserving of a vigorous young partner should be best appreciated by an older husband.

Now that he'd had a chance to get used to the idea, Edmund could hardly wait to introduce Julianna to Abbot's Leigh. He'd never taken his first wife there. She would have hated the old place. Julianna, on the other hand, would shine like a rare gem in a perfect setting. With a smile of mingled contentment and anticipation, Edmund fell asleep.

Julianna would not have cared to live through another such week. Supervising the packing in Brock's absence. Pleading with the seamstress to have her summer gowns made up in time to take them along. Shopping for items she might not find available in the country. All this she'd done in addition to spending hours with Sir Edmund.

Alternately scolding and cajoling, she had spared no effort to ready him for his walk out the door of Fitzhugh House. Their progress had been frustratingly slow at first and she'd begun to despair of his making the walk under his own power. Though she had accurately assessed the weakness of his limbs, she had not reckoned with his strength of will. Whenever she applauded his courage, his reply was typically self-deprecating.

"Tush! I believe half of what is vaunted as courage is no more than stubbornness, plain and simple. That is one virtue you'll warrant I have in ample supply."

Courage or stubbornness, Julianna was glad she had been able to tap his reserves. From the bed to the chair they'd shuffled, time and again, Sir Edmund leaning heavily upon her. After a rest stop at the chair, they would stumble to the door, turn and make for the bed again. For the first time, she was thankful he had lost more than a stone in weight since his illness.

Their final walk out of Fitzhugh House proved longer and more difficult than any Sir Edmund had previously attempted. Not surprisingly, Julianna found him badly winded and white as a sheet by the time they gained the carriage. He'd breathlessly jested of how good it felt to wear shoes and breeches again. She had winced to see how loose Sir Edmund's coat hung on his broad shoulders. For a moment her optimism faltered and she wondered if country air would prove potent enough medicine to revive him.

As Sir Edmund dozed on the seat opposite her and Gwenyth, Julianna watched the outskirts of the city give way to the shaws and hedgerows of the open countryside. She inhaled the bracing spring air, allowing her natural buoyancy to reassert itself.

After a time, the carriage passed through Guildford, turning off the highway and taking an older road. The track was rougher and the coach's jostling soon wakened Sir Edmund. The sleep appeared to have restored him somewhat.

"I marvel at your ability to sleep under such circumstances," said Julianna. "No doubt you managed under worse during your days at sea. How do you feel?"

"Like I had been mauled by a Sumatran tiger." Sir Edmund chafed his legs. "Where are we now?" He peered out the carriage window. "On the road to Marlwood?"

"We just passed through Guildford this half hour." Julianna picked up the hamper that rested at her feet. "Are you hungry? Mrs. Davies packed us a lovely lunch for the road—Cornish pasties, cheese, biscuits. Even a jug of cider."

"It all sounds good. Pass me over whatever comes to hand. I'm glad we have a fine day for traveling. This time of year, a heavy rain can make these roads well-nigh impassable."

Julianna watched with approval as he eagerly consumed several biscuits. "It is a beautiful day. I have been drinking in all the pastoral splendor since we left London."

"Come October you'll be glad enough to get back to town, I expect. Life can be rather dull out here at times."

"That may be." Julianna cast him a doubtful look. "But I mean to enjoy the novelty for the present." She was glad to have him awake at last. She had been bursting with questions. "Sir Edmund, you must tell me more about your part of Surrey. For a start, how did Abbot's Leigh get its name?"

"I couldn't say for certain," he admitted with a shrug. "Perhaps because the present house lies near the hill where Marlwood Abbey stood—Abbot's Tor, they call it. Parts of the old abbey still stand, but only as a roost for owls these days. As a child, I used to go there and pretend it was a fortress. It is so peaceful there, like a remnant of the twelfth century lingering on the frontier of the modern world."

"Has the estate been in the family long?"

"Yes, indeed. The earliest part of the house was built in the

fourteenth century. Like many such dwellings, portions were
added to the original later. There is a small chapel dating from
the first house, with the old family crypt beneath it. The whole
place is covered so densely with ivy, in the summer it is often
difficult to distinguish from the surrounding trees and gardens.''

"I can hardly wait to see it," said Julianna. "Tell me, why
do the Bayards no longer live there?"

"My, but you are full of questions." Sir Edmund yawned
and stretched. "It all goes back to the Civil War. You see, the
Bayards were royalists in their sympathies, though they took
care not to broadcast the fact, as most of the south had declared for the Puritans. When the war began to go badly for
King Charles, the queen fled for the Continent. All of this area
had fallen into Cromwell's hands, making it a difficult and
dangerous journey. Her party kept to the old back roads to
avoid armed patrols on the highway. My grandfather gave
them sanctuary at Abbot's Leigh."

Obviously it was a long-standing Bayard tradition, helping
ladies in distress, Julianna mused as she watched Sir Edmund
demolish one of Mrs. Davies's pasties in two bites.

"After the Restoration," continued Sir Edmund, "King
Charles rewarded those who had remained faithful to his family, during their time of persecution. In remembrance of Ri-
chard Bayard's assistance to his mother, the King created him
Lord Marlwood. The title came with additional land and rev-
enues, so his son Laurence built Bayard Hall. It is much
grander than the old place. My grandmother continued to live
at Abbot's Leigh, and after her death, it passed to me. I believe
I see Bayard Hall coming up on the right."

On their progress from London they had passed a number
of grand houses, glimpsed in the distance. Several had been
larger than the one now in view and most decidedly more
ostentatious. However, none could match Bayard Hall for
symmetry and elegance. Two wings swept forward from the
central house, each with a tower facing into the courtyard.
Three lower towers rose from the rear of the main house. A
magnificent lawn fronted the house, while soaring elm trees
framed it on either side.

"Quite a place, isn't it? Uncle Laurence never did anything

by half measures. The present Lord Marlwood is also named Laurence. If he does not look sharp and marry soon, Bayard Hall may pass to some other branch of the family."

Julianna took his discreet glance to mean Crispin.

"This Laurence, did you tell me he's a cousin of Crispin's?"

"The boys were born within weeks of each other and always considered twins for looks. I expect that comes from their double kinship. I never had any trouble telling them apart. Laurence doesn't come often to Bayard Hall, except when he brings a hunting party in the fall. Our paths seldom cross in London, for he considers himself a gentleman of fashion." His dismissive tone told Julianna what he thought of the "beaux."

She was still curious to meet this "twin" of Crispin's. Though she treasured her miniature as a beautiful reminder of her distant love, it was no substitute for a living model. She was about to ask Sir Edmund to tell her more of young Lord Marlwood when he announced, "There's Abbot's Leigh, now. The old place looks just as it has from my earliest memory."

Unlike Bayard Hall, Abbot's Leigh had no symmetry whatsoever. There was a low main building with a taller structure to one side. Four smaller outcroppings along the front appeared to have grown like limbs from a tree trunk. Green veins of ivy wandered over the dressed stone. In another month, when the leaves made their full growth, Julianna imagined the house would look like one giant topiary sculpture.

The grounds were laid out as haphazardly as the house, with trees, hedges and beds of flowers arrayed in no discernible pattern. For all that, Julianna thought the old estate gracious and charming, making the elegant Bayard Hall seem spiritless and artificial by comparison.

As their carriage halted in a side courtyard, a sheepish-looking Mordecai Brock awaited their arrival, standing behind a wheeled chair. Seeing that Sir Edmund had spied him also, Julianna braced herself for the inevitable explosion.

Instead, he laughed with apparent delight. "My grandmother's chair! I have not laid eyes upon that old contraption in almost thirty years. Where did you find it, Brock?"

The steward appeared most relieved by the reception, "It was

Mrs. Tully's idea, Captain. She minded how old Lady Marlwood went about for years in this chair. Then it was only a matter of sifting through all those attics to find it.''

Smiling to himself, Sir Edmund shook his head. ''When I was a child, I often wanted to ride in Grandmother's chair. Who'd have thought I'd be in it, after so many years?''

''You must tell me more about her!'' Julianna demanded. ''Have you her picture?''

''Hers, and many others. We can save that for a rainy afternoon—studying the old family portraits and airing all the scandals. In the meantime, Mr. Brock, will you lend me your stout arm?''

As Julianna crossed the low-eaved threshold of Abbot's Leigh, pushing Sir Edmund's chair, she smelled beeswax, dried lavender and old wood. For the first time in her life, she experienced the warm, enveloping sensation of homecoming.

Chapter Eleven

May sunshine beamed into Julianna's bedchamber, gently filtered through thick glass panes knit together by a tight lattice of lead. Stray rays lit on a bed strewn with discarded gowns and a floor randomly littered with caps, combs and hair ribbons. The soft lighting did little to mellow Gwenyth's cross expression. One hand rested on her hip, the other wielded a hairbrush.

Peering into the looking glass with a vexed face, Julianna pulled her hair free of yet another dressing. "No, Gwenyth. This will not do—too prim. Think how Sir Edmund will tease!"

"Then sauce him back as you always do!" Gwenyth threw down the brush. "How many ways do you think hair can be done? You're not going to meet the king, just the village vicar and his wife. That's no cause for all this fuss and bother."

Julianna's dismay at this tirade soon gave way to amusement. "Gwenyth Jones," she jestingly threatened, "have a care or you will become as notorious a scold as Mrs. Tully."

Gwenyth's pique evaporated in a gale of girlish laughter, in which her mistress joined. Though Sir Edmund might be titular master of Abbot's Leigh, his housekeeper effectively ruled the estate. A broad-jawed countrywoman of ample proportions, Myrtle Tully had a sharp tongue that did little to mask her bountiful heart. Even Mr. Brock deferred to Goodwife Tully with wary respect.

"Oh, Gwenyth, I *am* a goose to fuss so over a simple call on the Trowbridges. But this will be my first chance to meet the village folks. These are Sir Edmund's people and I want to look my best. Not that it will make any difference.'' She remembered her cool reception in London at the Handel concert.

''Sit down and stay still.'' Gwenyth grudgingly relented. Picking up her brush, she tugged the bristles through her mistress's hair with vengeful vigor. Discretion told Julianna to hold her tongue. As Gwenyth worked, she let her thoughts wander.

The days of the past month had tumbled away like bright, luminous beads off a thread. Every day, Julianna had fallen deeper under the spell of Abbot's Leigh. She'd explored it from root cellars to attics, on each prowl discovering some fresh delight: a half-hidden window seat on the back-stairs landing; a trellised walkway; a low, old-fashioned well in a shaded corner by the scullery. The place had an endless catalog of charms.

True to his word, Sir Edmund had introduced her to his Bayard ancestors, via the portraits that crammed the walls of Abbot's Leigh's many galleries. In cool or damp weather they had stayed indoors, sharing tales of Bayards past and enjoying their usual pastimes of reading and chess by the drawing-room fire.

On fine days, they'd spent their time in the walled arbor, which opened directly from the Great Parlour. This cozy little nook was a wonder, with cherry and plum trees already well in bloom, and a riot of flowers in the most vivid hues. It was the special pride of Nelson Tully, a grizzled, laconic fellow whose hawk nose bespoke a strong dash of Norman blood. Under his tutelage, Sir Edmund and Julianna were both trying their hands at gardening. Julianna had come to enjoy the smell and feel of the freshly turned earth, though Gwenyth warned her continually and to no avail that she must wear gloves or risk ruining her hands.

As Brock had predicted and as Julianna had hoped, the atmosphere of Abbot's Leigh had worked wonders on Sir Edmund's health. He had used his grandmother's chair for a while after they arrived. Finding it difficult to maneuver through the doorframes, he had become frustrated with the cumbersome conveyance, abandoning it in favor of walking. Between his exertions and the wholesome country air, he had been eating enough for three men and reported sleeping deeply and restfully.

In the context of Abbot's Leigh, all the contradictions of Sir Edmund's nature came into focus for Julianna: the pride and scholarly solitude of the Fitzhughs warring with the Bayards adventurous wanderlust, leavened by the humor and poetic whimsy of his grandmother's people. He was the most fascinating man she had ever known—well worth the effort she had made to cultivate his friendship.

When Gwenyth pronounced herself finished, Julianna surveyed her latest hairstyling—demurely swept back, with three little ringlets falling from the rest. Tossing her head to give the curls a saucy waggle, she awarded her reflection a pert smile of approval. After discarding virtually every gown in her wardrobe, she returned to her first choice. A simple but pretty little dress, without hoops or panniers, the creamy muslin bore a gay print of green leaves and flowers. A smartly pressed white apron and cap completed her ensemble, with a wide-brimmed straw hat and a parasol to protect her fair skin from the sun. Giving her reflection a final nervous glance, Julianna clutched Gwenyth in an impulsive embrace and skipped away.

Edmund was exercising a stocky black pony around the kitchen courtyard. From the driver's seat of the trap, he shot an impatient glance at Julianna's window. What in blazes could be taking her so long to dress? He hoped she wasn't decking herself out in too grand a fashion. The village folk wouldn't care for that at all.

Edmund hated to admit how anxious he was for Julianna to make a good showing today. Having grown up in Marlwood, he cared more for the opinion of his old neighbors than all the stuck-up noses of his London acquaintances. Charlie Warbeck had been at him for years to bring a bride home to Abbot's Leigh. What would Charlie make of his young wife?

Edmund inhaled a deep draft of spring air—the best tonic in the world. Like the old oaks of Abbot's Leigh putting out fresh shoots, Edmund felt himself quickening. He woke each morning with a sense of anticipation he hadn't known in years. He looked toward Julianna's window again, this time with an indulgent smile, for it was she who had revived him. In her company, every activity took on a sweet piquancy. She'd infused his bland, somber existence with color and music and perfume. And he had come to love her for it. Not in any improper way, of course. He would have denied such a notion to his dying breath. He loved Julianna as he had loved Alice and Crispin— no more and no differently. Or so he continually told himself.

The Dutch doors of the kitchen flew open. Out breezed Julianna, looking so blithe and beautiful Edmund feared his heart would burst with pride. Unable to bear the vulnerability of such tender emotions, he sought defense in feigned severity.

"Two minutes more, young lady, and I'd have gone off and let you walk into Marlwood. What on earth can take a woman so long to dress for a call on the local vicar?"

"Sir Edmund, did your grandmother never tell you if you pulled such a face it would stay that way? Smile this instant and admit I look tolerably well. I know you can hardly wait to show off your bride to the village. I would not have taken so long, but I want to make a good impression, for your sake."

What defenses could stand against such disarming candor? "My dear, can you not take a bit of rallying? Imagine if I showed up in the village without you. The old gossips would turn me out of the trap and tear it to pieces looking for you."

He swept an appraising look over her. "Yes, I will admit you look quite charming this morning—refined and ladylike but not too toplofty, as we say in these parts."

Laughing and chatting, they drove down the long lane from Abbot's Leigh, lined with linden trees in their virginal riot of soft fragrant blossoms. Almost before Julianna realized it, they had arrived in Marlwood. Several thatched cottages squatted on either side of the main road, which opened into a small square. The church and vicarage stood at one corner of that square, where a narrow lane turned off toward Aldershot. Two or three older folk, working around their homes or sitting out front, called greetings to Sir Edmund as the trap rolled by. He acknowledged each by name, with a promise that they would return for a proper introduction after their call. Though Julianna could feel many eyes upon her, she sensed no ill will in the people's frank curiosity.

The vicar was a tall, stoop-shouldered man who put Julianna in mind of the vague but kindly Parson Adams of Mr. Fielding's book. When he spoke of his work in the parish, visiting the sick and elderly, educating the children and helping the poor, his long, homely face glowed with the light of Christian charity.

She took an immediate fancy to the vicar's wife. From their brief introduction, she gathered Mrs. Trowbridge had enjoyed a upbringing similar to her own—educated by a learned father. Though only a few years older than Julianna, the lady was clearly an efficient manager of her husband's social ministry.

"Now that you have settled in for the summer, Lady Fitzhugh, perhaps you would care to help me with some of my parish work. Several times a week I pay calls and bring aid to the sick, the poor and the elderly."

"I'd be happy to join you, Mrs. Trowbridge. Let me know when next you'll be going and what I can bring. Perhaps one day, when you have time free from your duties, you could call at Abbot's Leigh. I believe we might share some common interests."

"That would be a treat, Lady Fitzhugh. I gain great satisfaction from my work, but it would be pleasant to exchange views on history and literature with another woman."

She slipped a friendly arm in Julianna's. "Has Sir Edmund taken you to see the new almshouse he endowed a few years ago? It is a well-run place…a great boon to the parish."

An almshouse, the Foundling Hospital, the Westminster—was there a more generous man in all of England than her husband? Julianna wondered. Or one more concerned for the plight of the weak and helpless?

"Actually, Mrs. Trowbridge, concerning my husband's charitable endeavors, I am the right hand that does not know what the left hand is doing."

The vicar's wife conducted Julianna on a tour of the house. Though Sir Edmund had been born and raised there, she could feel no mark of him upon the place as she sensed at Abbot's Leigh. The old stone church she found very quaint. Seeing the graveyard beyond, she resolved to visit to the graves of Sir Edmund's sister, mother and grandmother with flowers from Abbot's Leigh.

As Sir Edmund had promised, he and Julianna stopped to pass the time with several people on their return trip. At each stop, she could see more villagers emerging from houses farther down the road. She felt their movement was taking on the aura of a royal progress. The affection of the Marlwood folk for Sir Edmund was evident, as was his for them. He never missed a name and often had some remembrance of an incident past for each new face they met. Julianna saw none of the tight-jawed politeness with which he was wont to greet people in the city.

One toothless old fellow called out from his chair in a cottage yard. "Shame on you, young Fitzhugh, for not bringing a bride home to Marlwood before this! I see you were biding your time to find a very peach, and that she is."

Sir Edmund positively beamed as he tendered a warm reply. "I had to find the best to bring home to Marlwood, Mr. Warbeck. I am glad you approve my choice."

"Aye, so I do." The old man handed a small object to a much-freckled youngster seated beside him. The boy then ran pell-mell with it toward the trap. "Our Jimmy's bringing you a wee charm, missus," Mr. Warbeck called.

The object, deposited in Julianna's lap by the child, was a tiny straw wreath, cunningly braided and trimmed with a sprig of aromatic dried flowers.

"Don't tell vicar I've been witching you," cautioned Mr. Warbeck. "Just keep that nailed to your lintel post, and you'll have a babe in your arms before a year is gone."

Feeling her cheeks redden, Julianna cast a sidelong glance at Sir Edmund. Without losing his good humor, he joshed the old man. "Is that how you got your twelve, Mr. Warbeck? Foolish me! I thought there was a bit more to it than that!"

At another stop, a bashful little girl, all curls and dimples, offered Julianna a handful of posies. Touched by the kind reception of these good people, Julianna promised herself she would not stint in helping the vicar's wife minister to them.

The Fitzhughs finally cleared the last cottage, waving behind to a group of children who had followed them down the road. Sir Edmund plucked the straw wreath from Julianna's lap.

"Don't think ill of Charlie Warbeck. He always was a bit cheeky with folk from the big house—scolding them about this or that, offering unsolicited advice. Mrs. Tully is his sister."

Julianna nodded sagely over this information. No doubt Mrs. Tully's brother looked on the village as his personal fiefdom, just as their housekeeper looked upon Abbot's Leigh as hers.

At the foot of the lane, Sir Edmund made to throw the little charm into the hedgerow. Julianna snatched it back.

"It is a pretty piece of work and offered with the best of intentions. I am sure everyone who knows us, high or low born, believes we are eager to have a child." Thinking aloud, she added, "I will save this until Crispin returns home."

Sir Edmund laughed. "When Crispin comes home after two years at sea, I doubt you'll need a charm of that sort."

"Perhaps not." Julianna smiled to herself. "But I mean to keep it, nonetheless. Now, what shall we do this afternoon? Eat our lunch under one of the cherry trees in the garden?"

"I thought we might do some fishing. There's a good spot not far from the house. Have Mrs. Tully pack us a lunch we can eat there. We'll amble down to the stream at whatever pace I can manage and one of the footmen can come after us with the food and gear."

"What a marvelous idea!" Julianna clapped her hands like an excited child. "I've never seen a live fish before, and certainly never imagined catching one. This will be an adventure."

"First, though," warned Sir Edmund, "you had better change into something more suited to the occasion."

Julianna scampered toward the kitchen door, Mr. Warbeck's wreath tucked in her apron pocket. "Just give me a minute to change clothes and speak with Mrs. Tully."

She heard Sir Edmund call crisply after her, "See that your minute is shorter that the one you took to dress this morning!"

Chapter Twelve

As the small punt drifted downstream, Edmund dipped his pole into the water and gave a powerful push. His exertion was not strictly necessary. The river's lazy, inexorable current would pull the craft along well enough. Yet, as his healing body surged with renewed strength, Edmund enjoyed calling forth this robust effort of thew and sinew. The muscle of his upper arm swelled beneath his light shirt, responding with welcome vigor.

Her amber curls unbound, Julianna reclined in the bow of the craft, one graceful hand half-immersed in the water. With the summer solstice approaching, the air felt pleasantly warm. The succulent perfume of woodbine wafted on a faint breeze. An avenue of towering elms bordered the stream, creating a vaulted canopy of green over the water. In the lofty arching branches of the elm trees, a linnet piped. Odd shafts of sunlight pierced the leaves, shooting rays of transparent shimmering gold. When one of these touched Julianna, her hair glowed like a halo.

"'Bless the Lord, O my soul,'" Edmund quoted in the reverent silence. "'Who stretchest out the heavens like a curtain; who layeth the beams of his chambers in the waters; and maketh the clouds his chariot, and walketh upon the wings of the wind....'"

Julianna closed her eyes, as if to savor the words. "Oh Edmund, that is so apt and eloquent it thrills my heart." Her smile of delight quirked into an impish grin. "Did you ever think of following your father into the church?"

"Never." Edmund's voice was honed to a fine, cool edge. "By the time I discovered the God of that psalmist, my feet were set upon a different path. Growing up with my father nearly soured me on Scripture for life. Only after I joined the navy and went to the Orient did I begin to read the Bible Alice had given me."

Uttering his beloved sister's name, Edmund's tone warmed once more. "At sea, time can hang very heavy on one's hands. A ship's berth is hardly the place for an extensive library. I came to appreciate the breadth of fine literature contained between the covers of that single volume. It has words to give voice to a man's deepest passion, fear or woe." His last word trailed off in a sigh.

They lapsed into companionable silence again, contemplating the pastoral grandeur. Julianna could not recall when she had felt so happy. It was a strange, sweet mingling of exhilaration and contentment. The contentment, she knew, sprang from a wholesome sense of belonging. She felt as though Abbot's Leigh had always been her destined home, biding its time to welcome her.

The Marlwood folk had taken her unreservedly to their hearts and she had reciprocated. Twice or thrice a week she accompanied Mrs. Trowbridge on calls about the village. Before these calls, Julianna labored in the kitchen of Abbot's Leigh, under the dubious eye of Mrs. Tully, compounding broths, jellies and water-gruel for the elderly and invalid. Thanks to Winnie's tutelage in the housewifely arts, none of the recipients had ever turned up their noses at Julianna's offerings.

After they paid their calls, Arabella Trowbridge often accompanied Julianna home to Abbot's Leigh. There, they would take tea in the library or in the garden and talk of books and music, philosophy and history. Julianna found the vicar's wife very clever and forthright. She admired Mrs. Trowbridge's dedication to her parish duties, which the lady regarded as a personal vocation rather than simply an extension of her husband's work. Her devotion to the earnest and uncomely Mr. Trowbridge, Julianna found more difficult to fathom. Then again, who truly understood that alchemy of the heart that bound any two people in love?

Julianna's exhilaration in her new life stemmed from the host of novel pursuits she and Edmund shared. Each occupation seemed more absorbing than the last. They went for long rambles in the meadows and forests around Marlwood. Though she never had fished before her advent in Surrey, Julianna now considered herself as inveterate an angler as old Izaak Walton. She enjoyed the peaceful solitude and leisure of angling, even when she caught nothing. Some days they abandoned the shore, taking to the water in this small punt.

At a slight stirring of the breeze, Julianna opened her eyes, catching glimpses of blue sky through gaps in the foliage overhead. She hoped this fine weather would continue, for she was reveling in her days out of doors. She never bothered to put her hair up, except for visits or in the evenings. Having surrendered in the fight against freckles, she had also ceased to fret about ruining her hands. If she was not sure it would thoroughly scandalize the household, Julianna would have shed her skirts altogether in favor of breeches and boots!

She glanced at Edmund. Absorbed in thoughts of his own, he was aware of neither her appraisal nor her smile of proprietary satisfaction. The change that the past weeks had wrought in his constitution was better than she had dared to hope. The gaunt hollows of his cheeks had filled out handsomely as he regained all of his lost weight. Edmund Fitzhugh now strode about Abbot's Leigh like a strapping fellow half his age.

More than a fortnight ago, he had mounted a horse for the first time in almost a decade. He had seldom been out of the saddle since. Edmund had encouraged Julianna to take up riding so she could accompany him on his wider peregrinations. However, after several days of bumps and scrapes from tumbles off her placid old mare and a rump bruised black and purple from jostling in her saddle like a sack of meal, she had grudgingly admitted defeat. Nelson Tully must have taken pity on his woebegone young mistress as the master rode off alone—albeit at her insistence. The next day he produced an ancient saddle, with a wide, flat pommel that made a somewhat precarious perch for Julianna in front of Edmund. Galloping across the open ground with the wind in her hair, the steady gait of the horse beneath, and Edmund's stout arms encircling her, she would lean back against him and lose herself in the pleasant dichotomy of adventure and security.

Edmund rested for a moment, letting the punt drift, only dipping his pole into the water to keep the boat on a straight course. When Julianna was not looking, he cast a doting glance over her. In three short months, she had integrated herself so smoothly into this world that no one could imagine Abbot's Leigh without her. She'd knit their household into a family— the kind of large congenial family he had longed for as a boy.

She would invite Brock and Gwenyth or the Tullys for a set of whist, with more chatter and laughter taking place than actual card play. They would entertain the household with an evening of madrigal singing or consort music—Edmund upon the clavier and Julianna with her harp. Nelson Tully proved a fine fiddler, though he complained of stiffness in his fingers. Julianna had even coaxed Brock to unearth his old hornpipe. Together, they formed a spirited if somewhat rustic orchestra. Playing the most familiar old tunes, their performances met with eager approval. Their play readings were likewise quite popular, principally due, Julianna insisted, to Edmund's talent for mimicking accents.

Some evenings they were content to sit quietly by the fire, reading or talking. Edmund found it hard to fathom how two people who spent so much time together could continue to find fresh food for discourse. Even after a whole day spent in conversation, they would often sit up late into the night still talking, loath to leave off until morning. At times Edmund would find himself wishing…things he had no earthly business wishing.

As their punt glided along, Edmund saw Julianna reach for a water lily floating on the still surface of the stream. He opened his mouth to warn her against such dangerous antics in a boat. Before he could call out, she lunged for the flower. The punt lurched sideways, throwing them both into the chilly water.

Edmund retained just enough self-possession to dive clear of the boat. He did not want to risk braining himself when he rose to the surface. Thrusting his head out of the water, he gasped for air and looked frantically around for signs of Julianna. The overturned boat was continuing its progress downriver without regard for the fate of its passengers. In the narrow channel, a cluster of bubbles broke the water surface. Edmund struck out toward them, all but disemboweled by a stab of nauseating fear.

He dove down, but could see nothing in the brown cloudy depths. In a mad panic he flailed about, hoping to find Julianna by touch. Of all the dangers he had faced in his life, nothing had ever terrified Edmund Fitzhugh like this sudden prospect of losing her. He knew, in that moment, that he loved her as he had never loved another human being. Better to die himself than to contemplate life without her.

Just as Edmund feared his lungs would rupture for want of air, Julianna's hand struck his and clung like grim death. In a joyous, dizzying burst of strength, he grasped her under the arms and hoisted her up. A few short strokes brought them to shore. He flung her onto the bank and vigorously slapped her back. Coughing and gasping, she spewed out a stomachful of water.

"You confounded little ninny." Edmund gasped, water streaming down his face. "I should shake you until your teeth rattle! What do you mean by tipping a boat when you can't swim a stroke?"

Julianna struggled for breath. "I'm sorry…Edmund. So stupid. I was going after…a flower."

"Stupid is right!" He fell back onto the grass, panting. "A flower! You would drown yourself over a flower?" His voice began to crack with laughter, in spite of him. "Well, it appears your flower has found you."

Following his pointing finger, Julianna reached up into her bedraggled hair and touched the petals of her water lily. Gazing down at her sopping gown, her own laughter welled up—tinged with mild hysteria. She fell forward beside Edmund. Together, they lay on the bank in a tiny oasis of sunlight, laughing and laughing. When one would subside, panting for air, the other would continue until they were both at it again.

"If anyone sees us like this," Julianna gasped, "there will not be horses fast enough to cart us off to Bedlam." The thought of them being rushed to the madhouse shrieking with mirth, only served to make them howl the louder. At last, they lay still—exhausted. Somehow, Edmund found Julianna's head resting against his chest. Before he could stop himself, his arm protectively encircled her shoulders.

"It is so beautiful here," she whispered. "I wish I never had to leave."

Edmund clenched his teeth against the confession that he also wished to stay like this forever. He fought the mounting urge to tilt Julianna's face toward him and kiss her. No chaste, paternal peck would suffice. He wanted to probe and awaken her with a lover's kiss.

"I could lie here," she continued dreamily, "and let night fall around me. Then watch a fresh new morning dawn." With a decisive note, she added, "I believe I shall. Not today, of course, or I would catch my death in these wet clothes. Before the summer is out, though, I resolve to sleep under the stars."

"By all means." Edmund strove to sound indifferent. "You are your own mistress at Abbot's Leigh. I would suggest waiting until the nights become warmer. I also advise you to sneak out after the household is asleep. Otherwise, there could be talk about whom you were meeting."

She gave an indignant sniff. "As if I would. Come with me, then. That way there'll be no talk, even if I am caught out."

"Oh really, Julianna, I have slept out of doors more often than I care to recall. I can tell you it is generally deucedly uncomfortable. These bones of mine take enough abuse in the run of a day that a goose-down mattress is like heaven at bedtime."

"Oh please, Edmund!" Her tone of wistful supplication could melt stone. "Please!"

"Very well," he grunted. "I am an indulgent fool. My back will pay for this whim of yours, mark my words!"

Edmund kept his promise. On a clear, moonless night in early July, he and Julianna slipped out of the darkened house like two conspirators. In a nearby field, mowers had cut the first crop of hay. Edmund pulled some of the sweet-smelling chaff from a stack and laid Julianna's blanket atop it for a mattress. His own blanket covered them, though the night was hardly cool enough to warrant it.

Julianna marveled at the strange beauty of the darkened countryside. Above them, the night sky hung like a black velvet welkin studded with glittering diamonds.

"It was these stars that finally brought me home," Edmund said in a quiet, thoughtful voice.

"The stars?" Julianna asked with a hint of amused disbelief.

"Oh yes. You see, south of the equator the stars look very different. One night, I looked up into that southern sky and my heart yearned for the Dippers and the Pole Star. Other things influenced my decision, of course. We'd had several close calls with the Dutch and I had taken another attack of that cursed fever. In the end, though, what prompted me to give up the South Seas was my longing for this familiar sky. I had lived my childhood fancy to explore the world, only to discover there was no place more beautiful than my own home."

Was Crispin now looking up at those southern constellations and longing to see the Pole Star over Abbot's Tor? Julianna wondered. Finding herself vaguely annoyed that Crispin had intruded upon her thoughts at that moment, she instantly chided herself for harboring so disloyal a sentiment.

In truth, the only blight upon her happy weeks at Abbot's Leigh had been the creeping conviction that Crispin was slipping away from her. The eight months of his absence felt like eight years. He was retreating into the mists of memory and, worst of all, Julianna could not force herself to care. Only in dreams did he still come to her as a lover, his face always shrouded in shadow, or turned away. She knew him only by the rich, mellow cadence of his voice.

Edmund chuckled quietly. "Just looking at the night sky made me think of that tune about an old woman sweeping cobwebs from the sky." He hummed the opening bars.

Julianna knew the melody well, a favorite from her nursery days. She recalled often singing it to Edmund while he was feverish—when she had exhausted her memory of anything else.

As the last notes died away, Edmund spoke again. "I can almost swear I do see strands of gossamer trailing from star to star. As a little boy, I used to make Alice sing me that song every night before bed. I thought my grandmother must be the old woman with the broom."

Rolling onto her stomach, Julianna rested her chin on one hand. "The old woman could not possibly have been your grandmother," she chanted in a tone of childish mockery. "Because the old woman was my grandmother. She was a witch, you know. And my grandfather was a pirate."

"Blood will tell," quipped Edmund.

In defense of her family honor, Julianna plied a long strand of cattail grass as a switch.

"I merely meant that heredity must account for your spirit and bewitching charm." Fending off her "attack" with raised hands, he laughed.

"Well recovered," she grudgingly allowed, assaying a final swipe at his nose.

"You have always been so curious about my family and early life." Edmund turned suddenly serious. "I just realized how little I know of yours. I have heard you mention your father but never your mother. Do you remember her at all?"

"No." Julianna fiddled absently with her stalk of grass. "Like yours, my mother died when I was born."

He fumbled for her hand, then gently squeezed it.

"No need for condolence at this late date," she said, but her voice sounded small and plaintive. "What I never had, I never missed. Besides, there was always Winnie and my grandmother. I don't recall being aware of my mother's absence, until after my grandmother died and my father remarried."

She hesitated. Edmund's arm stole around her, drawing her head to his shoulder. "Tell me," he whispered.

For a time she was silent, feeling the coarse weave of his shirt against her cheek. She recalled their wedding night and how she'd wept in his arms. Try as she might to bite them back, the words came on in spite of her, hot with shame and resentment.

"I was just six years old when Jerome first came to our house. I remember being left alone with him to get acquainted. He walked right up to me, smiling that loathsome smile, reached around and pinched me very hard on the bottom. I cried out, of course, and everyone came running. I told them he'd pinched me, but when they asked to see the mark, I was too embarrassed to show anyone or to tell where it was. Jerome protested his innocence, and they…my father…"

"Took Jerome's word?" Edmund's voice sharpened with indignant rage.

Julianna could only nod. She blessed the modest cover of darkness that shrouded her confession, making it a harmless whisper of words on the wind.

"In a way, I think he wanted to believe me. But it distressed him to hear of our quarrels. Having no sons of his own, he had taken Jerome to his heart. Papa would not admit he had any faults. Because I worshiped my father, I was prepared to do anything to spare him. So…I stopped…trying to tell him and simply did my best to avoid Jerome."

"The most contemptible bully," Edmund muttered, almost to himself. "I knew it from the moment I laid eyes on him."

"Perhaps I should have insisted my father listen to me and believe me, but I couldn't bring myself to. Afterward, when it got worse, I was far too ashamed to tell anyone."

"Got worse? How? You don't mean…? He didn't…?"

She reached out, pressing her fingers against his lips.

"No, he didn't. Though he tried often enough. The year I turned fourteen, when he came home from school on holiday, I saw that look in his eyes. He began stalking me, pulling me into shadowy corners. Kissing me in frightening ways a child should never be kissed. Groping at my…bosom and under my skirts…"

She was trembling now, with all the helpless terror she had felt during those shameful encounters. Edmund pulled her close to him and held her for what seemed like hours, offering her a refuge from the past, asking nothing in return. For the first time in many years, Julianna felt truly and completely safe.

At last she grew calm enough to draw a deep breath and finish her story. "On the eve of our wedding he tried one last time." When she finished her tale of Jerome's last abortive rape attempt, Julianna felt as if a pressing weight had been lifted from her chest.

The muscles of Edmund's arm tensed and she could hear a choked savagery in his voice. "The blackguard! To think I let him sit at my table. I should have called him out the moment we were safely married."

Julianna smiled in the darkness. In his present condition, he certainly would present a formidable challenge to her stepbrother. However, Jerome would have made short work of the ailing gentleman Edmund had been on their wedding day.

"It is all past now. Thanks to you, I have nothing to fear from Jerome Skeldon. Do you know, this is the first time he has crossed my mind since we came to Abbot's Leigh."

Edmund might not realize the import of that statement but it came as a revelation to Julianna. Never before had a day gone by without some twinge of memory or a furtive glance over her shoulder. Fear of Jerome had become an unpleasant habit, like a sinister, rumbling bass note in the symphony of her thoughts. Now she was free of him, and she had only Edmund to thank.

"We must deal with your stepbrother." His tone brooked no argument. "Soon. If anything should happen to me…"

"Nothing is going to happen to you, Edmund." The very thought chilled her. "Besides, Jerome is a dangerous man."

"He is no match for you and me, together."

"We do make a rather formidable pair," she agreed. "But for now, let us not spoil our lovely night by talking about Jerome."

"Very well." Edmund considered for a moment. "Let us add a course in astronomy to your prodigious education. See there, opposite the Great Dipper, is the chair of Cassiopeia."

"The mother of Andromeda?" Julianna asked, eager to make a break from the painful revelations she had shared with him.

"Yes. And there is the tail of the scorpion. Over there is a constellation just for you. See that bright star? That is Vega of Lyra, the harp.''

"Harp?" Julianna studied the configuration of stars for a moment. "Yes, I believe I can see it."

On they talked into the night, of stars and lullabies, and fairy lore. Julianna began to yawn and nod. Finally, she could no longer concentrate on the sense of Edmund's words, and they washed over her dreams like ripples of water caressing the strand. Her head still resting in the hollow of his shoulder, she was lulled to sleep by the rich, mellow cadence of his voice.

Julianna's breathing slowed and deepened. When he was certain she had fallen fast asleep, Edmund cautiously pressed his face into the fragrant froth of her curls. They smelled as sweet and clean as an April breeze, mingled with a tantalizing feminine warmth. For this one night, Julianna was his to hold, and protect, and cherish.

Thinking of all she had told him of her early life, and safe in the knowledge that she could not hear him, he murmured, "I swear I'll never do anything to make you afraid of me, Julianna."

The stars shimmered in the heavens—beautiful, but cold and remote. With a sigh so deep it shook his tall frame, he added, "Not if I have to die from wanting you."

Chapter Thirteen

A bead of sweat slid along Julianna's damp hairline, dropping from the nape of her neck onto the moist indentation in her pillow. She twitched at the ticklish sensation, waking from a fitful doze to the stifling heat of her bedchamber. With a groan, she rolled over, seeking a patch of sheet that was dry if no cooler. How in God's name could the weather remain so hot for so long? For the first time since coming to Abbot's Leigh, Julianna actually longed for London. There, hot weather usually provoked a cooling fog from off the Thames.

St. Swithin of Winchester was responsible for the present heat wave—or so said Nelson Tully.

St. Swithin's Day, if it dost rain,
For forty days it will remain,
St. Swithin's day, if it be fair,
Then for forty 'twill rain no more.

He had quoted the local proverb to Julianna on the previous day.

"Then we have another month of this heat to endure, Mr. Tully?" Julianna asked, desperately plying her fan.

"Aye, that's so." Nelson Tully leaned on his hoe. "They say when old Bishop Swithin lay a-dyin'," he said as how he wanted to be buried out in the churchyard where the 'sweet rain of heaven might fall upon his grave.' Well, the monks never took no notice, it seems. After he passed on, they planned to do him the honor of laying his bones to rest inside Winchester Cathedral. Then, on the day they was to move his body, it began to rain and kept up for forty days. The monks finally figured they'd better honor the old fellow's wishes, or so my gammer told me.''

''That is quite a tale,'' Julianna sighed with a wilted smile.

''So it is.'' Nelson Tully stroked the stubble on his chin with the back of a gnarled hand. ''Course, most times on St. Swithin's Day the weather will be cloudy or changeable. Then who's to say what it'll go on like. This year, there were no doubtin' it were fair and hot as you please. We're in for a few more warm days, before the forty have run their course.''

The thought of several more weeks like the past fortnight, made Julianna writhe. For a time, the old stones of the house and shade from the surrounding trees had kept it bearable indoors. However, for the past day or two, the stones had baked right well through the day. At night they gave off their heat like an oven. Julianna could cheerfully have roasted the sainted Bishop of Winchester on a spit!

Even lying naked beneath a sheet she got no relief. She dreaded rising in the morning to don her clothes, for the lightest gown felt tight, sticky and suffocating. She heartily despised Edmund and Mr. Brock their ability to withstand the current heat wave. They had become inured to hot weather during their years in the tropics. Any complaint on Julianna's part would send them into the most dreadful reminiscences about the extreme temperatures they had once stoically endured.

If she stayed one moment longer in her room, Julianna feared she would fricassee like a tough joint of mutton. Donning her thinnest shift and gown, she could not bear to light a candle and create even that tiny amount of additional heat. Barefoot, she stole down a back staircase, trying to emulate Edmund's catlike tread. The air outside was warm and still, but compared to the stifling atmosphere in the house, it felt almost cool. With a sigh of relief, she set off across the meadow, toward the brook. There, she would bathe her feet and watch the sunrise.

By the time Julianna reached the trees, the birds were tuning up for their morning chorus. The transformation of the landscape from darkness to dawn fascinated her. She found it difficult to catch the elusive threshold between night and day. It came by such gradual degrees, she scarcely noticed the transition. She just looked up one moment to realize that morning had broken around her.

When she reached the water, Julianna dipped a toe in. A thrill of delicious coolness rippled through her. Succumbing to an adventurous impulse, she decided to explore farther up the stream toward Abbot's Tor. As she picked her way along the bank, Julianna discovered the vegetation growing more densely in and around the stream. In places water had collected in little pockets by the bank. There, reeds and tussocks of sedge flourished, and the still surface of the water was spread with a patchwork coverlet of emerald lily pads.

If she could just get around this old silver maple… As Julianna clung to the trunk, the tree's roots, long since deprived of earth by the action of the stream, gave way. It swooned into the water, taking her along. After the first shock of falling, she was relieved to find the brook shallow enough to touch bottom. One near-drowning a summer was quite her limit. Refreshed by the cool flowing water, Julianna threw back her head, soaking her face and hair. Holding the fallen maple trunk for support, she relaxed her body, delighted to discover she could float—weightless and ethereal as a young naiad.

Thinking of those water nymphs made Julianna long to lose the sodden weight of her gown. She scanned the stream on either side, looking for a clearing where she might slip out of her soaked clothes. A yard or two away, the bank and part of the water were obscured by the trailing wands of a large willow. Intrigued, she parted the leaves and entered…a fairy's arbor!

Of the many beauties of nature Julianna had experienced since coming to Abbot's Leigh, this alone threatened to stop her heart with its wonder. The verdant curtain of hanging willow encompassed a shallow pool, where the stream had begun to cut a wider course. Around the foot of the tree grew swaths of moss and fern, sweetbrier and late-blooming marsh marigolds. The secluded little nook was so thickly shaded, the very air shimmered vibrant green. A faint breeze stirred the lush valance of willow branches, carrying upon it the sweet tang of wintergreen.

Entranced by the subtle witchery of the place, Julianna waded over to the foot of the tree, wallowing onto the bank in a clumsy manner quite unbefitting her elegant surroundings. Struggling out of her drenched, clinging gown, she wrung out the skirt and spread it to dry on the splayed limbs of a fallen sapling. Then, unencumbered save for her lightest cambric shift, she set about to savor the delights of her sylvan bower. Gathering a bouquet of brier roses and oxlips, she inhaled their intoxicating perfume. Alternating the blossoms, she fashioned a garland of pink and gold. So exquisite was the result, that when Julianna set it in her hair, she thought an empress crowned with mere diamonds and rubies might envy her chaplet of riverbank roses.

Within arm's reach, a dainty rill cascaded over an outcropping of rock, spilling into the pool below. Each bead of water upon water echoed like a note of some haunting canticle. Cupping her hands, Julianna gathered a draft of the icy brew. Cold and sweet, every drop made the flesh of her throat tingle. Never was a carpet woven so soft and plush as the velvety mantle of moss that overlay this hidden verge. With voluptuous abandon, she sank back, offering herself to the blissful cool of its caress. Whether because she had consumed some fairy potion from the waterfall, or because several sleepless nights had suddenly caught up with her, she was overcome by a delicious drowsiness.

A faint noise brought her half-awake. Had she slept the merest instant, or like some who quaffed the wine of Oberon's court, for a hundred years? Julianna knew she could not be fully conscious. Yet how strange it felt to be so self-aware in the midst of a dream. Her dreams were often set in times of classical mythology, as this one surely was. Her surroundings had not changed—the uncanny beauty of the willow pond lent itself easily to Olympus. In the midst of this fey vision, it seemed altogether natural to watch the figure of a faun or merman rise from the still water.

Though his face was shadowed by an overhanging branch, his naked torso looked lean and well muscled, its mat of dark hair beaded with moisture. Having seen several such statues in the wall sconces at Fitzhugh House, Julianna had been innocently intrigued by the naked male form. However, to perceive the warm tones of flesh, the sweep and shadow of underlying sinew, was a thousand times more provocative. As she gazed at the tempting creature before her, Julianna felt the first stirring in her blood of hungry desire for a man.

Lazily, she brushed the back of her hand across her eyes. Surely merry Puck had stolen upon her as she slept and anointed her eyelids with his master's beguiling purple flower. Why else should she feel pulled by so powerful a tide of attraction to this stranger? Smiling to herself—after all, it was only a dream, so what the harm?—she raised her arms, to draw the alluring satyr into her embrace. He placed a finger to his lips, and emerged from the water with soundless, sinuous grace.

Julianna's mouth dropped open and her eyes widened. Rather than merman's scales or goat hide, she saw a pair of firm bare calves and thighs clad in familiar buckskin breeches. Edmund? Then she was not dreaming! Queen Titania, wakening in the embrace of the yeoman ass, Nick Bottom, could have experienced no less intense instant of shock and bafflement.

Edmund knelt behind her, his arm outstretched, forefinger pointing to a narrow gap in the curtain of willow branches. Glancing through the leaves, Julianna caught her breath. A doe and two young fawns were drinking daintily from the stream. The animals appeared completely unaware of their audience. Julianna was free to study the beautiful creatures to her heart's content.

Instead, she could scarcely draw her eyes away from that arm, strong and supple with its nimbus of fine dark hair. She was also intensely aware of Edmund's bare chest lightly pressed against her back. Cool at first, it soon warmed with the contact until it burned like a brand. The sensation of his breath upon the nape of her neck made Julianna faint with temptation.

Though she tried vainly to control it, her own breathing came fast and shallow. If he now touched his hand to her hair or grazed her bare shoulder with his cheek, Julianna knew she'd be incapable of resisting the lust in her heart. She would turn on Edmund with a kiss of such feral abandon that it would sear his lips.

Suddenly, a bird stirred the underbrush causing the deer to startle. They skittered away, perhaps to resume their drink farther upstream. The mute intimacy of their moment shattered, the watchers startled also. Edmund and Julianna flew apart as if driven by some natural force of repulsion. She could not bear to meet his gaze or to speak, lest some avid light in her eyes or a catch in her voice betray her inner tempest.

Edmund broke the silence. "Quite a sight, that. I was moving in for a closer view when I chanced upon your recumbent form. I fully expected you to stretch, yawn and ask, 'Who wakes me from my flowery bed?'"

"Do you not mean '*what angel* wakes me from my flowery bed?'" Julianna corrected him, sensing safety in jest.

Edmund ignored the bait. "How did you find this place?"

"By the most delightful chance. I fell in the water and landed nearby. Do I take it that this is…"

"Yes. The 'bank whereon the wild thyme blows.'" Edmund spoke King Oberon's words.

"I have seen no thyme, but there is wintergreen nearby. I smell it quite distinctly. Now would you kindly explain why you have kept this place a secret?"

"I had no idea it still existed." Edmund's voice died away to a bemused murmur. "Thirty years is a long time. I was sure the elfin nook of my childhood had disappeared. The stream might have undercut this old tree or the course of the water might have changed, leaving this little pool a stagnant bog. I could hardly believe my eyes when I came upon it again today, even more lovely than I had remembered."

He looked up suddenly, a silver twinkle in his gray eyes. "Complete with a slumbering Titania in her diadem of rosebuds. A very pretty touch."

Julianna could feel her composure rapidly deserting her. "What are you doing here at this hour?"

In spite of her abrupt interrogation, Edmund replied with a good-natured laugh. "I came on the same errand you did, obviously—looking to escape the heat. Abbot's Leigh is one great stone oven at present and I felt my bones had stewed enough for one night. So I came down for a swim before breakfast. Speaking of which, we should be getting back soon."

Julianna nodded absently, secretly loath to leave Titania's magical bower and risk breaking its spell.

"You look quite lost in thought, my dear," said Edmund in an odd, almost solicitous tone.

She had become so used to thinking aloud in his presence that her words tumbled out, uncensored. "I was just wondering why such an attractive man as you never married before?" Realizing what she had said, Julianna clamped her lips together in case something worse might follow.

"I appreciate the compliment." Edmund grinned ruefully. "But I was married once."

"Well, I would hardly count your 'little birds.'"

Edmund shook his head. "No, not them. I mean properly married—'till death us do part.'"

Dumbfounded, Julianna felt curious and rather envious of whatever lady had claimed the young Edmund Fitzhugh. Curiosity won out. "Why has no one ever mentioned her to me?"

"I am not sure anyone of our acquaintance remembers Amelia. She was not from Surrey, and she had been dead for some time when I first met Brock. I doubt if any of the staff knew I was a widower. Crispin would have been too young to remember."

"Tell me about her," Julianna prompted.

Edmund was no longer looking at her, but off into the willow draperies, as if gazing backward into his own past. She was free to stare at him as much as she liked. Seeing him with new eyes, she drank in the excellence of his form. Admiring. Desiring.

When, at last he began to speak, Edmund's voice sounded like a faint echo resonating from bygone days. "My first marriage was short-lived, unhappy and long ago. My father's doing and her mother's, in the main. I was going to India and Father considered it unwise to send a young man off to temptation among the exotic pagan females half a world away. Whatever made me fall in with his wishes, I will never understand. It was the first and only time, and I certainly came to regret it.''

Edmund fell silent. Julianna watched unaccustomed emotions play across his features. Then, speaking more quietly still, he resumed. ''We were totally ill-matched. I made a very poor husband. Too bookish, too solitary in my habits and too much interested in anything novel or foreign. Worst of all, I was far too blunt-spoken.''

Called back to the present for an instant, he looked up at her with a wry grin. ''You may have noticed that the intervening years have not cultivated my ability to suffer fools gladly.'' He shrugged. ''There is little more to tell. Amelia died of a fever shortly after we arrived in India. I honestly cannot say I grieved much for her. After her death, I had neither the opportunity nor the inclination for further adventures in matrimony. I doubt womankind was any the worse for that.''

''Nonsense!'' cried Julianna. ''You are a wonderful husband. Any woman would be…'' She almost blurted out her belief that any woman would be lucky to have him. Yesterday she would have told him so without a qualm. Today she did not dare.

''I mean,'' she stammered, ''you're quite agreeable in spots.''

''I doubt Amelia would have concurred.''

For a time they sat in silence, Edmund clearly still absorbed in regretful memories. Julianna's thoughts skittered like the deer, not daring to examine too closely her sudden physical attraction to this man. Though technically her husband, Sir Edmund Fitzhugh was, first and foremost, a dear friend. Why did it please her to know he had not cared for his first wife?

Edmund abruptly broke from his bemusement. ''Enough woolgathering. I'm starved, and the household is likely in an uproar over our absence. Get dressed and we'll go.''

Her shift! She had been so engaged by the novelty of viewing her husband's unclad body, she had entirely forgotten her own less than modest apparel. Jumping like a scalded cat, Julianna threw herself behind the shelter of the willow's wide trunk. Blushing furiously, she pulled on her damp gown.

Edmund merely laughed and called after her, "If you go home dressed like that, it will be all over the county in an hour that Edmund Fitzhugh has been trysting in the woods with his young wife! Such a flattering, if undeserved, reputation for carnality might make me quite insufferable."

She knew the jape was directed more at himself than at her. Nonetheless, it hit uncomfortably close to her own forbidden desires. Too flustered to parry Edmund's verbal thrust, Julianna poked her head out from behind the willow tree. She pitched her garland of flowers at him with a lame, "Oh, get away with you!"

Chapter Fourteen

Brock and Mrs. Tully had their heads together when the master and mistress of Abbot's Leigh returned home, damp and lightly clad. The quizzical cock of his steward's eyebrow was not lost on Edmund. Neither was the shrewd grin flashed in answer by his housekeeper. He acknowledged them with a curt nod.

"I'll join you for breakfast," he muttered to Julianna, setting off in the direction of his bedchamber. Brock cleared his throat loudly to call his master's attention, then withdrew a sealed letter from his capacious waistcoat pocket.

"This arrived last night, sir, after you'd retired."

Edmund took the paper and moved off down the corridor, casting Julianna a look that invited her to follow. After scanning the missive, he pulled a sour face. "My cousins have decided to honor Marlwood with their presence. We are invited to dine at Bayard Hall this evening. I must say, she wastes no time."

"She?"

Edmund rolled his eyes. "Vanessa." His voice rose to a nasal tenor, diction overly precise. "The dowager countess of Sutton-Courtney." With a derisive chuckle, he dropped back into his own warm baritone. "I believe that is her proper title. The invitation bears Laurence's signature but I have little doubt Vanessa contrived it. That feckless ninny is as much under his sister's thumb as he was under his mother's."

Ignoring his contemptuous tone, Julianna asked eagerly, "Is Laurence the cousin reckoned to be Crispin's twin?"

"Some see a likeness. Personally, I consider accounts of their mutual resemblance decidedly exaggerated. Shall I send our regrets to vex them?"

"Edmund Fitzhugh!" Julianna sputtered. "Do you mean to vex your cousins or to vex me? Of course we must go."

"As you wish." He capitulated with a smile and a shrug. "Brock, send to the Hall, accepting my cousins' kind invitation with our compliments." He wagged his finger at Julianna. "Never say I didn't warn you, my dear."

Once Julianna had gone on her charity rounds, Edmund had his horse saddled for a solitary ride. He kept an easy pace, not wanting to wear out his mount in the heat. His arms felt empty without Julianna perched before him. Of late he'd used the hot weather as an excuse not to go riding with her. There were limits to his iron self-control, after all. Nothing tested those limits as severely as Julianna pressed against him, her wild hair blowing in his face.

Ever since he'd acknowledged his love for Julianna, Edmund had found his composure challenged at every turn. His returning vitality only made the situation worse. Suddenly, he was achingly aware of Julianna as a woman. The gentle undulation of her walk, the implicit invitation of her lips, the fine distraction of her wayward tresses—all racked him with desire. In the past years, his monkish existence had brought him only the most superficial contact with the fair sex. Ill health had made him largely indifferent to their charms. The slumbering hunger Julianna had awakened now gnawed at him with sharp teeth.

He knew he'd been playing with fire that morning on the riverbank. The sight of Julianna, a thousandfold more alluring than the fairy queen of his imagination, had robbed him of breath and movement. How long had he stood in water not cold enough to quench his lust, imagining how he would make love to her if only he dared? When she'd opened those bewitching eyes, he'd been powerless to resist his need to touch her. Thank God the deer had spooked. Otherwise, Edmund might have acted on an answering attraction he'd sensed in Julianna. He would have taken her there, in the willow bower, hushing her protests with avid lips, pretending to mistake her struggles for responding passion.

Her words had sobered and wounded him more than he cared to admit. She found him "quite agreeable in spots." She didn't see a man restored to robust prime. To Julianna, he would always be the pitiful invalid, old before his time. She cared for him in the same kind, nurturing spirit she spared for her other charity cases. He was a duty she owed to Crispin. Unless he wanted to betray the two people he loved most in the world, Edmund knew he'd better get a firm grip on his insurgent emotions.

That was why he'd invited his cousin to come—not that he'd ever admit the fact to Julianna. A lively creature, Vanessa would provide a welcome distraction. If only she hadn't brought that brother of hers along. Too handsome for his own good, Laurence was always up to mischief where women were concerned.

For Julianna, the day passed quickly. Thankfully, the heat had lessened and a strong breeze had risen out of the east. She felt certain it boded ill for the continuation of their torrid St. Swithin's weather. The heat of the past weeks had taken its toll on the sick and elderly of the parish, though. She spent several busy hours with Arabella, paying calls and providing what aid they could. Welcoming the diversion, Julianna threw herself into her duties. She dreaded the quiet moments, when her errant thoughts strayed back to her daybreak encounter on the riverbank.

Puzzled by her sudden, unaccountable attraction to Edmund, she feared the powerful, forbidden emotions her memories evoked. Perhaps, she told herself, it was only the elusive glamour of time and place, or the result of Crispin's long absence. It would do her good to spend some time with people nearer her own age, like the Bayard cousins.

Almost before she realized it, evening had come. Scrubbed, coiffed and arrayed in her green silk, Julianna faced Edmund's relatives in the elaborate drawing room of Bayard Hall.

"Julianna, may I present my cousins—Laurence Bayard,

Lord Marlwood, and Vanessa, the dowager countess of Sutton-Courtney.''

Julianna could only stare dumbly. This woman was easily the most beautiful she had ever seen. A frothy creation of lace, voile and lavender silk complimented her delicate, gracefully rounded figure. Large, densely-lashed green eyes brimmed with mirth and mischief, while a perfect rosebud mouth had undoubtedly broken many men's hearts. Julianna particularly envied the dowager countess her hair. Dressed high in the latest style, it was thick, lustrous and the color of dark honey.

Making a deep curtsy, Julianna glanced up to find herself in the openly admiring scrutiny of young Lord Marlwood. Despite Edmund's opinion to the contrary, she thought Laurence Bayard the living image of Crispin. Any differences were minor and superficial. Lord Marlwood was shorter and slighter than his cousin and followed fashion by favoring a powdered wig over his own hair. His eyes, lacking the warm brown of Crispin's hazel, were a glittering emerald like those of his sister. Julianna could barely stifle a sigh of admiration.

Edmund took the sleek, perfectly manicured hands of the dowager countess in his own. Suddenly, Julianna was acutely conscious of her own long, thin fingers, browned and coarsened by the pleasures of the summer.

'''The Queen of Love was pleased and proud,''' Edmund quoted his old friend Swift. '''To see Vanessa thus endowed. She doubted not but such a dame through every breast would dart a flame.'''

Edmund's cousin withdrew her hand, slapping his with gentle coquetry before clasping it warmly again. ''Cousin Edmund, the manners of a Cavalier and the morals of a Puritan, as ever! You are so impossibly gallant, a lady might imagine you mean it.''

Her velvety voice turned sweetly petulant. ''Pray do not remind me of Godfather Swift's wretched ode! At one time, I thought it novel and amusing to be named for his creation. Now, it serves only to date me in a most unflattering fashion. As for that detestable title—dowager indeed! It makes me sound like an aged hag. I suffer it from enough people, so I insist within the family at least, it is simply Vanessa.''

She offered her cheek for a kiss, which Edmund stooped to deliver. Then she moved past him to grasp Julianna by the hands. ''So here is the pretty child who has made a benedict of our old bachelor!'' she gushed. ''Langston Carew has been broadcasting word of your fresh beauty to all our set for half a year now. I must say, I do share his admiration. Of course, the one subject I would take that old reprobate's word on is a lady's good looks. Such a complexion! Oh, for the dewy innocence of adolescence!''

Julianna pulled back her hands abruptly. ''I am every day of twenty, Your Ladyship. And I can hardly imagine Mr. Carew having anything to say of me, as we met on only one occasion.''

''That was all it took, I gather. I recall hearing he noticed you at the theater and could hardly keep his eyes upon the stage.''

She affected a wounded tone. ''It positively broke my heart to hear Edmund had taken a wife without inviting Laurence and me to the nuptial celebrations.''

''I'm afraid our wedding was a very modest and quiet affair,'' said Edmund, ''Julianna's father having died but shortly before.''

''I met your father once, Cousin Julianna,'' said Laurence Bayard. His voice had a light pleasant tone, but not the deep warm resonance of Edmund's—or Crispin's. ''I was at Lloyd's with my cousin, Crispin Bayard, when we spied Francis Underhill with your father. I believe he had planned to invest in Crispin's expedition to the Far East. I gather you spent some time in Crispin's company before he left.''

Julianna cast Edmund a questioning glance. Surely with his own family they could drop the deception and explain the true nature of their expedient relationship. His answer was a subtle, but decisive head motion to the negative. He responded to Laurence's implied question.

''Yes. In fact, it was Crispin who introduced me to Julianna. Our courtship was somewhat precipitated by Mr. Ramsay's untimely demise.'' He took her arm and added with a warmth that sounded a trifle forced, "Like many couples, we have had to become closer acquainted after our marriage. Quite an agreeable experience for me. However, my sudden illness this winter may have caused my wife to reconsider her wedding vows."

A servant signaled that the meal was ready. Laurence took Julianna's arm and Vanessa took Edmund's, escorting them to table. Vanessa continued the flow of conversation. "Yes, that dreadful fever. We called 'round when we heard you were ill, Edmund dear. Your implacable Mr. Brock wouldn't let us across the threshold. The next we heard, you had decamped for Surrey. Dear Julianna, how terribly worried you must have been!"

Though Vanessa's tone was emphatic and ingenuous, she obviously doubted Edmund's young wife had cared at all. "Do give us an account of the whole dreadful business!"

Over the soup course, Julianna related the story of Edmund's illness, de-emphasizing her own role in his recovery. Edmund, however, was quick to interrupt with details of his wife's devoted attendance and superb nursing skills. When they had finished the tale Vanessa shook her head.

"To think how close we came to losing you, dear Edmund. How very fortunate that your wife has such a cool, mature head upon those young shoulders. Then to spend weeks amusing you with chess and music and reading! My sweet child, I had no idea you were so terribly accomplished. Of course, when word of your marriage first came out—" Vanessa rolled her eyes, a light trill of laughter bubbling from her lips "—you can imagine the talk it engendered! I said, 'You may be sure if Edmund Fitzhugh has taken a child bride, she will hardly be some callow girl, but a young lady of refinement and excellent understanding!' Besides, children mature so quickly these days."

Though Julianna felt she should acknowledge this backhand compliment, she was growing heartily impatient with the countess's unremitting references to her youth. The best she could tender was a tight and fixed smile. She breathed a silent sigh of relief when the lady turned her attentions upon Edmund.

"To hear the talk, dear cousin, one would think you were quite in your dotage, rather than a fine figure of a man in his

prime.'' She placed a sleek finger to her lips. ''If you would
only bend to fashion and affect a good wig, no one would take
you for more than two-and-thirty!''

Julianna would have preferred a more general topic of conversation. Lady Vanessa, however, appeared intent on pursuing
the subject of age for some time to come.

''I would defend any woman's choice of an older husband.
Why, I married a young man and where did it get me? Wed
no time at all and the whole family fell ill. My husband survived
his father only long enough to inherit his title and brand me a
dowager countess as his very young widow. Then, the estate
passed to some distant relation and I was left penniless....''

Laurence tried to laugh. Instead he choked noisily on the
morsel of oyster in his mouth.

His sister cast him a disparaging look. ''Well, comparatively
penniless. My advice to any sensible woman—get a man of
mature years with a proven constitution, who will not expire at
the first sniffle.''

Julianna breathed more easily when talk turned to the London
social scene and thence to the struggle among the European
powers over the Austrian succession. Soon it was on to the
subject of politics—a thorough airing of the Tory views of the
Bayards and their set. There was speculation about the intentions of the Young Pretender. Vanessa hinted the young man
might soon move to reclaim the English throne for the Stewarts.
Edmund dismissed such talk as wishful nonsense. Politics had
never been a topic of interest in the Ramsay household, so
Julianna was unable to contribute anything to the conversation.

Glancing to her left, she was pleasantly disconcerted to find
Lord Marlwood's eyes upon her. His sister, who missed nothing, shifted her speech in midsentence. ''Dear Julianna, you are
making a conquest of my brother. I can see it. You must be
terribly firm with him or he will break his heart over you. Then
I shall never get him married off! Well now, I see the men are
being brought their port. We can retire to the drawing room,
Julianna, and get better acquainted.''

The gentlemen stood as the dowager countess ushered her
out. Julianna cast Edmund a furtive glance of supplication, urg-

ing him to drink up quickly. She doubted how long she could cope with his voluble cousin on her own.

As the ladies withdrew to the drawing room, Vanessa whispered to Edmund, "Do talk to Laurence. His gambling debts…his love affairs…I can do nothing with the wretched boy. Perhaps he'll pay heed to you."

Edmund doubted it. Having intensely disliked Vanessa and Laurence's self-important mother, he had clashed with her frequently over the boy's ruinous upbringing. He'd never been able to fathom Crispin's affection for his foppish cousin. Moreover, he resented the way Laurence had been ogling Julianna all evening. Taking up his port, he began to pace the length of the dining room, surveying the paintings. Personally, he wouldn't have given most of them houseroom. Behind him, a fatuous little click heralded the opening of Lord Marlwood's snuffbox.

"I must say, I admire your taste in women, Cousin Edmund."

Before he could reply, Laurence added, "And your nerve— pouching Crispin's little pigeon so smoothly."

"What blather are you talking now, boy?"

Dipping a pinch of snuff, Laurence delicately touched his nose with a lace-trimmed handkerchief. "Oh, don't be coy, old fellow. Surely you knew Crispin meant to marry the girl. What will he say, do you think, when he finds out? Do save me a ringside seat. Why, it'll be jollier fun than a cockfight!"

"Have you managed to settle your gambling debts yet?" Edmund growled, disdaining to pursue Laurence's avenue of conversation.

"Heard about that, did you?" Laurence arched an eyebrow. "How bad news spreads. Yes, I've managed to pay off the worst."

"Really?" Edmund stood over his young cousin, glowering paternally. "Where did you get the money?"

Holding out an exquisite cloisonné snuffbox, Laurence offered him a pinch. "Oh, generous friends. One isn't completely lost if one still has one's charm."

Edmund declined the snuff with a derisive flick of his hand. "Whose wife were you charming this time?"

Lord Marlwood grinned and touched a finger to the side of his nose. "Now, now, old man, mustn't kiss and tell, you know."

Edmund turned away, vaguely nauseated to consider their common ancestry. "How unwontedly honorable of you," he muttered. Then he added in a louder voice, "Tell me, did the lady pay you to keep her husband from hearing? Or was it the husband not wanting anyone to know you'd cuckolded him?"

Laurence let out a high giggle that set Edmund's teeth on edge. "Oh Cousin Edmund, you are a caution!"

Bolting the last of his port, Edmund set his empty glass on the sideboard. He had no inclination to prolong this postprandial chat. "I suppose it's hopeless to expect you'll grow up one day. Marry a respectable lady. Do something with your life."

"Faugh, but everyone is anxious to marry me off. What a dreadful bore! I mean to follow your lead, Cousin Edmund— sow my wild oats while I'm able. Once I get useful for nothing else, I'll put myself out to stud with some amusing young filly."

Edmund felt his stock growing tight around his neck. The blatant insult to himself he could let pass. "Are you comparing my wife to a horse, Laurence?"

"Not in any derogatory sense, I assure you! I simply meant good bloodlines—spirited—a real 'trier."

"See that you don't *try* anything with my wife."

His young cousin giggled again. "Steal her from you like you stole her from Crispin? My dear fellow, I have not your craft! Not that I blame you, of course. Why, those eyes, those lips—they could induce any man to lose his scruples."

Laurence always had loved to bait him, Edmund recalled. The young fool had probably picked up the habit from his mother. Usually he managed to put the cocky cub in his place with a few stinging words. Tonight Laurence had him on the run. The sly young dandy had spotted his weakness.

Changing tactics, Edmund tendered a dignified reply. "If you had either sense or taste, you would see that my wife's face is only the beginning of her beauty."

Laurence raised his glass as if in a toast. "Oh, I'm not blind to her other charms, I assure you."

Lord Marlwood appeared not to realize how close he was to a sound drubbing. In the interest of family harmony, Edmund tried to remain civil. "I refer to her wit, her character, her generosity—qualities you could not possibly appreciate."

Tossing back the last of his port, Laurence rose from the table. "Perhaps we should join the ladies."

As he held the door for Edmund, Laurence added archly, "Perhaps you are right, Cousin Edmund. We young fellows do have an eye for face and form when it comes to women. It takes an old duffer like you to treasure their less tangible attributes. Vanessa's right, though, marriage has spruced you up. No one would ever guess your real age. You must be every day of—what? Five-and-fifty?"

"Forty-one next birthday," Edmund snapped. "Not quite in the league of Methuselah, yet."

"Only that? Really?" Laurence winked. "Well, I'll back up your story if anyone asks."

As they drew within earshot of the ladies, Laurence asked, loudly, "Were you a first cousin of my grandfather or my great-grandfather, old fellow? I have such a poor head for genealogy."

While the men were taking their port, Vanessa joined Julianna on the drawing room settee. There was scarcely room for them both, with Vanessa's wide and elaborate skirts.

"My sweet pet." Vanessa patted Julianna's hand. "Now it is just we women alone, you must tell me all. How are you managing with such a man of the world as our Edmund, you innocent babe?"

Remembering that she must maintain the fiction of their marriage, Julianna was flustered by the intimate implication of Vanessa's question. She feigned ignorance. "In what way, Your Ladyship?"

Edmund's cousin chortled. "Oh dear, so modest! Please, do call me Cousin Vanessa. 'Your Ladyship' makes one feel so old. I know you would never cast my age up to me."

You, on the other hand, thought Julianna, *would never hesitate to cast mine up to me—and everyone else.*

Vanessa continued in a throaty, sensual tone. "I mean, has he taught you any of the amorous secrets he learned in the East? If Langston Carew is to be believed, your husband once had a full harem. I have often thought a wealth of passion must simmer beneath that monkish exterior Cousin Edmund presents to the world."

All day Julianna had been stubbornly trying to keep such thoughts from her mind. Yet, here was the dowager countess of Sutton-Courtney scrutinizing the sensitive area, like one's tongue probing a sore tooth. In neither case was the resulting sensation a pleasant one.

"You must remember, Cousin Vanessa—" she tried to sidestep the question. "—Sir Edmund...I mean Edmund, has been very ill all winter, and..."

"Langston Carew implied that too much exertion during your honeymoon was to blame! Besides, Edmund is looking very fit and virile these days. Far better than he has in years."

She slanted a secretive, sidelong smile. "You know, I often thought if I ever decided to remarry, Edmund might make a splendid choice. You are fortunate, my angel, that I make it a positive point of honor never to poach on my friends' husbands."

She slowly moistened her lips with the tip of her tongue. "Unless they are simply too delectable to resist, of course." Her feline eyes twinkled with laughter and malice.

As the men rejoined them, Julianna overheard Lord Marlwood pose a courteous query about their degree of kinship. Edmund responded with thunderous umbrage. Honestly, he could be such an old badger by times! Still, the men's presence came as a welcome respite. Julianna could bear only so much of Vanessa's prying and barely concealed interest in Edmund. The dowager countess had surpassed that limit by a mile.

The Fitzhughs stayed on for several sets of cards—the countess partnered with Sir Edmund and Julianna with Lord Marlwood. Vanessa continued to entertain the company with her sparkling badinage, occasionally supported by the gentlemen.

Though she appeared to give no thought to the game, her hand was always flawlessly played. Thoroughly unnerved, Julianna made mistake after foolish mistake.

At length Edmund yawned. "I believe you'll have to excuse us, Vanessa, Laurence. I know the evening has barely begun for the two of you. However, Vanessa's flattery notwithstanding, I am an old fellow who needs his rest. You must come visit us soon at Abbot's Leigh. You always enliven a place, Vanessa."

They exchanged the usual parting pleasantries, lingering in the forecourt for some time. At last, Edmund and Julianna were alone in the darkened carriage on their way home. Leaning heavily back, Edmund pulled a hand down his face. "Dear Lord, I had forgotten how exhausting that woman can be!"

"You gave every appearance of finding her company most agreeable and enlivening," Julianna observed tartly.

"My dear!" he protested. "Some measure of civility is required in all social intercourse."

"And your infamous blunt speaking?"

"Never with a lady, surely!" Edmund rapidly switched topics. "What did you make of my cousins?"

"I thought Lord Marlwood a very fine-looking man, and exceptionally agreeable company. I can certainly see his resemblance to Crispin."

Edmund snorted. "At least Laurence has learned to keep silent when he has little worth saying. Nothing resembles a wise man like a fool who keeps his mouth shut. And Vanessa?"

"Your cousin is undoubtedly the most beautiful woman I've ever seen." Julianna's tone heated. "She is also the most irritating woman I have ever met. If she'd mentioned my age one more time, I'd have risen up and wrung her graceful neck!"

Edmund replied with the most annoyingly indulgent laugh. "She did harp on the subject, didn't she? I agree she is quite a comely creature in an artificial way. Still, I expect she is beginning to peer back over her shoulder. When a woman's looks are her calling card, it must be worrisome to find a whole new generation of pretty girls coming on the scene." His voice turned soft and serious. "I rather pity her."

"Save your pity for those who need it. If a lady is wealthy, witty and beautiful, she has no one but herself to blame if she is not happy."

Edmund clucked his tongue and quoted *King Lear* in mild reproof. "'So young, and so untender.'"

Julianna felt her eyes sting. She bit back Cordelia's heartless reply. "So young, my lord, and true." Instead, she observed waspishly, "Your cousin certainly showed you a more than familial interest. Like a cat with a bowl of cream. I can't think why she hasn't gobbled you up long ago."

Again, Edmund gave a wry laugh and shook his head. "Being a bachelor, I could have been invisible for all the attention Vanessa paid me. As a married man, I now come within her selected purview. It is all a game to her."

A game? thought Julianna. Lady Vanessa's game was not one she cared to play.

Chapter Fifteen

A warm, yeasty aroma permeated the kitchen of Abbot's Leigh, mingled with the tang of dill weed and vinegar. With harvest beginning, Myrtle Tully's sunny domain had become a beehive of domestic industry. Gwenyth cut cucumber at the table while at the corner rolling board, Julianna kneaded a spongy mass of white dough with a vigor bordering on violence.

Edmund had gone up to London, where his old friend General Oglethorpe was facing court martial. The founder and governor of the Georgia colony had been one of Edmund's few close friends at school. After the boys parted, one to join the army and the other the navy, they had managed to maintain sporadic contact. Edmund could barely contain his outrage at critics who questioned the governor's role in repulsing Spanish invaders from Georgia soil. He planned to extend Oglethorpe every assistance in answering the preposterous charges.

When he'd halfheartedly offered to take her along, Julianna had declined. All too soon they would be returning to London for the winter, she'd reminded him. Until then, she wanted to spend every possible moment at her dear Abbot's Leigh. In truth, she'd felt the need of some time away from Edmund, to concentrate on quelling the unwelcome feelings that roiled within her. Perhaps with Edmund gone, Vanessa would cease haunting the place.

During the past fortnight they had entertained the Bayard cousins on several occasions. Far too many occasions for Julianna's liking. The dowager countess had monopolized Edmund. An expert horsewoman, she'd usurped Julianna's place riding with him. She'd been sweetly patronizing of their evening entertainments. "Like Phyllis and Corydon, with your bucolic pleasures!"

Julianna's Welsh temper smoldered when Vanessa had insisted on taking the lead roles in their play-reading. She'd discovered one flaw in Vanessa's perfection, however. Unlike her cousin Edmund, the dowager countess of Sutton-Courtney had neither the ear nor the voice for singing. Oblivious to the fact, she had patently demonstrated her lack of talent again and again, to Julianna's secret amusement. Unfortunately, that lone shortcoming only served to throw Vanessa's many other skills into sharp relief. Around Edmund's beautiful cousin, Julianna felt callow and gauche—the foil to Vanessa's ripe perfection.

To hear her talk, the dowager countess was on near-intimate terms with everyone of consequence in London. Her every word and action suggested life was an exciting, ridiculous game, which she played with effortless skill. Her references to Julianna's youth were as frequent and pointed as ever. So were her fawning attentions to Edmund, all fluttering eyelashes and teasing sidelong glances. He'd appeared amused by his cousin's blatant coquetry, responding with lavish compliments to her eyebrow—or her elbow. Julianna could cheerfully have throttled him! As for that she-cat, Vanessa—the simpering doxy—the brazen bawd!

"Miss Julianna!" Myrtle Tully's laughing interjection brought her up short. "If you do not leave off pummeling that dough, old Gammer Drummond will break the last of her teeth on the tough crust of your bread!"

Julianna cast Gwenyth and the housekeeper a rueful glance. "Too right, Mrs. Tully. My thoughts were elsewhere—a dangerous pastime in the kitchen."

Setting her bread with a gentler touch, she could not keep her thoughts from returning to Edmund and Vanessa. Why should she even care if the calf-eyed fool made an ass of himself over that strumpet? After all, he was not her husband in any real sense. Still, it galled Julianna beyond bearing that Vanessa might gloat over stealing Edmund's affections.

"Look sharp now, girl!" Mrs. Tully sternly admonished Julianna as though she were a scullery maid, rather than mistress of the manor. "You've burned your arm on the kettle, smashed two pieces of my good crockery, and like as not that bread'll barely be fit for the swine. Moonin' and mopin' about since the master left. If you can't spare his company a day or two, you should have gone with him and good riddance."

Heaving an exasperated sigh, she shook her apron to dispatch Julianna like a stray goose. "Be off where you can't do no damage and let me finish my work in peace."

"Don't be cross, Myrtle," Julianna coaxed. "I haven't been myself lately. It's all the company, I expect. I promise to stay out of your way until I can better concentrate."

"There now, my dear, no real harm done. You run along. Gwenyth and I'll see to the cookin'."

Mooning and moping. Mrs. Tully was too perceptive for Julianna's liking. Eager as she'd been to see Edmund go, she found herself missing him dreadfully. Life felt very flat without their late-night chats and private jokes. Laurence Bayard's call, two days after Edmund's departure, promised a welcome distraction—especially since his sister did not accompany him.

Vanessa had so dominated their previous encounters, Julianna had been unable to gain any perspective on Lord Marlwood. Unfailingly gallant, he seemed reasonably well informed. She couldn't fathom why Edmund had such little regard for Laurence, while stubbornly maintaining a good opinion of his vixen sister.

"Cousin Julianna, I'm delighted to find you at home. Though I did think it unlikely Cousin Edmund would take you to London, under the circumstances. I've been left on my own as well, so we can club together for company. It's the deucedest thing. You can't think how vexing it is to be always patronized and bossed about by one's sister. Yet she does leave a vacancy in one's life when she's gone."

Julianna could well appreciate the vexation of being patronized by the dowager countess of Sutton-Courtney. She could hardly imagine bearing the brunt of it on a continuing basis. Her heart warmed with sympathy for young Lord Marlwood.

"How kind of you to call, Cousin Laurence. Shall we share a drink in the back garden? Mrs. Tully makes a marvelous cherry cordial."

"A delightful suggestion." Lord Marlwood inhaled a pinch of snuff. "I have longed to meet and talk with you alone, Cousin Julianna. Your husband has that haughty, self-assured way about him that always makes one feel an utter dunce. When he fixes me with those icy eyes, I know he believes I have never talked a word of sense in my life. So, I generally keep quiet around him. Then, I get the impression he considers me terribly backward!"

Laurence Bayard ended his confession with a rueful snigger. Julianna laughed, too. She recognized the feelings he had described as similar to her own abashment with Vanessa.

"You mustn't mind Edmund. I know he can seem rather stern at first, but he likes it when people stand up to him—to a point. Besides, you underestimate his opinion of you. He commented to me, quite recently, that you show admirable sense in not being too free-spoken." Julianna surreptitiously crossed her fingers at this slight readjustment of the facts.

Laurence thrust out his lower lip. "Well, the devil with what anyone thinks of me, I say." Cradling his chin in his hands, he gazed raptly at her. "Let me hear something about you, Cousin Julianna. You are so restrained and modest compared to Vanessa. It makes one avid to hear more from you. Do you also have an overbearing sister who keeps you in your place?"

"I have no family at all since my father died, other than my cousin, Francis Underhill…and my stepbrother."

"Is your stepbrother older or younger than you?"

"Older. By several years."

"That is almost as bad, isn't it?" Laurence held up his hands in mock horror. "Vanessa constantly nags me to find a wife and beget a son to inherit the title. Duty to the family and all that rot. Truth to tell, I find the title business a dreadful bore. I wish Vanessa had been a boy and become Lord Marlwood, instead of me. She cares much more for that nonsense. I sometimes feel she is rather jealous of me for being the heir. That, and Mama's obvious partiality. I cannot see why Vanessa should resent something so natural. After all, I was Mama's only son, the baby of the family and posthumous to boot. Vanessa and Mama never got on well together, even before I was born...."

As Lord Marlwood talked on and on of his childhood, raised by an indulgent, domineering mother, his voice took on an obnoxious, whining tone. Occasionally, he paused long enough to ask Julianna a question. After paying scant attention to her reply, he began another tedious monologue about himself. As the afternoon dragged to a close, Julianna struggled to maintain the appearance of interest and to stifle her yawns.

At last, Laurence regretfully observed, "I must be going, delightful as this has been. May I call upon you tomorrow?"

Julianna's attempt at a smile missed somehow. "Much as I would like that, Cousin Laurence, I will be busy tomorrow. On Thursdays, I assist Mrs. Trowbridge with her parish work."

Laurence clucked his tongue. "How tiresome for you, having to play lady of the manor! Well, Cousin Julianna, if you are unavailable through the day, may I invite myself for dinner?"

"No need for that. I would be happy to invite you." The pained courtesy in her own voice reminded Julianna of Edmund in uncongenial company.

"Until tomorrow, then." Lord Marlwood took his leave with a very mannered and gallant kiss on her hand.

Reflecting upon her interview with him, Julianna could see how little resemblance Laurence bore to Crispin in character and outlook. Still, certain of his mannerisms reminded her of Crispin so acutely, it took her breath away. For those scarce instants she would suffer his company.

On Julianna's parish rounds the next day, the subject of Laurence Bayard rose from an unexpected quarter.

"God rest you, milady...reverend missus!" The irrepressible Mr. Warbeck accosted the ladies. "Busy with all your good works, I see. The vicar tells us God saves by grace alone. A pity some folk use that as an excuse to leave off being charitable to their neighbors. I hear as how His Lordship is up at the big house these days, what, Lady Fitzhugh?''

Julianna seldom missed a day in the village without her budget of gossip from Old Charlie. It was no secret he doted on Sir Edmund's young bride and his fondness was amply reciprocated. ''Yes. Mr. Warbeck. Lord Marlwood and his sister came down over a fortnight ago.''

Mr. Warbeck blew his crimson-veined nose. ''That's one young coxcomb, what?'' he chortled. ''Clean spoiled by his stuck-up mother. Miss Vanessa was a merry lass when she were young. I mind how she's quite a little minx now though, getting up to three kinds of mischief in the City. Mark you—'' he wagged his forefinger ''—they were once a fine family, the Bayards. The branch with the best of that old blood is Captain Fitzhugh's. Be a sad shame to see it die out.''

Julianna had suffered enough heavy-handed hints from Charlie Warbeck all summer to know where this was leading. She placed her hands decidedly upon her hips, in the manner of Mrs. Tully.

''If wishes could get babies, Mr. Warbeck, I know your good auspices would see Abbot's Leigh with a full nursery. However, as that is not the case, you had better leave the matter to my husband and me.''

The old fellow cackled and slapped his knee. ''You're not half a tart one, lass! I knew the captain wouldn't suffer no meek, mewling mouse of a wife. A good job you're winsome enough to get away with all. 'pon my word, I won't open my mouth about babes again. You'll not stop me prayin' on it, though.''

When Julianna turned back to the vicar's wife, Arabella was shaking her head. ''That one never stands on ceremony, does he? I believe I like the old demon all the better for it.''

No sooner had she pronounced that sentence than the blood drained from the woman's face and she slumped against a nearby stile.

''Arabella!'' Julianna flew to catch the vicar's wife in her arms and ease her to the ground.

''Mr. Warbeck!'' she cried. ''Have someone go for the vicar!''

Rather than call for one of the children, the stooped old figure scurried off in the direction of the vicarage. Arabella's eyelids were beginning to flutter when her husband marched up and scooped her into his arms. Without a word to Julianna, he carried his wife back toward their home, crooning her name. Julianna followed behind, embarrassed to intrude upon their intimacy but concerned that he understand what had taken place. She hovered in the vicarage parlor for some time, until Reverend Trowbridge descended the stairs. He appeared surprised to find her waiting.

"Lady Fitzhugh, how kind of you to call."

"Mr. Trowbridge," she said, with more than a hint of asperity, "I was with your wife just now, when she fell into a swoon in the middle of the village. Is there anything I can do for her? Should I summon medical help?"

Understanding dawned upon the vicar's gaunt face, together with the hint of a smile. "That will not be necessary. My wife is early with child, and I'm afraid the duties she so loves are becoming a bit too much for her."

"Congratulations!" cried Julianna, her spirits buoyant with relief. "Tell your wife she is under my orders not to stir from bed for several days, at least. I can carry out her duties with help from Gwenyth and Mrs. Tully. I'll stop by to see her tomorrow."

As she sauntered along the road to Abbot's Leigh, thoughts of babies cooed and tumbled through Julianna's mind. She'd had almost no experience with the little creatures, until recently. During the winter, she'd paid several calls on the Underhills and their infant daughter. Now Arabella was to become a mother. The Marlwood folk reminded Julianna subtly but constantly that she should be carrying a baby, too. She could not help but think on what a doting father Edmund would have made.

Oh, the tedium of dining with Lord Marlwood! As a substitute for Edmund's stimulating companionship, the foppish young beau left much to be desired. Without his sister to monopolize the conversation, or fear of Edmund's silent censure to keep him quiet, Laurence could certainly manage to talk. Although glib enough, his opinions were merely borrowed from others, without any true understanding. While Lord Marlwood made free with his flattery, he denied Julianna the true compliment of listening to what she said. She longed for the evening to end.

"I have a delightful surprise planned for us tomorrow," Laurence announced on his way out. "Have you seen the abbey ruins on the tor?"

"I wanted Edmund to take me. He was not strong enough at first and lately I believe it has slipped his mind."

"Will you go with me, then? I have scouted it out. A rough trail winds up the southwestern slope. We will have to walk, of course, but I can bring a pony to carry our lunch. What do you say?" Laurence's eyes rounded and his voice fell to an eldritch whisper. "I could tell you all about the Mad Abbot of Marlwood."

"Oh, that does sound—interesting," Julianna replied, diplomatically. "Unfortunately, I have a great deal to do tomorrow, with Mrs. Trowbridge indisposed. Thank you for your kind offer, but I'll wait and go another time with Edmund."

Laurence Bayard's handsome mouth curled in an unattractive sneer. "How charming! The faithful wife, waiting on a husband who is off in London enjoying a dalliance with my sister."

"What are you saying, Laurence?"

"I'm saying, don't let him play you for a fool, Julianna. Vanessa left for London the same day Cousin Edmund did. And she made no secret of her reason for going. My cousin is the fool, to leave your side for any other woman. In your position, I'd go on a little excursion without him. It does a husband good to know he cannot take his wife for granted."

Julianna's thoughts whirled. Edmund and Vanessa? He would not dare! Of course, he'd been amused by her attentions and the lady was both beautiful and available. Damn him! Without realizing what she was doing, Julianna bade Laurence goodnight, promising she would accompany him to Abbot's Tor the next day.

Chapter Sixteen

Early on Friday morning, Edmund set off for Marlwood. By riding horseback instead of taking the carriage, he meant to avoid the congested thoroughfares of London and strike out on a more direct route, cross-country. Keeping a steady pace through the rural districts of Kensington and Hounslow, he hoped to cross the Thames at Weybridge no later than noon. After a quick bite at some convenient public house, he'd race south toward Marlwood. With the comfortable knowledge of a week's successful endeavor, Edmund had hankered for Friday to come. He couldn't wait to get home to Julianna.

Between consulting lawyers and calling in favors on Oglethorpe's behalf, he had pondered the problem of his marriage. He'd considered a discreet liaison with some highly paid courtesan to appease the appetite Julianna had whetted. In the end he'd rejected the idea with a shudder of distaste. He wanted only one woman. No other would serve. Besides, he'd vowed to cleave only unto her. His puritan morals would not countenance adultery—even if his marriage was a pretense.

Early in the week, he'd made grim resolutions to keep Julianna at arm's length. She belonged to Crispin, Edmund constantly reminded himself. Circumstances had entrusted her to his loyal stewardship. Despite his recent impure thoughts, he must do nothing to betray that trust. However, with each passing day he had missed his young wife more keenly. Even her brief, temporary amputation from his life maimed him. Longing for

Julianna besieged his stubborn resolve, demolishing it to smoking rubble.

As he drew nearer to Abbot's Leigh, Edmund's pulse quickened and he urged his mount to a faster pace. The droning bees sang to him. The fragrance of ripe berries tantalized him with thoughts of sweet red lips. The warm rays of sunlight caressed his face like a woman's gentle fingers. He could imagine Julianna looking up in answer to his call, flying toward him in rapturous welcome, flinging herself into his arms.

Laurence Bayard's offhand barb about Vanessa and Edmund had succeeded in murdering sleep for Julianna. No matter which way she turned or how she tossed from side to side, images of the lovers had taunted her. She'd pictured the two of them laughing and talking over dinner, their hands clasped across the table. She'd imagined Edmund helping Vanessa from a carriage, holding her too close and too long. She'd writhed at the thought of them in his chamber, Edmund easing Vanessa's sleeves off her shoulders and whispering bits of poetry to her every perfect feature.

The disquiet of the night told upon Julianna the next morning. When she stopped at the vicarage to check on Arabella's condition, it was the vicar's wife who expressed concern for her.

"You do not look well, Julianna. Was that the reason you sauced Charlie Warbeck yesterday?" Arabella's pale face lit up. "Are you expecting a baby, too?"

Julianna had no blushes left for such questions. "No, Arabella. I'm sure that is not the case." She immediately changed the subject. "How are you feeling?"

"Wretchedly ill, I'm afraid. I cannot get my stomach settled. Old Mrs. Drummond claims it is the sign of a healthy baby— drawing all of its mother's strength. I wish my little companion would leave me just a bit. I hate to give up my parish work."

"Only until you are stronger," said Julianna. "When our Lord told his followers to deny themselves, I doubt he meant an expectant mother should deny herself a well-deserved rest."

Arabella laid her hand upon Julianna's. It looked alarmingly delicate, almost transparent. "You are a good friend, Julianna, with much more common sense than one would expect...."

"In a girl not come to years of discretion? Not you, too, Arabella. I hear nothing of late but reminders of my immaturity!"

"You're far too sensitive, dear heart. I meant to say you show more common sense than one would expect from a city girl."

As it turned out, Gwenyth and Julianna had only a few calls to make that day. Julianna returned to Abbot's Leigh in plenty of time to change clothes before Laurence's arrival. It was a sublime day for exploring the tor—sunny and warm, with a fickle little breeze.

Laurence had his coachman drop them at the end of a lane in the village. The path soon narrowed into a track up the hill. While the tor's steep eastern slope supported only a stunted crop of box and yew, the gentler incline Julianna and Laurence traversed was well wooded with poplar, holly and hazel. From all her walking and fishing that summer, Julianna was in excellent condition, able to make the climb with little difficulty. Leading a well-laden pony, Laurence found the going more onerous. His exertions left him little spare breath for talking, a situation for which Julianna was profoundly grateful.

The view from the summit of Abbot's Tor proved well worth the climb. Off to the east, the slender spire of Guildford Cathedral pointed men's eyes toward heaven. Westward, the ancient ramparts of Farnham Castle loomed protectively over the town. Marlwood nestled at the foot of the hill, buildings and people dwarfed by the distance. The common stretched beyond the village like loosely draped folds of bright green muslin, tufted with white sheep. Julianna thought it little wonder those first Cistercian monks had built their abbey here, so many centuries ago. The place gave her a feeling of separation from the world, an almost celestial perspective.

They soon set to work exploring the ruins of the abbey. In the stillness of the deserted cloisters, Julianna fancied she could catch a faint echo of padding feet, whispered prayers and mellifluous chants. Part of the chapel roof had fallen away.

Strangely, it made the place feel even more consecrated. A prayer uttered from that altar must surely ascend into the infinite blue, directly to the ear of God.

By and by, they discovered a low stone wall that might once have enclosed a garden. There, Julianna and Laurence decided to dine. She was grateful he had not broken the venerable spell of the ruined abbey with too much idle chatter. Having forgone his wig for the day, Laurence resembled Crispin to an unsettling degree. *Oh Crispin,* Julianna thought, *why must you be so impossibly far away?* Try as she might to hold him, he slipped away from her a bit more each day. Foolish fancies were taking his place—foolish and dangerous fancies.

Edmund rode into the kitchen courtyard of Abbot's Leigh about midafternoon, pleased by the good speed he'd made from London. He leapt from the saddle, affectionately tousling the hair of a young stable boy who rushed forward to catch the reins of his horse. The top half of the kitchen door stood open, letting savory smells waft into the courtyard.

Edmund strode to the door. "Julianna, I'm home!" No three words could have given him more joy to utter.

"Captain, good to have you back." The sonsy figure of Mrs. Tully appeared in the doorway, wearing a broad smile of welcome.

"Good to be back, Mrs. Tully." Edmund didn't bother to disguise the eagerness in his voice. "Is my wife around?"

A look of apprehension deepened the furrows in the housekeeper's brow. "No. She's gone off with His Lordship on a little outing. Up the tor," she added, as though determined to make a clean breast of disagreeable news.

Up to Abbot's Tor? With Laurence?

"Did the countess go along?" He could not imagine Vanessa climbing that hill in all her elegant frippery.

"No sign of Her Ladyship all week." Mrs. Tully wiped floury hands on her apron, avoiding his eye. "Master Laurence has been hanging about a good deal, though." Her tone left no doubt of Mrs. Tully's disapproval.

"Has he, indeed?" Edmund could feel the rage building from

his toes. He struggled to keep his tone neutral. "It is a fine day for such an expedition. I believe I'll join the party."

Turning sharply from the housekeeper, Edmund bellowed for his horse. Pulled from its stall with no more than a mouthful of water and oats, the beast snorted and pranced as he remounted. Mouth grimly set, Edmund gained the saddle and applied his crop to the gelding's glistening flank. In a hail of pebbles, the horse wheeled and galloped off down the lane.

Mordecai Brock and Nelson Tully stood in the shade of an old oak that grew between the scullery and the stable. Silent and unseen, they had witnessed the events of Sir Edmund's homecoming.

"I'd not care to be in young Marlwood's boots just now. Would you, Mr. Tully?"

Swiping a gnarled knuckle across the stubble on his chin, the gardener slowly shook his head. "That I would not, Mr. Brock. That I would not."

After their walk and in the fresh air of such a spectacular setting, the food Laurence had brought from Bayard Hall tasted particularly toothsome to Julianna. It was simple fare: a small loaf of bread, new cheese, early grapes and plums, cold roast fowl, accompanied by a light ale. When Laurence talked about subjects other than himself, Julianna found he could wax almost as amusing as his sister.

"More ale, Julianna?" Laurence held up the jug. "What a delightful day to come here! I have not been since I was a child. Very little has changed in the meantime. Shall I tell you the tale of the Mad Abbot? I did promise, after all."

"Is there a ghost?" Julianna held out her cup for a drop more ale. "How romantic!"

"Oh, the story is romantic enough. It was an old yarn, even at the time of the Dissolution. They say this place was once ruled by a clever young abbot who went mad. Began riding down into the countryside at night, calling at the windows of young ladies, enticing them out for moonlit trysts. They say he had the face of a fallen angel and was so sweet-spoken no lady could resist his invitation. Sounds perfectly sensible to me," he added, in a sardonic aside. "Though one does expect better of the clergy."

The remark caught Julianna by surprise. Laughing, she sputtered her drink. Laurence continued, his voice quieter. "This went on for some time with none the wiser. Then, one of his young paramours was discovered heavily pregnant on her wedding night—the dress of the times making it difficult to tell any earlier. It made a terrible scandal, of course. There was talk of witchcraft until one of his other young paramours confessed the whole story."

The carnal tone of Laurence's tale made Julianna squirm with embarrassment. She took another drink and poked through the luncheon basket to avoid his eyes.

"A mob of villagers rode to the tor to have it out with the abbot. During the encounter, someone threw oil of vitriol in his face. His beauty marred and his secret exposed, the Mad Abbot flung himself from the priory tower. The spot where his body landed never raised a flower or blade of grass from that day on."

Laurence Bayard has considerable power as a storyteller. As he finished the tale, Julianna's neck pricked with gooseflesh.

"Since then, the specter of the Mad Abbot is said to ride out on Michaelmas Eve. Cowled and masked, he calls beneath the windows of young ladies."

Laurence broke the unearthly stillness with a guffaw. "Personally, I think the poor wretch is finally at rest. But his ghost has taken the blame for the odd aborted elopement or a married woman discovered on her way to a late-night assignation."

While they were laughing over this quip, Laurence reached for Julianna's hand, his tone lighthearted. "So, if I come to your window on Michaelmas Eve in the guise of the Mad Abbot, would you come away with me, Julianna?"

She tried to extract her fingers from his grasp but he held them all the tighter. "Really, Laurence," she said sharply. "That jest is not especially amusing."

He dragged her hand to his lips, an ardent note creeping into his voice. "Because I have never been in such passionate earnest." Gripping her hand in an iron hold, he bestowed incongruously delicate kisses upon each finger. "I have been besotted with you since the first day we met, Julianna. That vivid, lustrous hair, those strange mesmerizing eyes and those luxuriant lips—what man could possibly resist you?"

His likeness to Crispin was so strong, even his endearments were the same. However, Laurence Bayard's words inflamed Julianna not with love, but with cold anger. Pulling hard, she wrenched back her hand. "I will not listen to this foolishness, Laurence. You have known from the moment we met that I am a married woman. The wife of your kinsman, no less!"

He fondled the hem of her skirt, his tone quiet and reasonable, if slightly wheedling. "Ah, Julianna, I above all men know that many married women have desires unsatisfied at home. More than once, I have seen a look in your eyes that betrays your attraction to me."

Julianna opened her mouth to speak. How could she reply to that? Tell Laurence the only passion he awakened in her was the longing for Crispin she wished to recapture? "You are mistaken, Laurence. Or you are seeing what you want to see."

"I think not. I've played this game many times. If it salves your conscience to protest and pretend reluctance, that makes my conquest all the more piquant. As for my relation to your husband, nothing could give me greater satisfaction than stealing Edmund Fitzhugh's young bride." His voice turned hard. "Prick his arrogant hide."

His hand slipped under her gown, coiling around one ankle. "Besides, any man fool enough to leave your tender arms for my strumpet of a sister, is asking for whatever comes his way."

Julianna could scarcely believe what she was hearing. When Laurence's words finally sank in, her temper reared. "If you think my protests are counterfeit, you are very much mistaken, Laurence Bayard! Now, take your hands off me!" She kicked out.

Laurence did loosen his grip on her ankle, only to grasp her about the waist. She could feel his lips on hers—a sickeningly familiar sensation. Unlike Jerome's, Laurence's importunities provoked more rage than fear. With every ounce of strength, she pushed him away and gained her freedom.

The fool only laughed and panted. "You are every bit the hot-blooded vixen I imagined. I can hardly wait until you drop all pretense and channel the passion of these denials into fiery lovemaking!"

She dodged behind the stone wall. He vaulted over it, catching her again. "I doubt your cold fish of a husband has ever ignited this fervor in you. Listen to your heart, Julianna. Give yourself to me!"

"For the last time, Laurence, take your hands *off* me!" She twisted out of his embrace, delivering a sound slap to his cheek. "You have no idea what feelings I have for my husband. Edmund is ten times the man you will ever be, you conceited dandy!"

Her words erased the laughter from Laurence's face. It was replaced by petulant rage. "We'll see about that, shall we? I mean to have you, Julianna, willing or no!"

Laurence leapt at her, knocking Julianna backward to the ground. His weight pressed the breath from her lungs. She could feel his lips on her neck and bosom. She heard the fabric of her bodice tearing. She felt his fumbling hand push aside the cloth. Blood pounded in her ears. *How dare you, Laurence Bayard* it pulsed. *I will kill you if I have to!*

Edmund's horse raced through the village, scattering irate poultry in its wake. He managed to ride halfway up the tor before the peril of low-hanging branches forced him to dismount. Springing from the saddle, he charged up the path. As each long stride carried him toward the crest of the tor, the heat of his wrath intensified. Small wonder his young wife had packed him off to London with such obvious relief. Small wonder she'd refused to accompany him in the first place. Wanted to keep up her charity work, had she? Wanted to help Mrs. Tully, had she? Bah! Did she think he'd just tumbled off a turnip barrow?

What she'd truly wanted was a clear field to indulge her girlish fancy for that unprincipled cub, Laurence. Edmund had seen all the signs—the covert glances, the flirtatious smirks exchanged when they'd thought his back was turned. He paused for a moment to tether his flagging horse. A sound floated down from the summit of the tor, amplified in the stillness. At first Edmund thought it was the peal of a bell. Then, sick with outrage, he recognized Julianna's laughter.

Without knowing what he meant to do, Edmund advanced up the path. As he approached the abbey clearing, he hung back in the shelter of the trees. With the stealthy tread he'd learned in the South Seas, Edmund circled the clearing, following the sound of voices. At last he could see them. Julianna sat on the grass, resting against a low wall. Laurence reclined beside her, holding her hand to his lips. Edmund watched in horrified fascination as Julianna drew her hand back with counterfeit modesty. So this was the manner of shallow gallantry that wooed women nowadays, he reflected bitterly. The poetic quotations of a middle-aged scholar must seem pathetically quaint courting by comparison.

Just then, Lord Marlwood let out a hoot of derisive laughter. Edmund knew they must be enjoying a private joke at his expense. Part of him longed to skulk away and go to ground like an injured animal, nursing his wounds in private. Yet he could not tear his eyes away from the painful scene before him. Laurence slipped his hand under Julianna's skirt to fondle her ankle. To Edmund's surprise, she spoke sharply and kicked Laurence away. He lunged forward, kissing her hungrily. Pushing him off, she scrambled to her feet, putting the wall between them. Laurence sprang over it and caught her, laughing at her pretended reluctance. Twisting out of the bold buck's embrace, she dealt him a resounding smack on the cheek.

"Laurence, take your hands off me!"

The obvious sincerity of her words released Edmund from his paralysis. However she might have encouraged him, Julianna obviously had not reckoned Lord Marlwood for the utter cad he was. No matter how she had hurt him or played him a fool, Edmund would not suffer the likes of Laurence Bayard to lay hands upon her in such a way. He had already broken cover, bearing down on them like the righteous fire of damnation, when Laurence knocked Julianna to the ground and mounted a more determined assault.

* * *

Bringing her nails up to rake his face, Julianna felt Laurence's body lift off her. As her vision cleared, she could see Edmund holding him by the collars of his shirt and waistcoat. She had never heard Edmund's voice like this—throaty, with fierce savagery barely held in cheek.

"What do you think you are doing, Laurence?" With each word he shook the younger man.

Inches off the ground, Lord Marlwood's feet flailed. "Truly, Cousin Edmund, this is all a misunderstanding. Julianna—"

"Shut your mouth!" Edmund snarled "Never let me hear my wife's name upon your lips again. If I do, so help me, I will cut your tongue out and feed it to you!" His voice died away to a hoarse whisper. "If you ever lay hands upon my wife again, can you guess what I will do?"

"Kill me?" Laurence squeaked.

"That goes without saying," Edmund replied, his voice soft and reasonable, chillingly at odds with his murderous threats. "But I warn you, it will be a leisurely and imaginative death."

With that, Edmund hurled the younger man some distance. Laurence landed heavily. Julianna's last sight of him was a scuttling crab-walk, to remove himself from Edmund's sight as fast as humanly possible.

Not bothering to watch his cousin's ignominious departure, Edmund turned on Julianna, his eyes blazing. Following his gaze, she realized that her naked bosom was clearly visible through the tatters of her bodice and shift. Before she could bring her hands up to cover herself, Edmund removed his coat. Flinging it to the ground at her feet, he pointedly turned his back. Julianna hastily pulled it around herself.

"Edmund, how fortunate you arrived when you did!" she gasped. "However did you find us?"

He swung back to face her. "Mrs. Tully told me where you had gone." His tone blasted her like hoarfrost. "And with whom. Was it fortunate for you that I arrived? What exactly were you playing at, accompanying a man like Laurence to this distant spot? Small wonder he expected to have his way with you."

Julianna's rage at Laurence had not had time to dissipate. Edmund's tone infuriated her further. She breathed deeply, trying to calm herself. "Laurence called on me while you were away. He was very amiable company. As a married woman and a member of the family, I had no reason to suspect his intentions."

Her explanation did nothing to mollify Edmund. "Naiveté can be a charming quality, Julianna. But in your case it borders on stupidity! Did you not realize that Laurence makes a specialty of seducing married women? As for family connections, you of all women should know there are men for whom that is no impediment."

He would cast her at fault in this?

"Forgive me for believing the Bayards a more honorable breed of men. I spent a good deal of time in Crispin's company, unchaperoned, without any fear of his taking such liberties. You have been scrupulously respectful toward me in all the time I have lived under your roof. Even with every legal right to—"

"You would do well in future not to overestimate any man's honor where women are concerned. You needn't play the innocent, either. I have watched these two weeks, while you have preened and flirted with that young jackanapes." The volume of his voice rose with each word, and with each word he stepped ominously toward her. "I am sure he expected you to greet his attentions with enthusiasm."

He grasped her by the shoulders. Through the light fabric of his summer coat, she could feel his powerful fingers pressing implacably into her flesh.

"Is this the way you keep faith with Crispin? For, by Heaven, if it is—you can leave my house within the hour!"

Julianna had been held thus before, by men hungry for the pleasures of her body. With Jerome her reaction had been terror. With Laurence, rage. But as Edmund held her, his fierce gaze boring into her very soul, she felt only a rush of aching surrender. She wanted him to commit every unseemly act she would have died denying Laurence or Jerome. She wanted Edmund to take her, to use her as he had used Vanessa.

She flinched at Edmund's words and at the thought of him

with another woman. She hated herself for the carnal desire that coursed through her. She hated him for kindling this forbidden fire in her blood. Most of all, she hated Edmund for not wanting her as she so desperately wanted him.

"I thought—" Julianna looked pointedly at the hands that clenched her "—you held yourself a cut above any cowardly dog who would harm a woman."

Edmund's grip slackened and his arms fell to his sides. "There are wounds that have nothing to do with blood or bruises."

Their quarrel might have ended there, but Julianna's passions were aroused. Verbal combat was her only safe outlet for the explosive mix of fervor and fury Edmund had ignited in her.

"If Laurence gave himself any excuse for trying to seduce me, it was surely that a cheated wife might wish to have revenge upon her husband in kind."

"Cheated wife?" Edmund looked over his shoulder, lip curled. "What foolishness are you talking?"

"I am neither a fool nor a child." A rebellious Julianna returned fire. "Have any woman you like, Edmund Fitzhugh, but don't insult my intelligence by skulking off to London to indulge in your philandering."

"Now you are talking like a child. Making up nonsense."

"Don't bother to deny you went up to London to bed Vanessa. Laurence told me as much."

"After this, you would trust his word?" Edmund laughed scornfully. "If I intended an assignation with some other woman, would I have asked you to come with me to London? I assumed Vanessa was here in Marlwood during my absence. I never laid eyes upon her the whole time."

She had no answer for that. Edmund pressed his advantage. "Furthermore, I will have any woman I care to. Depend upon it, I will not bother with a hot and troublesome journey to London simply to spare your delicate sensibilities."

A smarting blush rose in Julianna's cheeks.

"Come." Edmund surveyed the darkening sky. "We should get home while there's light to negotiate the path."

"No, thank you." Pulling his coat more tightly about her,

Julianna swept past Edmund with all the hauteur she could muster. "I will find my own way home, as I would have done if you never had intervened. What makes you think I was in such desperate peril? I've preserved my virtue against a man far more capable of violating it than that fatuous puppy! If Lord Marlwood had persisted, I'd have made certain he left Abbot's Tor incapable ever of siring an heir to his title."

As she made her way down the hill, unshed tears of indignation stung Julianna's eyes. Her cheeks burned. With every step, Edmund's damning denunciation rang in her ears—*Is this the way you keep faith with Crispin?*

Chapter Seventeen

As Julianna swept past him with regal disdain, Edmund stood transfixed, shaking with the effort to fight down his own fury. How dare she turn on him, after he'd come rushing to defend her dubious honor? What presumption. What audacity. What a woman! He couldn't stifle a grudging flicker of admiration as he watched her stalk down the path without a backward glance.

Most women who'd been through what she had—physically assaulted by one man and verbally abused by another—would have taken refuge in a swoon or a fit of hysterical tears. Julianna had stood her ground, battling him to a bloody draw. As for Lord Marlwood, on calmer reflection Edmund admitted his intervention had likely saved Laurence from more harm than Julianna.

Stirred from his musing, he raced to retrieve his horse and to follow her at a discreet distance. A rising tide of chagrin rapidly quenched his anger. He had allowed jealousy to make him break his promises to Julianna—never to lay violent hands upon her and never to make her fear for her virtue. He had seen the momentary spasm of fear in her face as he'd held her. He'd felt the tremor of her body beneath his hands. Feminine instinct must have warned her that in spite of his self-righteous protestations on Crispin's behalf, he'd wanted her for himself. Once again, he'd been ready to wrest by force what she never would surrender willingly. Did that make him any less a cad than his cousin?

Edmund winced at the memory of his behavior. On top of everything else, why had he ever uttered that callow conceit about bedding any woman he cared to? Pitiful excuse for a libertine he'd make—pining for the one woman he never could have, yet prepared to accept no substitute. Foolish as he felt for having said it, Edmund had no wish to take back his empty boast. Perhaps it would distract Julianna from recognizing his obvious desire for her. A darker purpose he could scarcely bring himself to admit—that his words might tempt Julianna to see her reserved, middle-aged husband in the unlikely role of lover.

Fortunately, the villagers were all indoors, tucking into hearty harvest suppers as Edmund and Julianna passed through Marlwood, quiet as ghosts. Otherwise, Charlie Warbeck's gimlet eye would surely have picked up signs of discord and they'd never have heard the end of it. On the long walk down Abbot's Tor, Julianna's temper had deserted her, leaving only cold humiliation in its wake. She doubted Edmund would lie to her about Vanessa. Laurence, on the other hand, had every reason to lie, hoping to goad her into a spiteful betrayal of her husband.

Her cheeks blazed as she recalled Edmund's blistering denunciation. Could it be true? He had accused her of leading Laurence on. Laurence had said as much himself. Jerome had always maintained that she provoked his horrid importunities. Was she no better than a careless wanton, prepared to make a conquest of any man who came within her reach?

As she made her way up the lane to Abbot's Leigh, the proud tilt of her chin began to droop. She could hear Edmund leading his horse a ways behind. Only the thought of his gaze upon her kept Julianna from breaking into a run and hurling herself into the comforting arms of home. She might be a Fitzhugh in name only, but the Ramsays were not without their own pride.

Certain that Julianna had gained the safety of Abbot's Leigh, Edmund stabled his horse, gruffly dismissing the stable boy he'd greeted so affectionately a few hours before. After loading the manger with a liberal measure of fodder and a double ration of oats, he unharnessed the beast and groomed it meticulously. That minor act of contrition accomplished, Edmund slipped into the house through a side door. He cursed under his breath as he met Brock on the stairs. Refusing to meet the steward's inquiring stare, Edmund grunted that he was too tired to take supper and that he planned to retire immediately. Fortunately, Brock had enough discretion not to press him about the events of the afternoon, or ask the whereabouts of his coat.

With a sigh of relief, Edmund gained his bedchamber and began to peel off his riding clothes. Brock had evidently anticipated his needs after a long, dusty journey, for a tub of water was set up in the corner of the room. Easing himself into the tepid bath, Edmund took up a cake of Mrs. Tully's goose-grease soap and vigorously scrubbed himself. Could any amount of washing expunge the stench of lust and jealousy he exuded? Edmund doubted it.

With each swipe of the wet cloth across his skin, Edmund acknowledged his own responsibility for what had happened. He should have known better than to leave Julianna alone at Abbot's Leigh with a predator like Laurence sniffing about. He should never have given his cousin reason to think Julianna a disgruntled wife—fair game for his attentions. He'd been a fool, Edmund chided himself, lapping up Vanessa's flattery.

What if Julianna had fallen sincerely in love with Laurence? Could anyone expect better of a mere girl, separated from her fiancé for almost a year? Many years older and wiser, Edmund had come to love where he had no business loving. It ill-behooved him to sit in judgment. Yet he had judged. Had condemned. Had threatened to cast her out. Might she take him at his word? Suddenly, Edmund's bathwater felt icy-cold. He shivered. What if Julianna decided she could no longer stay where she was not trusted or respected? Edmund Fitzhugh clapped an iron hand to his mouth. Dear God, what had he done?

"Milady, your pretty gown—whatever happened?"

"Do go away, Gwenyth, and mind you say nothing about this to anyone. Tell Mrs. Tully I won't be down for supper."

"Aye, ma'am." Gwenyth hurried off without further warning.

Casting off Edmund's coat as though the cloth burned her

skin, Julianna threw herself on the bed and indulged in a brief spate of passionate tears. Having vented her feelings, she wiped her face and began to undress for bed. Catching a glimpse of herself in the glass, she paused for a moment to take stock. Her upper arms had begun to bruise where Edmund's fingers had dug into her flesh. The creamy rounding of her breasts showed through the wreck of her shift, one tawny pink nipple flaunting itself. Though she blushed fiercely at the thought of Edmund seeing her thus, Julianna could not help wishing the sight of her body had moved him—excited him.

Closing her eyes, she imagined what it might be like, giving herself to Edmund. She could almost feel his hands, strong and supple, exploring the sweet secrets of her body. She could almost taste his kisses. She could almost hear him caressing her with the warm, mellow cadence of his voice.

Julianna's eyes flew open. The voice she'd heard in her dreams for months now—the voice of that shadowy lover she'd assumed to be Crispin—had belonged to Edmund all along. In a flash of anguished clarity, Julianna understood. What she felt for Edmund was no fancy. She'd called it gratitude at first, dismissing a definite physical attraction as mere curiosity. Later she'd called it pity and duty. Finally, she'd clothed it in the deceptive cover of affectionate companionship. She'd fooled herself with that innocuous label, until the green pulsating dawn at Titania's Bower had made it a mockery. Still she had tried to defend herself against the truth, calling it lust. Infatuation. Madness. Reluctantly, Julianna realized that she had long since fallen in love with Sir Edmund Fitzhugh.

How could this be? Edmund was her sanctuary, her companion, her friend. *Your husband,* whispered a mocking little voice in the back of her mind—Vanessa's voice.

True, but she still belonged to Crispin. How could she have let herself fall in love with another man, particularly this one? Why hadn't she seen what was happening and stopped herself?

Vanessa's voice came again. *Because you are a child, and have no experience in such matters.*

Julianna turned from the glass with a shudder. She half fancied she could see Vanessa's exquisite features mocking her from her own face. Tearing off her shift, she donned a modestly enveloping nightgown and crawled into bed. Sleep would not come.

What would she do? In Edmund's eyes, she was his nephew's wife. Her love for him amounted to adultery. If either man ever suspected the truth, all three of them would suffer. The disdain she had seen on Edmund's face today would be nothing to his reaction on learning that she had betrayed Crispin. Knowing Edmund, he would take the blame upon himself and feel besmirched by her inconstancy. She would have caused an irreparable breach between them. Neither Edmund nor Crispin would ever forgive her.

Only one course lay open to her, though Julianna shrank from the prospect. Methodically, assiduously, she must root out this foolish yearning for Edmund and concentrate on rekindling her love for Crispin. She had every confidence she could do it. After all, contrary to popular custom, she had educated herself the equal of any man. She had survived years of Jerome's abuse and escaped his plans for her downfall. She had braved the enmity of the Fitzhugh servants, rescued Edmund from the brink of death and won her enemies round. Now, Julianna's whole future rested on her ability to make her heart submit to her will.

Perhaps she should start by encouraging Edmund to look elsewhere for female companionship. The hurtful words he'd hurled at her on Abbot's Tor suggested he was already thinking in that direction. Julianna had heard of wives who condoned, even chose, their husband's mistresses as an exercise in power and security. Certainly, she knew of one woman well disposed to such an arrangement, attractive and close at hand. Yet, rather than watch Edmund take Vanessa as his mistress, Julianna was prepared to let him cast her out.

In the empty hours past midnight, Edmund woke in a state of rampant arousal. Throbbing with insatiable need, he shrank from recalling the dream that had induced it. He'd dreamed himself on the tor again, watching Laurence seduce Julianna. Rage had boiled in him. Pulling his cousin off Julianna, Edmund had begun to beat him viciously. Gradually he'd realized he was striking not Laurence, but Crispin. That knowledge did nothing to ease his blood lust. He'd hit Crispin again and again, until the lad had crumpled at his feet.

Julianna had thrown herself over Crispin, shielding him with her own body. Her eyes had blazed with hate as she'd called Edmund a madman and a murderer. He'd reached out to calm her, but his hands had yielded to the tender temptation of her flesh. Her face contorted in a grimace of loathing, she had pulled away from him. "Villain! Lecher! You're no better than Laurence and Jerome—using kinship to coerce me into your bed!"

Before Edmund could open his mouth to protest, Crispin rose behind Julianna. This time, he bore the cold, grim aspect of his grandfather and Edmund's father, the Reverend Crispin Fitzhugh. Pointing a long bony finger of accusation, the clergyman thundered, "Thou shalt not covet thy nephew's wife."

The shock of facing eternal damnation, in the shape of his fiercesome father, jolted Edmund awake. Heartsick, he acknowledged the repellent truth—love for Julianna had made him Crispin's rival. The young man he'd loved like a son and a brother, he now envied with all his heart. In the dark silence, Edmund Fitzhugh gave a bitter, mirthless laugh, remembering how he had dared denounce Julianna for breaking faith with Crispin.

Julianna slept fitfully and woke the next morning with a sense of foreboding. Remembering her quarrel with Edmund, she wondered if there would even be a friendship to salvage. Could he possibly forgive her silly flirtation with Laurence or her malicious accusations about his conduct with Vanessa?

His head buried in the pages of *Gentleman's Magazine,* Edmund was eating his breakfast when Julianna came down to the dining room. He did not bother to look up when she sat down at the table. As the silence between them swelled, Julianna picked at her porridge and fruit. She cleared her throat once or twice, trying to draw his attention so she could begin her apol-

ogy. He continued to ignore her, occasionally reaching around
his magazine to help himself to more coffee.

Finally, Julianna's temper flared. "Damn you, Edmund Fitzhugh!" She threw her cutlery down on her plate, making a
terrible din.

Gentleman's Magazine lowered an inch or two. The gray
eyes that peered over it were fully attentive. They held something else as well. In anyone but Sir Edmund Fitzhugh, Julianna
might have mistaken it for fear.

"Scold me. Lecture me. Throw me out the front door. But
at least have the courtesy to acknowledge my existence!"

Edmund closed his reading and laid it to one side of his plate.
"I thought," he replied quietly, "that after my churlish outburst
yesterday, you would be on your way back to London, com-
plaining of my treatment to your stepbrother."

Was Edmund prepared to own some of the blame? Then he
might accept her apology after all. Overwhelmed with relief,
Julianna began to laugh.

"Complain of you to Jerome? Hardly! Perhaps, if you had
squeezed my neck rather than my arm…"

Seeing an answering look of relief in his eyes, she added.
"Besides, if I did anything to encourage Laurence, you had
every right to be angry. I swear he means nothing to me. I
never would have gone with him, had I guessed his intentions.
I used poor judgment, for you warned me often enough what
kind of man he is. He looks so much like Crispin, I couldn't
believe he would do me any harm."

Edmund rose from his place and moved toward her, taking
her hand. "You are gracious to excuse me so easily. I shouldn't
condemn my cousin when I have behaved so badly. I am heartily ashamed of myself and I beg your forgiveness."

Julianna looked away, not trusting herself to answer those
beseeching eyes. Purging this man from her heart would be far
more difficult than she had imagined.

"There's fault on both sides." Giving his hand a reassuring
squeeze, she quickly withdrew her fingers. "I never should have
repeated those lies Laurence told me about you and Vanessa."

She silently pleaded with him to deny Laurence's charges, to refute them so totally she would have no choice but to believe.

"I promise you," Edmund said softly, "I saw nothing of Vanessa while I was in London. Perhaps she did have something planned, much as I doubt she has any real interest in me. I can see where Laurence would have seized upon the situation, to press his advantage with you."

She did believe him and it was balm to her soul. "I was foolish to listen to Laurence." Julianna gave a brittle laugh. "I admit I was rather jealous to think of the two of you together." She tried to keep her voice light, to disguise the truth of her words. She'd always found a subtle reinterpretation of fact more believable than flat denial. "It's terribly childish, but that woman gets at me in the most disconcerting way. I couldn't bear the thought of her taunting me with having stolen my husband."

Apparently taken in by her explanation, Edmund pulled a wry face. "I may have let my feelings of pity for Vanessa blind me to what she has become."

"Pity?" Julianna shook her head. "You mentioned that once before and I still do not understand. The dowager countess of Sutton-Courtney has everything a woman could want."

"Everything but what she wants most. Though you would hardly believe it, hearing her talk now, Vanessa cared very deeply for the young husband she lost. One subject of which you will never hear her speak is the child she lost. Vanessa was a favorite of my dear Alice, who feared for her reason at the time. Since then, Vanessa is as you have seen her—beautiful, charming company, but shallow and empty. A sad waste."

Julianna couldn't think what to say. This revelation skewed her whole picture of Vanessa. Had she known of it before, she might have made allowances. But after all that had passed, she doubted anything could soften her attitude toward the voluble, predatory creature.

The breach between them mended, at least superficially, Edmund and Julianna returned to their breakfasts, now grown cold. Julianna fell to musing upon the events of the previous day.

She did not realize that her face had broken into a sardonic smile, until Edmund brought her up sharp.

"Pray, what do you find so droll in Mrs. Tully's porridge?"

"I was minding the look on Lawrence's face, when you were shaking him about...like a rat caught in the jaws of a mastiff!"

Edmund replied with a throaty canine growl, followed by a rueful chuckle. As Julianna joined in his laughter, the intense feelings of the previous day were dissipated, at least on the surface.

Would she ever be truly at ease with Edmund again, Julianna wondered wistfully, now that her heart was engaged?

Chapter Eighteen

Loath to leave Abbot's Leigh, Julianna pressed her nose against the carriage window to catch a final glimpse of the dear old place. Her breath left a patch of fog on the cold glass. Though she reminded herself they would be back again in a few months, it still hurt—bidding farewell to this joyous summer. Better they return to London, she conceded reluctantly, if she hoped to make good her vow of distancing herself from Edmund. In the dying weeks of summer, she had struggled to pull herself from the emotional vortex into which she'd so innocently slipped.

Undertaking all of Arabella's parish work had been her excuse for spending less time with Edmund. She'd spent her mornings in the kitchen. Concentrating ruthlessly on the tasks at hand, she'd compounded calves'-foot jelly, apple butter and other delicacies. Mrs. Tully had never again found cause to scold her for "mooning and moping." In the afternoon Julianna had paid her calls in the village, dispensing the parting gifts she'd prepared. She had contrived to have company every evening, and to the request for a play reading, she'd quickly suggested the unromantic *Macbeth*.

Twice only, had Julianna abandoned her self-imposed penance—at the harvest ball and the Michaelmas Fair in Farnham. The latter had been a rare, sweet day. She and Gwenyth had run about eager as children, with Edmund and Brock trailing behind like two indulgent, often exasperated sires. There had been interesting wares for sale and all manner of refreshments. Entertainment had included a racing meet, morris dancing and a Romany fortune-teller. Late in the afternoon, as Edmund and Brock openly scoffed, Julianna had paid her coin and extended her palm to the old woman.

"You are musical. You play a lute—or a harp?" The woman poked a plump finger, none too clean, at Julianna's hand. "Also very clever, reading and writing."

Julianna shook her head in wonder. Many women played musical instruments, but the harp was unusual. As for being literate, that was too uncommon to be guessed. Then she noticed a faint stain of ink on one knuckle and the telltale harper's calluses on her fingertips. Julianna smiled to herself.

"Your mount of Apollo, very full. This mean wealth."

Julianna thought for a moment. Her thick gold wedding band would certainly suggest affluence. She found it amusing to second-guess the palm reader.

"See this line?" the old woman continued. "It mean long life. These marks mean children—one, two, three. Your mount of Venus is very strong and you have also the ring. You love too much. Joy it will bring, but also much sorrow. See where line of fate cross your heart line? You will have important choice that will mark your whole life. You must follow your heart."

A chill went through Julianna. Snatching her hand away, she fled the fortune-teller's tent. When the others had questioned her, she replied lightly, "Just the usual foolishness... riches...long life. What anyone would wish to hear."

To herself, Julianna had scoffed. Follow her heart? That capricious, inconstant organ was no fit guide.

As they drove past Bayard Hall, the carriage gave a lurch on the muddy, rutted road. The Hall had stood empty for several weeks, ever since the evening Lord Marlwood had skulked down from Abbot's Tor and made a hasty departure. The dowager countess of Sutton-Courtney had never returned from her sojourn to the city.

Edmund pressed the soles of his boots against the heated

bricks on the floor of the carriage. The weather had grown cold in the past week, with the ominous threat of approaching winter. His relationship with Julianna had taken a markedly cool turn as well. Ever since that day on Abbot's Tor, when he'd frightened her by betraying the true nature and intensity of his feelings, Edmund had felt this cautious chill descend between them. It had cut him to the quick.

Julianna had once felt safe with him, as she had never felt safe with any other man. In his remorse, Edmund knew she had trusted him more than her own beloved father, who had blindly harbored his serpent of a stepson, or Crispin, who had abandoned her to unforeseen calamity. He had shattered that fragile trust by momentarily exposing his passionate desire for her. Since then, he'd tried to keep his distance. It had not been easy.

Against his better judgment, he'd let her cajole him into resurrecting the old tradition of a harvest ball at Abbot's Leigh. Julianna had thrown herself into the preparations, tantalizing him with glimpses of their former sweet camaraderie. She'd had all the furniture moved from the Great Parlor and the floor sanded for dancing. She'd engaged musicians, ordered down provisions from London and played kitchen maid to Mrs. Tully—cooking up a sumptuous buffet.

An autumn rainstorm had not dampened the enthusiasm of the large crowd who turned out, all decked in their modest finery. The Trowbridges had come, the vicar's wife looking pale but quietly radiant, eager to enjoy the evening's society. Thinking of his own mother and fearing for the health of Julianna's friend, Edmund had casually suggested hiring a curate to take over the lady's parish duties. Julianna had greeted his simple gesture with extravagant gratitude.

Throwing her arms around his neck and pressing her cheek to his, she'd exclaimed, "Oh Edmund, you are the kindest man alive! Anyone can give what is asked. You care enough to recognize the need and supply it before anyone thinks to ask."

She had quickly drawn back, perhaps frightened of rousing his unwelcome ardor with her impulsive embrace. He had stammered and reddened and dismissed his offer as a trifle. To himself, Edmund admitted that he'd gladly fund a whole battalion of curates, if it pleased her so. The light of Julianna's smile cast a warm glow over the whole evening. When he'd led off the first dance with her on his arm, it was all he could do to keep from thrusting out his chest and strutting like a proud old cockerel. He'd forgotten how much he enjoyed dancing. One of his few social graces, he'd often employed a dance invitation to fend off the treacherous intricacies of polite conversation.

As they concluded a lively round of "All the Flowers of the Broom," a flushed and breathless Julianna cast him a mischievous glance. "Why, Edmund Fitzhugh, you have been withholding on me! I never imagined you had such a light step on the dance floor."

During the evening he kept a weather eye out for Julianna, who often seemed to be in several places at once. She'd be passing the time with Charlie Warbeck and old Mrs. Drummond, encouraging their tales of bygone days evoked by the portrait-hung walls. Then he'd catch her refreshing someone's glass at the puncheon. The next minute, she'd be prancing through a set of "Linden Lane," cheerily suffering the clumsy dancing of a stout yeoman or his overgrown son. Once or twice, Edmund managed to catch her eye and exchange a wink or a conspiratorial smile. The rest of the time, he was content simply to watch her. Though she might never be his wife in the truest sense, Edmund took comfort in knowing Julianna was truly mistress of Abbot's Leigh.

As their carriage rattled over the last mile of old road approaching Guildford, the silence and tension between Julianna and Edmund lengthened unbearably.

Edmund cleared his throat. "Now that we have a bit of time and privacy, perhaps we should discuss your stepbrother and what we are to do about him."

"I've given it some thought." She seized upon the topic eagerly. "I believe Jerome stole from my father all the time he was supposed to be managing his affairs. He must be made to pay for that…as much as for anything else."

Edmund shook his head. "With your father dead and Jerome one of his principal legatees, it would be hard to prosecute."

"I see what you mean." Julianna lapsed into pensive silence. They were well along the Guildford road to London when she spoke up again.

"If he was mismanaging Papa's money and properties, perhaps he is stealing from others as well."

"I don't doubt it," replied Edmund. "Though that could be difficult to prove. He is probably far more careful to cover his tracks when dealing with strangers."

"Could we catch him in a ruse? Offer to let him invest part of your fortune, then wait for him to help himself?"

"A fine suggestion, but that would take longer than I am prepared to wait. I want that blackguard brought to justice as swiftly as possible, so he will no longer pose a threat to you. Besides, I managed to convince him of my goodwill once. I doubt my acting skills would extend to an encore performance. Particularly now that I recognize what a specimen of vermin he is."

Julianna heaved a sigh. The outskirts of the city were just coming into view when her head snapped up, a golden gleam of triumph shining in her eyes. Edmund knew that gleam all too well from their chess matches. It meant checkmate.

"Papa's will," she announced. "Jerome forced me to marry you by claiming my dowry had gone to pay Papa's debts in bankruptcy."

Understanding dawned on Edmund. "Of course. It may have been just a ploy to do you out of your inheritance, and to punish you for not giving in to him. If there were no substantial creditors, and no bankruptcy, then I can prosecute him on your behalf." He thought for a moment. "I will enlist the help of your cousin, Francis, to…"

"What of me?" Julianna cried. "What can I do?"

"You have conceived of the plan, my crafty chess strategist." Edmund could not keep the warmth from his words. "Is that not enough?"

"No." A troubled frown creased her creamy brow. Edmund longed to smooth it away with a kiss. With many kisses. "I must play an active part in this. Can't you see that, Edmund?

I have to prove to Jerome—to myself—that I am no longer a child he can torment and terrify.''

''I know what it is to be held hostage by the past,'' he replied in quiet earnest. ''Very well. I promise you whatever part you can carry out without arousing Jerome's suspicion.''

Julianna stared out the window, her attention captured by the teeming life of London. As they progressed along the wider, more sedate thoroughfares of Westminster, Edmund spoke up again. ''Can it be only six months ago we left for Surrey? I, exhausted from the effort of walking down a flight of stairs?''

An unexpected smile illuminated Julianna's face. It took his breath away. ''Nowadays, you could easily run up those stairs with a hundredweight of coal slung over your shoulder!''

They both laughed at the mild exaggeration.

''Abbot's Leigh was your salvation,'' she chided. ''When I think of the fuss you raised against going...''

Edmund rolled his eyes. ''Women! Is it not enough they are always right, and so intolerably smug on that account? They have to rub a poor fellow's nose in it at every opportunity. 'Didn't I tell you?' and 'Wasn't I right all along?''

''No worse than men, who think they know best in everything. When a woman does manage to move heaven and earth to persuade them and it works out as she predicted—they pretend the idea was theirs all along. They never offer a word of thanks for avoiding the catastrophe that would have befallen if they had held to their own course.''

Laughing, Edmund held up his hands before her onslaught. ''I surrender. Charged and found guilty.'' He could not resist leaning forward and taking her hand. ''Besides, Abbot's Leigh deserves only part of the credit for my recovery. You have been my salvation, Julianna. Have I ever thanked you properly?''

He saw a brief quiver of panic erase her smile. Silently he cursed his own lack of restraint.

''Every day, in a hundred ways,'' she replied in a strained tone, pulling her fingers away. ''Look, we are home at last.'' There was no mistaking the relief in her voice.

Seeing Fitzhugh House, Edmund suddenly recalled what he'd wished, shortly before Julianna had come into his life. He had desired only the restoration of his health and a reason to live. In granting both those wishes, his winsome young wife had made him long for so much more.

"Look, we are home at last." Even as those words passed her lips, Julianna knew that nowhere but Abbot's Leigh would ever be home to her. Yet she welcomed the sight of Fitzhugh House. If Edmund had held her hand a moment longer, she might have lifted his hand, pressed it to her cheek and begged him to kiss her.

As she alighted from the carriage, Julianna recalled her first arrival in this courtyard, almost a year ago. Her extravagant sorrow and fear on the day of her wedding now seemed laughably childish. Brock ushered them in. He grudged Julianna a smile in return for her effusive greeting.

"Someone to see you, Captain—milady. In the parlor. Her Ladyship, the dowager countess of Sutton-Courtney."

Brock had barely made his announcement when Vanessa descended upon them. "Edmund! Julianna! My darlings, home at last! When Mr. Brock told me you'd be home today, I could do nothing but wait to welcome you. How was your journey? Roads too dreadful, no doubt? What a relief it must be to return to civilization. I have been starved for the sight of you. Edmund, I declare you grow younger with each passing day. At this rate, Julianna will soon be the one accused of robbing the cradle. Speaking of Julianna—my sweet child, I believe you have grown taller since we last met. Still growing up—how unutterably precious!"

The barrage of patter stunned Julianna speechless.

"Do close your mouths, my dears." Vanessa wagged a finger. "You look at me as if I were a trained bear, performing tricks in your parlor. Surely you didn't expect me to ignore your return to London? I know Laurence has behaved like an idiot and made himself thoroughly unwelcome. Does his banishment extend to me, as well?"

She turned to her cousin. "If you will recall, Edmund, I warned you that my brother would make a fool of himself over your charming young bride. I was mortified when I heard how he'd disgraced the family with his churlish behavior. Though I'd have given anything to see you both put the young coxcomb in his place.''

Julianna welcomed an interruption by the steward. ''A word with you, ma'am, if I may?''

''Certainly, Mr. Brock. Vanessa, will you take tea with us?''

''Too kind of you, my sweet, but I mustn't. You simply can't think how many calls I have yet to make. I meant only to stay long enough to welcome you and to invite Julianna along with me to my dressmaker's tomorrow. Your own seamstress does lovely work *à la mode anglaise,* my pet. But for the engagements of the coming season, I would suggest true haute couture.''

''But we have no engagements planned.''

''Oh, my angel!'' Vanessa threw up her hands. ''I have already filled the calendar on your behalf for months ahead. The lucky few who have met you are simply dying for want of closer acquaintance. The rest are avid for introductions. The first opera of the season opens this week at Covent Garden, and Drury Lane has a marvelous program planned. Lord Peterborough is hosting an evening of chamber music at month's end and I could not begin to oblige all the dinner engagements offered. So you see, a fashionable new wardrobe is the order of the day.''

She cocked her fan at her cousin. ''Pray, don't glower so, Edmund. If you would take half the money you lavish upon those myriad charities and put it toward your wife's costume like a true gentleman, there's not a lady in London could rival her. Tomorrow then, Julianna.''

As his cousin breezed off, Edmund chuckled. ''She is well wound today. At times like this, an encounter with Vanessa is like a spell of bad weather at sea! Don't feel that you must humor her with this fashion nonsense or the social whirl. Just give the word and I'll put a stop to her high jinks.''

''No need,'' Julianna replied. ''I should have some new dresses made and I'd be foolish to refuse the tutelage I could receive from Vanessa. Much as she irritates me at times, I admit your cousin is always elegantly turned out. If we must winter in London, we might as well enjoy ourselves.''

As promised, the dowager countess called the next day shortly after noon. She eagerly accepted Julianna's offer of a cup of tea before they ventured out to her dressmaker. Knowing something of Vanessa's tragic past, Julianna tried to make allowances for her. In spite of that, there were times when the lady's patronizing speeches goaded her beyond endurance. Once or twice she had risen with a hot retort, only to lapse back into stunned bemusement, unable to get a word in.

''Your own suite of rooms—how heavenly! Every woman in a civilized household should have a little pied-à-terre. I would never have recognized them as Cousin Alice's. After she died, Edmund kept her rooms exactly as she left them. And so many books! Cousin Alice would have been at home with them, being so well read herself. A woman of simple tastes but the most understanding heart.''

It was the first time Julianna had heard the dowager countess utter a sentiment that sounded wholly sincere. Vanessa appeared to catch the slip, for her next remark was obviously calculated to divert. Raising her hand to twitching lips, she cast a sly glance at the door. ''Do you not find that drafty old gallery a terrible bother? Getting back and forth between your apartment and Edmund's, I mean. Tell me, does he come to you to avail himself of a night's pleasures, or are you summoned to him?''

This again? Julianna opened her mouth to offer her usual blushing, maidenly evasion. Then, some imp piqued her to reply archly, ''What makes you think I do not summon my husband to attend me?''

''Well done, my dear!'' Vanessa laughed heartily. ''Well done, indeed!'' Julianna wondered if she had just caught Edmund's cousin in another unintentional display of sincerity.

Their afternoon with Vanessa's modiste proved an education for Julianna. The dowager countess never minced matters.

''Remember, Clothilde, Lady Fitzhugh is my special protégée. You must ensure that she is the sensation of fashion this season. Her husband has more money than he knows what to do with, so expense is no object. See that your fabrics are only the finest. None of that refuse from Spitalfields!''

As the seamstress compiled some sketches and swatches of cloth, Vanessa turned to Julianna. ''Clothilde is always up on the latest Continental fashions. We met several years ago when I was in Paris. She and her sister were in business together, though how they managed, I will never know. The French are such charming people, unequaled in elegance and wit. However, the aristocrats make it a point of honor never to pay tradesmen.''

Vanessa contemplated a bolt of olive-green brocade, then shook her head decisively. ''I persuaded Clothilde that she would fare better in London. Marie-Charlotte stayed behind in Paris and sends her sister word of the latest French fashions. Clothilde obliges likewise. The French are positively mad for anything *à la mode anglaise.* As we seek to emulate their elegance, they wish to recapture our simplicity.''

''It seems difficult to imagine,'' Julianna offered.

''Just so!'' Vanessa rolled her eyes. ''Yet it is the same in everything. Why, when I was there, can you guess the latest rage in the ballrooms of Paris? Nothing but the rude country dances I learned as a child in Surrey. Of course they were called *contredanses* and performed at a slower pace with certain refinements. Still, they were nothing more than the old 'Greensleeves' and 'Sir Roger de Coverly.' I pray this wretched Austrian succession soon gets resolved, so I may return to the salons of Paris. *C'est triste, n'est-ce pas, Clothilde?*''

''*Ah oui, Madame la Comtesse,*'' agreed the dressmaker. ''Now if I may show young madame this color in a thick satin with a striped underdress. *Mais* for something *plus formal,* an ivory brocade, shot with thread of gold…''

The sketches all looked equally enchanting to Julianna, but Vanessa proved a most discerning critic.

''No.'' Her Ladyship tossed one sketch aside. ''The cut would never suit young madame. It would make her look positively consumptive. I quite like this one, perhaps with more contrast in the underdress. What can you show us by way of a *manteau?* We must see the milliner and the ferrier as well,

Julianna. And you do need gloves. Whatever have you been doing with your hands?''

Before Julianna knew it, they were leaving Madame Mercier flushed and smiling with a considerable order in hand, and an appointment for fittings within the fortnight. Vanessa seemed pleased with the afternoon's labor. While Julianna might have chosen one or two of the gowns Edmund's cousin had rejected out of hand, she admitted that Vanessa's choices would likely prove the more becoming.

Bidding Vanessa farewell at the door of Fitzhugh House, Julianna hurried to her rooms to remove her wrap. She could hardly wait to tell Edmund all about her outing. As she bustled back to join him for tea, the sound of voices stopped her at the top of the stairway.

''...between Clothilde and myself, we shall make our *jeune fille,* Julianna, into a true lady of fashion.''

Why was Vanessa still hanging about?

''There is nothing wrong with my wife as she is,'' replied Edmund. ''So do not meddle overmuch, Vanessa.''

''Of course not, Edmund darling. Just a bit of polish.''

''To paint the lily—''

Vanessa cut him off. ''Never without an apt word to quote, are you, my love? Can you truly be satisfied with this slip of a girl? I always thought you a man who would admire a some-what riper beauty.'' Her voice was low and seductive. Julianna did not have to look to know that Vanessa was standing very close to Edmund. Impossibly alluring—perhaps irresistibly so.

Edmund's answer was not what she had expected. Offhand, slightly impatient, he replied, ''You may dispense with this pose, Vanessa. I wonder that you bother when no one is about to hear. Practicing, are you? The only reason you even play this ridiculous charade is the absolute assurance I would never take you at your word. A single amorous advance from me and you could not run away fast enough. We both know that.''

Vanessa had moved to the foot of the stair. Her whisper floated up to Julianna quite distinctly. Not intended for Edmund's ears and certainly not for his wife's, the words sounded bitter, yet somehow wistful. "Then perhaps you know less than you think, Edmund Fitzhugh."

Edmund could not have heard, for he continued in the same vein. "Furthermore, this whole mock flirtation is embarrassing to me, irritating to my wife and quite unworthy of a Bayard. Therefore, it will cease immediately. Is that clear?"

An instant of silence was shattered by the crack of a sharp slap. "There is a limit to what I will take, Edmund, even from you!" Feet flew across the marble floor of the entry hall and the heavy front door thudded shut.

Gingerly, Julianna peeked out over the balustrade. Looking thoroughly bemused, Edmund stood there, holding a hand to his offended cheek. "And I from you, Vanessa."

Chapter Nineteen

Some days later, as the autumn sun was sinking, Edmund strode into the common room of the Chapterhouse, his latent military instincts roused to vigilance. Looking around, he recalled how, in this very place, he'd maneuvered Jerome Skeldon into letting him marry Julianna. With any luck, their new intrigue against that foul bounder would meet with similar success. A welcoming fire blazed in the front hearth, pots of coffee and chocolate steaming on the hob. Their appetizing pungency permeated the room, along with tobacco smoke and the odor of damp woolens.

Edmund edged his way between two of the narrow trestle tables that ran the length of the room. Clusters of men sat smoking pipes, talking in muted tones, drinking their coffee and reading newspapers by the flickering candlelight. Scanning the crowd, Edmund noted the presence of many regular patrons with approval. It was unlikely anyone would recognize the man whom he awaited, or grasp the significance of their meeting.

"Upon my life, Sir Edmund Fitzhugh. I almost didn't recognize you." Mr. Millar, the bookseller, clasped his hand warmly. "I heard you'd returned from the country looking fine and fit. Glad to see for myself the truth of those reports. Marriage certainly agrees with you."

Edmund smiled warmly and easily. "I would be the last man on earth to deny it."

Lowering himself into his accustomed corner seat, he ordered a cup of chocolate and a copy of the *Craftsman,* keeping his eyes trained upon the door. His surveillance soon bore fruit, when Francis Underhill peeked into the room, looking for all the world like a hare poking its twitching nose out of a thicket. Catching Edmund's eye, he raised his brows questioningly. Edmund replied with a slow nod. The coast was clear.

Turning, Francis signaled to someone lurking in the shadows behind him. Fortunately, at that moment a brace of writers entered the common room, talking in loud, animated tones. Francis and his companion trailed in their wake, eyes downcast and hats held to obscure their faces. They slid onto the bench opposite Edmund, hunching guiltily forward.

"Good news, Sir Edmund," Underhill hissed excitedly, his pale blue eyes glittering behind his spectacles.

"Not now." Edmund snapped his fingers and called for two dippers of punch. The last thing this jittery pair needed was a dose of strong Chapterhouse coffee. He cast a wary eye over Underhill's confederate, a small, sharp-featured fellow of indeterminate age with bad teeth and worse breath.

"Good news," Underhill repeated when the hostess had returned to her booth after dispensing their drinks. He shoved a much folded scrap of paper across the table. "That's the accounting from Baker's on the auction of Uncle Alistair's effects."

Edmund's eyes widened as he read the total. It was mostly his own money, to be sure. He'd instructed his agent to spare no expense in buying up any item that might conceivably have sentimental value for Julianna.

"I have made discreet inquiries in the City." Edmund pocketed the auctioneer's account. "I can find no evidence that Skeldon ever filed for bankruptcy on behalf of his stepfather's estate. If I could only lay hands on the probate of the will…"

"It's not with the bishop?"

Edmund shook his head. "Did your cousin have property in another part of the country, perhaps?"

"That's it!" Francis snapped his fingers. "The Cornish property from Julianna's mother."

Their eyes met. "Canterbury," they said together.

"I'll call on His Lordship the Archbishop within the week," said Edmund. "Then perhaps we can get to the bottom of this."

"Sounds like you two gents have Mr. Skeldon all sewn up between yus," said the third man. "Where do I come into it? That's what I want to know."

Edmund turned his no-nonsense, sea captain's gaze upon the fellow. "You are in Skeldon's employ?"

"Was. Got the sack, didn't I?"

"So there's no love lost between you."

"Not hardly." The man sniggered.

"There is a peculiarity in dishonest men, Mr...."

"Sloan. Bill Sloan."

"Mr. Sloan," Edmund continued. "They tend to be very mistrustful. I believe your former employer would want every ha'penny of his money accounted for. But he doesn't dare put the real figures into his public ledger. Have you ever known him to have a special account book, one he tries to keep hidden?"

A wide grin spread across Sloan's narrow face, exposing his revolting dentition. He jerked his head toward Francis. "Like I told your friend, there's a big book what he carts home with him every night. He must lock it up in the house somewheres, for he don't have it on him when he goes off for the evenin'."

Edmund laid a small leather pouch on the table between them. Sloan's clawlike hand snaked out and grabbed it. "Half now—half when you get the book?"

"Perhaps there has been a misunderstanding, Sloan," said Edmund. "I don't wish you to...*acquire* Mr. Skeldon's secret ledger. It is enough to know that he has one and where he keeps it. You'll find there the full sum you negotiated with Mr. Underhill. Spend it wisely."

The fellow drained his punch dipper in one long draft, then scrambled up from his place at the table. "Upon my life I shall, sir. And I hope you gents give Skeldon what he's got coming."

Before they could reply, he was gone. Edmund took a sip of his chocolate. It had gone cold, but the sweetness of it washed away the foul taste in his mouth.

Francis grinned. "This whole business looks more promising

by the minute. If you can unearth the probated will from the court at Canterbury, we can go a fair ways to proving Jerome did Julianna out of her rightful inheritance. His secret account book would secure the case. Why didn't you just engage Sloan to steal it?''

''We must leave that to Julianna.''

''You can't be serious?'' Francis objected. ''Jerome Skeldon is not a man to be trifled with. Besides, there has always been...something most unsavory about his conduct with Julianna.''

''Which is precisely why she needs to do this. Your cousin is an extraordinary woman. I have every confidence in her.''

The young man drained his punch. ''I must admit, I had my doubts initially how you two would get on together. I'm pleased to see how well this arrangement has turned out. You truly have managed to fill the empty spots in each other's lives. She's temporarily taken Crispin's place with you, and I suspect you have permanently filled the void left by her father's death.''

That thought irked Edmund out of all proportion. He leapt up and jammed on his hat. ''And speaking of my *wife*...'' He could not keep himself from accenting that last word. ''I must be getting home.'' Realizing how brusque a dismissal this sounded, he added in a more amiable tone, ''We have an engagement this evening and she will twit me if I'm late.''

''Cecily will be expecting me, too.'' Francis rose and extended his hand. ''Farewell, Sir Edmund. Give Julianna my best regards and warn her to have a care when dealing with Jerome.''

Underhill had barely cleared the door when a large party of gentlemen entered. One small round figure detached himself from the loudly conversing group and made straight for Edmund.

''Fitzhugh, old boy!'' cried Langston Carew. ''Just the man I most wanted to see. Have you a moment to spare an old comrade?''

''For you, my friend? Always.'' Edmund settled back into his seat and called for two more dippers of punch. ''You don't need me to stand your second, I hope?''

"Haw, haw!" hooted Carew, slapping his thigh. "You always were a master of the dry quip, Fitzhugh. No more duels for me," he added in a tone almost regretful. "Most husbands these days take an attitude of indulgent amusement concerning my admiration for their pretty wives. Cheeky pups!"

The two men lifted their glasses in a toast to younger days.

Carew turned suddenly serious. "Your skillful machinations on Oglethorpe's behalf this summer have not gone unremarked in the corridors of power."

Edmund shrugged. "It won't be the first time I've made enemies, and I doubt it will be the last."

"Enemies? Hardly. You've won considerable admiration for your principles and for your masterful deployment of influence."

"It helped that the charges were pure rubbish."

Carew shook his head so forcefully that his periwig fell slightly askew. "That's neither here nor there. The point is, you sprang into the fray and routed your opposition without even soiling your hands. Made a number of people sit up and take notice. The Whigs have asked me to sound you out about standing for a seat in the House."

"Parliament?" Edmund felt his jaw drop. "Me? I think they've got the wrong man."

"Not a bit of it!" The vehement bobbing of Carew's head caused his wig to slip a little farther. "A few discreet inquiries unearthed your support for a number of worthy causes. The only caveat was your low social profile. Now you've solved that—popping up all over town in the very best company with a charming young wife on your arm. They want you, dear fellow, and I for one don't blame 'em. Don't refuse without thinking on it."

"Very well, Langston. I'll give the notion all the consideration it deserves. Now, unless you have any other momentous news to deliver, I must be pushing off. Have to make myself presentable for this evening, and there's an errand I must run before the shops close."

Carew straightened his wig. "I'll let you go, then. Mull the idea over and get used to it. I relish the prospect of unleashing your trenchant wit upon those dull dogs in the Commons.'' With a wink of his one good eye, he added, ''And do give my most ardent regards to your fair lady.''

Edmund chuckled over Carew's parting remark as he hurried down Ave Mary Lane, toward the shop of a certain skilled jeweler. This very day, one year ago, Julianna had breezed into his life and captured his heart. The anniversary might hold no special significance for her, but Edmund could not let it pass without some private gesture of acknowledgment.

The jeweler held out his handiwork for Edmund to admire, the loupe still screwed up in his right eye. ''As fine a set of matched pearls as ever I've seen, my dear sir. Brokered in pairs or small lots, they would have yielded you a king's ransom.''

Edmund dismissed the suggestion with a decisive shake of his head. '' 'Who can find a virtuous woman?' '' he asked, quoting the proverb of King Lemuel. '' 'For her price is far above rubies.' ''

Removing the glass from his eye, the little man beamed. '' 'The heart of her husband doth safely trust in her,' '' he countered, '' 'so that he shall have no need of spoil.' '' Shutting the velvet-covered box with a sigh, he handed it over to Edmund. ''You are fortunate to have a lady worthy of such adornment.''

Answering the jeweler's compliment with a polite nod, he tried to quell a nervous flutter in his stomach.

Enchanted with her new gowns from Madame Mercier, Julianna found it difficult to choose which she should wear that evening. They would be dining with Mr. and Mrs. Makepeace, more friends of Vanessa's. After much debate with Gwenyth, she settled upon the buttercup-yellow satin, with a cream and gold striped underdress. Gwenyth used the natural thickness and curl of her hair to coif it with flattering little tendrils. Julianna felt she could almost equal the dowager countess of Sutton-Courtney.

While Gwenyth scurried below stairs to fetch a cap, Julianna pondered the problem of jewels. Her emerald pendant was completely wrong for this costume. Of late it had become a constant reminder of the uncomfortable split in her loyalties. As it bore

Crispin's likeness, she often felt hypocritical when she wore it, yet guilty when she left it off.

Hearing a stir at the door of her dressing room, she called out. "I hope you have brought more than one, Gwenyth, for I cannot decide which...."

Glancing in the mirror, she stopped short. Edmund stood in the doorway, splendidly handsome in a coat of black and gold brocade. What a fine-looking couple they would make tonight!

"Come to help with my hooks, have you? Or is it the husband's perennial complaint, that his wife is taking too long to dress?" Julianna tried to keep her voice light. Having him here in her most private sanctum, the candlelight low and intimate, made her suddenly light-headed with suppressed desire.

"No expense of time can be too great, when the result is so exquisite. Neither have I come to fill in for your lady's maid. I'm here to remind you of what day it is, and to give you this."

He reached around her to deposit a slim box upon the bureau top. As their gazes locked in the glass before her, Julianna hated to look away.

"What day?" The timbre of her voice sounded entirely foreign to her—high-pitched and breathless.

Edmund gave a half smile of fond mockery. Julianna felt the blood in her veins turn to molten butter—warm, rich and sweet.

"Tsk, tsk, forgotten so soon. Today is the first anniversary of our wedding. Please accept this token in remembrance."

How could she have forgotten? For an instant Julianna's thoughts slipped back to the first time she had sat before this glass, quaking at the prospect of sharing her bed with the remote stranger who had just become her husband. If only she'd foreseen how she would come to feel about that man, Julianna knew she would never have let him leave her on their wedding night.

Her fingers trembled as she lifted the lid from the box. Nestled in cotton lay a string of luminous, creamy pearls, some of the largest she had ever seen. The necklace encircled a pair of earbobs, each composed of one large round pearl with another, drop-shaped, hanging down. As she let out a gasp of admiration at their beauty and obvious value, it cost Julianna an effort of will to look back at Edmund, if only his mirror image.

She feared her voice would break. "Edmund, thank you. They are...beyond words."

"A few of the best from the Soulay Sea." His voice sounded hearty with satisfaction at her obvious pleasure. "May I?" He indicated the ornaments.

"Please." Julianna replied in a whisper, daring no more. She tilted her head as Edmund deftly clipped an earbob to each lobe. Then the pearls rested warm against her throat. Edmund fastened the clasp, momentarily resting his hands on her shoulders. Without thinking, Julianna raised her own hands to lay on his and press them into her hungry flesh. She was a heartbeat too late. Before she could reach him, Edmund had backed away.

The gems complemented her costume perfectly. Julianna knew she would treasure them always. Still, she would have cast them aside in an instant, in exchange for one brief kiss.

"Get to your feet, girl, and let us see the full effect."

Julianna's tension vented in a nervous trill of laughter. Rising, she faced Edmund and executed a little twirl to flare her skirt. With a finger pressed to his lips and an ever so slight shake of his head, Edmund's admiration was palpable.

"Now which do you think, milady? This wee scrap of a one, or the..." Gwenyth bustled in, headgear in hand. "Excuse me, sir—milady. I shall just leave these here, shall I?"

"No, Gwenyth," Julianna called. "We are running late as it is. Perhaps my husband can lend his opinion. Which do you think, Edmund?"

Edmund cocked an eyebrow and puckered his forehead. "That one is altogether too pert. You will be breaking enough hearts tonight. This one, I think." He took the cap from Gwenyth and handed it to Julianna. "When Makepeace and his Whig cronies clap eyes on you tonight, they won't give me a minute's peace until I stand for Parliament...all for the pleasure of seeing you grace the ladies' gallery."

As Gwenyth pinned her cap in place, Julianna gave him a searching look. "Edmund! Are you serious? Parliament?"

He nodded. "Langston Carew hunted me down at the Chapterhouse this afternoon to advance the idea."

"How marvelous!" Julianna searched through her dressing room clutter for a fan. "Of course you've agreed?"

"Do you think I should?" Edmund took Julianna's *manteau* from Gwenyth and slipped it around her shoulders. "I can't say I ever fancied myself a politician."

She spun about and caught his hands in hers before he could back away. "But think of all the good you could do. For the foundlings, and the hospitals. One man's fortune can only stretch so far in easing social ills. The country needs men like you to guide it. Men of honor and compassion. Say you will?"

"My dear. You'll set me blushing." He tucked her hand in the crook of his elbow and ushered her through to her sitting room. "I suppose if you're so fond of the idea, I can give it more serious thought. Now, we must be off. Vanessa tells me that Makepeace is a stickler for punctuality."

"I almost forgot," said Julianna as they hurried down the gallery. "You were supposed to meet Francis at the Chapterhouse today. What news of Jerome?"

"Promising news," replied Edmund. "I'll tell you all about it on the way and we can plan our strategy."

Chapter Twenty

The manservant cast a suspicious glance over the woman who stood in the doorway of his master's house. Feeling like an idiot in a gaudy mask of face paint, Julianna twitched open her cloak to reveal a daring expanse of bosom, artificially plumped by the most excruciating corset she had ever worn. As the suspicion in the young man's eyes gave way to naked lust, Julianna fought down the familiar sensation of suffocating panic. This was precisely the reaction she'd hoped for, the one she was determined to turn to her advantage.

Relieved to find he did not recognize her in the hideous black wig, she fluttered her eyelashes in a perfect parody of Vanessa, stretching her reddened lips into an encouraging smile.

"I'm just tellin' you what I was told, lovey." She prayed the hours of Edmund's tutelage had perfected her Cockney accent. "Your guv told me to meet him here at five bells. It must be gettin' on for that now. Are ye goin' to let a lady freeze to death on yer doorstep, or will ye be a gent and ask her in?"

The fellow reluctantly shifted his gaping stare from her décolletage to glance furtively up and down the street. "Mister Skeldon'll be here any minute now. He don't invite his…ladies home as a rule, but I guess it won't do no harm for ye to wait for him inside. Seein' as how it's a mite chilly out."

"Ta, lovey." She traced a finger redolent of cheap scent from one of the boy's prominent ears to the center of his pockmarked chin. "No wonder your guv don't bring his…ladies 'round here. Don't want 'em settin' eyes on a handsome cove like you. Did ye say ye'd slip me a splash of gin and lemon, lovey?''

She and Edmund had practiced this part over and over, but it was not the same. As she'd whispered those words in Edmund's ear, oh so seductively, it had taken every ounce of self-control she possessed not to slip her arms around his neck and behave exactly like the harlot she was playing. Faced with Jerome's rancid, randy footman, it was all she could do to hold her gorge.

"Gin?" He eyed her up and down, a speculative smile lighting his spotty young face. "Don't see why not. Half-a-mo'."

Julianna forced herself to count ten, until she was certain the boy was occupied below stairs. Glancing around to make sure there were no maids lurking about, she whispered a prayer of thanks that Jerome found it so difficult to keep female servants. Slamming the front door with all the force she could muster, she turned and bolted up the staircase. Once out of sight of the entry, she crept into the spare bedroom and hid in the narrow space between the wardrobe and the corner of the room.

Sometime later she heard Jerome pass by, arguing with his footman about the woman who had arrived and then disappeared so mysteriously. She heard movements in the room next door and the rumble of voices. *Hurry up, Jerome,* she silently urged him. *Get yourself dressed and out on your round of debaucheries before this corset permanently disfigures me.*

She heard the two men out in the hallway again, talking over Jerome's plans for the evening.

"…and if she shows up again, make sure to detain her until I get back. This promises to be a dull night. I could do with a bit of sport…." Jerome's words trailed away down the staircase.

Still she waited in her hiding place, cramped and chilled, until she was certain the servants would be eating their evening meal. At last she took as deep a breath as her corset permitted and eased out from behind the tall wardrobe. Treading quietly, as Edmund had taught her, she stopped still and held her breath whenever a floorboard gave even the faintest creak. The short distance from the guest bedroom to Jerome's chamber seemed to stretch on forever, as Julianna concentrated fiercely on listening for sounds that would warn her of possible detection.

Once out in the dimly lit hallway, she sacrificed a measure of stealth for greater speed. The fine hairs on her neck prickled as she slipped along the corridor. It was just such shadowy, deserted places where Jerome had so often accosted her. Her taut nerves stretched to a new peak of quivering sensitivity. Why had she ever insisted Edmund let her do this?

Lit only by the embers of a dying fire, the room was crowded with deep, yawning shadows. Jerome's smell hung in the air— a mix of sour brandy and the sweat of lust. She could almost feel him hovering over her with his vicious, greedy hands and mouth. A spark popped in the fading fire. A scream rose in Julianna's throat, but she strangled it to a mere squeak.

It was no use. She couldn't do this. She must sneak away before anyone caught her. Run. Hide. Cower in Edmund's arms.

Then she spied the strongbox beside Jerome's bed. The thought of Edmund had momentarily calmed her so she could think rationally. If she failed now, after coming so close, Jerome might suspect something. He might take steps to hide his secret accounts more securely. Perhaps he would destroy the book altogether, and the precious evidence it contained.

Concentrating on thoughts of Edmund, as she might have clutched a talisman, Julianna forced herself to kneel and examine the lock on the strongbox. From a secret fold sewn into the hem of her cloak, she extracted a small assortment of iron picks, rolled into a length of thick flannel to keep them from jangling against one another. Carefully, she tried them one by one, listening intently for the faint sounds that signaled success.

With a satisfying click, the lock gave at last. Thrusting the lid open, Julianna grabbed the heavy book and slid it into another special pocket Gwenyth had sewn into her cloak. Quietly she closed the box and resecured the lock. Her heart hammered with the heady rush of success. Weighing the merits of a break for the front entrance versus a stealthier escape out a main floor window, she pulled open the bedroom door.

"Hullo! What have we here?" Jerome said, "I hoped you

might have come back again. I don't know how I could have forgotten a pretty little piece like you.''

He clenched her chin with his fingers, as he had on her wedding eve, pulling her face up for a closer look. If he recognized her, all was lost.

Fighting down her panic and the overwhelming urge to freeze or run, Julianna pushed herself toward Jerome. He had obviously not expected this response, for his grip slackened. She was able to plant her mouth on his, imitating what she could remember of his hungry, demanding kisses. His mouth fell open in response to the onslaught of her tongue and the provocative brush of her hand against his groin.

Turning Jerome's own tactics against him filled Julianna with an intoxicating sense of power. Her free hand closed over the heavy roll of lock picks. She whipped it back and sent it crashing against the straining bulge in his breeches. At the same instant, she bit down hard on his probing tongue. With a guttural bellow of pain, Jerome doubled over. Julianna swung her cloak and the heavy book hidden in its folds, bringing it down with deadly force on Jerome's head, just behind his ear. He collapsed into a senseless heap on the floor.

Dizzy with the ecstasy of conquest, Julianna fought the impulse to drag his bed curtains into the fire and rid herself of Jerome Skeldon once and for all. Justice, she reminded herself. She wanted justice, not vengeance.

Hearing the sound of running footsteps, she fled. She just managed to duck into the next room when Jerome's servants came pounding past, summoned by the sounds of her struggle. Once they were noisily occupied next door, she slipped out of hiding and flew down the stairs. A burst of frenzied energy carried her out the door and down the street to where a carriage waited.

''Julianna. Thank God!'' Edmund clasped her to him, as she wilted into his arms. ''I saw Skeldon come back. I was beside myself with worry. In another second I would have battered down the door. I should have known you'd get the best of him.''

''I got it!'' she gasped, as the carriage set off for Fitzhugh

House. Groping in the folds of her cloak for the book, she shoved it into Edmund's hands. "He caught me...just as I was leaving. I don't think he...knew who I was." She snatched the black wig from her head, a high-pitched giggle breaking from her lips. "No wonder you can't abide these wretched things."

She turned her back to Edmund. "Will you act as my tiring woman again? I can scarcely breathe in this torture of a corset. Oh, that feels better. I can't wait to get home and have Gwenyth draw me a bath. I want to wash off this face paint and this cheap scent."

"I hope no one saw you unfastening my clothes." The shrill, wild laughter shook her again, but her eyes stung with tears. "Quick frolic in your carriage with a common strumpet—no seat in p-p-Parliament for you."

Edmund gathered her into his arms again. "They'd probably give me a whole ministry," he said with a chuckle. "Hush now," he whispered as she began to sob quietly. "It's all over. You're safe. Jerome will never be able to hurt you again. Everything will be all right."

No, it won't! Julianna wanted to wail. *It won't be right because I can't stop loving you.*

Chapter Twenty-One

Why could she not stop loving him?

In an act of sullen contrition, Julianna dragged the bristles of the brush through her hair until her scalp stung.

"If you go on like that you'll tear every pretty hair out of your head." Gwenyth plucked the brush from Julianna's hand and gave her ruddy locks a gentle smoothing. "What's got into you today? Thought you'd be happy as a lark with the trial over and that wicked Mr. Skeldon finally getting what he deserves."

Julianna did not trust herself to reply.

"You should be pleased as punch with yourself after what you did. Walking into that house, bold as brass, and laying your hands on that book. I'd never have had the nerve."

In retrospect, Julianna could hardly believe her own audacity. Testifying in court had been easy after that. Oh, the satisfaction of taking the stand and giving her evidence, all the while meeting Jerome's baleful glare. Best of all, the judges had believed her. Gwenyth was right. She should be giddy with relief. She had every reason in the world to be content with her life and proud of her accomplishments. Every reason but one.

For three months she had fought to purge Edmund from her heart and resurrect her love for Crispin. And she had failed. Not for lack of effort, Julianna reminded herself. She had gone through all the proper motions, even paying dutiful visits to Crispin's rooms. Lately, however, the faint smell of his pomade provoked only a queasy spasm of guilt.

What did it matter the motions she went through during the day, when it would all be undone the moment she closed her eyes? Dreams that had once brought Crispin to her were no longer Julianna's allies. Now the traitorous nightly visions always placed her in Edmund's arms. Sometimes she dreamed them back at Titania's Bower. As he knelt behind her, she would turn on Edmund, sending them both sprawling onto a downy mantle of moss, his naked torso pressed against the moist, sheer cambric of her chemise. At other times, she pictured them back on the summit of Abbot's Tor. As his fingers dug into the flesh of her arms, Edmund would suddenly strain forward and forcefully claim her lips. Frequently, he would reach out for her on a mattress of new-mown hay, beneath a starlit canopy.

Such dreams often came in the early morning. As Edmund brought her to the tremulous brink of ecstasy, Julianna would awaken, unsatisfied. Writhing in her empty bed, she would bury her face in the pillows to muffle her howls of frustration.

"Have you thought what you'll wear tonight, milady?" Gwenyth's insistent question roused Julianna from her musings.

"Oh, choose something for me, Gwenyth." She sighed. "Nothing too heavy, for I gather there will be dancing."

Their host for the evening was an acquaintance of Edmund's from his years in Madras. The owner of extensive estates in the Caribbean colonies, he'd recently returned to England, ostensibly for his health. Vanessa, from whom few secrets remained hidden, had informed Julianna that their host's true purpose was to find husbands for his many daughters. Vanessa planned to press her brother in their direction.

"A new gown just arrived from the dressmaker's," said Gwenyth. "I think it's the loveliest yet. Shall I set it out?"

At her noncommittal nod, Gwenyth produced the latest Mercier creation. Julianna's black mood evaporated in a puff of rosebuds. The silk taffeta bodice and overdress glowed softly, like the blush on a ripe apricot, while the stiff damask underskirt was wonderfully embroidered in shades of gold and mulberry. A light tiffany fichu delicately draped the low-cut neckline. In this marvelous costume, she would breeze into the Pritchard's ball, the embodiment of a Surrey springtime.

When Julianna finally stood before her dressing room glass to survey the effect, Gwenyth simply gazed at her, dumb with admiration. At length she did voice one suggestion. "Might I try something different with your hair this evening, milady? The color of this gown will set it off so well. 'Twould be a shame to cover it up with a cap. What if you let me curl it at the back with some pretty feathers for an ornament?"

"Do let us try, Gwenyth. It sounds wonderful!"

In fact, the hairdressing proved no small labor. Gwenyth spent more than an hour with comb and crimping iron, until she was completely satisfied with the result. Julianna used the time to cleanse her mind of worries, longing and guilt, determined to enjoy herself thoroughly for this one night. Her toilette finally complete, she stood mute with wonder. Could that beauty in the glass truly be she? The rosy silk brought forth her color and the warm hues of her hair. When she walked, her gown rustled and whispered of glowing sunsets and cherry blossoms.

She had but one thought—to show herself off to Edmund. Thanking Gwenyth warmly for her ministrations, Julianna flitted down the gallery to her husband's chamber. She had not passed its door since their return from Abbot's Leigh. To think she had once spent every waking moment there and thought to go mad from confinement within its four walls. For a moment she stood silent, allowing herself to absorb some essence of Edmund that clung to his Spartan quarters. Then, softly, she called his name.

Edmund glared at his reflection in the dressing room mirror, directing his most baleful look at the hank of powdered horsehair atop his head. Did it make him look younger? He scowled critically. Even in youth, his face had lacked the handsome, boyish fullness of Crispin's. The wig subtracted a year or two from his age, he decided. Certainly no more than five—still an object of unthinkable antiquity to a lass of twenty. With a grunt of annoyance, Edmund fumbled with his neck linen. The stiffly starched lace of his jabot threatened to decapitate him.

He dreaded the prospect of this evening. A matrimonial fishing expedition for George Pritchard's daughters, the ball promised to draw a larger than usual crowd of young swains. The last thing Edmund needed was a bevy of fashionable beaux making sheep's eyes at his wife. With the passing autumn weeks, as Julianna had moved from one social triumph to another, the black beast of jealousy had goaded Edmund. If she had been a wife to him in more than name, if he'd been able to take her to his bed at the end of the day, he would have gloried in her success. As the situation now stood, Edmund resented every man who passed a casual word or an innocent dance with Julianna.

He'd been almost sorry to see Jerome Skeldon arrested and tried, so greatly had he enjoyed the sweet torture of preparing Julianna for her role.

"No. Hold your mouth this way to pronounce the word." He had gently coaxed her lips to form the proper shape, all the while willing his fingers not to tremble.

"Insert the pick like so...." He had covered her hand with his own, guiding her through the delicate motions, intoxicated by the scent that rose from her hair.

"Now, slide your finger along my face. Yes, just like that...and whisper in my ear the words we practiced." He'd fought to disguise the catch in his breath as she'd touched him in a convincing pretense of seduction.

Once or twice he'd sensed an echo of his own passionate longing—in her look...her voice...her touch. He'd feared that, true to his word, he would die from the pain and the pleasure of wanting her. Each time she had stopped short of acting upon whatever attraction she might have felt. After everything she had suffered at the hands of Jerome Skeldon, Edmund knew he must leave the choice with her. To initiate a more intimate relationship...or not.

Struggling with the recalcitrant jabot, his scalp itching from the unaccustomed periwig, Edmund gave his reflection a resigned grimace. This torture would all be worthwhile, he assured himself, if it made Julianna see him as a desirable mate.

"Edmund, are you dressed yet?" He started at the sound of her voice. Though his knees felt suspiciously weak, Edmund gulped a breath of air and squared his shoulders. Ready or not, the time had come to try out his new look.

"Oh, Julianna, running us late, am I?" He emerged from his dressing room, pulling distractedly at his neck linen. "Blame this damned jabot. I can do nothing with it. I'll wager the laundresses have put starch in it again. Can you help me out?"

Catching sight of her, Edmund stopped short. She looked so maddeningly desirable. Three long strides would carry him to her. He must take her in his arms at last. Before he could bestir himself, Julianna lifted gloved fingers to her twitching lips. Pointing at his head, she burst into gleeful laughter.

"Wherever did you get that silly wig? You don't mean to wear it out, I hope. It makes you look a fright!"

Edmund had never felt such a fool. He stood rooted to the floor, buffeted by a tempest of conflicting emotions.

Reining in her mirth, Julianna swept him a deep curtsy. "What do you think of my fine feathers?"

"You've become quite the doll of fashion, my dear." He dashed the words in her face, like ice water. "Do you expect the poor Misses Pritchard to have any chance of securing husbands, when every male in the place will have hungry eyes only for you?"

As Julianna let out a bewildered gasp, he held up the stiff fillets of lace. With pretended indifference, he asked, "See what you can do with my jabot, will you?"

"I am *not* your valet!" Spinning on the toe of her slipper, Julianna fled his room, slamming the door in her wake.

Erupting in a spew of graphic Balinese curses, Edmund snatched the wig from his head and kicked it clear across the room. Soaring in a graceful arc, it landed squarely in the unscreened hearth. It rapidly caught fire, making a merry blaze.

A pointed silence prevailed in the Fitzhugh carriage during the ride to the Pritchard premises in Hanover Square. Edmund and Julianna arrived at the same moment as Lord Marlwood, the dowager countess of Sutton-Courtney and a very handsome stranger. It was the first time since the summer that they had come into such close contact with Laurence Bayard. Edmund looked his cousin levelly in the eye, daring him to speak a word to Julianna.

Bent on far more important matters, Vanessa took no notice of the byplay between her brother and her cousin. "Julianna Fitzhugh, your hair! Confess, you sly minx—you've succeeded in poaching Lady Ardmore's French *friseur*. It is too bad of you. I've been after the fellow for months, to no effect."

Julianna patted a curl with pert satisfaction. "You know I let no one touch my hair but Gwenyth. This is her creation."

"Your little Welsh girl? Take care someone doesn't snatch her from under your nose. The paucity of good hairdressers in this city is a scandal! Now look, you have dazzled me such that I've quite forgotten my manners." Taking the arm of her escort, she embarked upon an emphatic introduction. "May I present my dear friend, Baron Felix von Auersberg. We met in Paris. Now he has turned up in London with the Austrian ambassador. Felix, my cousin, Sir Edmund Fitzhugh, and his wife, Julianna. Is she not a rival to half the courts of Europe?"

The baron disengaged himself from Vanessa and swept an exaggerated bow. Flourishing his tiny beplumed hat, he came to rest on one knee, kissing Julianna's hand. "My dear Lady Fitzhugh, I have heard much of the 'English rose,' but thought never to see one at this time of year. Now I understand that bloom is none but the fair flower of English womanhood."

Julianna caught her breath. The baron was a most handsomely favored gentleman. Fashionably pale in complexion, he wore a high wig with curls that twined round his ears. He obviously prided himself on his sartorial style, for every stitch of his costume reflected the latest in Continental fashion. His coat, a robin's-egg-blue velvet with silver frogging, opened over a lavishly embroidered waistcoat of the same brilliant hue. His jabot and cuffs boasted fully five inches of Brussels lace. The color of his attire served to emphasize the glacial blue of the baron's wide-set eyes. Behind his ingratiating salute, Julianna detected a razor edge of mockery. If this mincing macaroni expected her to swoon at his feet, he was in for a surprise.

Though her anger at Edmund's earlier rebuff still simmered, Julianna retracted her hand from the baron's and took her husband's arm. "Your compliments could easily turn a lady's head, sir. You might put them to better use with our hostesses. My husband has spoiled me for the flattery of any other man."

"Quite true, my dear Felix," said Vanessa. "Cousin Edmund has a treasure trove of literature from which he draws his sweet phrases." She wagged a finger at the baron. "You needn't get up to any of your little tricks, either. These two are so perversely devoted to one another, you can't think. As obscene a display of marital propriety as ever I saw."

"Is this your first visit to England, Baron von Auersberg?" Edmund asked. Once again Julianna intercepted the level gaze. She noted with satisfaction that the Austrian looked away first.

"It is, Sir Edmund. I must tell you how much my empress appreciates the alliance of England in securing her lawful succession. One finds it refreshing to deal with people who can be trusted to keep their word."

Edmund's left eyebrow cocked. The thin line of his lips twisted sardonically. "We are neither of us, Baron, so naive as to believe this war hinges on the honorable word of those who wage it. Though, for pure self-interest, it helps that we English are not affected by the Salic Laws. We know from experience that women can be very capable sovereigns. I grew up during the reign of Queen Anne—a period of peace and prosperity in this land. And no past British monarch of either sex is revered above Good Queen Bess."

Vanessa rolled her eyes. "If you must talk dreary history and politics, Edmund, I suggest you usher Felix through and introduce him to our hosts. I want a quick word with your wife."

As the men moved off, Vanessa drew Julianna aside and whispered breathlessly. "My darling, I am in such a tither. I cannot keep the news to myself a moment longer. The Marquis of Blessington has planned a grand ball for Twelfth Night. A masquerade, no less, and he has asked me to act as hostess! Promise you'll come? The marquis has decreed no unmasking at midnight. Each guest must come alone, their identity a complete secret from everyone else. Does it not sound *amusant?*''

''I can hear Edmund now.'' Julianna aped his most sententious tone. ''It sounds like the very prescription for uncontrolled mischief.'' She added brightly, ''Though I cannot answer for him, I wouldn't miss it for the world.''

What a strange turn her relationship with Vanessa had taken of late, Julianna mused. Much as it pained her to admit it, she owed a great deal to the dowager countess. Vanessa had skillfully shepherded her introduction to London society. She had only to watch Edmund's cousin for cues on how to conduct herself in any company. She had never heard Vanessa pass a further flirtatious word with Edmund, though the two were finally back on speaking terms. Despite all this, she could not bring herself to fully like or trust Edmund's glamorous cousin.

''I plan to make this an entertainment that will be talked of for a decade.'' Vanessa's emerald eyes glittered. ''Your invitations will arrive shortly, so I warn you to betake yourself to Madame Mercier, posthaste. Make sure you pack Edmund off to his tailors before they are overwhelmed with orders. Now, I suppose we should go in. You and I must support each other this evening, my dear. I fear there are few ladies present other than Mr. Pritchard's legion of marriageable daughters.''

Vanessa had not overstated the case. As Edmund introduced their hosts, Julianna beheld a receiving room swarming with men. She overheard Edmund mutter something under his breath about ''every young buck in London.'' George Pritchard took Julianna and Vanessa, one on each arm, and made the introductions of his seven daughters. A covey of colorless young ladies, virtually indistinguishable from one another, Julianna found them quite unremarkable except for their excessive timidity. Certainly they bore scant resemblance in either looks or spirit to their beautiful and dramatic names—Lavinia, Ophelia, Portia, Cordelia, Rosalind, Miranda and Juliet.

As they moved away from the receiving line, Vanessa whispered to Julianna behind the cover of her fan. ''What a mercy the Pritchards had no more daughters. Otherwise, we might next have met one named Lady Macbeth.''

Julianna laughed in spite of herself. She had been entertaining the very same thought. "Vanessa, you are a terror!"

A hint of kinship warmed Vanessa's gleeful reply. "I should hope so! I work very hard at it."

As Julianna moved to rejoin Edmund, she found her path blocked by a tall, florid lady wearing a brittle mask of face powder and a plum-colored gown of too young a cut for her figure.

The woman hailed Edmund. "Captain Fitzhugh. So much time has passed, but you are as handsome a gallant as ever!"

Edmund's eyes widened in recognition. "Miriam Pritchard, what a surprise!" Turning to Vanessa, he introduced the woman, who gave her name as Lady Lynwell, the sister of their host.

"Charmed, my dear!" Lady Lynwell greeted Vanessa. "What a pleasure to finally meet some of the captain's family. I was poor Amelia's dearest friend, you know. I understand that you've remarried, Captain Fitzhugh. Never too late, they say, though I thought your heart might be buried in India...."

Julianna could hear a note of tearful reproach in her voice. Edmund looked thoroughly lost for words.

"Well...that is..." Spotting Julianna, he spun Lady Lynwell in her direction. "May I present my wife, Julianna. My dear, meet Lady Lynwell—Mr. Pritchard's sister and an old friend."

Lady Lynwell's mouth moved, but no sound emerged. She looked like someone unexpectedly presented with a large dead fish in an advanced state of decay.

"A pleasure to meet you, Your Ladyship," said Julianna coolly. Handsome gallant, indeed.

Before Lady Lynwell could reply, two young men approached Vanessa and Julianna to make up a set for dancing. As they glided through a stately saraband, Vanessa raised her eyebrows meaningfully at Julianna, who swallowed an undignified giggle. The next hour passed in a continuous round of court dances. When one ended, new partners waited to sweep the ladies back onto the floor. Finally, Julianna begged a pause for some refreshment.

The bluff Mr. Pritchard came to her rescue. "A dipper of punch, Lady Fitzhugh?"

"How delicious, sir! I must confess that, parched as I am from dancing, I'd welcome a drink of vinegar." She drained the dipper in a single draft.

"My own recipe," the host boasted, ladling another generous measure. "I make it with rum and sugar from our plantation, together with assorted fruit cordials."

"Very refreshing." Julianna returned her empty cup. "Might I have another? It's so sweet, one would never guess it contained spirits. You must be proud of your pretty family, sir."

"They are good girls," he confided with a sigh. "This ball is my wife's idea and my sister's. Our Lavinia and the others were all born in the colonies and have led a simple life. I believe they're overwhelmed by London society. Now that we have a bit of money and property, nothing will do for Mrs. Pritchard but they have proper English husbands—no colonial bumpkins. I can't see that they're making much of an impression tonight."

Though inclined to agree, Julianna offered some reassurance. "I found fashionable society rather daunting at first, Mr. Pritchard. Only recently have I begun to find my feet. Perhaps your daughters would blossom socially in a more informal atmosphere. When the holidays are over, I'll invite them to tea at Fitzhugh House."

"Very generous of you to offer, Lady Fitzhugh." George Pritchard beamed. "More punch?"

"Just a drop. I fear we must save further conversation for supper. It appears I have a queue of dance partners forming."

Through the next brisk gavotte, Julianna began to relish all the male attention she was receiving. Perhaps her husband would realize that other men found her attractive. When she glanced in his direction, however, Edmund was taking no notice. He appeared deep in conversation with Lady Lynwell. Much as this annoyed her, Julianna could not help noticing how her husband stood apart from the other gentlemen.

His habit of black broadcloth, in a rather severe cut, showed his tall spare figure to striking effect. He had forgone the lace of his starched jabot in favor of a plain stock, and his Spartan attire admitted not even an inch of lace on the cuffs. His close-cropped hair served to accentuate his deep-hewn, patrician profile. Beside these young dandies, all powdered, patched, painted and periwigged, Sir Edmund Fitzhugh looked the very picture of uncompromising masculinity. Dizzy desire bubbled in Julianna's heart like sweet, unbidden laughter.

Chapter Twenty-Two

At the Pritchards' table that evening, dinner conversation lagged during the early courses. The timid Pritchard daughters seldom ventured a word. Sensing the purpose of the evening, the gentlemen were as skittish as horses, lest one of the marriageable ladies mistake their hollow flattery for sincere interest. Fortunately, Vanessa proved equal to any social situation and not averse to carrying on multiple conversations. Watching with envious admiration, Julianna drank more punch in preparation for the strenuous country dancing that would follow the meal.

As his guests nibbled at the final course, Mr. Pritchard stood and raised his glass. "Ladies and gentlemen, I give you the hero of Masulipatam, without whom my family and I would not be here to entertain you this evening. Here's to the good health and continued felicity of my friend, Sir Edmund Fitzhugh."

Edmund scowled as the party drank his health. His black look darkened further when Vanessa called out, "Good manners dictate you must respond, Cousin Edmund. Do honor us with an account of your daring rescue!" She turned to Mrs. Pritchard, speaking loudly enough for all to hear. "Inducing this man to tell of his adventures in the Indies is well-nigh impossible. I would know nothing of his exploits had I not set Langston Carew drunk and wrung him of all the details."

"Carew!" Mr. Pritchard thundered. "He got us into that

mess in the first place. Most indiscreet with his favors. Called down the wrath of the Subedar on every Englishman in India.''

Julianna noticed several of the beaux exchanging disbelieving glances and mouthing the name ''Langston Carew?''

''I shudder to think what might have befallen,'' said Mrs. Pritchard, ''if Captain Fitzhugh had not sailed to our rescue. The Hyderabadis and the French were practically on our doorstep, while George stubbornly refused to admit we were in any danger.''

''It is my earliest memory.'' At those soft words the company fell silent, astonished to hear Lavinia Pritchard speaking of her own volition. ''Captain Fitzhugh scooped me up and set me on his shoulder. I was afraid my head would bump the ceiling. Then he said something to Father about refusing to have the blood of innocent children on his conscience and stalked off with me.'' Miss Pritchard ducked her head, blushing, when she realized how large an audience her remarks had drawn.

Lady Lynwell took up the story. ''Of course, we couldn't let Captain Fitzhugh sail back to Madras with the child, so Abigail and I packed up the babies and followed. I can still see George jumping around the dock like a flea, raging about loading the tea. 'Damn the tea!' Captain Fitzhugh bellowed at him. 'Load your people!' We had just cast off when the attack came. They put the whole factory to the torch.'' She shuddered. ''One such close call was enough to last me a lifetime.''

A polite ovation sounded at the conclusion of the story. There followed renewed calls of, ''Reply. Reply, Sir Edmund.''

Realizing he'd have no peace until he acknowledged the toast, Edmund rose—a mite unsteadily, Julianna thought.

''This is yet another tale,'' he announced solemnly, ''that has grown in the telling. My role is much exaggerated. However, I am proud of the minor part I played in preserving our hosts from harm. George, I compliment you on your family. They are better than you deserve—fretting about your blasted tea.''

''For a man who counts pride as his besetting sin,'' Vanessa pointedly observed, ''you suffer from a tiresome excess of modesty, dear cousin.''

Laughter erupted, then died away again as Edmund raised

his glass. "I believe these fine damsels are far more worthy of our salute than a tiresome old sailor. Ladies and gentlemen, I give you Juliet. 'Beauty too rich for use, for earth too dear.'"

As the youngest Miss Pritchard tossed her head at Edmund's toast, Julianna noticed how lustrous a shade of butternut were those shining tresses.

"Miranda," Edmund continued. "'So perfect and so peerless...created of every creature's best.'"

This young lady, more diffident than her sister, brought up her hands to shield her blushing face. They were very pretty hands indeed, delicate and graceful.

By the time Edmund reached the third Pritchard daughter, an audible whisper of anticipation had built among his audience. "'Let no face be kept in mind,'" declared Edmund, "'than the fair of Rosalind.'"

Scattered applause greeted this. Rosalind Pritchard bit her lip, cheeks flushed. The suffusion of color enlivened her pale little face to such an uncommon degree that none of the company would have challenged the title "fair."

When Edmund saluted the next sister—"'Fairest Cordelia, that art most rich, being poor; most choice, forsaken, and most loved, despised.'"—the lady's gaze fell to her lap. When she looked up to offer Edmund a shy smile of thanks, her blue eyes shone almost violet and Julianna envied her luxuriant lashes.

Of the shortsighted Miss Portia, Edmund announced, "'She is fair, and fairer than the word, of wondrous virtues.'" She greeted his words with a peal of jubilant laughter so sweet that Julianna felt sure some present beau would be anxious to call it forth, for himself.

The party now grew very quiet. Julianna squirmed in her seat. She hoped Mr. Pritchard's rum punch had not induced Edmund to overstep the limits of his own scholarship. He'd done well so far, but Ophelia was next to come. Hamlet had spared few words of compliment for his lady—at least, none repeatable in polite company. As for Lavinia, her gory revenge tragedy was considered highly offensive to modern sensibilities. The less said of Titus's ravished and mutilated daughter, the better.

"'Oh rose of May! Dear maid, kind sister, sweet Ophelia!'"

Glasses raised, as much in tribute to Sir Edmund's peerless command of Shakespeare, as to Ophelia Pritchard, though few would fault that lady's charmingly dimpled smile.

The company held its breath and hung upon Sir Edmund's final words like an avid crowd watching a skilled conjurer.

"Lavinia," Edmund concluded with a flourish. "'Whose circling shadow Kings have sought to sleep in, and might not gain so great a happiness as have thy love.'"

Lavinia Pritchard clapped her hands delightedly, eyes starry, a whimsical twist to her lips. The other guests went quite wild, whistling loudly and banging upon the table until the glassware tinkled and the cutlery jangled. Edmund had performed a subtle, potent sorcery, Julianna reflected. His lyrical tribute had kindled in each lady a spark of self-regard—which had, in turn, illuminated her own unique beauty. Was it any wonder she had fallen fathoms deep in love with this eloquent poet-mariner? she asked herself, falling deeper still.

There was not enough of Julianna to satisfy all her would-be partners for the country dancing. She kept trying to claim Edmund for a turn around the floor, but each time she found him squiring the Pritchard sisters or their aunt. It suddenly dawned on her how much she counted upon Edmund's public attentiveness. His dereliction this evening was beginning to chafe.

Across the room, Edmund nodded absently, feigning interest in Lady Lynwell's reminiscences of India. The poor woman suffered under some bizarre delusion that he and Amelia had cared for each other—that he'd been heartbroken by her early death. If he'd been paying attention, Edmund might have had trouble biting back a scathing rebuttal. Loved Amelia? Absurd! Back then he hadn't known the meaning of the word. He knew it now.

Covertly, his gaze strayed to Julianna, treading the dance floor like thistledown borne on a summer breeze. He was vexingly aware of how many young bucks also followed his wife with their eyes. She'd made a triumphant conquest of every man present, his fair English rose. How like a rose she was—

vibrant, fragrant and beautiful beyond all reckoning. And if she bristled with the odd thorn—sharp wit, piercing intellect—did that not add to her allure? Part of the rose's charm was that she did not suffer herself to be plucked by any casual hand. Buttressed by her thorns, she yielded her favors only to the careful admirer.

As a set of "Linden Lane" concluded, Baron von Auersberg approached the musicians. Following a muted exchange, he took the floor, accompanied by Vanessa. "With your indulgence, ladies and gentlemen, I beg to introduce a courting dance from the mountains of my native Austria."

The baron clapped out a rhythm for the musicians, three-quarter time, with a strong initial beat. First the baron and his partner spun with hands clapping above their heads. Then, he took Vanessa's hand and twirled her under his arm. They circled each other back to back, clapping once again. The baron put an arm around Vanessa's waist while she placed hers on his shoulder. They clasped right hands together and began a spinning step about the floor, very quick and graceful.

As the dance concluded, the company applauded, whispering among themselves. It was mildly shocking. In no contemporary English dance did couples advance beyond a decorous touching of hands. As eager partners mobbed Vanessa, Edmund saw Baron von Auersberg approach Julianna. He couldn't bear to watch.

"What do you say, Captain Fitzhugh?" Lady Lynwell asked. "Shall we give this new step a try?"

Desperate for any distraction, he took her arm.

As they neared Julianna and the baron, his wife turned toward Edmund. "And here he is! How kind of you to fetch him for me, Lady Lynwell. I was telling Baron von Auersberg that the mild improprieties of this dance are not for married persons to share with others. Don't you agree? If you'll kindly lend me my husband, I believe the baron is looking for a partner."

She sounded exactly like Vanessa. Edmund barely managed to contain a groan of disgust. Dazed by the sudden turnabout, he allowed Julianna to lead him onto the floor. Privately, he fumed. What did she mean, abducting him so airily from Miriam Lynwell? Julianna needn't pretend she wanted his company when she had her pick of the young swains. No. She simply meant to keep him on a tight leash—the old hound, to warn off unwanted admirers. She'd spurn him fast enough if one of those swaggering pups took her fancy. Damned if he would tamely stand such use!

The music began. Fortunately the steps were easy and the beat of the music strong. Spin and clap. Edmund took his wife's hand. As she pirouetted beneath his arm, he inquired through clenched teeth, "What prompted that brazen display?"

As they circled back to back, Julianna fired a casual retort over her shoulder. "Merely a concern for appearances. You have been neglecting your wife something scandalous this evening, Sir Edmund. I wished to forestall gossip."

He pressed his hand against her back, crushing her to him. "You did not want it said that Lady Fitzhugh has tired of studying ancient relics and gone in search of livelier subjects?"

"I did not want it said that Sir Edmund Fitzhugh has forsaken a diet of green fruit in favor of something riper."

"I see." Edmund maneuvered them to the center of the floor. "Well, we can nip such talk easily enough."

As the final bars of the music died away, he bent his head and imparted a lingering kiss in the hollow of Julianna's throat. A hum of muted comment and surreptitious laughter rose from the other dancers. *Take that,* he thought.

Julianna's face burned scarlet and her temper sputtered like a fuse to gunpowder. How dare Edmund Fitzhugh insult her with his empty, calculated gesture? And how dare her own legs betray her by turning to jelly?

The novelty of the dance proved wildly popular. The gentlemen even clamored for the Pritchard sisters. Lady Lynwell took the floor on Laurence's arm, while Mr. Pritchard led his wife. The baron returned to Vanessa.

"Let us stand out this round," said Edmund. "The turning is making my head spin. That deceptive fruit cordial of Pritchard's may be the most potent beverage I've tasted in a while."

Indeed? Had Mr. Pritchard's punch set her drunk, then? It

was not an unpleasant sensation. Julianna felt entirely rational and self-possessed, though just a trifle giddy. In spite of her anger, or perhaps because of it, she found herself much aroused.

"Do I take it you are still indulging in your earlier sulk?" Edmund asked with studied unconcern.

She cocked an eyebrow, trying to mimic the arrogant expression of Baron von Auersberg. "I never sulk. I was pouting, and that is a different matter entirely."

"Forgive an ignorant old sailor." Edmund affected the Somerset buzz that always struck her funny—doubly so in her present mood. "I've not the wit to mince words like your learned friend, Mr. Johnson."

Helpless with laughter, she dealt the impudent rogue a tart tap with her fan. "Every ignorant sailor should have the benefit of an education at Eton and Oxford. Besides, you were mincing words quite cleverly with your 'old friend,' Lady Lynwell."

Edmund skirted those treacherous waters. "Then, are you still pouting, milady?"

Julianna thrust out her lower lip in an exaggerated moue. "Most certainly, and not a wife in the world would blame me. After spending all the afternoon primping for my husband, what do I get? Petted and praised as I deserve? No. Reprimanded, like some tart about to take to the streets."

"Am I to believe this is all for my benefit? I'm not nearly so ignorant as that." Edmund gestured to the dancers. "There is your intended audience. What can I add to their acclaim?"

Another round of music began. Partners changed and Julianna drew Edmund to the floor once again. Through the opening moves of the "Landler," she explained, "If I strive to look presentable in company, I only do it to make you proud of me."

"How could I be anything else?" Edmund gave a quiet chuckle—the kind that never failed to melt her heart. "Why, I am insufferable with conceit, to claim the fairest English rose as my own. Though I prefer the wild eglantine to the cultivated blossom. Your nose dappled with tawny freckles and your hair a cascade of coppery curls. Skirts kilted up, standing in water to the knees with a lively fish on the end of your line—I call that true beauty. 'Such sweet neglect more taketh me, than all the adulteries of art; they strike my eyes, but not my heart.'''

Around and around they circled, too breathless for more conversation. Oddly detached from herself, Julianna became acutely aware of certain sensations: the bare skin of her arm against the stiff fabric of Edmund's topcoat. His breath in her hair. The crush of her bosom against his chest. A pulse, beating in her ears, in time to the music. Beating his name, over and over. Somewhere in his secret, jealously guarded heart, Edmund Fitzhugh did care for her in a way he would never admit. Perhaps tonight she would make him acknowledge those feelings.

At last, with considerable deliberation, Edmund said, "I have not been this inebriated in years. And this is your first time, unless I miss my guess. We must get home to bed, my dear, before we make complete fools of ourselves."

Flashing him a coy smile, Julianna concentrated fiercely to keep from slurring her words. "By all means, get me home to bed."

While their hosts continued to dance, Edmund had a servant summon their carriage. "Tomorrow I'll make our apologies for stealing away. At present I don't trust myself to tender a coherent farewell."

Ensconced in the carriage, Julianna slipped into the seat beside Edmund, thankful that her skirts were not too wide. Emboldened by the mask of darkness and the effect of strong drink, she felt compelled to speak the words she had guarded for so long. Yet she could not coax her voice above a whisper.

"Edmund, there is something I must tell you."

"Yes?" His voice was mellow and husky.

"Say nothing until I have told you all," Julianna begged. "Please believe I never meant for this to happen. I could scarcely believe it myself at first. I have fought against it. You will never know how hard. But, at last I was overcome...by my feelings for you. What Lear's daughter said perforce and falsely, I say to you freely and with all my heart. 'Sir, I love you more than word can wield the matter, dearer than eyesight, space, and liberty; beyond what can be valued, rich or rare.'''

An unbearable pall of silence descended. Would Edmund

stop the carriage and throw her into the street? Might he take her in his arms and confess his own love for her? By and by, Julianna could stand the suspense no longer. "Edmund, what say you?"

Again silence fell, punctuated by slow, rhythmic breathing. Edmund had fallen asleep? She had poured out her heart to a man asleep! Julianna could not decide whether to weep with vexation or to laugh hysterically. In the end, it emerged an odd mixture of the two. As Edmund slouched in the seat, unconscious, Julianna stole the chance to indulge those impulses she had long held in check. Drawing off her glove, she let the back of her fingers slide caressingly over his smooth-shaven cheek. Bringing one to rest in the shallow cleft of his chin, she let another play tremulously across his lips. Still he slept on, while the carriage drew up to the door of Fitzhugh House. Home to bed.

Before Brock could utter a word, Julianna gestured for him to keep silent, pointing to his master's slumbering form. With some difficulty, she and Brock were able to drag Edmund up the stairs and hoist him onto the bed.

"I'll see to him now, ma'am," Brock whispered.

"I believe I am capable of tending my own husband, Brock."

First a mask of shock, the steward's face quickly slid into a sly smile. "Very good, ma'am. I'll see it's kept quiet in the morning for you and the captain. God rest ye, ma'am."

Though her head had begun to spin violently, Julianna managed to pull off Edmund's boots and stockings. Removing his coat and waistcoat, her fingers fumbled over the many buttons. His cravat and shirt shifted more easily. How he slept through her clumsy handling, she could not fathom. Neither could she puzzle how to separate the man from his breeches—so she let them be.

For a moment, Julianna stood looking at Edmund in the dim light of his bedchamber, letting her fingertips glide over the gently undulating musculature of his chest. Then, snuffing the candle, she wrestled herself out of her gown, pulling the pins and feathers from her hair in the process. Taking a deep breath, she slid beneath the bedclothes and into the arms of her husband.

Though deeply asleep, some latent instinct stirred in Edmund. He turned toward Julianna, bringing both arms to encircle her. One lay heavily across her waist, the other rested on the gentle swell of her buttocks. Sight and hearing were lost to her. She had entered a dark, silent world of touch and smell. Such sensations! Could there be a more delicious warmth than his skin upon hers? Greedily, she inhaled the rich, musky odor of a man's flesh. Tilting her head, she tentatively nuzzled Edmund's neck, savoring the delicate, briny taste. In answer, his arms tightened about her, pulling them even closer together. His lips were on her throat in a kiss that blotted out all memory of his earlier empty pretense.

Was it possible to die of desire?

So Julianna wondered, as she sank into blissful oblivion.

Chapter Twenty-Three

Stop the dancing, Julianna wanted to moan. She was twirling out of control, dizzy, stomach bilious. *For heaven's sweet sake, stop the dancing!* As she raised her hand to steady her spinning head, Julianna came to foggy awareness of her surroundings. Where were her clothes? What was this warm, weighty form draped over her? This was not her bed!

Slowly her memory unfolded...a whirling progress around the dance floor...a dark carriage ride...words of love... disrobing...entering Edmund's bed...Edmund's bed! Had she lost her senses last night? If he should wake and find her here, she trembled at the thought of his wrath. The imminent jeopardy pierced the fog in her brain. Slowly, she slid out of Edmund's embrace. Once he stirred and her heart all but stopped. He only rolled away from her in his sleep, and she continued to ease herself out of bed.

Naked in the icy darkness of Edmund's bedchamber, she searched the floor for her clothes. Her shift—a shoe—her cloak. This Julianna threw around her shoulders, for a little warmth. Feathers—petticoats—fichu—dress. Where was that other shoe? Her arms were full when Edmund began to toss and mutter in his sleep. This would have to suffice. As she groped for the door, Julianna tripped over the second shoe, falling noisily. The ensuing silence was total—ominous. She crouched on the frigid floor, clothes strewn about, her teeth beginning to chatter and her stomach growing more sour by the minute. It felt like an eternity before she could believe she hadn't raised the entire household with her racket. Collecting her scattered garments, cursing the door's squealing hinges, Julianna made her escape.

She barely gained the sanctuary of her dressing room before she was loudly and violently ill. When she was able to move once again, Julianna fumbled through the wardrobe. Laying hands on a nightshift and a heavy woolen dressing gown, she wrapped her numb body in the garments, then fell upon her bed, insensible.

Poised between sleep and consciousness, Edmund reached out for Julianna. Her absence brought him fully awake, uncertain which pained him most—his head or his heart. He'd dreamed of her in such vivid, sensuous detail, he could scarcely bear to wake and find her gone.

Scattered memories of the Pritchards' ball resurfaced to torment him. What a wretched fool he'd made of himself—spouting Shakespeare, kissing his wife in public. With a stab of fear, Edmund realized he had no recollection of leaving the Pritchards'. What further indiscretions had he committed, too painfully mortifying to remember? Had he drunkenly pawed his wife in their carriage on the way home? Had he lain his head on her lap and bawled out his feelings in mawkish self-pity? Contemplating all the humiliating possibilities left Edmund nauseated with embarrassment.

No use hiding away in his bedchamber, he decided at last. Better to face Julianna down, praying she'd ascribe his misconduct to the drink. With any luck, George Pritchard's rum punch might have dimmed her memory, too.

It was light when Julianna wakened. The spinning of her head had been replaced by an excruciating pounding. At painful length, she discovered it to be her own pulse. Her stomach still felt rancid and her mouth felt like the floor of a byre. Little wonder most folk of her acquaintance imbibed temperately. The heady sensations of last night were not worth so agonizing a price. Julianna swore she would never again let strong drink pass her lips. She couldn't afford to indulge her reckless impulses if she hoped to remain in this house and retain any vestige of Edmund's affection.

"Did I waken you, milady? I'm ever so sorry! I didn't expect you'd be here—that is, Mr. Brock said you'd…"

Why had she never noticed how high and shrill Gwenyth's voice was? Every word beat like a cudgel against her temples.

"Sweet Mother of God, girl, keep your voice down! Oohh!" Her own words exploded like a cannonade inside her skull.

"Is something wrong, milady?"

"Life is wrong, Gwenyth," Julianna groaned piteously. "Morning is wrong. My head is so wrong it may never be right again." Holding her throbbing forehead, she spit her orders. "Fetch me coffee, strong and hot—lots of it. And a clove to sweeten my breath. But no food or it will cost you your life."

Crawling from the bed, Julianna surveyed the havoc in her dressing room. Pulling on a loose old sack gown and apron, she closed the door upon the mess and stench. Fortunately the sitting room fire blazed. Pulling a chair near the hearth, she chafed her bloodless fingers. Returning with a full pot of coffee and several cloves, Gwenyth was gruffly dismissed. Julianna's hand shook as she poured the coffee. Slowly she sipped the bitter, scalding liquid, letting it cleanse her mouth. A pounding on the sitting room door sounded like the hammering of a blacksmith against his anvil. Her skull was that anvil.

The door swung open and Edmund lumbered in, dropping ponderously into a chair. "I smelled the coffee. Pour me a cup."

"Pour it yourself!" Julianna massaged her temples. "And keep your voice down, for heaven's sake!"

"'Ave pity on a poor old drunkard, ma'am."

Julianna laughed. Instantly she regretted doing so, as her head threatened to split from front to back. "Leave off your silly mimicry and shut those drapes. The light is blinding me."

"Suffering from a dose of 'next morning,' my dear?" Peering at her through half-shut eyelids, Edmund appeared to have trouble focusing. "I must confess." He rubbed his jaws. "I've felt better—like the time I was gored by the wild pig. A man of my years should know better than to drink excessively."

Roused slightly from her own misery, Julianna observed with grim satisfaction that Edmund looked quite as ghastly as she felt—unshaved, unkempt, pallid and somber. What a dissipated pair they must look. The thought brought Julianna a wan smile. Each wrapped in their own misery, they sat for some time, drinking several cups of the strong coffee, chewing the pungent cloves, and occasionally communicating in a series of uncivil grunts and barks. Edmund eventually regained himself enough to broach the subject of the preceding night.

"What were you and Vanessa conspiring about in the Pritchards' front hall?"

Julianna concentrated to retrieve the memory. "Something about a party. Vanessa is hosting a masked ball on Twelfth Night, for her friend—the marquis of…something."

"Blessington. Geoffrey Blessington." Edmund's tone conveyed no high regard for the marquis.

"Precisely. We are invited, or soon will be. It promises to be a very grand affair."

"Knowing Vanessa, I have no doubt of that. I haven't been to a masque in ages. How shall we go? A literary theme would be only fitting. Portia and Shylock? Macheath and Polly Peachum?"

As another crumb of memory surfaced, Julianna explained the proviso for secrecy.

"Sounds like a prescription for unbridled mischief," said Edmund, exactly as she had predicted. "I, for one, would not think of missing it," he added good-naturedly. "Since we must travel separately, I'll ride to Blessington's on my own. You may take your choice of the carriages. Should I consult a tailor?"

Julianna nodded. "Vanessa urged haste in that department, before every seamstress and tailor in London is overwhelmed with orders. I'd intended to visit Madame Mercier today. Under the circumstances, I may postpone it. One thing I do know—I shall avoid the punch bowl at the marquis's Twelfth Night revel."

At this, they both laughed weakly. Then, they groaned.

By midafternoon, Julianna had recovered somewhat. Though she still could not face food, the pain in her head had dulled and her eyes felt less sensitive. While Gwenyth fretted noisily over the state of her rose gown, Julianna breathed a sigh of relief that Edmund appeared unaware of her disgraceful antics the previous night. She prayed Brock would not let slip some sly remark to give her away. The more she reflected upon her outrageous behaviour, the more Julianna realized that drink was only partly to blame. Since returning to London, she'd tried so desperately to quell her feelings for Edmund, they had grown to obsessive proportions. Perhaps a safer course would be to find some harmless outlet—like the masked ball.

Carefully, she considered her costume, discarding one possibility after another. She wanted nothing to do with the conventional Columbine or Domino. Perhaps a literary theme, as Edmund had suggested. Even as she tried to rest, ideas ran through her mind. Only as she drifted off to sleep, did Julianna envisage the perfect disguise. It would be an undertaking beyond the skill of any mere dressmaker.

"You wanted to see me, Skeldon?" Glancing around the Newgate prison cell, Edmund wrinkled his nose in disgust. This was the last place he wanted to be, but knowing Jerome had friends in low places, he wanted fair warning if the bounder planned any retaliation against Julianna. "Keep it brief. I've little patience with your kind."

"My kind, is it?" Jerome sneered. "I don't think we're so different, you and I. Not when it comes to a certain redheaded temptress. I've seen the way you look at her. Whether you'll admit it or not, you're as hungry for that sweet flesh as I've been. Only I'm man enough to go after what I want."

Telling himself over and over that he must not let this man get to him, Edmund still felt befouled by such suggestions. "We are not in the least similar, Skeldon," he said quietly but firmly. "Now unless you have something sensible to say, I will not waste my time any further."

"You've as good as slit your own throat, you know."

Marching over to where Jerome Skeldon stood, Edmund stared down at him. "Are you making threats?"

Skeldon jabbed a blunt forefinger into Edmund's chest. "Just showing you your own folly, old man. How long did you think I'd take to figure out your little marriage ruse…keeping her safe and cozy for that pretty nephew of yours?''

''Long enough to get the church register signed, at least.'' Edmund cracked a faint smile.

''You're very amusing for a man who's just bent over backward to deny himself what he wants most in the world.''

''Prison has addled your wits, Skeldon. I hope for your sake the judge sentences you to transportation.''

''What if Bayard never comes back?'' Jerome whispered invitingly. ''Has that ever crossed your mind, you poor fool? You've removed the two things that would have tied Julianna to you for life—financial dependence and her fear of me. It's a dangerous enterprise, sailing halfway 'round the world…as you well know. Bayard could be dead now for all that. And if he is, you mark me—she'll be off before you can say her name twice.''

Edmund's right hand flew up, gripping Jerome's lower face. Tighter and tighter he clamped down, until he could feel the jawbone threaten to give way under the weight of his rage.

''Getting a taste of your own medicine in here?'' he growled. ''Seeing what it's like to be the prey instead of the predator? Finding out how it feels to fight off stronger hands than yours intent on lechery?''

Coarse features contorted in pain and hate, Jerome spit in Edmund's face. The warm spittle ran down his cheek like a tear. He did not bother to wipe it away.

''So you are?'' Edmund did not slacken his grip, but his voice fell to a calm, cold murmur. ''Good.''

Letting Jerome drop, Edmund bellowed for the turnkey to unlock the cell door.

''Got you convinced she cares something for you, hasn't she?'' Jerome snarled. Edmund tapped his foot impatiently as the jailer fumbled with his great iron key ring.

''Idiot! She's trained all her life to twist pitiful old men like you around her little finger. Just see how much she cares. Try to claim a single kiss or a touch from all the carnal pleasures she promises with those eyes.''

The cell door swung open. Edmund strode through it without a backward glance. Behind him, Skeldon still spewed his vitriol.

"She'll look at you like you're a piece of filth crawled out of the gutter. She'll fight you like a hellcat and make you want her that much more."

The long prison corridor seemed to stretch on forever. Edmund wondered if the other prisoners had purposely fallen silent to let Jerome's poisonous accusations dog his footsteps.

"I almost feel sorry for you!" Jerome was screaming at the top of his lungs now. Though Edmund had left him far behind, he could still hear the venomous tirade faintly in the distance.

"I may be locked up, or transported, or even *hanged*. But she will torture you for the rest of your life...."

Only when he could hear Jerome no more did Edmund pause long enough to wipe his cheek with a handkerchief.

Julianna's first thought upon waking was to secure her costume for the masque. The late morning hours found her in conference with Herr de Vos, a theatrical costumer for Covent Garden. She asked about his willingness to take on a private commission, only to find him already contracted to design several outfits for Blessington's ball.

She explained the type of gown and mask she had in mind, describing a willowy riverbank and quoting Shakespeare rather liberally. From a cluttered worktable, the costumer selected a large tablet of paper and several sticks of colored chalk. As Julianna spoke, he began to sketch. By the time she finished, he had completed a drawing that suggested her idea to perfection. She assured him that if his execution in silk was even close to the draft, it would be worth whatever price he saw fit to charge. Taking leave, she mentioned her desire for secrecy.

The man responded by laying a finger aside his nose. "Trust me to keep mum, Lady Fitzhugh. My other commissions are of an equally delicate nature. An indiscretion could cost my life."

As she was already about town, Julianna visited several shops to make Christmas purchases. For weeks, she had racked her brains to come up with a suitable gift for Edmund. Cost was no object, since Jerome had been forced to hand over the money from her father's estate. Julianna had her heart set on something special—to match the breadth of her affection for Edmund. At last an idea had come to her, but she would need expert advice about the purchase. Advice available from only one source.

Calling at Vanessa's town house, she found the dowager countess taking tea. Busy with a thousand details for the ball, Vanessa was eager to confide every one. When Julianna finally got an opportunity to mention Edmund's gift, Vanessa was patronizingly amused, but she made several suggestions, referring Julianna to a seller with whom she'd had prior dealings.

After following up on Vanessa's contact, Julianna returned home late in the afternoon, thoroughly exhausted. Drooping onto her sitting room chaise, she felt suddenly weary of all the effort to repress her true feelings. Retiring to bed on the pretense of a headache, she had Gwenyth inform Edmund that she could not join him at Covent Garden that evening.

How would she ever get through this Christmas, alone in the house with him for several days? Julianna fondly recalled the previous Christmas, seeing in retrospect the early germination of her love for Edmund. It had all been so naive and innocent. This year she would scrupulously guard every word and gesture, hoping the intimacy of their holiday would not induce her to commit some act of folly. She dared not dwell upon the blissful, misty memory of lying naked in Edmund's arms.

She will torture you for the rest of your life.

That threat echoed in Edmund's mind when he received Julianna's message. It only confirmed what he suspected already—she was seeing Laurence Bayard behind his back. Lunching at the Cocoa Tree that afternoon, Edmund had overheard Lord Marlwood discussing his latest conquest. The young rake intended an assignation at the Twelfth Night masque.

"There we'll be, dallying under the very nose of her frightful old husband. What spice! God bless Blessington!"

As Lord Marlwood and his cronies drank the marquis's health, Edmund tried to persuade himself that Laurence hadn't been talking about Julianna. He'd almost missed his cousin's next remark. Referring to his costume for the ball, Laurence had said something about a ''black knight.''

All day, with Jerome's malignant curse ringing in his ears, Edmund had struggled to quell his suspicions. Then, driving home at teatime, he'd noticed his own brougham parked in front of Vanessa's town house. He could not imagine his wife voluntarily paying a call there—unless she planned to meet another occupant of the house. Julianna's sudden withdrawal from their evening engagement confirmed Edmund's worst fears.

He penned a hasty note and rang for Brock. ''Have one of the footmen deliver this to Brigadier Thorburn, with my regrets.''

''Then you won't be going out this evening, sir?''

''It would appear not. Tell Mrs. Davies I'll take a cold bite in the library. And, Brock...''

''Yes, sir?''

''Let me know me if anyone calls, or if my wife goes out.''

''The mistress would hardly go out without you, would she, sir? Feeling a bit poorly, so I hear.''

''Kindly don't question my orders, Mr. Brock. I trust you did not learn such insubordination under my command.''

Brock opened his mouth to reply, then closed it again. Edmund steadfastly ignored the reproachful look on his steward's face. What business had a man of Brock's years looking like a kicked whelp with its tail between its legs?

Edmund spent the evening pacing his library. To his surprise, he received no reports of Laurence coming or Julianna going. He sent his cold supper back to the kitchen, untouched.

Had he suffered from drunken self-delusion the night of Pritchards' ball? Edmund wondered. His hazy recollections of that night were charged with the touch and scent of Julianna, the unmistakable invitation in her eyes and in her voice. Robbed of inhibition by George Pritchard's Caribbean rum, she had let herself want him. There was nothing he would not do to make her want him like that again.

The germ of an idea took root. Suppose Julianna and Laurence were planning a tryst at the Twelfth Night masque? Edmund had not decided on his own costume yet. Might he not look well in a suit of armor? The thought appealed to him more and more. He retired to bed with his mind made up. Twelfth Night would see two black knights vie for the favors of their queen.

Chapter Twenty-Four

"I says to Agnes at tea..." Gwenyth brushed a length of Julianna's hair around her fingers into a glossy ringlet. "I'd a merrier Christmas this year than any since I came from Wales."

Julianna glanced up. "We had a jolly time, didn't we? I must tell Sir Edmund you enjoyed our celebration. He'll be pleased to hear it. He felt badly you missed your holiday."

A great snowstorm had buried London just three days before Christmas, forcing the servants to cancel their holiday plans at the last minute. Edmund had stepped into the breach, as usual, suggesting they make a house party of it. For three days they'd made merry with music, dancing and games, fortified with the best food and drink Mrs. Davies's larder and Sir Edmund's wine cellar could provide. Julianna had watched the mounting snowdrifts with a mute sigh of relief, wondering what folly she might have committed if left alone with Edmund for those three days.

"Well, there's your hair done, milady." Gwenyth stepped back to admire the result. "Lovely it looks, if I do say so."

Julianna nodded her approval. It was not an elaborate coif. Her hair hung free around her shoulders, strategically curled to curb its general unruliness.

"Now where's your costume, ma'am? Fancy, I haven't a notion who you're going as."

Which is just the way I plan to keep it, thought Julianna.

"Never mind about that now, Gwenyth," she said. "I have a much more important task for you."

"Aye, ma'am?" Gwenyth peered at her expectantly.

"Go see if Sir Edmund has ridden out. I'd hate to spoil the secret of my identity by blundering into him in the corridor."

After Gwenyth had gone, Julianna bolted the door and opened a locked drawer in one of the wardrobes, pulling out a bulky parcel that had arrived earlier in the week from Herr de Vos. For days, her anticipation of this evening had grown. She had imagined it a hundred times. Safely disguised, she would seek out Edmund at the ball, turning on him the full potency of her charm. She would seduce him as no woman had ever seduced a man.

A time or two, her pretty daydreams had gone awry and she had realized the awful risk she was taking. Then, a sheen of sweat had broken on her brow and she had grown faint with apprehension. Care and stealth must be her watchwords if she meant to succeed in her plan.

Once she had donned her attire, Julianna tied up the ribbons of her mask, and looked herself over in the glass. Her costume should draw a few glances this evening, she decided. The cut of the gown owed nothing to contemporary fashion, but much to pure fantasy. Sewn from trailing strips of filmy, loose-woven silk in several verdant shades, it gave every appearance of real foliage. Without petticoats or panniers, following the natural lines of her figure in the most flattering way, it draped low at the bust.

A garland of lifelike silk blossoms, resembling the sweetbrier and marigolds of a Surrey riverbank, trimmed the plunging neckline. A chatelaine of those same flowers hung about Julianna's hips, while several strands falling from a chaplet were woven through her hair. The mask, of light papier-mâché painted a deep emerald hue, was cunningly wrought. It pointed upward at the corners to beguiling effect. So did Julianna envisage Titania, the fairy queen. She could scarcely recognize the entrancing creature looking out of the mirror as herself.

The doorknob rattled. Julianna gave a guilty start.

"Milady?" Gwenyth called. "Why is the door locked?"

"Never mind, Gwenyth." Julianna threw on her longest cloak, pulling up the hood to hide her hair. "Has Sir Edmund gone?"

"Aye, ma'am. A good half hour ago, Seamus said. "On the new horse you gave him for Christmas."

As she took off her mask and tucked it into the generous folds of her *manteau,* Julianna smiled to herself. How surprised Edmund had been on Christmas morning when she'd presented him with the handsome roan gelding. Agincourt, he had promptly named his new mount. When the Christmas snow had melted as rapidly as it had fallen, he'd taken every opportunity to go riding.

"Do you need any help getting into your costume, ma'am?"

"No, thank you, Gwenyth." Julianna pulled open the door, nearly sending her maid sprawling onto the dressing room floor. "I managed well on my own. Now I must be off before some other lady snares my husband for the evening. Don't wait up for me. If I know Lady Vanessa, this ball may not end before dawn."

As her carriage neared the Blessington estate, Julianna's heart began to palpitate wildly. Her stomach felt as if a colony of moths had made their home in it. A line of carriages moved up Blessington's long drive at the pace of a sedate largo, halting as each one stopped to deposit its passenger at the door. Julianna took the opportunity to tie her mask in place, and to murmur a desperate prayer that nothing would go amiss.

The Blessington mansion blazed with lights, the air humming with music, conversation and laughter. A servant in splendid livery received Julianna's invitation. Another took her cloak. She shivered, for the entry hall was drafty and her gown very light for the time of year. Some misgiving about her escapade might have been at work, as well. In the company of other new arrivals, she made her way toward the ballroom.

Pausing at the entrance, she caught her breath in wonder at the sight. Never had she seen so large a room in a private dwelling. It was lit by several large chandeliers, each of which held hundreds of candles, their highly polished crystals gently disbursing the light. A string consort played from a raised platform, while tables laden with food and drink ran the length of the far wall. Unable to guess how many people must be in attendance, Julianna could only marvel at Vanessa's powers of organization, to have produced such an extravagant spectacle.

The guests mingled freely, displaying their costumes. Several harlequins in gaudy patches frolicked among the revelers, along with a Punchinello in grotesque full mask and jester's cap. Julianna made her way among the press of guests, keeping a sharp eye out for one familiar figure. There he was! Near the refreshment table, draped in a voluminous white robe and crowned with laurels. Noble Caesar—what a fitting role. Approaching him from behind, she spoke just loud enough to catch his ear.

"Hail, mighty Caesar. Would the ruler of the Romans care to step a dance with the queen of the fairies?"

"By all means, madam."

Even as Caesar led her to the floor, Julianna's heart sank. The man spoke in a reedy tenor and stood a good head shorter than Edmund. As she moved mechanically through the steps of the minuet, Julianna's glance darted from one guest to another. By the time the music stopped, she felt sick with disappointment. She could not begin to count how many men had put aside their periwigs for the night. Even a short, corpulent Friar Tuck, who could be none other than Langston Carew, sported a tonsured scalp in keeping with his role.

Ducking into the crowd to lose her admiring dance partner, it suddenly occurred to Julianna how many elaborate headdresses might hide the head she sought. The bejeweled turban of that Eastern potentate. The feathered bonnet of an American Indian chief. The night-black cowl of—the Mad Abbot of Marlwood! No. There could be only one head beneath that cowl and it surely belonged to Laurence Bayard. Thank heavens he had made himself so conspicuous to her eyes. She would make sure to avoid him.

After accepting dance invitations from several men, none of whom had turned out to be Edmund, Julianna paused to fortify herself with a glass of wine. Downcast and frustrated, she berated herself for not spying him out before the party. Then another unpalatable thought struck her. She could see couples

pairing off—dancing, conversing, flirting. Was Edmund, even
now, whispering sweet words into some other ear, holding some
other hand, planning to kiss some other lips? Julianna cursed
her own short-sighted naiveté. She slammed down her wine cup
so sharply that a Blessington servant looked askance.

Edmund hung back on the fringe of the crowd. Arriving
early, he had taken up a position from which he could monitor
the entrance. Since he had begun his surveillance, three other
knights had come to the ball, though curiously none in black.

Flecked with silver paint, Edmund's woolen armor looked
passably like chain mail, but weighed almost nothing. Bless the
tailor's apprentice who'd suggested lining the suit with uncut
velvet. It added to the bill, but had saved him an agony of
itching. A tabard of the same black velvet hung down to his
knees. When the tailor had asked what emblem they should fix
to the tabard, Edmund had asked for the white forked cross, in
honour of his Crusader ancestor. Edmund prayed that Laurence
had not given Julianna too detailed a description of his costume.

Julianna! Edmund recollected himself. He hadn't been paying
close enough attention to the ladies entering the ballroom. What
if she had come in without his noticing? He looked up, and
there she stood. A sound escaped Edmund's lips—part sigh,
part moan. Blessington's ballroom and guests melted into a diffuse, glowing backdrop for Titania, queen of the fairies, gowned
in leaves and crowned with roses. Edmund could not bring himself to believe she had donned this guise for an illicit meeting
with Laurence Bayard. As boldly as she dared, Julianna was
signaling him, ''I am for here for you, Edmund.''

He knew he should go to her. More than anything, he wanted
to be with her. His legs had other ideas. They balked whenever
he tried to move in her direction, rooting him to the spot. He
watched her approach a man in Roman garb—a man she might
easily have mistaken for him. He needed no further convincing
of her intent. Yet his legs still refused to carry him to her. *Stop
and think,* Edmund's conscience warned him. *You will be walking straight into betrayal and dishonor. The harm you do tonight may never be undone.*

Ever since he'd realized the depth of his need for Julianna, fear of rejection had stayed his hand. With that obstacle suddenly swept away, he had to make a hard choice. Could he face Crispin, having stolen his bride? Wrestling with his puritan morals, Edmund wandered out onto a terrace. His legs raised no objection to going that way. He drew several deep breaths of the crisp winter air in a vain hope it might cool his desire.

At last he felt steady. The secret was to push Julianna from his thoughts, while concentrating on memories of Crispin. Edmund knew what he must do. He must leave the party, now. Tomorrow he'd set out for…anywhere. France. Italy. He would stay away until Brock sent word of Crispin's return. With a vestige of the self-possession that had deserted him the moment he'd set eyes on Julianna, Edmund strode back into the ballroom. In his haste to leave, he jostled one of the other guests.

"I beg your pardon." He bowed absently, desperately eager to be on his way.

"And I beg yours, Sir Knight," replied a merry, musical, teasing voice. "I had better mind where I am going." Julianna swept him a deep curtsy. Every burnished amber curl called to Edmund's fingers and to his lips.

One brief dance, he asked himself, *what harm can it do?*

The tall knight's stark habit in gray, white and black cut a sharp contrast to the vividly colored costumes of the other revelers. Wordlessly, he offered Julianna his hand. Intrigued, she took it. As they swept through a graceful bourrée, Julianna scrutinized her silent partner. A hood, of the same mock chain mail as his body armor, covered his head. She could not tell how much hair might or might not lie beneath that discreet hood.

As the dance ended, the knight bowed his mute leave of her. She laid a hand on his arm to stay him. "Your heraldic badge, Sir Knight? Is it the Maltese cross?"

"Correct, Your Majesty."

Was that Edmund's voice? Having strained so to catch its familiar cadence all night, she was no longer sure she would recognize it. "That is the emblem of the…"

"The Knights of the Order of St. John of Jerusalem, milady."

"Also known as the Knights Hospitaller?"

"That is so."

Again the knight made to leave. Julianna caught his hand.

"You addressed me as 'Your Majesty' just now. Can it be that I am recognized?" Without her telling, none of her other partners had guessed that she portrayed Shakespeare's fairy queen. Edmund, if indeed this were he, would know at a glance.

The knight hesitated a moment before answering. "Is secrecy your aim, my fairy queen, as you steal amongst this mortal company to dance a rondel? I pledge my life to guard your true identity."

"You are courteous and fair-spoken, Sir Knight," she commended him, still uncertain. "But you have found me out. Guard your tongue well, or I might collect upon that pledge and hie you away to my kingdom. Such a gallant, well-favored champion would make a welcome addition to my court."

He bent close, imparting his answer as a secret for her ears alone. "If you would truly see your secret safe, dear lady, threaten me not with a fate I so desire."

"You are too great a flatterer, good sir." Julianna found herself enjoying their flirtatious sparring. "For that offense, I sentence you to attendance upon me for this one evening."

The knight bowed low and kissed her hand. "I am yours to command, Lady Queen."

It must be Edmund. Who else could maintain this flow of poetic discourse with such ease? Though Julianna was not without her doubts, the company of this eloquent knight held far more appeal than continuing her vain search for Edmund among the masked throng.

She took his arm, pointing imperiously to the dance floor. "I command a minuet, gentle knight, followed by some refreshment and more of your pretty compliments."

"It sounds a pleasant program indeed, my liege."

So began an evening of rapture and allure. Keeping up the fiction of their identities, Julianna and her knight-errant flattered and flirted, the silken phrases and poetic compliments dropping effortlessly from their lips. They kept exclusive company, with eyes for no others—dancing, sharing a glass of wine, laughing at their own extravagant, fanciful coquetry. The whole experience was like a dream—sweet, elusive and far too brief. Around them, the company began to slip away, the candles burned low, and the Blessington servants nodded sleepily. The time had come to bid good-night. Julianna's escort drew her into a curtained alcove of the ballroom.

"Have a care for your virtue, Sir Knight. Are you not vowed to a monastic life?" Her question was light, gently chiding, in keeping with the tone of their evening's flirtation.

His reply, however, was urgent, purposeful and sincere. "Even so, yet mortal still—subject to the enchantments of Fairyland, and Cupid's merry malice." Eyes, shadowed behind his mask, were intent upon her face. His hands enfolded hers.

He was so near, and her hopes had been building to this moment for so long, Julianna's voice grew husky with emotion. "Your words are sweet as honey, and your voice as intoxicating as mead. A lady—a queen—even an immortal might lose her heart to you, though it be pledged elsewhere."

He leaned toward her. Julianna tilted her head to meet his approaching lips with her own.

"Her Majesty's heart could have no more tender keeping," he whispered as their lips made contact.

At that first tentative brush, a shiver ran through Julianna's body, like the chill of a searing fever. In all their time together, Edmund had kissed her hands, her forehead. They had exchanged affectionate touches of the cheek. But never, since that aborted kiss on their wedding night, had their lips met. Until now. As the first mild salute deepened and intensified, Julianna could only think it had been well worth the wait. She twined her arms about his neck. One of his arms stole around her waist, the other hand entangled itself in her hair.

His body tensed. His kisses grew fervid and adamant, as though driven by a barely controlled ferocity. She felt her pulse race out of control. The tide of her passion threatened to break its bonds in response to his raw, ruthless ardor. Julianna's turbulent heart exulted. Edmund was hers at last.

It was light when Julianna wakened the next morning. A secretive smile played upon her lips as she indulged in a voluptuous stretch. Giving a low, throaty chuckle, she ran her fingers through her hair as Edmund had done. Then she let her tongue glide lazily over lips still swollen from his kisses. Her flesh tingled with the memory of his touch and the desire for more.

Today her life would begin anew. Having proved to her own satisfaction that Edmund could love her, could want her, she would convince him. He might resist temporarily, as she had resisted. In time he would come to understand. Whatever unlikely circumstances had brought them to the altar, they were married in the eyes of the church. That love and passion had grown between them—was it not a sign they belonged together?

Where had Gwenyth got to? Julianna wondered. Probably using her sleep-in as an excuse to hang about below stairs with the other maidservants. Well, let them enjoy their gossip. Considering the nature of her coming interview with Edmund, it might be better if the servants were otherwise occupied.

Throwing open her wardrobe, Julianna searched for a gown. She briefly considered wearing her fairy queen costume, but finally decided against it. She meant to end her long masquerade this morning by revealing her true feelings to Edmund. It hardly seemed fitting to wear a disguise.

At last she chose a simple gown that Edmund had always liked, one she often wore for their quiet evenings at home. Practicing her speech in front of the mirror, she ran the brush through her hair but did not bother to pin it up. "Such sweet neglect more taketh me," Edmund had said in an unguarded moment. If it was sweet neglect he wanted, she would be happy to oblige.

Passing Edmund's bedchamber, Julianna wondered if he might still be sleeping. After last night, she had not the slightest scruple about stealing into his bed and softly rousing him with a kiss. She liked the idea of catching him in the first golden, drowsy moments of consciousness, before he had the chance to assume his invisible armor of reserve and frosty courtesy.

Unfortunately, his bed was cold and empty. "Edmund?" she called softly, peering into his dressing room. Judging by the temperature of the water in his basin, he had been up for some time. From the uncustomary clutter in the room, Julianna guessed that he had washed and dressed in a hurry. How odd?

Either he had not eaten yet, she decided, glancing into the pristine dining room, or else he had finished quite a while ago. Could he have gone out? Seeing the library door slightly ajar, she chuckled to herself. Apparently he did not intend to make this easy for her. If she wanted Edmund, she would have to beard the lion in his den.

He stood silhouetted against the bright winter sunlight streaming through the window. Stepping into the room and closing the door quietly behind her, Julianna pressed her back against it. She would not let him run off until she'd had her say.

"How does my ardent knight this morning?" she challenged.

With a start, he turned to face her. It was not Edmund after all, she realized with a shock of disappointment. Not only did this man have shoulder-length hair, he had a close-trimmed dark beard that gave him the air of a pirate or a cavalier. His blue velvet coat, strangely familiar, strained to contain the well developed muscles of his arms and chest. His wide stance suggested almost arrogant self-confidence.

"Julianna!" Her puzzled musings were cut short as he moved toward her, a blinding smile flashing on his handsome face. "My sweet, you are a hundred times more beautiful than I remembered."

The gentle bewilderment that had so far buffered her from the truth ripped painfully apart.

"Crispin?" Both her voice and her legs seemed to lose all power. Julianna felt herself melting to the floor.

He caught her in his strong arms, pulling her into a crushing embrace. Before she could voice any of the insistent questions that clamored in her mind, Crispin stilled her lips with a confident, possessive kiss. Dormant, scarcely remembered feelings surged to life in Julianna's heart. She did not know whether to fight them or welcome them.

Above the sound of the library door opening, she heard Edmund's voice. "I can't think where she has got to, Cris—"

Crispin released her lips, but his arms held her tight.

"You have found each other, I see." Edmund's indifferent acknowledgment struck Julianna like a physical blow.

She struggled against Crispin's implacable hold, searching Edmund's gaze with her own. Silently she pleaded with him to rescue her, as he had rescued her from Laurence. But Edmund made no move toward them.

"It's all right, my dear." Crispin chuckled indulgently, raining reassuring kisses on her brow. "Uncle Edmund and I have had a long talk. I know everything. I'll admit I was rather taken aback when he first told me the two of you were married. Of course, I should have known better than to question your loyalty...or his." He flashed Edmund a trusting smile. "Greater love hath no man than a confirmed bachelor like my uncle should let a woman in his life for my sake. I hope you haven't made too great a nuisance of yourself, my sweet."

Part of Julianna wanted to scream at him to stop treating her like a truant child. At the same time, her senses reeled from Crispin's nearness and echoes of her old longing for him.

"On the contrary." Bleak and cold, Edmund's reply might have been chiseled into a slab of granite. "We have managed to remain on quite civil terms."

Suddenly, Julianna felt like a little girl again, confronting her beloved father with the story of Jerome's first abuse. Without even a hint of the regret her father had plainly displayed, Edmund was turning his back on her—giving Crispin's wishes and future happiness precedence over hers. And she had fooled herself into believing he cared for her.

"Excuse me for intruding upon your reunion," said Edmund.

Before they could protest, he was gone.

"Civil terms." Crispin threw back his head, laughing. "He's just the same as ever—phlegmatic and imperturbable. I fear you have suffered a very dull year in my absence, darling one. There, there, my precious. No need to cry over it now."

Chapter Twenty-Five

"Here's the best part of the story." Crispin smiled at Julianna across the dining room table. "Brock, you old sea dog, come sit with us and hear all about it."

"Master Crispin, I fear it would not…" Brock demurred.

"Nonsense." Crispin waved away his objections. "Why, you're one of the family. Besides, I know you want to hear all about my exploits, so don't try to pretend otherwise."

With obvious reluctance, Brock took a seat.

"Now, where was I? Oh yes. We were just returning from a lucrative run to the Conchin coast. Sailing in Philippine waters, we spied plumes of smoke and heard cannon fire off in the distance. As we got closer, we could make out a British ship fighting for her life against a Spanish galleon. Seeing the British colors, we weighed in on the side of our countrymen."

"That's the spirit, boy!" cried Brock.

Crispin's voice rose to a dramatic pitch. "Night was falling. I guessed that the Spaniards had no notion of our presence. Approaching from the west, with the setting sun at our backs, we announced our arrival with a couple of well-aimed eight-pounders fair amidships. One stove in their hull right at the bilge line. I led a boarding party, which distracted the Spaniards from the other ship long enough for her crew to catch their breaths and realize reinforcements had arrived. Caught between two stalwart British crews, the Spaniards surrendered."

"I'll just wager they did." Brock beamed as proudly as if he'd taken a leading part in the skirmish.

Crispin savored the last morsel of his roast veal. "Brock, be sure to tell Mrs. Davies her cooking has not fallen a mite from its usual high standard. I can't tell you how good this tastes after months of salt beef, hardtack and pickled limes."

"Pickled limes?" Julianna's mouth puckered, just saying it.

"Pickled limes," Crispin repeated. "Your father suggested it as a preventative against scurvy. Some crackbrained theory put forward by one of his scientist friends. Worked like a charm, though. I lost crew to enough other ailments and accidents, but not a man to the scurvy. Poor Anson couldn't say the same."

"Anson?" Brock sat up sharply. "Do you mean that chap who set off to sail around the world? What do you know of him? There's been no word of any of his ships for the longest time. I'm sure they've all been given up for dead long ago."

"And rightly so for most of the poor souls," replied Crispin. "But, I'm getting ahead of my story. I was just coming to the best part."

"I thought you had already told the best part." Julianna could not fully censor a note of impatience from her voice.

"I apologize, my dear. Am I boring you stiff with all this talk of ships and fighting?"

"Of course not." Julianna relented. That errant chestnut curl, now gilded by the tropic sun, had fallen forward onto Crispin's brow. It gave him an endearing boyish look, in spite of his beard. "But I would like to hear how you came back to England so far ahead of schedule."

"Well, it is all wrapped up together, dearest. So humor me by listening a few minutes longer. When the smoke cleared, the captain of the other British vessel summoned me to extend his thanks. Who should it turn out to be, but Commodore Anson! He'd been reduced to a single ship and a fraction of his original sailors."

"Sir Edmund said Anson's expedition was an ill-advised stunt from the very beginning." Brock looked properly gratified at hearing his master's opinion vindicated.

"Speaking of Sir Edmund…" For the first time in months,

Julianna felt it necessary to use his title. "Where has he got to? I haven't seen him since yesterday."

Brock shrugged. "Out in the City on some urgent business, ma'am. Or so he said."

"Isn't that like him, though?" Crispin grinned. "It would take more than the unexpected return of his only nephew from the other side of the world to disrupt my uncle's sacred routine. But back to my story. As it turned out, the Spanish vessel we had captured was a richly laden treasure galleon. Anson graciously pledged me and my crew a share of the booty. He knew it would take his ship a while to limp back to England, so he dispatched me ahead with news of their coming. I already had a good cargo of spices aboard. So, with my fortune assured, I decided the time had come to return home and claim my bride."

Brock looked back and forth between Crispin and Julianna. "Your bride, sir?"

"My bride," affirmed Crispin, nodding toward Julianna. "Brock, do you mean to say she and Uncle Edmund never told you the reason for their sham marriage?"

"Sham?" the steward repeated, his face quite devoid of expression. If Crispin had picked up the poker from the dining room hearth and clubbed him with it, Julianna doubted Mr. Brock could have looked more dazed.

"We told no one, Crispin." Julianna spoke up, to give Brock a moment to digest the news. "In the beginning, Sir Edmund feared what Jerome might do if he found out he had tricked him."

Her explanation seemed to satisfy Crispin. "Surely a sharp fellow like Brock had his suspicions, though?"

"Well, sir," Brock replied haltingly, "I did wonder at your uncle getting married on the spur of the moment like that. Now I see things clearly enough."

He shot Julianna a searching look.

Where was he and how had he got here? Blearily peering around the ill-lit tavern, Edmund wrinkled his nose at the cloudy liquid pooled in the bottom of his cup. Did they call this grape effluent, wine? He remembered walking back from a late evening at the Chapterhouse. Taking an unfamiliar route, he'd passed this place. Noisy merriment had drawn him inside. Anything was better than roaming the damp cold streets, walking his body into a state of exhaustion that might buy his mind a few hours' rest.

He'd hoped to leave his cares outside in the winter fog. They had clambered in, hot on his heels. Bitterness, sorrow, shame—poor drinking companions. He'd tried to silence them with wine, but they'd howled even louder. Worse, they had beckoned another companion to the table—frustrated desire.

How could he still want that woman? Edmund raged at himself. She'd enticed him. She'd tempted him. She'd made him turn his back on Crispin. All the while, she hadn't cared a fig for him. The moment Crispin came swaggering through the door, she'd flung herself on him like a bitch in heat. Skeldon was right. Edmund rued the day he'd opened his home to that Jezebel with her provocative curls, bright and wild. Eyes and lips that could beguile a man to perdition. Damn it! He was doing it again. Would she never cease to torment him?

With a peremptory rap on the table, he called for more wine.

Julianna's eyes opened. She stared into the darkness. It must be three o'clock or thereabouts. Ever since Crispin's homecoming, she had wakened each morning at this bleak hour to grapple with questions that seemed to have no answers. Questions about two fine men—her feelings for them and theirs for her.

Among all her questions, she knew only one thing for certain. Crispin's feelings toward her had not changed. He was as gallant and ardent as ever. She was not sure her own love for him had altered a great deal. Who could resist Crispin's open, engaging charm?

And Edmund—what of him? Did he truly care for her? What had their Twelfth Night tryst meant to him? Had he been reaching out to her in his tentative, cautious way? Had he believed she was someone else? Or had he coldly and deliberately set out to test her loyalty to Crispin? Could that be the reason he had avoided her so pointedly since Crispin's return?

Her own feelings for Edmund were nearly as difficult to

fathom as his for her. The love that had grown in her heart like a slow-blooming rose—would it fade gently and quietly with time? Or would it thrust its roots deeper still, blighting any chance of happiness with Crispin?

As for the future, Crispin took it for granted that Edmund would immediately pursue an annulment. Once or twice he had expressed his impatience at never being able to catch his uncle to discuss the matter. Julianna was in no hurry to change her status. Whenever she looked ahead to an irrevocable parting from Edmund, a senseless panic engulfed her.

She would be a very foolish and willful creature indeed, Julianna scolded herself, to cling to a man who might care nothing for her, while turning her back on one who obviously loved her very much. Yet, in the days since Crispin's return, she had often found herself scrambling to the window hoping to catch a glimpse of Edmund coming home. Dressing with unusual care before meals in case he should attend. Retiring to bed early in anticipation of a provocative dream.

Oh, enough of this! Rising, Julianna donned a dressing gown and slippers. If she was ever to sort out her conflicting emotions she must know Edmund's feelings for her, clearly and truly. And she must make certain he knew of her feelings for him. How could they ever hope to talk candidly if he continued to avoid her, or if Crispin was always present, forcing them to pretend? Edmund must come home to sleep sometime. If he was home now, she would speak to him now. If he was not home yet, she would wait and speak to him when he arrived. Perhaps by catching him unawares, she might surprise a more honest admission from him than she could possibly get if he came prepared.

The house was dead quiet with no distant stirring from the scullery or the maids' quarters. Edmund's bed had not been slept in, Julianna discovered when she peeped in. A dim light beckoned at the end of the gallery, from low-burning candles in the entry hall below. Slumped there, sound asleep, snored Mordecai Brock. His presence could only mean that Edmund had not yet returned home. Julianna confirmed the time by the tall pedestal clock. It had, indeed, gone three.

"Brock." She nudged his shoulder. "Get yourself to bed. Since I'm awake anyway, I can wait up for Sir Edmund."

He startled at her touch. "No, no. I'm fine, ma'am. Just dozed for a moment." He pulled a hand down the crags of his face and blinked reddened eyes under his shaggy brows. Julianna marked the deep gray smudges under those eyes.

"How often this week has he been out so late?" Her tone brooked no prevarication. "Three nights? Five? Six?"

"Not six," Brock insisted. "No more than four."

"Four nights away until almost dawn?"

She was about to order him to bed once again, when the sound of voices erupted and the front door swung wide.

"There you are, sir. Delivered right to your front door." Julianna did not recognize the voice.

"Capital, my good fellow. Take your hire out of this, and a good-night to you." Edmund's voice boomed through the stillness of the entry with drunken bonhomie. He lurched forward, recovering his balance within inches of her.

"Good morning," she greeted him, her tone deceptively level.

He reeled back slightly. "Good morning, my dear," he replied with a befuddled grin. "You are abroad early."

Edmund made to step around her, but Julianna moved back and to the left, blocking his way. "No. You are abroad late."

As he squinted at the clock, she added, "You come and go these days whenever the whim takes you. Mrs. Davies never knows when to serve dinner. Brock sits up until all hours. It is not like you to treat your household in so cavalier a fashion."

His eyes narrowed. Julianna had often seen that look of inebriate belligerence on Jerome's face. It sickened her to see it on Edmund's.

"I have been without a mother since the day I was born," he growled. "I see no need to fill the vacancy at this late date."

Julianna winced. Edmund took her firmly by the arms, removing her from his path. Then he ascended the stairs with a heavy, deliberate tread.

"You may not need a mother," she called after him, "but if you go on like this, you will soon need a keeper!"

"Don't pay any mind, lass." Brock's voice was drowsy and dispirited. "A man never means the bitter things he says when he's in his cups."

Julianna recalled secrets she had confessed while in her cups. Though she would never have dared utter such words sober, they had been all too true.

"What were you up roaming the halls for, at this hour?" Brock asked.

"I needed to talk with him."

Brock nodded slowly. "Best let it wait on the morning now."

Julianna had no intention of trying to talk with Edmund in his present condition. But as she hurried past his door, she heard a single dry, retching sob. It was a sound more tormented than the weeping of any woman. Was Edmund as torn and bewildered by all of this as she? Before she could stay herself, Julianna was through the door and on her knees before him.

"Edmund, you must tell me what's wrong." She threw her arms around his waist, driven nearly to tears herself by the raw pain that radiated from him. "Is it me? Have I done this to you?"

Her touch set tongues of fire licking Edmund's flesh. With a savage will all its own, lust reared between his thighs like an unbridled stallion.

"Edmund, I'm so sorry. Believe me, I never meant for this to happen."

Looking into her eyes, he saw sweet, aching pity. The kind of pity she'd spared the ailing old man she had married. He'd been a fool to think she could feel anything else for him.

"Get out!" he roared. "I did not invite you here and I'll be damned if you are welcome."

"Please, Edmund, don't send me away. We need to talk."

Shrinking from her incendiary touch, he thrust Julianna back. "Get out, I said. I want nothing more to do with you."

"Edmund, I beg you, don't shut me out. I am your wife."

It took his breath away, that she should taunt him with so bald and cruel a lie. He ached to take her, break her, to crush her beneath him with a ferocity that would make Laurence's thwarted rape look tame and well mannered. Summoning a desperate measure of self-control, Edmund fought to check that raging urge. He feared it would not be long denied.

"You are *his* wife. That is all you have ever been. You are nothing to me!"

She seemed to shatter before him into a thousand jagged shards. A wild exultation possessed him. If nothing else, at least he had the power to hurt her. Julianna turned and fled. The flame of ascendancy in Edmund's heart was swamped and extinguished by cold wave of despair.

Oh, what now?

Edmund heard voices all the way from the entry hall, and the sound of brisk footsteps in the gallery beyond his door. His head felt swollen to twice its normal size. His memories of the previous night were even more blurry than his vision. Somehow he knew he must avoid recalling them more clearly.

He dressed hurriedly, fumbling with his clothes. What was Julianna up to now? Ever since he'd let her into his life, there'd been an endless parade of fuss and bother. Edmund made no effort to spare his throbbing head. The pain fueled his anger, and he wanted to stay angry. Anger was a strong, forceful emotion. He could live with anger.

"What's going on here?" he barked at a trio of maidservants, ferrying various boxes and bundles down the hallway.

"It's the mistress's orders," volunteered Agnes, her eyes suspiciously red. "Says she's leaving."

"We'll see about that." Edmund strode to the stairs. The entry hall was piled high with luggage, and Brock was nowhere in sight, blast him. Crispin and Julianna stood in the midst of the clutter—arguing, by the tone of their voices.

"Dearest, what is the meaning of all this?" Crispin gestured about him.

Edmund froze, halfway down the stairs, listening for Julianna's reply. She looked up, pinning him with her gaze.

"Surely you must realize, Crispin—" even as she addressed his nephew, her eyes never wavered from Edmund "—what an awkward position this puts me in. Living in the same house with the husband from whom I am seeking an annulment, *and* the man I plan to marry once that annulment is forthcoming."

"Oh, dear. I hadn't thought of that." After a moment's consideration, Crispin asked, "But why so abrupt and hasty? You might have consulted Uncle Edmund and me, instead of taking everyone by surprise like this."

"I saw no reason to consult you, as this is not your house."

Some rebellious quarter in Edmund's heart applauded Julianna's spirit.

"As for your uncle," she continued, her voice brisk and cold as the winter wind whistling outdoors, "he has been far too preoccupied with his *affairs* to spare any thought for my situation."

"Where will you go?" Crispin sounded none too pleased that she had taken matters into her own hands.

Edmund saw Julianna hesitate. Apparently she'd been so eager to get out from under his roof, she hadn't given much thought to her destination. He fought to quell a flicker of sympathy for her.

"I...er...that is..."

"She will come and stay with me, of course." Vanessa breezed through the door without even a knock. "Crispin, dear boy!" She conferred a glancing kiss on each of his cheeks. "I heard you'd come home covered in wealth and glory. My, how rugged you look. And I do like the beard. Enough to set any lady's heart palpitating, I declare."

"Oh, hullo, Vanessa," said Crispin absently. "What are you doing here?"

"A fine, mannerly greeting from a cousin I have not seen in more than a year." Vanessa swept a disapproving glance around the entry hall. "Why, this looks like the luggage room at a busy posting inn." She took Julianna's hand. "No call to shift all your worldly goods this very day, my pet. Just the necessities."

Spurred to action by Vanessa's arrival, Edmund descended into the fray, all flickers of admiration and sympathy for Julianna ruthlessly extinguished. "So the two of you have contrived this between you?" he challenged the women.

"Ah, Edmund. I wondered where you were hiding." Vanessa

made no effort to greet him with a kiss. "As for contrivance, I have never heard anything so ridiculous, even from you. I only just got wind of all this coil. Unlike you *gentlemen,* I could tell immediately what an intolerable position it placed poor Julianna in. So I am here, and not a moment too soon, as usual."

Leave it to Vanessa to seize upon the situation to settle some imagined score with him, thought Edmund.

"If she finds my house so intolerable," he snapped, "by all means let her be on her way." He turned and started back up the stairs. "And good riddance to both of you."

"Polish up your lovely manners, Cousin," Vanessa called after him. "They have deteriorated most scandalously of late."

"Don't pay Uncle Edmund any mind," Crispin advised the women. "You know how he hates a commotion and being caught off guard."

"I seldom pay him much mind," said Vanessa.

Behind him, Edmund heard Crispin and Vanessa laughing harder than her feeble quip warranted. He also heard slippered footsteps on the stairs, light and fleet.

"Edmund?" Julianna caught him by the coattail.

He wanted to wrench himself free of her, but he could not. Neither could he trust himself to ask what she wanted.

"This house was my sanctuary when I most needed one." She spoke quietly, as if bestowing a confidence. Every word went straight to Edmund's heart. "You were my protector when I had no other. I owe you past what I can ever repay. If you want me to stay, you have only to say the word."

If she had drawn a fixed bayonet and plunged it into his chest, she could not have inflicted so deep and gaping a wound. For a moment, Edmund could find neither the breath nor the courage to reply. Then the harsh lessons of his childhood came to his rescue. *Bury the hurt—bury it deep. Look and speak as though it does not matter in the least.*

Without turning to look at Julianna, he spoke as if her offer did not matter to him in the least. "Any debt you owe me may be discharged by making my nephew a loving and faithful wife. I will file an annulment petition before the week is out."

Her only response was to release her hold on his coat. Deliberately, one step after another, Edmund ascended the last few stairs. Deliberately, one step after another, he walked down the hall. Deliberately, he opened the door of his bedchamber and went inside. Over and over he told himself he was much better off to have Julianna gone from his house. And though he argued the point quite strenuously for the rest of the day, Edmund could not quite make himself believe it.

Chapter Twenty-Six

"**J**ust think of it, dearest." Crispin inhaled a deep breath of fresh spring air. "In less than a month's time we'll be married and on our way to the South Seas. I know you'll come to love shipboard life once you get used to it, and all our exotic ports of call."

April sunshine beamed down on the paths of Vauxhall and their vibrant borders of hyacinths and daffodils swaying in the warm breeze. The June-like temperatures of the past few days had accelerated the budding of leaves on all the trees and shrubbery.

"Slow down, please, Crispin." Julianna silently chastised herself for the sharpness in her voice. "I'm not sure Vauxhall was such a good idea. The weather is very fine, but these paths are a sea of mud."

To illustrate the problem, she lifted one foot. The platform sole and high heel of her shoe came free of the mire with a wet, sucking noise. The hem of her gown looked filthy.

Crispin laughed. "Well, if we can't walk, at least come sit for a while and enjoy the sun and the songs of the birds. Wait until you see some of the strange birds they have in the tropics. Such plumage. Puts our drab little swallows and wrens to shame."

The shrill cacophony of birds held little charm for Julianna. The grass looked drab and washed-out. Even the temperate south wind carried an odor of rotting leaves and horse manure. Before she could catch herself, she sighed.

"Dear me." Crispin stopped short in his lecture on tropical fauna, casting her a look of mingled concern and impatience. "I'd hoped an afternoon in the fresh air might shake you out of your doldrums. I'm sorry to see it hasn't had the desired effect."

"Doldrums? You'll be taking me there soon, won't you? Isn't there a place you sailors call the Doldrums?" Once again Julianna made an effort to appear happy and interested. The strain of holding a fixed smile was beginning to give her a headache.

"Not a place exactly." Crispin dove happily after her change of subject, like a spaniel chasing a stick. "They're a band of latitudes near the equator. Fitful breezes, lots of rain. A ship can find herself becalmed there for days."

They both fell silent for a moment. Then Crispin asked, "Do you recall the last time we came to Vauxhall?"

"How could I forget? You proposed to me here." Thinking back to that day, it seemed to her that Crispin had hardly changed at all. He was as sweet and attentive as ever. The frivolous, romantic girl who had accepted Crispin's proposal, she hardly recognized.

"So I did," said Crispin. "It was the happiest day of my life, when you agreed to be my wife. I've had only one happier since—the day I came back to you after those lonely months at sea. But I foresee another, happier still. Once we can get past this annulment tribunal." He snapped his fingers. "That's what's been troubling you, isn't it, my angel?"

"I'm sorry, Crispin. What did you say? The tribunal. It has been weighing on my mind, perhaps more so than I'd realized."

He reached out and took her hand. "You needn't worry, my sweet. Uncle Edmund gave his testimony last week, and he said it went well. Dry and tedious, I expect, but once it's over and the bishop's court declares you were never truly married, you and I can be together. Just as we planned when I proposed to you."

"How is your uncle these days?" Julianna struggled to keep a tremor from her voice. "I haven't seen him in ever so long."

"Fine. Same as ever. Keeps pretty much to himself, but that's nothing new. I don't think he was much pleased when that piece came out in the *Spectator* about the annulment and why the two of you had got married in the first place. Hates having anyone else know his business. Always did.''

"Does he ever ask after me?'' The question slipped out despite her most diligent efforts contain it.

"Now and again,'' replied Crispin. "Just the other night he inquired if Vanessa had talked your ears off yet. I assured him that not only were those exquisite, shell-like appendages still in their proper place on either side of your incomparable face, but they were still the most beautiful ears in all the world.''

Julianna tried to summon up the thrill with which she had once greeted Crispin's extravagant, poetic compliments. But all she could think of was Edmund's wry dictum: "Any currency thrown about too freely soon loses its value.'' She had learned the truth of those words during the long, bleak months of winter, as the annulment proceedings had dragged on. Crispin's constant flattery, though sincere and eloquent, had quickly paled. It was Edmund's sparing tributes that Julianna mused on, hoarding them in her heart like stolen gems—all the more precious for their rarity and for what they had cost him to bestow.

Tomorrow she would have to face the ecclesiastical tribunal and say she had been coerced into wedding Edmund, admit that their relationship had never been physically consummated, agree with his petition that the church declare their marriage null and void. Hard as she had tried for the past three months, knowing it was the wish of both him and Crispin, Julianna could not think of herself as the wife of anyone but Edmund.

In the tranquil seclusion of his library, Edmund leaned back in his armchair and took a long draw from his pipe. A slim volume of Shakespeare's sonnets lay open on his knees. Lately they had become his reading matter of choice. He took strange comfort in knowing that the great poet had also once been a middle-aged fellow torn between his love for a fair young man and a tantalizing woman. From the alchemy of his genius, Shakespeare had taken his own pain and passion, transmuting them into verse of immortal beauty.

As he slowly turned the pages, Edmund found two leaves of his book stuck together. Peeling them carefully apart, he discovered a slip of tiny wild lilies pressed and dried. Julianna's hand-iwork, no doubt. As he held the sprig of flowers in his hand, a faint ghost of their perfume awakened his sweetest memories of an enchanted summer at Abbot's Leigh.

Absently he brought the pipe to his lips. It suddenly occurred to him how disappointed Julianna would be to know he had taken up smoking again. That thought was enough to make him tap the ashes and lay the pipe aside.

His gaze wandered to the open pages of the book and he began to read:

When to the sessions of sweet silent thought
I summon up remembrance of things past...

One of Shakespeare's best, to be sure. The closing couplet of the sonnet resonated in Edmund's heart.

But if the while I think on thee, dear friend
All losses are restored and sorrows end.

It was true. His only happiness these days lay in his memories of Julianna. They had hurt at first, taunting him with mirages of what might have been. But gradually the bitterness had faded, until only the magic remained. Shakespeare had made him see clearly what he had only glimpsed until now. He'd been looking at everything the wrong way. Instead of resenting the fact that he could not have Julianna, he should thank Providence for the time and affection they had shared. He should delight in her happiness with Crispin. As for his withdrawal from society...

A tentative, almost fearful knock on the library door inter-rupted Edmund's musings.

"Come, Brock," he called. "Don't skulk out in the hall."

Mordecai Brock edged into the room, his nose wrinkled as though suspiciously sniffing the wind.

"Well?" Edmund cast his steward an expectant look. Lately, nothing short of mortal catastrophe could prompt his servants to disturb the solitude of his library.

"Someone to see you, sir. I told him you wouldn't like to be disturbed, but—"

"But," interjected Langston Carew, waddling into the room, "I informed your man that I didn't get where I am today by readily taking no for an answer."

"Come in, Langston. Good to see you." Edmund indicated the empty chair opposite him. "I wouldn't have denied you admittance, old friend. As it happens, I am badly in need of a breath of fresh air, which you always provide. And speaking of fresh air—" he signaled to Brock "—it's awfully close and smoky in here. Throw open the sash, will you? And kindly refrain from reminding me that you offered to do it two hours ago, at which time I nearly bit your head off."

Carew climbed into his seat, his feet dangling just short of the floor. He chortled. "Temper getting the better of you these days, old fellow?"

"I fear so," Edmund confessed, with a rueful glance at his steward. "But that is all about to change. Can I offer you a drink, Langston?"

"I wouldn't refuse a cup of your good claret."

"What brings you out at such an early hour?" Edmund asked his guest, after the claret had been poured and Brock had discreetly departed. It was nearly teatime.

"I've come with exciting news, old fellow. A by-election's been declared and one of the vacant seats is right in your home patch in central Surrey. You're as good as elected, man."

Edmund gave a faint, regretful smile. "That would have been very good news indeed. But I can't imagine the Whigs still want me to stand for that seat any more than I'm inclined to do."

He gestured toward a small pile of newspapers tossed disdainfully to the floor. "Ever since the *Spectator* published that scurrilous story about my marriage to Julianna, I'm sure I've become a general laughing stock, if not worse. Hardly the stuff of a winning political candidate, at any rate."

"Tut, tut." Carew lifted the current issue of *Gentleman's Magazine* from the side table. "You, my friend, are laboring under the misapprehension that there is such a thing as bad publicity. Why, the papers are so fiercely partisan these days that vilification in one necessarily means the others must rally round and raise you to sainthood. The secret is getting your name before the voters. Nothing worse can be said of a candidate on election day than 'Who's he?' Have you read this piece by young Johnson? So laudatory it's downright sickening. You couldn't ask for a more eloquent champion. I wonder if he'd hire out to write your speeches?''

Edmund considered for a moment. For every generous, high-minded soul like Samuel Johnson, there would be a dozen of Jerome Skeldon's ilk. Ready to snigger behind his back and ask each other how he could have played husband to the most desirable woman in London, but not been man enough to claim her. His pride could not suffer such humiliating scrutiny.

"I'm sorry, Langston. It's quite out of the question."

"Think it over." Carew swirled the last of his claret around the glass and bolted it in a single toss. "You could do a bit of good, you know. Not that I care for that sort of idealistic nonsense myself."

Just then, a breeze from the hedgerows of Hyde Park stirred the draperies and beckoned Edmund. Rising from the depths of his armchair, he sauntered over to the window. Another spring was warming the world to life, just as Julianna had once warmed him. By turning his back on the world, Edmund realized, he was denying the profound influence she'd had on his life—denying his love for her. He had done it once in rage and pain when he drove her out of his house. He would never do it again, no matter what the cost to his cursed pride.

From now on he would fulfill his love for Julianna in the only honorable way open to him—by being the man she had helped him to become and by living the kind of life she would want him to live. Slowly Edmund's lips spread into a broad grin. The expression felt unfamiliar, but not unpleasant. He turned back to Langston Carew with a single question.

"You'll manage my campaign?"

There was no use trying to sleep, Julianna decided as she tossed restlessly in Vanessa's guest bed. Tomorrow she must face those dry old clerics and give testimony that would permanently

sever her ties with Edmund. Soon afterward, she'd make vows
that would forever bind her to Crispin. Then she would sail away
out of Edmund's life, never to return. Though she would meet
her fate with womanly resignation, worries still gnawed at her
heart.

And there was no one with whom she could share those worries, no sympathetic shoulder on which to vent her growing dis-
content. Always she must conceal her true feelings, make every
effort to appear cheerful—just as she had while Jerome blighted
her childhood. Julianna recalled the overwhelming relief of telling Edmund her painful secret. If only she had someone to confide in now.

Vanessa? The very idea made Julianna laugh aloud in the dark.
True, she was grateful to the dowager countess for offering her
sanctuary when life at Fitzhugh House had become intolerable.
Her former irritation with the beautiful countess, once bordering
on sheer hatred, had moderated and softened with time. She now
felt a queer mixture of amusement for Vanessa's public persona,
and puzzled compassion for the unhappy woman she sensed
trapped beneath it.

But her budding friendship with Vanessa was tainted with a
sense of wistful envy. Once the annulment became final and she
had left England, Vanessa would have a clear field to pursue
Edmund. If the contrary old fool had any sense, he'd let her
catch him. Vanessa might be good for Edmund, Julianna grudgingly admitted. She wouldn't let him retreat into the isolation of
his library. She would keep him actively engaged with the world.
And if he did decide to stand for Parliament, as Julianna fondly
hoped, Vanessa would make an incomparable politician's wife.
Perhaps she *was* the logical choice for a confidante.

The night was still comparatively young for one of Vanessa's
relentless sociability. Rising from bed, Julianna donned a wrap
and slippers, resolved to wait up for her in the drawing room.
She might even help herself to a small ration from the brandy
decanter—just enough to relax the emotional barriers she'd
erected against Vanessa, and perhaps ease her to sleep later on.

The amber liquid splashed into an exquisite snifter of cut crystal, which matched the decanter.

"Pour me one while you're at it."

Julianna jumped and gasped as that casual request floated like a ghost in the empty drawing room. The compact figure of the dowager countess rose from a high-backed armchair.

"Vanessa, you scared the life out of me! Your lovely decanter came close to being a pile of broken glass and a puddle of brandy on the floor."

"In that case, I'll pour my own while your nerves recover."

Vanessa was her usual pristine picture, even well after midnight and a ridotto at the Austrian embassy. She wore a sumptuous velvet gown in her favorite shade of lavender, accented by a magnificent amethyst necklace. Even with so many other matters weighing upon her mind, Julianna could not suppress a familiar pang of envy. Perhaps if she had been so beautiful, Edmund might have loved her.

"What are you doing home so early, Vanessa? Did the party break up in a heated duel over your favors?"

"Not tonight." Vanessa smiled wryly, pouring herself a very generous tot of brandy. "But I had some serious thinking to do, and that string consort at the embassy is not in the least conducive to reflection. One of the viols is always sharp."

"Thinking? Reflection? This smacks of something very solemn indeed." Julianna teased. "Is Laurence in trouble again?"

"When is he not?" After a most unladylike swig of her brandy, Vanessa settled on the chaise. "Oh, he settled down for a while after Edmund put the fear of God into him last summer. Lately he's making up for lost time. Sneaking around with Colonel Harcourt's brazen chit of a wife. When I refused to rescue him from his latest financial calamity, the young idiot threatened to sell off Bayard Hall in order to settle his debts. But it's not Laurence I'm thinking about. I've decided to wash my hands of him until he grows up."

"Good for you, Vanessa." Julianna sank down onto the chaise, raising her own glass to toast the idea.

Vanessa rolled her eyes. "I hope he learns a little sense before some hot-tempered husband blows his head off in a duel."

"If not your wayward brother, what is the cause of all this

earnest contemplation?'' An impulse of genuine concern moved Julianna to add, ''You're not ill, I hope?''

''Only ill at ease.'' Vanessa took another drink. ''If you must know, I'm considering a marriage proposal.''

''Are you?'' Julianna tried to sound casual. ''Anyone I know?''

''Clive Farraday.''

Julianna blinked in surprise. A handsome, soft-spoken man with kind eyes, Mr. Farraday had been a frequent caller in recent weeks and a fixture at most of Vanessa's social engagements. The countess had barely condescended to acknowledge his existence.

''I hear he has a large fortune,'' said Julianna. ''Perhaps he could buy you Bayard Hall for a wedding present.''

Vanessa fixed her with a look of mild contempt. ''You sound far too much like me, Julianna. Don't cultivate the tendency, I beg you. And don't make fun of Clive.'' Her voice died away. ''He's a very dear man.''

''If you care for him, what is there to think about, Vanessa? Accept his proposal.''

''How easily you say it. Accept his proposal. Step in front of a runaway team of horses. Throw yourself off a cliff.''

''You aren't making much sense, Vanessa. Perhaps you shouldn't drink your brandy so fast. If you don't care for Mr. Farraday, turn him down, by all means.'' Months of pent-up exasperation sharpened Julianna's voice.

Vanessa's rose-petal complexion went white as snow. ''I'll thank you not to take that tone with me, young lady. It's all very well for you. You'll soon be wed to the love of your life and sailing off to paradise.''

''He is *not* the love of my life,'' Julianna protested before she could stop herself.

One delicate brow arched. ''Indeed? Why are you putting everyone through all this ado to marry him then?''

Knowing she had said too much already, Julianna hung her head wearily. ''Because he wants me.'' Somewhere between a sigh and a whisper, her answer was addressed as much to herself as to Vanessa. ''And Edmund doesn't.''

''What do you want?''

''It hardly matters, since I want what I can never have.''

Vanessa reached out one alabaster hand, tilting Julianna's chin to meet her insistent gaze. ''Wrong on both counts,'' she said softly. ''In the first place, what you want matters a great deal. You cannot control how Edmund or Crispin feel. You cannot even know for certain. Therefore…''

'' 'To thine own self be true'?'' Julianna's tone dripped venomous sarcasm.

''Trite advice, I know.'' Vanessa shrugged. ''Sound enough, though. Being true to yourself may not guarantee you'll be true to everyone else. But if you are not true to your own heart, how can you be true to others? You can't possibly make Crispin happy if you are miserable.''

''Perhaps I won't always feel this way. Once this wretched annulment is over and Crispin and I are together all the time…''

''Do you honestly believe that?''

Julianna's gaze faltered before the fondly pitying look in Vanessa's eyes. She shook her head.

''Neither do I.''

''It's too late to do anything about it now,'' Julianna insisted.

''It's never too late for love. You taught me that.''

''I haven't the faintest idea what you're talking about, Vanessa. I appreciate your advice. I'm sure you mean well.…''

From a hidden fold in her voluminous skirts, Vanessa drew out a miniature in an exquisite frame of gold filigree. Julianna gasped. Staring at the tiny portrait was like looking into a mirror and seeing a reflection of her childhood self. The little girl in the painting must be Vanessa's daughter.

''You see the resemblance, I gather?'' whispered Vanessa. ''The two of you have more in common than your red-brown curls and wide doe eyes. Like you, she had a heart enraptured by trifles and cast down, not easily, but so very deep. Every time I look at you, some long-buried memory of her rises up to pierce my heart.''

Hearing a catch in Vanessa's voice, Julianna glanced up from her intense contemplation of the miniature. The sight that met her eyes was one she had never expected to see. One by one, tears, like beads of crystal, slid silently from beneath Vanessa's closed eyelids, down the sculpted ivory contours of her cheeks. There was nothing artificial about the perfection of her face at that instant. Every lineament was imprinted with a depth and purity of sorrow that only served to refine her beauty.

Feeling like an intruder upon Vanessa's private pain, Julianna ached to offer comfort. Reaching out slowly, she brought her hand to rest upon the older woman's.

Vanessa drew several breaths, increasingly controlled. When her eyes opened at last, they were vague, fixed and inward-looking. Her voice, when she began to speak, was hardly recognizable—deeper in timbre, devoid of animation or inflection. Like one reciting a lesson conned by long and concentrated rote.

"When Langston Carew first began singing your praises, I thought it would be easy to hate you—so young and winsome."

Vanessa envied her? Julianna's imagination could scarcely compass the idea.

"When I met you for the first time, your very likeness to my daughter stung as deeply as any intentional affront."

Julianna understood. "So you stung back."

Vanessa nodded. "But how could I hate anyone so like my darling baby? You have this infuriating capacity to inspire affection, Julianna."

With a rueful grin, Vanessa came to herself, impatiently brushing the tears from her cheeks. "My eyes will be all red and puffy tomorrow," she scolded herself. "And you'll look like the very devil, too, unless you get some sleep."

"How can I sleep? I still have no idea what to do."

Vanessa leaned forward and kissed her on the forehead. Washed by earlier tears, her eyes were pools of liquid emerald. "I think we both know what we have to do, my dear." Her voice faded to a reflective whisper. "The question is, can we find the courage to do it?"

Chapter Twenty-Seven

"Shall I rephrase the question, Lady Fitzhugh?"

"I beg your pardon?" With an embarrassed start, Julianna realized she had been treating the august dean of St. Paul's to a slack stare, while her thoughts wandered a million miles away. Neither her talk with Vanessa nor the potent brandy had helped her sleep. Now she felt dazed and disoriented.

"You told this court how your stepbrother coerced you into wedding Sir Edmund Fitzhugh," said the dean, audibly impatient.

That much Julianna did remember. She nodded.

"I have asked once, and now I ask again, were you and Sir Edmund intimate at any time during your marriage?"

Julianna opened her mouth, but no words came forth. Her heart began to pound frantically, as though she had suddenly opened her eyes and found herself poised to step off a sheer precipice. Voices echoed in her mind.

Any debt you owe me may be discharged by making my nephew a loving and faithful wife.

It was the happiest day of my life, when you agreed to be my wife.

You can't possibly make Crispin happy, if you are miserable. What do you want?

Once again Julianna became aware of the dean's pale gaze upon her. Before he could ask his question a third time, she gasped her answer. "Yes."

Vanessa's words drowned out all the others. *It's never too late for love.*

"Lady Fitzhugh." The dean spoke slowly. He sounded as if he was tempted to add mental incapacity to Sir Edmund's list of grounds for annulment. "Perhaps you misunderstood. My question was, were you and Sir Ed—"

"I heard your question, sir." Suddenly the rapid beat of her heart felt strong and exhilarating. "And I understood it fully. You want to know if I ever shared Sir Edmund's bed in the time we were married. And the answer is yes."

The wraithlike dean went white. His fellow clerics went red. They put their heads together, whispering feverishly amongst themselves. Finally the dean turned back to Julianna.

"It is possible for a couple to share a bed without...that is..." The dean's pale face was beginning to redden also.

Julianna responded quickly, for she did not want to tell an outright falsehood. She had shared Edmund's bed. Had slept with him on more than one occasion. As for intimacy—were not the confidences they had shared as intimate, in their way, as the physical intercourse of most married couples?

"I have lain naked in my husband's arms, sir," she said in a calm, firm voice. "I have felt his hands and lips on parts of my person that modesty forbids me to name."

The dean looked ready to swoon.

One of the other clergymen spoke up. "But Sir Edmund assured us...."

The third produced a handkerchief and began to wipe his sweating upper lip.

Suddenly Julianna found herself enjoying their obvious bewilderment. "I'm not certain my husband remembers the night in question. We attended a very gay party that evening and I fear we partook too liberally of the refreshments. One thing led to another, and before I knew it, there we were in his bed...."

The dean's prominent Adam's apple bobbed furiously above his clerical collar. "I believe you have answered the question most satisfactorily, madam. Why, may I ask, have you kept this information to yourself and allowed this hearing to go forward?"

"I felt bound to respect my husband's decision to seek this annulment, gentlemen." No need to stretch the truth on that point. "But I will not sit here, under oath, and deny the deep and abiding love I bear him."

After consulting his brother clerics, the dean declared, "The court must now recess to consider this new evidence."

As the tribunal adjourned in consternation, Julianna caught her breath and tried to quell the insistent flutter in her stomach. Unless she misunderstood canon law, her testimony had destroyed any chance of Edmund getting an annulment. If he wanted to be rid of her so badly, he would have to take the matter before Parliament.

Facing down the tribunal had been an act born of desperation. Surprisingly, once she had begun, it had not been as difficult as she had imagined. The difficult task still lay ahead—to shatter the fragile happiness of a sweet, trusting man by breaking the news that she could not marry him.

He was waiting for her when she returned to Vanessa's town house. At the sight of his eager, expectant smile, Julianna's courage deserted her.

"My darling, you're as white as a sheet. Come sit down. Was it so very awful?"

Julianna let him lead her to the chaise. If only Vanessa had been there to ease the awkwardness with her banter.

"Cheer up, my sweet." Crispin patted her hand encouragingly. "The worst is over now."

Julianna wished that were true. *Postponing this will not make it any easier,* she reminded herself. Avoiding Crispin's sympathetic hazel eyes, she drew a deep breath and plunged ahead.

"There won't be an annulment, Crispin. I can't marry you."

"Surely you're mistaken, my love." He chuckled. "I expect those dusty old priests frowned a good deal and asked you all sorts of embarrassing questions, but that's their job. You mustn't think they mean to refuse Uncle Edmund's petition."

"They will not grant the petition...." Julianna pulled her hand away. She could not bear the warmth of his touch. "Because I told them I did not want it. I'm sorry, Crispin."

"There's someone else, isn't there?"

Julianna nodded.

"I knew it. I could feel it. You're not the gay, carefree girl I left behind."

"I was never carefree, Crispin." She raised her head to look straight at him. "But you couldn't see that."

His gaze faltered for a moment. "Will you tell me his name? I think I have a right to know that at least."

"Yes. I suppose you do." She was barely able to squeak those words out of her constricted throat. Having told Crispin she could not marry him, she had thought the worst was over. It was not. The worst, the hardest part, would be breaking the news that she had fallen in love with his trusted uncle.

"I didn't intend for this to happen. You must believe that, Crispin. At first I only wanted to be his friend, because he seemed so lonely. It came on by such gradual degrees, I had no idea. He never did anything to win me—not intentionally at least. So you must not blame him. It is all my fault."

"Julianna, I cannot make head or tail of what you are trying to say. Will you kindly be plain and tell me his name?"

Was he being deliberately obtuse? She had hoped he would come up with the name himself, rather than forcing her to say it. "Your uncle. Edmund."

Julianna held her breath, waiting for his reaction.

"Well, if you refuse to tell me, I suppose I can't make you." He sounded annoyed. Did he not believe her? "I'm forced to conclude you are not proud of the connection. Which suggests you are not quite so smitten with this fellow as you believe. Come to your senses, Julianna. If you come with me to the South Seas, I know I can make you forget all about him in time—"

"Did you not hear me, Crispin? I cannot go away with you or anyone else. I am married to your uncle, as I wish to remain."

"Please don't insult my intelligence with this pack of nonsense about a love affair between you and my uncle. To hell with the annulment, anyway. You and I know you were never truly married, and that's what matters. If we run away together, Uncle Edmund can go to Parliament for a divorce. It'll make a terrific scandal, I suppose, but I don't care if I ever set foot in this dreary country again. Please, Julianna, don't throw away the life we can have together for some momentary infatuation.''

"Crispin!" Sheer vexation overwhelmed all Julianna's feelings of remorse. "Listen to me. What I feel is no passing fancy. I care about you as much as I ever did, only now I realize it is not enough for a lifetime. And I am in complete earnest when I tell you I love Edmund.''

"I know what you're trying to do. You're trying to protect this cad. I consider it in very poor taste, using my uncle as a ruse after all he's done for you. At great personal sacrifice, I might add. I had no idea how glad he was to be rid of you at last. He's a changed man these days—in better form than I've ever seen him. Out and about the town, taking a more active interest in his investments and his charities, talking about standing for a seat in the Commons.''

Julianna flinched as if he had struck her. Deep in her heart she had nursed the hope of a future with Edmund, once he understood that she could not marry his nephew. Was she throwing away her only hope of love for the sake of an impossible fantasy?

"That does not change how *I* feel, Crispin. I cannot marry you."

Abruptly Crispin rose from the chaise and marched to the door of Vanessa's drawing room. There he paused.

"We sail in three weeks, Julianna. And I don't expect to return for many years. If you change your mind—"

"Crispin, dear fellow!" Laurence called from out in the hallway. "Just the man I wanted to see.''

"Ah, Laurence." Crispin slipped out of the room. Julianna could hear the two men's voices drifting off toward the conservatory. "What are you up to these days?" Crispin's cousinly concern sounded strained and wooden.

"Besides up to my ears in debt, you mean?" Laurence giggled. "A very tight spot at the moment, I'm afraid.''

A door closed in the distance, and Julianna could hear no more of the conversation. Drained of emotion and energy, she reclined on the chaise. She had not expected this confrontation with Crispin to leave her feeling so empty. And yet, she felt something else too—as if, having shed a rigid, constricting corset, she could breathe once again.

Edmund acknowledged the warm applause at the end of his speech with a formal little bow, followed by a self-conscious wave. He was not one of life's natural orators, Edmund reflected ruefully as he shook hands and exchanged a friendly word with several familiar people. With practice he was getting better. If he imagined Julianna standing at his elbow, radiating support and encouragement, drawing everyone's eye and bewitching them all with her smile, it banished his nerves entirely.

As the hand he was shaking clung to his, Edmund suddenly came to himself and realized it belonged to Crispin. His "campaign smile" warmed into a more sincere expression.

"Dear boy! How good to see you. What are you doing here in the country when you've wedding plans to make and a ship to ready?"

"Not here, Uncle Edmund," Crispin muttered. "Something serious has come up. I must talk to you."

"Yes, of course." What had happened to Julianna? Had Skeldon escaped custody and come after her? Edmund felt his internal organs tying themselves into reef knots. With barely civil haste, he bade his supporters good-night and hauled his nephew out of the tavern that had hosted his political rally.

"This way." They followed a narrow path until they had left the noisy merriment of the Olde Boar's Head well behind them. Edmund leaned against a stone fence, his back to the setting sun.

"Out with it. Something's happened to Julianna, hasn't it?"

"Only that she's lost her mind," burst out Crispin. "The little fool fancies herself smitten with some other fellow. Flat-out refused to marry me."

"You're sure there's someone else? She told you that?"

Crispin thrust out his chin. "Admitted it bold as brass. Had the face to claim she cares for me as much as ever, only it isn't enough now. Women!"

"Did she say who?" To himself Edmund wondered if it could be anyone but Laurence Bayard.

"That's the worst of it." Crispin strode back and forth in front of him, gesturing vigorously as he spoke. "She wouldn't tell me. Mark my words, he's a bounder and she knows it. I have a nasty feeling he has designs on your fortune, Uncle."

That certainly sounded like Laurence. "What makes you think so?"

"Somehow or other, she's ruined your chances of getting an annulment. You'll hear about it soon enough. The papers will go wild with this once they get their hands on the story."

He was still Julianna's husband. Having resigned himself to losing her, that thought sent Edmund's senses reeling.

"Why...why should she do that? Doesn't she want to be free, in order to marry Laur—this other man?"

"Dear Uncle." Crispin shook his head slowly. "You are such an unworldly fellow. Can't you see? Her new 'beau' has put her up to it. He may be planning a convenient accident for you, after which he can console your fair and wealthy widow."

Edmund caught his nephew by the lapels of his coat. "I will never believe such a thing of her."

"No, of course not." Crispin gingerly disengaged himself from Edmund's indignant grip. "He's probably persuaded her to wait until after you're dead...not bothering to mention that he means to speed the process."

"Thank you for the warning. I promise to watch my back from now on." Edmund took Crispin's hand. "I'm sorry things have turned out this way, my boy. What can I do for you?"

The handsome young face registered relief and reliance. "I was hoping you'd offer to help, Uncle Edmund. You must talk to Julianna for me. Make her see reason. Bring her to her senses. I know she looks on you as a kind of substitute father. Convince her to quit England and this tinpot Romeo of hers, and come away with me to the South Seas."

It was a tempting thought. He had struggled long and hard to reconcile himself with losing Julianna to his beloved nephew. Could he bear to watch her throw herself away on some unworthy fellow? Crispin was right. She might listen to him, heed his paternal advice.

"I suppose…" he began. "No. I'm sorry, Crispin. I can't do it. Julianna has a right to be happy, and if she doesn't believe she can find happiness with you, I will not gainsay her."

"Please don't refuse me, Uncle. You're my only hope now."

From a nearby perch, a nightingale warbled a few notes of his bittersweet song. Edmund cast a comforting arm around his nephew's hunched shoulders.

"A woman's presence in your life means nothing, unless she comes to you of her own accord. Deep down, I think you know it too. Still planning to go back to the South Seas?"

In the gathering spring twilight, Edmund could see the young man nod glumly. "Now, more than ever. It will take me a long time to get over her. Will you promise me one thing?"

"If I can."

"Watch out for her. Don't let her make a mistake she'll come to regret."

"Mistakes and regrets are all part of living, Crispin. It's how we pick up the pieces and go on with our lives that counts ultimately. Or so I believe. But I promise you I will always be here for Julianna—if she will let me."

"Vanessa, what is it?" Julianna cried out.

A letter clutched in her trembling hand, the dowager countess looked quite overcome with emotion.

"It's from Laurence. He's given me power of attorney over his affairs until he returns."

"Returns?" Julianna moved closer and began reading over Vanessa's shoulder. "Where's he gone? When's he coming back?"

"The South Seas," replied Vanessa, evidently dazed by the news. "He's bolted. Gone off with Crispin. Who knows when they'll return?"

Julianna took her arm. "Come into the drawing room and let me pour you a drop of brandy. Look on the bright side, Vanessa. I doubt Colonel Harcourt will pursue him all the way to

Java to demand satisfaction.'' Rumors of an imminent duel between the two men had been flying for days.

"I suppose you're right.'' Vanessa accepted the brandy snifter from Julianna. "He won't be able to run through his income, either. If he stays away long enough, he may even find himself solvent upon his return.''

Julianna gave Vanessa's shoulder an encouraging pat. "That sounds more like the dowager countess of Sutton-Courtney.''

"It's all so unexpected, though,'' said Vanessa plaintively. "I had no idea he was planning anything so drastic. I never got to say goodbye.''

"It'll all work out for the best, Vanessa. You'll see. A voyage to the South Seas may be exactly what Laurence needs to make a man of him. He'll glut himself on adventures, like a greedy schoolboy on jam tarts. And when he does come home, I expect he'll be only too happy to settle down and lead a respectable life.'' In an effort to cheer her friend, she quipped, "By then everyone will have forgotten all his old scandals and you'll be able to make a splendid match for him.''

"The selfish little wretch. Going off without a word. He's the only...family...I have left.''

"There, there.'' Julianna dropped to the chaise and pulled the weeping woman into her arms. The once imperious Vanessa felt small and vulnerable as a child. Since their talk on the eve of the annulment tribunal, the balance of their relationship had shifted subtly. More and more of late, Julianna felt a sense of responsibility and solicitude for Vanessa.

"You still have Edmund,'' she reminded Vanessa. "And me.''

"Have I?'' Vanessa raised her tearstained face. "Then what are all those trunks and boxes doing in your room?''

This was the first mention Vanessa had made of her packing, though it had been going on steadily and openly for several days.

"You know I can't stay here forever. Time doesn't stand still, Vanessa, no matter how much we want it to. Besides, I have a feeling you won't be alone for very long.''

As though on cue, Vanessa's butler appeared at the door to announce Mr. Clive Farraday.

"Oh dear! Tell him to wait a moment, Mills. Oh, Julianna, I must look a fright. You go speak to Clive. Tell him I'm indisposed. Ask him to come back this evening."

Julianna replied with an impulsive embrace. "Never fear, Vanessa. I'll see to everything."

She found Mr. Farraday pacing the entry hall. "Lady Fitzhugh." He bowed.

"You'll find Her Ladyship in the drawing room." In a few words, Julianna explained the situation. "She needs someone kind and loyal to rely on just now."

"I assure you, madam, it would be an honor and a joy to render Her Ladyship whatever small comfort I may." He looked so touchingly earnest.

"She cares for you a great deal." Would Vanessa resent her betraying a confidence? Suddenly Julianna didn't care, her scruples swept away by the craving for one happy ending.

"I have worshiped her for as long as I can remember," Clive Farraday mused aloud.

"All the better." Julianna found herself actually pushing him toward the drawing room door. "Now go in there and don't come out until Vanessa has promised to marry you."

Shoving him over the threshold, she closed the ornate drawing room doors with hopeful finality and returned to her packing. She had just finished when Vanessa wandered into the room, flushed and starry-eyed as a young girl.

"Will you stay in London one more day?" Vanessa asked.

"If I have a good enough reason."

"My wedding?" She sounded frightened to say the words aloud.

"The best reason in the world." For once Julianna's mouth hardly seemed wide enough to smile as broadly as she wished. "And will you look what I've found—at the bottom of one of my trunks." She held up a little straw wreath, cunningly braided, adorned with an aromatic spray of dried wildflowers. "From Mr. Warbeck, in Marlwood."

Tenderly placing the wreath in Vanessa's hand, she dropped

a light kiss on her friend's cheek. "Nail it to your lintel post, and you'll have a babe in your arms before the year is out."

As the coach wound its way up the lane to Abbot's Leigh, a west wind blew among the linden trees, sending blossoms wafting down like warm, fragrant snow. Spotting Nelson Tully at work, Julianna waved. Dropping his shears, the gardener pulled off his cloth cap, brandishing it above his head in great sweeping arcs.

News of her arrival spread like wildfire. By the time she alighted in the kitchen courtyard, practically every servant and worker on the estate was on hand to welcome her.

"Look at you." Myrtle Tully gathered Julianna to her motherly bosom. "There's naught to you but skin and bones. Do they not feed you up in London?"

"It isn't the same without an appetizer of fresh Surrey air, Mrs. Tully." Julianna pulled off her hat, to let the breeze ruffle her curls. "Besides, I'd trade every crumb of pheasant in aspic and French pastry for one slice of your good seed cake."

"Bless my soul, didn't I just take one out of the oven. You shall have some with your tea, my dear, and a saucer of cream."

Smelling the cake and fresh baked bread, Julianna suddenly felt hungrier than she had in months. As the housekeeper bustled off to prepare a festive tea, the others crowded around Julianna to exchange greetings and the odd scrap of news.

"Parson's lady is lighter of a fine son," said Nelson Tully. As Julianna clapped her hands and exclaimed how she must visit the vicarage, he added, "The lad's a longshanks, like his sire."

Julianna laughed at the description, all too apt she was certain, of the infant Master Trowbridge. "Ah, Mr. Tully." She clasped his gnarled fingers warmly in hers. Her fond gaze lingered over every shrub and outbuilding, as she inhaled a deep draft of the moist, loamy air. "It's good to be home."

Only after the others had dispersed to resume their duties did Julianna notice Brock hanging back by the kitchen door, watching her. After her abrupt departure from Fitzhugh House, what would Edmund's trusty steward make of her precipitous return to Abbot's Leigh? His thick brows bristled as fiercely as ever, but as she approached, Julianna detected a suspicious softness in his eyes.

"I knew you'd come back again," he said quietly, gripping her hand as though he never meant to let it go.

She hadn't the heart to tell him how brief her stay would be. After much soul-searching, she had decided that Edmund deserved an explanation for her recent actions. Once she had spoken with him and said proper goodbyes to her old friends in Marlwood, she would be off to Wales to begin a new life.

"Will Sir Edmund be home in time for tea?" she asked.

Brock shook his head. "Election's only three days away, ma'am. He rides out before daybreak and often doesn't get back until after dark. Some nights, if a meeting goes very late, he stays put and hires a room at an inn."

Julianna was sorely tempted to postpone her discussion with Edmund until after the election. That way she could pay her visits and enjoy her last days at Abbot's Leigh. But what if she was overcome by cowardice and skulked off without a word to him?

"There's an urgent matter I must discuss with him, Brock. If he comes home tonight, whatever the time, I wish to be informed."

"Very good, ma'am." Brock nodded. "In the meantime, let's get you some tea. Mrs. Tully's right. You want feeding, lass."

And feed her they did, until Julianna feared she would explode in a barrage of cream and caraway seeds. It was a feast for the soul as well, with an eager exchange of news and gossip—Vanessa's wedding being the most sensational.

It was only when Mrs. Tully had returned to her kitchen, Mr. Tully to his pruning and Brock to superintend the airing of her bedchamber, that Julianna had a moment's solitude to realize how much she had missed them all. And how very much she would miss them and dear Abbot's Leigh in the future. She could almost feel the old house enfolding her, reluctant to let her go.

Impatiently, she tried to dismiss such wistful thoughts by

concentrating on the new life ahead of her in Wales among her grandmother's people. Reunited with Winnie, she would set herself to learn Welsh in earnest. She would walk the stark cliffs and listen to the dirge of the Irish Sea. She would visit the legendary haunts of her grandmother—Talesin's Tomb, and the bards' gathering at the eistedfodd. One day, perhaps, she might find her fancy taken by a pair of dark Celtic eyes, and forget those other eyes of Norman gray.

Darkness fell. Only after Brock had voiced grave doubts of his master returning that night, did Julianna begin to prepare for bed. She had just finished brushing her hair, about to plait it for the night, when a firm tap sounded on her door.

Opening it a crack, Brock called through. ''Beg pardon, ma'am. You did say to serve you notice when the captain arrived, whatever the time. Well, he's come ten minutes since. You'll find him in his bedchamber if you mean to see him tonight.''

So the moment had arrived at last. Julianna's mouth felt dry, and her heart threatened to hammer its way out of her chest. She must not think. She must act—turn a knob, put one foot in front of another, knock on a door.

Chapter Twenty-Eight

There was something strange about the night, Edmund thought as he rode for home. He might have called it enchanted—if he'd still believed in such things. It was warm for May, even with a west wind blowing. The full moon hung low over Abbot's Tor like an enormous wheel of unripe cheese, casting a bright spectral light over the sleeping countryside.

One of his supporters had offered him lodging for the night, but he had declined. He never slept well in a strange bed. Better to ride the hour back to Marlwood, using the time and solitude to calm his nerves after the commotion of speech making. Then, drowsy from the fresh night air, fall into bed and sleep soundly until the morning, when he'd be back on his rounds again.

As often happened on these late-night rides, Edmund found his thoughts straying to Julianna. He had heard nothing of her since Crispin had come to him. For all he knew, she might have come to her senses and decided to join Crispin at the last minute. Or perhaps she was dallying in London with Laurence, wondering impatiently how long she'd have to wait to inherit his fortune. No, Edmund chastised himself, there was nothing mercenary in Julianna's makeup.

As he rode up the lane, Abbot's Leigh looked dark and silent. Evidently the servants had given up hope of his returning for the night and had taken to their beds. With a mild grumble, Edmund stabled Agincourt himself. Letting himself in the side door closest to his bedchamber, he saw Brock standing at the top of the stairs, in his nightshirt with a candle held high.

"Get back to bed." Edmund waved his steward away. "I can pry off my own boots for one night."

Brock opened his mouth as if to say something. Then he closed it again and settled for a nod. Leaving his candle on top of the flat banister post to light Edmund's way, the steward shuffled off to his own rest.

Parting the high riding boots from his feet proved an awkward procedure, but Edmund soon managed it. Other articles of clothing followed rapidly. At the end of a long, busy day, his bed looked most inviting. He was just unbuttoning his shirt when he heard a timid tap on his door. Who could it be at this hour?

"Come in." He didn't bother to disguise the impatience in his voice. Surely whatever it was could wait until morning.

Julianna pushed the door open, then hesitated on the threshold. She had obviously caught Edmund disrobing for bed by the light of a single flickering taper. His boots and stockings lay slumped at the foot of the bed, his waistcoat and surcoat flung over the back of a chair. The lappets of his jabot hung limp and wrinkled from his neck. A deep wedge of bare chest showed through his open shirtfront.

The sight of that tightly thewed flesh triggered intense flashes in her memory. She could feel Edmund pressed against her as the sun rose over Titania's Bower. She ached with the delight of lying naked in his embrace after the Pritchards' ball. Not for the first time did she fight to retain her composure in his presence. Biting hard on her lip, she willed her ragged breath to slacken, praying the dim light would mask her blushes.

"Lady Fitzhugh. To what do I owe this unexpected pleasure?" He greeted her with the immaculate courtesy he would have spared any chance-met acquaintance.

Perhaps he thought she had come to foist her unwanted company upon him. She would straitly disabuse him of that notion.

Striding into the room, she closed the door firmly behind her. "I'm sorry to barge in on you like this, but Mr. Brock assured me it was the only time I'd be likely to catch you."

"You might have waited a few days until this infernal election is over," he replied casually. "One way or another, I shall have time enough on my hands then."

"I haven't a few days to spare. I only stopped here briefly on my way to Wales."

His eyes widened and some trick of the candlelight made his face appear to blanch. But he said nothing.

"I mean to make my home there. But before I go, I thought you might require an explanation for my recent actions."

"I require nothing you do not wish to give." Edmund's voice warmed and his features lapsed into the half smile Julianna so loved. "Though I'll admit I am curious."

She almost wished he'd stayed remote and glacial. A choking lump of regret rose in her throat. The gray eyes she had once thought so cold and unaffected, she had seen since, changeable and evocative—in anger, dark as a thunderhead or flashing with cold iron; in curiosity and laughter, like quicksilver; in affection, as soft as the mist of a warm summer rain. What would she see in his eyes once she'd had her say—disillusionment, censure, contempt?

Edmund waited for her to speak, asking himself if she was real or only an apparition of this enchanted night. He hadn't been prepared for how intensely the sudden sight of Julianna would affect him, after all these months. She looked so soft and virginal. Was she a virgin still? Edmund wondered, hating himself for wondering.

Her power over him had not waned during their separation. If anything, it had grown. The power to make him whole. The power to rip his heart, still beating, from his chest. He could have faced an entire fleet of Celebes pirates more calmly. His mouth went dry and his legs suddenly felt unreliable. Leaning back against the bedpost for support, he crossed his arms over his chest to still the trembling of his hands.

"Out with it," he prompted her. In truth, he didn't want to hear, but neither could he bear the suspense.

She cast her eyes down, reluctant to meet his. "I expect you're angry with me for the way I treated Crispin."

"He's a fine man. You loved him once." An unspoken question hung in the air between them.

"I did. At first I thought my love for him was strong and deep enough to build a marriage on. I discovered it wasn't."

Edmund wanted to ask, scathingly, if she had found any strength or depth of love with the weak, shallow Lord Marlwood. He didn't get the chance, for Julianna rushed on.

"I'm sorry I wasn't able to repay my debt to you, as you asked—by making Crispin a loving and faithful wife."

All thought of Lord Marlwood fled from Edmund's mind. "I was wrong to ask such a thing. As if your wishes in the matter signified nothing. Besides, if there is any debt between us, the obligation is entirely mine." It was too late to make amends now, but it was important to him that she realize his sincerity. "Crispin came to me shortly after you refused to marry him. He hoped I would urge you to reconsider."

She glanced up. "Why didn't you?"

"Because I want you to be happy. Because I trust you to find your own way."

"You do?"

He nodded. "I won't lie by pretending I enjoy seeing you throw yourself away on a worthless scoundrel like Laurence Bayard. But if any woman is capable of reforming him..."

"Laurence Bayard?" She spit the name as though it left a bad taste in her mouth. "Where did you ever get such an idea? Laurence stowed away on Crispin's ship to escape his creditors and a duel with Colonel Harcourt. Hadn't you heard?"

Before he could answer, she added hotly, "Do you think so little of me to imagine I could care for that fatuous...conceited...swaggering..."

As she searched her vocabulary for further invective, Edmund tried to reconstruct his picture of Julianna's future—without Laurence. "Crispin told me there was another man."

"Just as I told him. I also told him who it was, though he refused to believe me. Perhaps you won't believe me, either." She took a deep breath. "Knowing and loving Crispin spoiled me for any other man—save one. And I fear you have spoiled me for any other in the world."

Edmund shook his head. His ears were playing tricks on him. "I...I don't...understand."

"Don't understand?" The impatience in her voice was unmistakable. "Or don't *want* to understand? Which is it, Edmund? From the very beginning you have turned a blind eye to my feelings for you. Is it because you didn't want to betray Crispin's trust, or because you can't return my love?"

What could he say? Edmund wondered warily. There she was, in his chamber, at night, saying words he'd only dreamed of hearing from her lips. It was like an enchantment, but he'd succumbed to the lure of such enchantments before. At Titania's Bower. At the Pritchards' ball. At the Twelfth Night masque. Each time he'd been cast back down to cold, hard reality. Each time from greater height, with a more painful impact. Could he survive another such fall? Jerome Skeldon's parting curse echoed in his thoughts: *Idiot! See how much she cares. Try to claim a single kiss or a touch from all the carnal pleasures she promises.*

And what delight she promised. High young bosom rising and falling with her rapid breathing. Long, shapely legs silhouetted beneath the light fabric of her nightshift. Slim, graceful hands whose touch had by turns inflamed and assuaged him. Had she come looking so bewitching, saying such impossibly wonderful things only to torment him? There was only one way to find out.

For God's sake, take her! Edmund's aching body urged. *Never against her will,* his heart insisted, gently but implacably.

Stirring himself, he slowly advanced on her. "I want to understand, my dear. Truly, I do. Are you saying you once cared for me...as a man...as a husband?"

She reached out, clasping his right hand in both of hers. "You must have known that," she whispered.

He hadn't known. He'd hoped. He'd doubted. He'd despaired. Now he knew and his heart rejoiced, for she had loved him once. Did that make his next question easier to ask—or harder?

"With everything that's happened between us, could you ever care that way again?"

"I'm here, aren't I?"

"So you are." With aching, breath-bated restraint, he brought his face closer and closer to hers, sensitive to the slightest flinch or tremor of aversion.

At the last instant, as his lips prepared to make the most tentative contact with hers, Julianna lunged toward him, assailing him with a kiss more intense than any he'd ever felt. Her lips parted, releasing a gush of tender breath. A gasp and a sigh mingled, it was the sound of longing and thwarted hope rewarded at last. Like a spring zephyr, it blew through the frozen barrens of Edmund's heart. Thawing. Healing.

Julianna had loved him. In spite of everything, she loved him still. Edmund's blood ran cold as he thought of all he had done to drive her away, and of how close he had come to succeeding. Plunging his hands into the tangle of her russet curls, he clung to her like a lifeline. Thirstily imbibing her kisses, he tasted the sweet brine of Julianna's tears. Or were they his own?

As he moved toward her, Julianna silently prayed he would not turn aside at the last minute. What was taking him so long? This was not some dream. Not some masked paramour who might or might not be Edmund. This was the man she had longed for, yearned for so passionately in spite of her most strenuous attempts to repress those feelings.

She could stand it no longer. As he hesitated, so close she could feel his breath on her face, Julianna threw herself at him, planting her lips on his with fierce, possessive ardor. For a brief rapturous eternity, she could think of nothing beyond her delight in the long-forbidden sensation. Then, recalling how he had pushed her away when she'd kissed him on their wedding night, she felt a stab of fear. Would he despise her wanton behavior?

He raised his arms. Not to ward her off, but to enfold her. Crispin had been wrong. Edmund did love her. Now she was no longer kissing him—they were kissing each other. No light confections, but kisses of salt and bread and potent red wine.

Even as they satisfied one need, they ignited others. As if sensing her desire, Edmund clasped her to him, running his hands over her eager body. How glad she was that night had fallen, and they were alone in his chamber. Clad only in her nightshift—no lacings, no hooks, no cumbersome corsets would impede their lovemaking. Edmund loosed a strand of ribbon at her throat, and Julianna shrugged off the garment. It fell delicately and deliberately, disclosing more and more of her naked flesh to his eyes and hands and lips. She trembled in anticipation.

Edmund stirred from his intimate scrutiny. Holding her close he whispered, "Don't be afraid, Julianna. You need never be afraid with me."

His lips tickled her ear, and his reassurance tickled her comic sense. Done with dissembling and prim evasions, henceforth she would speak her feelings, no matter how brazen they might sound. Nuzzling his ear, her voice husky with desire, she replied, "I don't fear you, Edmund. I want you."

Throwing back his head, he gave a gust of hearty laughter. "Want me?" he crowed. "Then by God, woman, you shall have me!"

Catching her up in his arms, Edmund tossed her onto the cool, fresh-smelling sheets. He paused to cast off his remaining clothing, then turned back to her, his own desire gratifyingly evident. He handled her body deftly and gently, but with a touching, boyish eagerness. After so many months spent aching for his touch, Julianna responded eagerly.

In a pang of sweet fire, they coupled at last. Their first movements together were tentative and awkward. Gradually, in the grip of their overwhelming need for each other, they fell into the rhythm of that ageless dance—the way of a man with a maid. Like surging billows driven before a restless wind, pleasure swelled, mounted, crested and broke over them.

Afterward, Julianna lay wrapped in her husband's arms, limbs lazy with contentment. The past year's longing and heartache had fallen from her as easily as her nightshift. She felt suddenly curious and playful. Reaching out her forefinger, she gently traced the outline of Edmund's lips.

"Why did you never tell me—?" she began, half in jest.

"—that I was blindly, daftly in love with you?" he finished. "I never imagined you could return my love. I can scarcely believe it yet. Even in my youth, I was never a favorite with the ladies.'' Edmund reached up and ran a hand over the smooth crown of his head. ''I did not consider the passage of years had done anything to render me more attractive to a blithe and bonny lass like yourself.''

Quoting Doll Tearsheet's endearment to Falstaff, Julianna answered in tender earnest. '''I love thee better than I love e'er a scurvy young boy of them all.''' Then, by way of emphasis, she planted a kiss on the top of Edmund's head, another on his brow, a third on the tip of his nose. Soon, their lips were locked together in a kiss that threatened to renew their passion. For the moment, curiosity won out over a lust so lately appeased.

''But when...?''

''From the very moment I laid eyes upon you,'' Edmund interjected. ''Though I did not guess the truth of it until much later. I remember our wedding day and the marks on your face from your stepbrother's handling. That brutalized beauty appealed to every protective instinct in my being.''

Recalling their wedding day, and the weeks thereafter, Julianna was not convinced. ''But you acted so cold and stern.''

Edmund gave a rueful chuckle. ''It is no easy task, to break from a lifelong habit of reticence. Besides, I found myself behaving like a tongue-tied schoolboy whenever I was around you. That should have warned me of my true feelings. Our first Christmas together, I began to feel more at ease. When I fell ill, it galled—having you see me so helpless. During the weeks I was confined to bed, when we spent so much time together, you managed to pick the lock on my heart, steal in and make yourself at home. By the time I realized what had happened, I was powerless to evict you.''

Julianna stroked Edmund's arm with the back of her hand, thinking how he had crept into her heart that very way.

''All the while,'' he continued, ''I was telling myself I did not care for you any more or any differently than I had cared for Alice. Or for Crispin. Imagine.'' He laughed a trifle bitterly. ''A man my age not knowing he is in love—with his own wife?''

For a time Edmund lapsed into silence, then he began to speak again. ''When we came to Abbot's Leigh, and my strength returned, I felt the stirring of needs and desires I had not experienced in many years.''

As he spoke, the events of the past months unfolded before Julianna with a new clarity. Reliving those moments through Edmund's eyes, warmed by the delicious ache of their love-making, she could finally begin to believe what she had thought impossible.

''I recall so many times from those golden months—that day-break on the riverbank. To find you there, slumbering amid the flowers, seemed the most natural thing in the world. I'm not sure how long I stood watching you, making love to you a thousand times in my mind.''

He sounded so wistful, Julianna could not bear it. Lifting her head she nuzzled Edmund's ear, imparting a faint, seductive whisper. ''I trust you enjoyed it?''

Edmund's arm tightened around her, perhaps to prove to himself that it was all true, and she did belong to him, at last.

''The day I found you with Laurence on Abbot's Tor, I finally awoke to the true extent of my feelings. I burned with such envy I wanted to kill him, there, with my bare hands. That day he looked more like Crispin than I ever believed possible. Suddenly I knew I would feel no differently if it had been Crispin. Seeing you with any other man...'' His voice trailed off.

Julianna shook her head in sadness and disbelief. ''To think all that time I was jealous of you and Vanessa.''

''From that day on,'' Edmund confessed, ''I could never let down my guard for an instant, fearing that you would guess my secret, and regard me as another carnal opportunist like Jerome or Laurence. How hard it was, living each day with the woman I loved most in the world, affectionate and close, but always with a boundary that I never dared overstep.''

Julianna pushed out her lower lip in a mock pout. ''You hid your feelings far too well.''

''The habit of a lifetime, my sweet,'' Edmund admitted with a rueful sigh, and a gentle kiss upon her outthrust lip. ''I came close to giving it all away that night at the Pritchards'. After a few glasses of punch, I began to imagine you were flirting with me. Like a self-deluded drunkard, I fancied you might have some feelings for me other than dutiful affection. Who knows what might have happened if I hadn't fallen into an intoxicated stupor? That night I had the most vivid dream. You were lying naked in my arms—''

Julianna could not resist. ''So I was.''

''What?''

''You were not the only one to overindulge at the punch bowl that night, and my flirting was not your fancy.'' Between volleys of laughter, Julianna blurted out her tale. ''It was like heaven dancing with you. I simply lost my head. Driving home in the carriage, I poured out my heart—how desperately I loved you. Quoting Goneril, if you please! Only to hear you snoring as I finished my drunken oration. I can hardly imagine how I kept on my feet long enough to help Brock drag you up to your room, then to undress us both. When I finally did steal into your bed, I lapsed unconscious before I could enjoy the fruits of my adventure. When I wakened, I was so shocked by my own behavior, and terrified of your reaction, that I fled.''

''You were right to fear my reaction.'' Edmund's response sounded strangely quiet, slightly menacing as he raised himself on one elbow and slid his body over, pinning her beneath him. ''For I would likely have reacted thus…'' His kiss was fierce and demanding. ''And thus.'' His lips trailed down her neck, rough and unrestrained.

Julianna arched herself toward him, and they began another tempest of lovemaking, even more fervid than the one before. It was as if they were in contest to prove whose frustration had been the greater, whose thwarted passion the keener. Even as she gasped Edmund's name in urgent ecstasy, Julianna was forced to admit defeat—exultant to plumb the depth of his feeling for her, reluctant to believe his suffering could have exceeded her own, saddened to think what the past months had meant for him.

When they lay quiet once again, Edmund passed a forearm across his sweat-soaked brow with a self-deprecating chuckle. ''See why I refused the tempting invitation to remain with you on our wedding night? This is rather taxing for a man of my years.''

Impishly, Julianna lowered her head, running the tip of her tongue from Edmund's hip to his ribs, convulsing him with laughter. ''Perhaps if you had not been such a reluctant bridegroom, we wouldn't have a year and a half of suppressed desire to burn off in one night.''

Abruptly his laughter ceased. Edmund cupped Julianna's chin in his hand and looked deep into her eyes. ''Let us not spend ourselves all in one night.''

''Never fear. There's plenty more where that came from.''

Lying there, quiet, spent and utterly contented, sleep began to steal upon Julianna. Coherent thoughts flowed into tantalizing dreams. From one such, rosy and lyrical, Edmund called her back. ''Before you drift off, my love, I beg one indulgence.''

Julianna replied with a drowsy kiss and a wanton murmur, ''Anything…''

Rising, he draped her with her nightshift. After pulling on his breeches and shirt, Edmund held out his hand to her. ''Come.''

''Edmund! It is the middle of the night. Come where?''

He drew her from the bed, catching her in his arms, and spinning them once around. With a saucy, secretive smile, he tweaked her nose. ''Humor an eccentric old man.''

''Very well, on one condition,'' Julianna conceded charily. ''Never let me hear you refer to yourself as an old man again until you are at least ninety! It irritates me almost as much as people disparaging my youth.''

''Agreed.'' Removing an object from his bedside table, Edmund slipped it into his pocket. Then he paused to light a taper for Julianna from the lone candle that had flickered throughout their tryst. ''I wonder how many young bucks of our acquaintance could ravish their pretty mistresses twice in a single hour.''

''I doubt if most of those smart dandies could manage it once with any degree of pleasure for the lady involved.''

Edmund offered a gentle, pretended spank. ''Wanton wench!

Now hush, unless you want the entire household awakened on us.''

Barefoot, arms about each other, their path lit by the candle flames, they stole through the sleeping house on their clandestine errand, whatever it might be. Bayard ancestors looked down from their portraits. Their expressions, Julianna fancied, ran the gamut from shocked disapproval, to amusement, to benediction. At length they entered the old chapel. Their very breath echoed in the stillness. The leaded glass in the narrow windows caught and reflected the faint light of their candles.

At the altar, Edmund removed the side tapers from a three-branched candelabrum, motioning Julianna to join him in lighting the central candle. This done, they placed their candles in the two vacant arms. Drawing Julianna down beside him, Edmund knelt before the altar.

''Call it the caprice of an ol—'' He caught himself. ''That is, the caprice of a man in love. Ever since we married, I have looked upon you as Crispin's wife. I know you made our wedding vows to him, in your heart. I made mine on his behalf. Now, if you will, let us say those words again—this time to each other. Perhaps then I can truly believe you are my wife.''

With a touch no heavier than a summer breeze, Julianna caressed his cheek. ''The time we have shared, the joys, the sorrows, the illness and the healing, the longing and the consummation, have made me your wife in a way that no words, even holy oaths, can do. It is true, I meant those first vows for Crispin, but I have lived them with you. Still, I am too much a romantic to resist the idea of midnight solemnities in this beautiful old chapel.''

The adoring smile Edmund bestowed upon her eclipsed the light of a thousand candles. ''One last request. Will you remove your wedding ring, and take another? He drew from his pocket a delicate gold band, set with a single diamond. ''This belonged to my grandmother. In her later years she could no longer wear it upon her poor fingers, but on a chain around her neck. She gave it to me shortly before she died. I know from the way she always spoke of him, that my grandmother was the happy wife of an ol—of a husband who doted upon her youthful exuberance.''

The thick gold circlet slid off Julianna's finger. After so much time, she felt strangely naked without it.

''I, Edmund, do take thee, Julianna, to my lawful wedded wife…'' The vicar's son knew every word and had to prompt Julianna once or twice on her vows. As a warm wind sighed around the old stones of the sanctuary, Julianna wondered how many Bayard brides had plighted their troth before this altar. Not one happier than she.

''With this ring, I thee wed. With my body I thee worship…'' A sly smile and a roguish glint in Edmund's eyes made Julianna smile also, and blush, to think of the delightful form such worship would take. Then, when all the words had been spoken, Edmund took her in his arms, and kissed her in the way she had once dreamed of—tenderly, almost reverently.

''And so, to bed.''

As one, they turned and blew to extinguish the middle taper. All three candles guttered and failed.

Laughing in mock dismay, Julianna protested, ''How shall we ever find our way back to bed now?''

She felt Edmund slip his hand into hers. From out of the shadows she heard his voice, warm and caressing. ''It hardly signifies. As Marvell's Mower said to the Glow-worms:

Your courteous lights in vain you waste,
For Julianna here is come.
And she my mind hath so displaced,
That I shall never find my home.''

''Oh, Edmund.'' Reaching into the soft, velvet darkness of a spring night, Julianna found his lips and kissed him once again.

*　　*　　*　　*　　*